WET DESERT

Lower COLORADO RIVER

NEVADA

UTAH

LAKE POWELL

Glen Canyon Dam

LAKE MEAD

GRAND CANYON

Hoover Dam

LAKE MOHAVE

Davis Dam

LAKE HAVASU

Parker Dam

Headgate Rock Dam

CALIFORNIA

Palo Verde Dam

ARIZONA

Imperial Dam

Delta

PACIFIC OCEAN

MEXICO

GULF OF CALIFORNIA

WET DESERT

*Tracking down a terrorist on
the Colorado River*

GARY HANSEN

HOLESHOT
PRESS.COM

HOLE SHOT PRESS

This book is an original publication of Hole Shot Press. www.holeshotpress.com

Note: This book is a work of fiction. Although many of the places referenced in the book are real, some characteristics have been changed to fit the story. Some real historical characters and events have been mentioned to enhance the story. However, the characters and events in this book are products of the author's imagination or are used fictitiously. Any resemblance to actual persons, living or dead, is entirely coincidental.

Printed in the United States of America
First Printed – 2007 / Paperback Edition
Second Printing – 2008

Library of Congress Control Number: 2007922620

ISBN-13: 978-0-9793521-0-2
ISBN-10: 0-9793521-0-X

www.wetdesert.net

To Kelly, Kevin, Jennifer and Allison

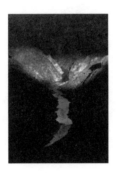

DAY ONE

Monday, June 21

CHAPTER 1

12:00 noon - Porcupine Canyon, Colorado

Grant Stevens braced for the explosion. He felt tightness in his stomach and up the back of his neck. He glanced sideways at his friend Bruce Godfrey and saw wild eyes and a tense smile. Bruce stared unflinchingly at the bombsite across the canyon. Neither of them would have missed this for the world. Grant looked back just in time.

The bombs detonated. Grant's entire torso flinched. Porcupine Dam exploded as particles jettisoned in soaring arcs above the structure. The concrete face of the dam came to life, bursting outward. A dust cloud expanded from the rubble, obscuring the entire structure of Porcupine Dam. Smaller clouds mushroomed out of the large one, in what seemed like a series of secondary explosions. Some of the rocks and pieces of concrete were propelled high in the sky, with trajectories like fireworks on the Fourth of July.

For an instant, Grant panicked. He was far too close. The onslaught of rocks and concrete would rain down on him, and kill him instantly. He would have no chance of escape. But then, as if on cue, the outward energy died. The particles reached the apex of their eruption and fell back to earth. Grant would not be killed after all, and he felt like an idiot for thinking it in the first place.

He relaxed. The explosion had been far more intense than he had expected, making him forget that they had not yet heard the noise. When the sound wave reached him, he ducked again. The loud impact made him feel like his chest might be crushed or his head split. He reached instinctively to cover his ears, in spite of the expensive twenty-decibel ear protection, clutching them tight to his head 3until the sound dissipated.

Only the dust was visible now, churning on itself like a thundercloud, and covering the carnage underneath. Although the dam's concrete structure was completely decimated by the explosion, and reduced to rubble, no flash floods or waves of water could be seen. In fact, no water could be seen at all in the streambed, or anywhere else below the dam. No reservoirs were released downstream by the demise. The canyon below the dam remained dry.

Grant realized he had never seen anything so spectacular in his life. He felt goose bumps on his arms and a grin spreading across his face. He stared at the fog of dust covering the far side of the canyon. A sound from behind startled him. It was a mixture of clapping, yelling, and a few whistles. Grant looked around and saw Bruce and the others applauding towards the demolished Porcupine Dam. At first, the cheering seemed foreign and wrong, but he slowly realized he felt the same way, and after a moment he joined in and clapped enthusiastically.

He glanced around at the others who were in attendance. Standing next to him on a flat plateau across Porcupine Canyon from the dam was a group of managers from the Bureau of Reclamation, representatives from the U.S. Department of Interior, and a large number of local politicians and various other VIPs from the Denver metropolitan area, including the governor of Colorado. The plateau, which acted as a grandstand for the large group, was conveniently located a half-mile downstream from the dam.

Below the plateau, sprinkled up and down the slopes, were the non-VIPs. This much larger group, which Grant estimated at a few thousand, was made up of non-managerial staff from the Bureau, farmers who had once irrigated using the water from Porcupine Reservoir, curious local residents, and a group of environmentalists with a banner that read: *Free the Rivers, Kill the Dams*. A scattering of deputy sheriffs infiltrated the group to keep peace between the environmentalists and the farmers.

While he stood and stared, he was vaguely aware of someone collecting the ear protection in a large basket. When the man, a Hispanic in a maroon tuxedo, approached, Grant deposited his ear protection in the basket with a mumbled "thanks." He looked back at the demolition site. The change was incredible. He had never seen anything like it. He rubbed his hand on his chest and admitted it still felt tight. He peered down into the canyon, but the dust frustrated his ability to see much of anything. If only the wind would blow the cloud away. However, that afternoon, Porcupine Canyon was devoid of any wind or even a breeze.

This event, which had drawn so many spectators up Porcupine Canyon on a hot Monday, was the culmination of five years of lawsuits, political jockeying, and environmental studies. Ironically, the Bureau of Reclamation, which had fought hardest against decommissioning Porcupine Dam, was now in charge of the event, and celebrating the dam's demise. Grant felt hypocritical. In spite of the excitement of witnessing the explosion, ultimately Grant wanted to build dams, not blow them up. As a manager for the Bureau of Reclamation, he detested the thought of destroying a working concrete dam. Although Porcupine Dam was not in the same league as the bigger, more well-known dams in the west, its sheer simplicity made it remarkable to an engineer like him – just a sweeping concrete arch, with two rounded spillways sculptured right in the middle.

Bruce Godfrey, his friend from the River Hydraulics Group, slapped him on the back. "What'd ya think?" Bruce had been unable to talk about anything else for weeks.

Grant pointed in the air. "For a second I thought some of the pieces were going to hit us."

"Yeah. Me too. It was awesome!" Bruce pumped his arm in excitement. "And it was way louder than I thought it would be. Even with the earphones," he said, motioning to his ear.

Grant pointed down in the canyon. "I wish I could see better. There's too much dust to see how much of the structure . . ."

"Give it a few minutes to settle," Bruce said, motioning toward one of the hospitality tents and a table of drinks in ice. "Let's get a drink."

Grant nodded and they both headed towards the table. He wondered if events like this were his future. How many more dams would the Bureau demolish over the next ten years?

Grant had worked for the Bureau for eighteen years. He had joined the Bureau to build dams, big concrete ones like Hoover and Glen Canyon. Their sheer size and power hypnotized him even after all these years as an engineer. As a child, he had toured Hoover Dam with his family while they vacationed in Las Vegas. At the age of seven, while looking down the six hundred foot face, he had announced to his parents that he would build dams when he grew up. But unlike most children, Grant had not stopped with his childhood dream. Instead, he had let his passion propel him through college – first a bachelor's degree in civil engineering, then a master's, all focused on the chemistry of concrete, structural analysis, and ultimately, dam building.

When Grant first started working at the Bureau of Reclamation in the early eighties, he had advanced quickly, gaining recognition both for strategic decisions and common sense. He garnished awards and promotions. It was not until his career was set and he had worked for the Bureau for over ten years that he finally realized the truth. It came in the form of disapproval for a dam proposal he engineered for the Snake River. It wasn't the disapproval that bothered him, because almost all his proposals had been denied. It was the lack of concern from his management at the Bureau. They had expected it to be refused.

The day the proposal was rejected, Grant's mentor Henry Petersen, who had helped design the Glen Canyon Dam in the late fifties, looked Grant in the eyes and said, "Face it, Grant, there ain't gonna be no more dams in America. It's over. It's not considered environmentally correct to build dams anymore."

It was at that moment that Grant's conscious mind grasped what his subconscious had known for years – he was too late. America's dams were already built. His dream would never be fulfilled. The Bureau of Reclamation had become a maintenance organization, content to monitor water usage. And, as the final straw, the Bureau was now decommissioning the dams it had built in the first part of the twentieth century.

When they reached the table, Bruce grabbed a cream soda and popped the top. "You all packed and ready to go?"

Grant smiled at mention of the trip. His luggage was packed for a flight that evening. "Yeah, as ready as you can be." He sorted through the sodas, and picked out a Diet Coke.

"How late are you guys leaving?" Bruce asked.

"Nine," Grant said.

This was a trip Grant was really looking forward to. The flight would take him first to JFK, then Paris, and then Nairobi, Kenya. After that it would be small propeller planes and cars to the dam site on the Tana River. Unfortunately for Grant, elephants would not be necessary, since there were actually paved roads to the site.

Since all the big rivers in the United States were already dammed, most of Reclamation's engineering work was now done in foreign countries. The Bureau consulted around the world on how to harness water resources. This particular trip to Kenya was a weeklong international symposium on dam building. Engineers, including Grant, would be attending from many of the giant projects around the globe, including the most impressive dam of all, the Three Gorges Dam in China. Grant had traveled to foreign countries before for business, but never a trip of this magnitude.

"You cleaned and oiled your rifle yet?" Bruce had a large smile on his face.

"Yeah right, like I could get a rifle through customs."

After the symposium in Kenya, Grant would vacation for an additional week around Kenya and into Tanzania. Who knew when or if he would ever get to Africa again? Bruce had been joking with him for weeks about going on a safari and shooting some big game, which he just might do. If he did, though, it would be with a loaner rifle, as he certainly had no intentions of trying to check his deer rifle in and out of airport security, border crossings, and customs.

Bruce laughed. "If you get me a Black Rhino head, I'll hang it on my living room wall."

Grant smiled at the image. He saw himself in customs with his hands cuffed behind his back, the unwrapped head of the endangered black rhino sitting on his luggage. But even as the image faded, another replaced it of seeing animals like the rhinos, elephants, zebras, and lions in their natural habitat. What an opportunity, an opportunity that comes only once in a lifetime. He was excited about the symposium itself too. Where else would he get to talk to engineers about real dam projects like Three Gorges? Certainly not in Denver.

Bruce frowned. "I can't believe Howard didn't try to horn in."

Grant scanned the crowd for his new boss and thankfully couldn't see him. "Even Howard knows he'd be out of place in Africa with a bunch of civil engineers at a dam symposium."

It was the first time in Grant's career he had reported to someone younger than him. But age was the least of Howard's problems. Historically, the Bureau's management consisted of civil engineers like Grant, who had worked their way up through the system. Howard, however, was a spy, and everyone knew it. In the U.S. government, the Bureau of Reclamation fell under the Department of the Interior. And Howard had come from Interior six months before. He was neither recruited nor interviewed. At the Bureau, it was inconceivable to become a manager without an engineering degree. But, by the early eighties, as the Bureau became less engineering oriented and more water management oriented, managers with MBAs had become the norm. Yet, Howard was neither an engineer nor a businessman. His education was the worst sort of training for actually accomplishing anything in life – he was a lawyer. The rumor was that a Senator had arranged for his position, one who wanted to find out how the Bureau of Reclamation worked, then gut it. Nobody at the Bureau seemed to know who the mystery senator was, but they knew that when the gutting started, Howard would be the one pointing the knife.

Life had been hell since Howard came aboard. He knew nothing about dams and water management. Worse, he came with the pre-conceived notion that everything the Bureau did was wrong. He ridiculed and scoffed at everything. Most frustrating, however, was that upper management seemed unaware or unconcerned. They let him roam through middle management unencumbered, allowing him to hand out endless busy-work and make decisions that could only be described as uninformed. Management either did not notice, did not care, or were afraid to do anything about the work efficiency problems or drop in morale.

Bruce reached over and scooped some salted nuts from a bowl. "Yeah, but I'm still surprised they left him in charge while they're gone. Roland should know better than that."

Roland Blackwell occupied the top position in the Bureau, the Commissioner. Besides managing most of the dams in America, and the Denver office, Roland flew back and forth across the country securing political support and funding. But at least Roland had once been a civil engineer, even if he hadn't been very good. Bruce's concern was legitimate – it was inconceivable that the Bureau would leave Howard, the spy, who couldn't build a dam in his flower garden, in charge while everyone was in Africa.

Grant shook his head. "It doesn't matter. Nothing's going to happen while we're gone."

Bruce put up his index finger. "Yeah, but what if it did?"

Grant shrugged. "Like what?" He turned and walked back toward the ledge where the remains of Porcupine Dam were finally becoming more visible through the dust.

Bruce hurried alongside. "Who knows? What if they had a catastrophe at one of the dams? Howard would have no idea what to do."

Grant shrugged. "What kind of catastrophe? The dams are practically automated."

Bruce hesitated, trying to think of something, then smiled. "What if they ran out of grease at one of the generating plants? The friction could damage the turbines."

Grant laughed and started walking again. "Sounds like a perfect job for Howard, greasing the turbines."

When they reached the ledge they stopped and looked at the remains of the dam. Although still partially obscured, it was obvious the precision charges had done a near-perfect job of reducing the concrete dam into a neatly stacked pile of rubble. By the end of the summer most of the debris would be gone, hauled down the canyon in trucks. Then the canyon would look more like it had before, except for the long scars where the dam had butted into the canyon walls.

Grant and Bruce dallied for an hour admiring the scene, eating and mingling. As managers for the Bureau, they had been allowed to attend the decommissioning with the VIPs, but both knew they were not important enough to rub elbows with politicians. That was the job of Commissioner Blackwell and his cronies. It was Grant and Bruce's job to stay out of the way, something Grant was more than happy to do.

After they both ate their fill of the appetizers and finished rehashing the explosion, they started back to their car. A gravel road snaked back and forth through some trees for almost a half mile down to where the cars were parked. They had just started down the road when Grant heard someone call his name.

"Stevens. Stevens. Hang on a second." Grant's boss Howard ran toward them, waving his arms. His forehead protruded and his bushy eyebrows grew together, making him look like he was constantly furrowing his brows.

"Our favorite guy," Bruce whispered.

When Howard got within ten yards of them, he shooed Bruce away with his hand. "Go on ahead Bruce. I need a few words alone with Mr. Stevens."

Bruce gave Grant a consolatory look and then continued walking to the car.

"What's up?" Grant asked, not really caring since he would be gone for the next two weeks.

"Grant, I hate to be the one to tell you this, but . . ."

Grant knew what he was going to say before Howard finished. They couldn't do this to him.

". . .but plans have changed. It seems the commissioner doesn't think I've been here long enough to run things with . . ." He looked around as if he didn't know how to finish. ". . .you know, with everybody out of the country so long."

Grant interrupted. "Are you trying to tell me you're canceling my Kenya trip?" He felt all the muscles in his face tighten.

Howard backed up a step and smiled. "I thought you would be happy to be left in charge."

Grant wondered if he had missed something. How could Grant be in charge, if both he and Howard were in America together? And then it hit him. Anger returned. His brows furrowed and he gritted his teeth, barely able to speak. Bruce had been right. "So you're taking my place?"

Howard shook his head and actually waved his finger back and forth. "No. No, Stevens. You've got it all wrong. I'm not interested in Kenya. Who wants to hang around with a bunch of boring engineers? I'm leaving. I decided to take vacation next week." Howard shrugged. "Then you can manage America's dams without my interference. Besides, ever since I came out west, my wife's been nagging me to take her to Yellowstone, so we decided—"

"How long have you known about this?" The thought of not going on the trip made Grant feel sick. He would kill to be able to discuss the challenges of building the Three Gorges Dam with the Chinese engineers. What about his safari in Tanzania? What would he tell his wife? Grant had spent a fortune on reservations for the week of personal travel. He had thought of nothing else but this trip for months.

Howard read his mind and waved his hands back and forth. "If you're worried about your personal money, don't. The Bureau's gonna pick up the tab. I told

Roland about your vacation and he said the Bureau would reimburse you. He's already approved it."

That mitigated some of the anger, but not the emptiness. The disappointment was overwhelming. He needed to sit down. He kicked at a loose rock on the road.

Howard pursed his lips in an expression that actually showed compassion. "Look, I know you don't like this."

He didn't say anything. He knew Howard didn't care.

His boss, who had never even attempted to talk to Grant as a friend, now confided in him like they were pals. "Hey, I'm not happy about this either. They told me that I didn't have enough time at the Bureau to be in charge. They wanted us to switch roles, me report to you for the week. But I told them to stick it, and took some vacation."

Grant couldn't believe what he had just heard. They had actually suggested Howard report to Grant for a few weeks? Maybe Roland did know what he was doing. But even if the Bureau suddenly figured out they needed to leave a real engineer home, why did it have to be Grant? Roland and Grant had never seen eye to eye. Grant felt like Roland was too much of a politician, and Roland always thought Grant was too much of an engineer. Besides, unlike most of the others attending the symposium, Grant actually cared about the speakers, and the panels. He wouldn't be there just to schmooze.

Howard continued. "Anyway, Roland's admin will brief you in the morning about any issues that could come up in the next ten days." Howard's eyes softened until they reminded Grant of a puppy. "And if anything does come up, here's my cell phone number." He handed Grant a card. "You can call me anytime. I'll be in Yellowstone with my family."

Grant nodded. It seemed for a moment as if Howard was begging him to call, like a call might validate him somehow. It didn't matter though, because Grant wouldn't call Howard if his life depended on it.

Grant pocketed the card. They stood and stared at each other for a moment longer, even though the conversation seemed to be over. Howard checked his watch. Grant turned to go.

"Don't hesitate to call," Howard said.

Grant walked away with his fists clenched. He resisted the urge to pick up a rock and throw it. He felt like screaming, but he held his composure. He walked stiffly for a few minutes before a thought struck him. Did Howard say he would be vacationing in Yellowstone? Grant smiled. Hadn't he read about grizzlies being re-introduced into the park? Grant smiled as he pictured Howard focusing his camera while a huge grizzly charged toward him.

* * *

12:30 p.m. - Grand Canyon, Arizona

The water looked cold and dangerous. Only an idiot would dare swim out beyond the shallows without a life jacket, or some other flotation device. It would be suicide. The strong undertows would grab you, and pull you to the bottom before you knew what was happening. And then? Well, there wouldn't be anything after that because once the river had you, it would never let you go.

The solitary man reached down and touched the river. He rolled the wetness between his fingers to determine the texture. Unable to detect any silt with his fingers, his hand went to his face, and he inhaled, smelling it. Nothing. He dipped his hand again, and this time licked the tips of his fingers, tasting. Ah, now he could just discern the silt in the water, his tongue finding a few small particles and detecting the expected salty flavor.

Still crouching, he looked across the Colorado River to the other side, taking in the size, sensing the power. It was alive. He felt it. The river radiated power, especially the rapids. Unfortunately, even here in the Grand Canyon, the river was shackled, bound like a prisoner, unable to show its full strength. Others didn't notice, but he did. The concrete dams held it back. Sure the river ran a little stronger today than yesterday. But that only meant the flow through the turbines at the Glen Canyon Dam, some hundred and seventy-five miles upstream, had been increased, most likely due to a "hot one" in Phoenix, when the Arizonans cranked up the air conditioners. More electricity from the turbines meant more water downstream. It was as simple as that. The mighty Colorado River was a slave to man, caged and controlled.

He stood and looked up the rock canyon walls rising thousands of feet on both sides of the river. Although he often visited the Grand Canyon, the immensity always inspired him. He tried to imagine the river carving the canyon over millions of years, an image that was impossible to visualize. But he knew it hadn't been this river; it had been a wild untamed river, over eight times larger during spring runoff, much dirtier, and powerful enough to constantly re-arrange the huge boulders.

The best way to describe the man, if anyone cared to, was that he seemed unremarkable in every way. No facial features worth remembering, a plain face with plain brown hair. His clothes showed his familiarity with the desert outdoors, but again they were not fancy and were well worn. The only attribute that anyone would likely remember if they tried to recall the man was his build. He was uncommonly skinny. Skinny enough that almost all would remember it, if questioned. Then there were his eyes. Some might be unsettled by them, and they would be recalled as wild eyes.

If anyone actually knew the man, they would likely describe him as obsessed with the Colorado River. He had studied it for years. He knew its history. Nobody cared more about the river than he did. Although he made a living as a technician in Las Vegas, keeping the casino lights flashing was only a job, secondary to his first love. Weekends and vacations were spent in the desert, the National Parks: Zion, Arches, Bryce, Canyonlands, and the Grand Canyon. Not just on the roads either, but in the backcountry. He knew them all, like a rancher knows his spread.

At that moment the man worried about the Colorado River, about what it had become. Most Grand Canyon tourists thought the river looked impressive, but they had never seen it before the Glen Canyon Dam destroyed it.

Before 1962, travelers described the river as a wild animal with rapids three stories high. The pre-dam Colorado was extremely dirty, carrying millions of tons of silt and mud. When the river receded from high flows, giant sand dunes were left deposited on the banks, creating the perfect environment for wild flowers and swallows that used the mud for their nests. Now, without the spring floods, the sand had eroded away, and the wild flowers and swallows had disappeared. The silt, meanwhile, was trapped behind the dam, slowly filling Glen Canyon.

He crouched back down and touched the water again. This time he held his fingers under the cold current. He didn't need a thermometer to know the temperature was in the forties. Too cold to bathe or swim comfortably. Since the dam was erected, it was always in the forties, forty-degrees Fahrenheit, plus or minus two, twenty-four hours a day, three hundred and sixty-five days a year. The temperature never changed at the bottom of a six hundred-foot dam.

One advantage of a colder river was that it benefited the rainbow trout introduced by the park service after the dam was completed. Rainbows love cold water, and the oxygen it carries. Unfortunately, the native humpback chub, which had lived in the Colorado for thousands of years, did not like it. Almost extinct now, the chub all but disappeared after the river turned cold, their exit accelerated by competition from the rainbows.

The man opened his pack. He gingerly moved the detonators and wires to the side, and reached for a clear Plexiglas container the size of a soda can. He uncapped it, and dipped it into the water. He recapped it and looked through it. Given some time, the silt would settle to the bottom, and he would be able to see exactly how much sediment was in the water.

He heard footsteps on the gravel behind, and he whirled to see two hikers, a man and a woman, approaching from upstream. He lunged to his pack, quickly covering the detonators, and almost dropped the water sample in the process. Had the hikers seen the detonators? He did not think so.

He studied their eyes to see if there were any signs that they had seen anything. The two did not look familiar, but that didn't mean they were not staying in the same campground. He had not talked to anyone. Leaving Las Vegas right after lunch the day before, he had driven straight to the North Rim, parked his truck, then made the long descent from the North Ridge via eight miles of winding trails to the river below, arriving in camp after dark. As the couple approached, the lady waved.

"Hi. It's a beautiful morning, isn't it?"

The skinny man stood and moved in front of his pack. He wiped his wet hand on his shorts and tried to think of a response. He didn't want a long discussion. "Yeah."

The woman's smile seemed to connect both ears. She had a few highlights of gray just visible under the straw hat. She and her male partner both wore khaki shorts and new hiking shoes, most likely purchased for this trip. The bearded man with her kept looking around at the canyon with his hand on his chin. He looked as if he would be more comfortable with a pipe in his mouth.

Neither the man nor the woman seemed particularly interested in his pack. Could that mean that they had not seen anything? Or were they just good actors?

The lady asked another question. "See any rafters on the river yet this morning?"
He looked across the river to avoid eye contact. "A couple."

"You're staying in our campground around the corner, aren't you?" She pointed upstream. "We saw you walk past our tent. You like to get going early, don't you? Where you from anyway? We're from Los Angeles. It's our first time in the Grand Canyon."

He wasn't sure which question to answer first. He hesitated then answered, "I like the peaceful mornings."

Maybe she was asking so many questions because she had in fact seen the detonators. What if these two were really undercover agents from some law enforcement agency? Or more likely, maybe they were just snoopy people who would report what they had seen to the first person they saw.

He quickly considered what to do. There was too much at stake to do nothing. What if he had to kill them? His knife was in the bottom of his pack and unreachable. He scanned the ground and saw multiple rocks the size of softballs. He looked up at the couple. The man was still gazing up the canyon walls. He was distracted. The woman seemed relaxed. What if he grabbed one of the rocks and bashed her in the head? That would do it. His hand twitched while he imagined her lying on the ground with a bloody crater on her head. He wondered if he would be able to get the man after the woman. The man's defenses would be up by then.

"What are you doing with that water?" She pointed at the plastic container of silty water in his hands. "You're not going to drink it, are you?" She stuck out her tongue in distaste. The woman made it hard not to look in her eyes, as if her eyes were hunting his.

He realized suddenly that these two had not seen the detonators. They were not a threat, and he would not need to kill them. They were just a couple of curious campers, happy to be in the Grand Canyon for the first time. Regardless, the encounter had made him nervous. He needed to move away from them and clear his head. He wondered how to end the conversation. "Well, I better go." He leaned down and zipped up the backpack, lifted it onto his shoulder, and walked past them. He held the water sample carefully in his hand.

She yelled after him. "Okay, we'll catch you later in camp or something."

From behind, the skinny man heard the man say to his wife, "I don't think he wanted to talk."

"Really? Why would you think that?"

He walked upstream around a bend in the river, away from the couple, away from people, until he was alone and could see a mile upstream. His heart was still beating fast. That had been too close, he had almost done something stupid, something that could have jeopardized everything he had worked so hard for. He had carried the detonators with him because he was too nervous to leave them in the truck, and that had almost screwed everything up.

He gazed upstream. He tried to picture the dam. He couldn't see it, of course; it was almost two hundred miles upstream. But he knew what it looked like. The Glen Canyon Dam rose over six hundred feet and completely blocked the canyon. It trapped Lake Powell behind it, with houseboats, water ski boats, and jet skis, all buzzing around like bees, with over three million visitors per year.

What he had never seen, unfortunately, were the canyons themselves, under all the water. Only about a thousand people ever had, before the dam buried them forever. He read accounts of people lucky enough to have explored them including John Wesley Powell himself. They declared Glen Canyon one of the most beautiful places on earth. They described pink undulating sandstone walls, some striped, with rain forest-like jungles in some of the side canyons, and green fractures high on the walls nourished by seeping springs. The endless carved rock canyons contained lush overhangs and rock amphitheaters. But now it was all gone, forever. It made his stomach tighten every time he thought about it.

Instinctively, he knew that it would be impossible to build the Glen Canyon Dam or most of the other fifty-three Colorado River dams today. Environmental impact studies would never allow them. Unlike in the early 20th century, modern politicians feared environmentalists.

But, even though the government had stopped building dams, and society had decided dams were detrimental to the environment, they left the big ones standing. Now built, the dams were forgotten. Even the environmentalist groups like the Sierra Club or GreenPeace didn't waste resources trying to get rid of the dams. There were too many other issues brighter on the radar.

Not that the man hadn't tried. Over the years, he had made his rounds in all the major environmental groups including the "Glen Canyon Institute," a group dedicated specifically to decommissioning the Glen Canyon Dam and restoring its canyons. But he finally realized the groups were all pissing into the wind. The issue didn't even register with today's politicians. Since lawyers had won most of the legislative seats in Washington and taken over the House and Senate like a virus, no risks were taken, no big decisions were made, good or bad. The bureaucracy was impenetrable. Decommissioning the Glen Canyon Dam was a fantasy.

That's why, if it was to be done, it would need to be done another way. After much contemplation, the decision had been made. Preparations took over a year. The logistics were planned in excruciating detail. The Glen Canyon Dam would finally be decommissioned the next day, on Tuesday, June 22. The man would be there for the ceremonies. In fact, he would be in charge of the events. Because he was going to blow it up.

CHAPTER 2

2:00 p.m. - Lake Powell, Utah

Julie Crawford took a deep breath. "Hit it!" she yelled.

The ski handle in her hands jerked savagely. It felt like her arms were being pulled from their sockets. As her body dragged forward through the water, spray from the ski hit her directly in the face. She held her breath and closed her eyes as she always did. She could hear the roar of the boat accelerating. As the ski started moving through the water beneath her, she stood up in one fluid motion. The spraying water disappeared as the ski came up on plane. She caught her breath while the boat gradually accelerated to just under twenty miles per hour. She took a second to adjust her swimsuit. She could see the other five in the boat: her husband Greg, Greg's brother Max and his wife Darlene, and her best friends Paul and Erika Sanders. Julie's husband had a big smile on his face.

Julie leaned back and slightly right. The ski reacted to the wedge and skied to the right. She cut over the wake of the boat, absorbing the bump with her knees. Outside of the wake the water was as smooth as a mirror. She traversed to the right until she was at a 45-degree angle to the boat. She reversed her lean and cut back toward the boat's wake, spraying water behind her. As she approached the wake, she reversed again and cut back right, more aggressively this time. The water was incredible. Only Lake Powell had water this smooth in the middle of the day.

The hot, dry desert air warmed her body. She relaxed and adjusted her hands on the rope handle. She took a second to glance up at the rock walls of the canyon. She loved the atmosphere. On her right side, a vertical rock cliff climbed toward the blue sky. The canyon walls, with their astounding variations of texture and red color, contrasted perfectly with the blue sky and cool water. They were miles back in one of the countless side canyons of the lake. Although there were probably thousands of boats at Lake Powell, they had not seen anyone else for hours.

On Saturday, after picking up the rented houseboat, they had motored for hours upstream from the marina, towing the Mastercraft behind. They passed numerous canyons, but Greg wanted to go farther upstream where there were fewer boats. No one had objected. The leisurely tour up the lake had been relaxing. It gave the six of them time to catch up.

Paul and Erika Sanders had been the Crawfords' best friends for years. They met when both couples lived in Irvine, California where Greg and Paul worked as computer programmers. After being introduced by their husbands, Julie and Erika connected immediately and the friendship was sealed. When they first met, they were newlyweds, but over the years the Crawfords added two boys and the Sanders one girl.

Greg's brother, Max, was almost ten years older than him. Max and Darlene lived in Las Vegas with their three kids, the oldest being a teenage boy who was going to come with them to Lake Powell, but ended up going to Boy Scout camp instead.

For this trip all three couples had farmed their children out to friends and family. Lake Powell would be a vacation away from runny noses and diapers, at least until the kids got a little older. Besides, it was sort of a reunion for the two younger couples, the first time they had reunited since Greg and Julie moved from California to Phoenix in February.

During Saturday's trip upstream, Julie and Erika shared pictures of their kids and recounted stories since their separation. Paul and Greg talked work and sports as if they had never been separated. The older couple, Max and Darlene, both avid readers, dove into novels from a whole box they had brought. Julie told Erika about life in Phoenix and how it was different from Orange County.

All three couples had looked forward to the week at Lake Powell. When Julie first met Greg, he already had a ski boat. It was a lifestyle that she readily adopted. Likewise, Paul and Erika were easily converted, and the couples had vacationed together on every body of water that allowed water ski boats within three hundred miles of Irvine. Occasionally, Max and Darlene came with them. Once a year, they planned a big trip, and the last three years it had been Lake Powell. Lake Powell was a water-skier's paradise. At almost two hundred miles long, with thousands of miles of shoreline, isolated canyons, and red rock cliffs, it felt like a different planet.

Julie tightened her grip on the rope and cut back to the left. This time she did not stop at the wake, but cut through it. On the left side she cut back and forth, each time gradually increasing her aggression. After a while, she felt the muscles burn in her back and arms. She knew she could push harder, but then again, they had the whole week ahead, so she tossed the rope into the air and coasted to a stop. As her body sank down in the water, she leaned back, floating on her back and letting her head rest in the water. She took a moment and looked up in the blue sky at a solitary white cloud. It reminded her of an oversized bed, covered with white blankets, and big pillows. Something was perched on top of the bed, a harp maybe. Yes, that was what it was.

Julie deserved this. Like the thousands of other boaters spread out in the countless canyons of Lake Powell, Julie Crawford intended to make the most of her getaway. She would relax and purge all her stress. What else was there to do?

* * *

3:00 p.m. - Grand Canyon, Arizona

"RIGHT SIDE PADDLE! RIGHT SIDE PADDLE!" Keller screamed from behind. "Come on right side, we need you. DAVID, HELP OUT!"

It took all David's willpower to consciously reach his oar ahead and grab more of the cold frothy water. His strength was gone and his hands were shaking. Where was Judy? A second ago she had been paddling just in front of him. Then the river had snatched her from the raft and swallowed her. How long could she hold her breath? Maybe she was dead. David blamed himself for organizing the trip, something he would now regret for the rest of his life.

"DAVID, PADDLE!"

He pulled hard on the oar and the raft slowly came back around into position, although he felt sure Sam, right behind, was doing most of the work.

Keller yelled from behind. "That's it, Judy. Hang on. We'll get you in a second."

David caught a glance of a bobbing head and a blue life jacket somewhere to his right, but he didn't dare look. His right foot, the one hanging in the low-forties water, was freezing cold as he straddled the right pontoon of the silver raft. He couldn't imagine how cold Judy felt. He hoped she was okay. He caught another glimpse of her, and relief warmed his body, but he kept his eyes straight ahead, focusing instead at the next wave downstream. Suddenly, her head popped up next to the boat. Before he could blink, Keller reached over him and grabbed her, dragging her up into the boat. He abandoned her immediately and resumed his position in the back. Judy sputtered some water, coughed, and amazingly looked up and . . . smiled!

The raft rolled through the next wave and this time stayed nose forward. Nobody fell out. David looked down as Judy scrambled to grab onto something. She looked rattled, but physically okay. David could feel his confidence coming back. The muscles in his arms began to respond again. He braced for another big one just ahead.

"Keep it straight, guys and girls," Keller reminded them from behind. "Right side paddle. Left side paddle."

David felt the boat drop as the hole sucked them down. They shot back up again, climbing the wave, then hesitated, almost stalling, then at the last minute the current grabbed the raft and pulled it over the top. He felt the raft bend as it crested. With the big rapids behind them, they slid through a series of smaller waves without incident.

After the river calmed, David finally got a chance to catch his breath. He willed his heart to slow down. The shaking in his hands gradually resided. Keller maneuvered the raft to snag Judy's paddle, which had followed the raft through the rapids. Afram reached out and grabbed it.

"Judy, you okay?" Keller reached up and patted her on the blue life jacket. "That's the best ride we've got out of Sapphire in a long time."

Judy finally spoke. "Awesome."

Everybody started to laugh. She shivered.

Sapphire Rapid, although not the biggest, was the wildest they had encountered so far on the trip, definitely the first one where someone fell out. One minute they were in perfect shape, the next the front of the boat went right. With the boat sideways, the next wave almost flipped them. The rapid was littered with truck-sized boulders scattered in the middle of the river. The canyon walls climbed steeply on both sides, but the texture was all boulders, apparently from eons of rockslides. Sapphire Rapid was located at mile 101 of the Grand Canyon. David had learned that river miles in the Grand Canyon were measured downstream from Lee's Ferry, the last place where boats could get access to the river, and just fifteen miles downstream from the Glen Canyon Dam and Lake Powell.

Sapphire was one of the jewels, a series of rapids named after gemstones. They included Crystal, Agate, Sapphire, Turquoise, Ruby, and Serpentine. They stretched from mile 98 to mile 106. Crystal was rated the most advanced, and was generally considered one of the best rapids in the Grand Canyon. But it was Sapphire that pulled Judy out of the boat, and almost capsized them.

Monday was the group's sixth day on the river with Colorado River Foam, a white water group David found on the Internet. There were two rafts in the company, six paddlers in each raft, plus the guide, Keller, who mostly steered and barked orders from behind. Their boat was made up of David's group of five and George, who came with the group of six in the other boat.

David's group of five included himself, Judy, Sam, Becky, and Afram. They worked together in El Segundo, California, just minutes from LAX, and had been planning this trip for almost a year. To get reservations to run the Colorado River through the Grand Canyon during peak season usually required well over six months notice. David had never heard of Colorado River Foam, but he saw the opening and grabbed it. Some of his co-workers had tried to book a trip the summer before but started too late to find anything.

After Sapphire, the river turned calm for the next few miles. The calm periods gave everyone a chance to catch their breath, get a drink or a snack, relax, and enjoy the scenery. The intermissions between rapids also gave them a chance to talk.

Afram turned toward Judy. "We thought we lost you. I only saw you bob a couple of times. Were you scared?"

Judy nodded. "Every time I went under, I wondered if I would ever come back up, but just when I thought I was going to die, I'd pop up. Now I know why Keller makes us wear these life jackets."

Everybody laughed nervously. David wondered if the others worried like he did, that she might have drowned.

Keller, constantly the boss, made the situation a teaching opportunity. "That happened because, the boat got out of shape. As long as the boat hits the wave head on, we're usually okay."

"Why only usually?" Sam asked from behind David.

Keller motioned downstream. "Hey, the river has a mind of its own. Sometimes we hit the wave perfectly with both sides paddling, and still get sucked down, pulled under, and spit out. Just wait, the best stuff is yet to come at Lava Falls."

"I can hardly wait," Judy said, climbing back into her position in front of David. "Bring it on."

Afram was shaking his head. "You are one psycho chick."

"She's got the right attitude," Keller said, pointing at Judy. "You guys paid your money. You might as well enjoy it."

David laughed. For a moment he had forgotten this trip was supposed to be fun. The first few days on the river had been easy, no real rapids, just a relaxing drift down the canyon. But today was different, multiple series of big rapids culminating in nearly capsizing and losing Judy. It had scared him. He realized the river now intimidated him. To begin having fun again, he needed to change his attitude. He looked across at Afram who was laughing to himself about something. He looked back at Sam and Becky who seemed more concerned with each other than the river. Even Judy, if he had to describe her, seemed more excited than scared, as if she had just completed her first sky dive or bungee jump. He seemed to be the only one freaked out.

David willed himself to relax. He had organized this trip. It was his idea. Besides, they weren't even halfway done yet. They had a week to go. He forced himself to remember the way they had looked forward to the trip, the nights spent camping on the beach, the lazy days floating. He remembered craving the rapids. The memory was like the clouds parting and the sun breaking through. He would enjoy this trip. No, he would love it. It was just a river, and thousands ran it every year. Then, just when David started to relax, he was jerked out of his thoughts.

"Get ready, rafters," Keller yelled. "Another jewel. This one is called Turquoise. It doesn't look too bad, but last year it flipped us. Right side paddle! Left side paddle!"

* * *

5:00 p.m. - Grand Canyon (North Rim), Arizona.

The man reached the crest of the long hike at the North Rim of the Grand Canyon. He turned and looked across to the South Rim on the other side, and down to the river below. The eight-mile trek from the river left him both winded and exhilarated. Spending a night in the canyon before he started his quest had been a great idea. There was a good possibility he would not survive to do it again. And even if he did, it was unlikely that he would be free to hike around in the Grand Canyon. No, this was almost certainly his last hike up the canyon, and he had enjoyed it tremendously. He had taken his time, stopping often to look at plants and the panoramic views. As he envisioned, the time had strengthened his resolve to do what he had to do.

The only difficult part had been seeing the other hikers. Would they be able to get out in time? He had not foreseen his concern for others. They were similar to him. Not as knowledgeable, of course, especially about the politics and environmental damage caused by the dams. But like him, they loved the canyon, and the river. Many of them were environmentalists like himself.

Surprisingly, he had been unable to make eye contact with them, and had avoided interaction when possible. Killing individuals was an unfortunate outcome of what he had to do. He was uncomfortable with it, and wished it were not necessary. Or if it was necessary, why did it have to be other environmentalists, instead of the bureaucrats who built the dams and screwed up the river? He would feel much less guilt about killing them. A scene played in his mind where a giant wave of water washed over the top of a large yacht, while dozens of bureaucrats on deck raised their arms to fend off the water and their ultimate death. That scene felt good. Unfortunately, the politicians were in Washington, not on a yacht in the river. It was his people down by the river.

He likened himself to a general sending his soldiers to battle. He hopes they all will live, takes every possible precaution, but knows inevitably some will die. He knew exactly how this great responsibility felt. It was a heavy burden.

Finally, unable to enjoy the scenery any longer, he turned and walked into the parking lot. When he reached his pickup, he removed his backpack and laid it carefully in the bed of the truck, careful not to jar the detonators. The truck was a late-model, three-quarter-ton white Chevrolet Silverado pickup. He rummaged in one of the side pockets of the backpack and found his keys. After opening the door, he transferred the backpack to the front, and climbed in. He grabbed a fresh t-shirt out of the bag on the floor and changed out of the sweaty one he had worn in the canyon.

With a twist of the key, he started the truck and backed out. As he drove to the end of the line of parked cars, he was afforded one more glimpse of the canyon. He slowed. The view was awe-inspiring. He never tired of it. He wondered how different it would look in the morning. He had a long drive ahead, so he resisted the temptation to stay for an extended look. Instead, he turned and headed north toward the exit.

Tonight would be a marathon. There was much to accomplish. Many things could go wrong. If everything proceeded as planned, the Grand Canyon would never be the same. He would do something that environmentalists would talk about for decades. The Colorado River would run wild in the canyon once more. His spine tingled at the thought. Exiting the parking lot, he accelerated up to speed.

* * *

5:30 p.m. - Denver, Colorado

Grant walked in from the garage, slammed the door, and threw his briefcase on the couch. He was unbuttoning his shirt as he walked down the hallway toward his bedroom.

His wife Melanie poked her head out of their son's room. She looked concerned. Doors were almost never slammed at the Stevens' home. "What's wrong?"

Grant gritted his teeth. "Guess."

She looked confused.

"What've I been preparing for for weeks?" he added.

Her face showed shock. She held both her hands up to her face. "Kenya?"

He didn't say anything. He walked past her into the bedroom where he removed his shirt and threw it at the hamper.

She followed him into the bedroom and put her hands on her hips. "What happened? They can't just take that away from you. What about your vacation?" She reached out and put a hand on his arm.

He grabbed a worn t-shirt from a drawer and pulled it over his head. "Oh, the Bureau'll reimburse my personal expenses for the vacation."

She shrugged. "Well, at least . . ." Her voice tapered off.

At 38, his wife Melanie was still a beautiful woman. He could see the compassion in her eyes. Her face, always her greatest asset, had stayed young over the eighteen years of marriage. Her eyes twinkled, she had perfect teeth, and you had to look close to see the grays mixed in with her blond hair.

She grabbed his shoulder. "Who decided this? Is this Howard's doing?"

"It's hard to tell." He kicked off his shoes. "He's the one who told me." He talked while removing his slacks and replacing them with a pair of worn Levis. "He told me Roland decided that Howard couldn't be in charge with everyone else gone. Howard said they made him take vacation."

She smiled and reached up to hug him. "So they're leaving you in charge? That's good. Isn't it?"

Grant glared at her. "In charge of what? That's the whole point of Kenya. There's nothing to do here." He pointed east as if Kenya were only a couple miles away. "There are going to be engineers there, real engineers with real projects. I was going to work with the Chinese from Three Gorges." He pressed his fingers into his forehead, rubbing up and down.

She reached around his waist and pulled him close. "Look, I know how disappointed you are." She hesitated, choosing her words carefully. "But this could end up being a good thing for you."

He rolled his eyes at his wife—the eternal optimist.

She jerked him closer and raised one eyebrow, mimicking John Belushi. "They sent Howard away so he wouldn't bother you. Maybe they're on to him."

Grant shook his head. "Maybe it was Howard's idea and he's blaming it on Roland." He pulled away from her and headed back toward the family room.

She followed, still talking. "Why don't you call Roland and find out?"

He stopped and turned around. "Yeah, right."

"Why not?" she asked.

His wife thought he could fix anything just by talking to the right person. She had been out of the workforce too long. In business, some things were intentionally not communicated. "I'm not calling Roland."

He walked into the family room and grabbed the remote, then headed for the lazy-boy. After pushing back, he closed his eyes. Melanie wanted him to get rid of the chair, but over the years it had worn into the exact shape of his body. The feeling was one of comfort and security. In that chair, he could deal with anything life threw at him.

"Well, one advantage," Melanie said carefully, "is that now we can use the week of vacation for the family."

The last thing he wanted to talk about was where to vacation instead of Africa. "Whatever," he responded without opening his eyes.

"Isn't there someplace else you want to go?"

Why was she doing this to him? He opened his eyes and looked at her. "Hmm. How about we go to Australia, spend some time in the outback checking out crocodiles? We could hit the Great Barrier Reef while we're there. Hey I know, how about Mount Everest? We could fly into Nepal, then—"

She recoiled. "I'm trying to be serious."

"So am I," he retorted, a little too aggressively.

"Well, if you're going to act like . . ." She turned and walked into the kitchen.

Grant felt guilty for snapping at her. It wasn't her fault. She was just trying to put a positive spin on it. He knew he should chase after her and apologize, but he didn't have the energy. Not now. Besides, getting up out of the chair at the moment was unthinkable. He vowed to make up with her later. But at that moment he needed to be left alone.

He reclined and glanced around the room. He guessed it looked like any other middle-class TV room in Denver. A thirty-two inch TV sat in the cabinet, not a big-screen. The couch reclined, but the kids had broken the left side, so it slouched slightly. The veneer coffee table was nice enough, but didn't match the oak entertainment center, something that bothered his wife, but Grant couldn't care less about. Everything about the room was unremarkable.

When he thought about it, he realized he didn't know a single person who'd been on an African safari. That would have been something different, something special. Now what? Would they spend a couple days camping and roasting wieners instead? In Africa, he had a chance to see an elephant in the wild, or a cheetah. Now, if he was lucky he might see a jackrabbit. Then there was work. Talking to the Chinese engineers could have made up for a year of paperwork. Now what? For all the excitement he expected in the next couple of weeks, he could manage the Bureau from his recliner.

He leaned back in the chair and aimed the remote at the TV. The channel came up on some court TV show. He flipped through various channels, seeing nothing that interested him. He passed a channel showing an expanse of water he recognized. He went back to it. It was Lake Powell. The camera panned across the horizon of the lake, showing the red rock cliffs surrounding a large bay. It zoomed slightly and focused on a large rock formation that Grant recognized as Castle Rock, which separated Wahweap Bay from Warm Springs Bay. Two houseboats meandered through a shallow cut between the two bays. He turned up the volume so he could hear the woman reporter.

"The below-normal spring runoff in the west has contributed to what was already a multi-year drought."

The camera, again panning the horizon, zoomed quickly to a narrow rock channel snaking back and forth. A water-ski boat motored next to the vertical rock cliffs.

"As you can see, water levels at Lake Powell are well below normal."

The reporter referred to a bleached white band surrounding the lake. The contrast between the red rock and the white band left no doubt as to where the water levels had previously been. Grant didn't remember ever seeing the lake that low.

"Water allocation, already a problem on the Colorado River, has become more complicated."

The camera angle, obviously shot from a helicopter, showed the upstream side of the Glen Canyon Dam. In one fluid motion the helicopter flew over the crest, allowing viewers to look straight down the face of the six-hundred-foot dam. The next camera angle showed the dam with Lake Powell stretching for miles behind it. The Glen Canyon Bridge, a modern, silver-arched structure just downstream from the dam, stretched across the top of the screen, and framed the view perfectly.

While working at the Bureau for the last eighteen years, Grant had traveled to the Glen Canyon Dam many times. Like every civil engineer, he loved to look at it. However, in spite of his many visits, he had never actually been on the lake. His wife wanted to know where to vacation; maybe Lake Powell was the answer. They could rent a houseboat and get lost on the lake for a week. Of course he didn't have a ski boat or any equipment, but he supposed you could rent all that stuff.

The reporter continued. "Although the Glen Canyon Dam is equipped with eight huge turbines, capable of generating enough power for over a million homes, low water has limited releases from the dam, forcing the Bureau of Reclamation to shut off four of the turbines. This has added to the power shortage in the west, just when households need it the most, during the air conditioning season."

Grant tried to remember the name of the new guy in charge of operations at Glen Canyon. Wasn't he scheduled to be at the symposium in Kenya? Maybe he could take Grant's spot at the Three Gorges discussion. Gee, maybe he could even take Grant's place on the safari.

The TV showed an aerial shot of another huge concrete dam, which Grant immediately recognized. "Similar circumstances exist downstream at Lake Mead and Hoover Dam – water levels and power output are both below normal."

The television showed the reporter in studio. She was a striking blond in a blue business suit worn over a red blouse. Her lipstick matched the blouse. A large flat screen monitor behind the reporter showed a close-up of a three-story houseboat towing two water-ski boats. The exposed part of the second deck carried six personal watercraft, with a large crane to lower them into the water. On the top deck, four bikini-clad women waved to the camera. Grant tried to focus on one, but the reporter's head moved in front of the scene.

The reporter furrowed her brows and looked directly into the camera. "The drought has everyone along the Colorado River nervous, especially the farmers. There are reports of cattle farmers in Utah and Arizona selling out due to lack of water for their herds."

A man's voice spoke, and the camera panned to show another reporter on the woman's right side. "Laura, how much rain do they need?"

She glanced at him for a second, before looking back at the camera. "That's a good question, Jim. The people I talked to at the Bureau of Reclamation say it rarely rains around these dams, that the Colorado River comes mostly from snow pack in the Rocky Mountains, not from rain."

The man turned to the camera. "So this problem isn't likely to get solved anytime soon then, is it?"

The camera zoomed in on the woman again. She shook her head, then stared into the camera. "No, Jim. It will take a wet winter, or more realistically, more than one, to get water levels back to normal on the Colorado."

The camera now moved to the male reporter. "Thanks for the report, Laura. In other news, a neighborhood in Boulder is suing the city for not responding to their complaints about –"

Grant pressed the button on the remote to shut off the TV. He stared blankly at the dark screen. Although he already knew the west was in another drought, he hadn't actually seen pictures of Lake Powell. The low levels had shocked him, especially the one showing the boats passing through the cut next to Castle Rock. Normally that whole area was underwater. He remembered seeing low water before, but only in the fall, never in June. At this rate, by the end of the summer, the Castle Rock channel would be impassable, forcing boats to go the long way around Antelope Island, through the main river channel, an extra sixteen miles around from the marina.

He sat in his chair for a while, thinking. Finally he stood and walked into the kitchen. He took a glass from the cabinet and filled it with water from the sink. He held it up and looked through it, before taking a drink. Out the window, excess water from his neighbor's sprinklers sprayed into the street. A small rainbow sparkled in the mist. Water ran across the sidewalk and into the gutter. Grant leaned forward and looked up and down the neighborhood. His neighbors all kept their lawns watered and green. He wondered how many of his neighbors were concerned about a water shortage in the west.

It was not unusual for the Colorado River to be in drought conditions. After all, the Colorado and its tributaries watered the bulk of the southwestern states, from Wyoming to California, including Los Angeles, Phoenix, and Las Vegas. Grant knew about the drought even before the reporter said so. But obviously his neighbors either didn't know, or didn't care.

He glanced sideways and saw his wife bent over rearranging stuff in the fridge. With the khaki shorts hiked up her legs, he could see the contrast between the beginnings of her summer tan and the white flesh above. The position emphasized the muscles in her legs.

He went to her and placed his hands on the back of her thighs. She jumped then straightened up. When she was upright he let his hands go under her shirt to her stomach in an embrace from behind. She leaned her head back on his shoulder.

"What happened to mad Grant?" she asked

"He's still here."

She smiled. "Let's try not to wake him up, then."

She turned around and faced him, putting her arms around his neck. Her lips were very close to his. "I'm sorry about your safari."

He pulled back. "It was more than a safari. I would have had a whole week with the Chinese engineers."

She pulled him back. "I'm sorry about everything."

She reached up and kissed him, a tender kiss of compassion. He pulled her close and kissed her back.

"They'll be gone a week, right?" she asked.

He nodded.

"Maybe we can have a safari here."

"What do you mean?"

She smiled mischievously. "You'll see."

CHAPTER 3

6:00 p.m. - Lake Powell, Utah

Julie Crawford and Erika Sanders paddled their kayak leisurely along a stretch of water next to the cliffs in an isolated rock canyon. The yellow kayak was the sit-on-top variety, and had been purchased specifically for Lake Powell. It was especially fun in the late afternoons when they could paddle next to the cliffs and stay in the shade. Their water-ski boat was resting, tied to the houseboat, which in turn was tied to the rocky shore only a hundred feet away. Their husbands, along with Max and Darlene, were lounging under the shaded deck of the houseboat.

The two women stopped paddling. Julie dipped her hand in the water, and wiped the wetness on her cheeks. "Man, can you imagine being out here before the lake was here, when it was dry?"

Erika nodded. "Yuk. I'd die. I already feel like I'm going to burn up if I don't get in the water every few minutes." She pointed at the others. "I can't believe they're not in here too." She looked over her shoulder at Julie. "By the way, how long will we be out of the water tomorrow while we're hiking?"

The plan for the next day included an excursion to "Hole in the Rock", a spot made famous by a group of pioneers in the 1800s who were looking for a shortcut. They had blasted a trail and transported their oxen and covered wagons down a mile-long grade to the Colorado River. Although the bottom of the original grade was buried under Lake Powell, Hole in the Rock was a popular spot. Hikers who could manage the steep climb were rewarded with a panoramic view, a monument, and a close-up perspective of what it would have been like to move oxen and wagons down the hill. The husbands had hiked to the spot before, but Julie and Erika never had.

"I think Greg said it was about an hour to the top."

Erika considered the information. "So an hour up and an hour down. That's two hours out of the water. What if I die?"

Julie laughed. "Going down shouldn't take as long as hiking up. Although, I guess if we rest for a while at the top, we might still be out of the water for two hours."

Erika rolled her eyes.

Julie pointed toward the houseboat. "That's why Greg's making us leave so early in the morning. We'll get up there and hike it before it gets too hot, and be back by noon."

"I think Darlene has the right idea," Erika said.

"There will be plenty of time during the week to sit around and read," Julie argued.

Max and Darlene had elected to stay behind the next morning. Darlene said she was too fat to climb the hill. The other two couples had argued with them, but to no avail. Darlene could stand to lose a few pounds and the hike was just what she needed. It would do her good. Greg had even suggested they modify the plan to go someplace less strenuous, like some of the rock cathedrals up the Escalante Branch of the lake, but both Max and Darlene had declined, insisting that the two younger couples needed some time together. Julie suspected that Darlene was already absorbed in her book, a romance novel.

"And we're stopping at Rainbow after?" Erica asked.

Julie shook her head. "No, before. On the way."

Since the trip to Hole in the Rock ran right past Rainbow Bridge, they planned on a quick stop to see the huge rock arch as part of the next morning's activities. Rainbow was by far the most famous attraction at Lake Powell, and was visited by almost two hundred thousand tourists every year.

"Wouldn't the hike be cooler if we did it first, before Rainbow?"

Julie had wondered the same thing. "Yeah. I agree. But Greg says if we try to stop on the way back, the tour boats will already be there and it'll be too crowded. Plus we would be all sweaty."

In the summer, large boats from Wahweap and Bullfrog Marinas arrived at Rainbow Bridge by 10 a.m., spilling tourists out and changing the serene atmosphere to one more like Disneyland. Julie had been there at the same time as the big boats before and agreed that it ruined the experience.

Erika nodded as if that made sense. "Are we going to ski on the way?"

"We could, but it would take longer. Ya know, all the stops and everything. Besides, it's no fun to ski in the main channel. It's too rough."

Erika flicked some hair off her face. "I remember Rainbow being huge. How tall is it?"

"I don't remember the exact dimensions; I think around three hundred feet high. They say you could fly a 747 through it."

Erika reached down in the water then ran her fingers through her hair. "Isn't it one of the seven natural wonders of the world?"

"I don't know about that, but I read that before Glen Canyon was flooded, only a couple thousand people ever saw it, not counting the Navajos. It was so remote. The hike down to it was over twenty miles in burning heat. Many of them rode mules. When environmentalists protested the flooding of Glen Canyon, the government pointed out that most of the protesters had never even seen the arch. The environmentalists couldn't even argue. Now, supposedly, over a hundred thousand people see it every year."

"Not as remote as it used to be, huh?" Erika said.

Julie slid over and let herself drop off the kayak into the water. Erika followed. While Erika held on, Julie dove underwater to wet her hair.

Julie swam back and draped her arms over the kayak like Erika. "You'd think the environmentalists would be happy that the area is more accessible. I mean, I understand they covered up some stuff with the water, but at least now, people can get there."

Erika cocked her head. "That's not the way they think. They don't want people to see it, or enjoy it. Didn't you hear? They want to eliminate cars from Yosemite, and snowmobiles from Yellowstone. They want to ban motorcycles from the desert. They use words like undisturbed, and pristine. They think that only they should be able to see it. The rest of us should be satisfied with pictures."

Julie smiled. "Wow, I didn't know you felt so strong about it."

Erika continued, "You know why it pisses me off? Because I consider myself an environmentalist. I'm against big businesses dumping garbage into the rivers, air pollution, and all that other stuff. But the environmentalists in the news are over the top. Shutting down logging over an owl, sleeping in trees, lying in front of bulldozers and trains. They're nuts. They believe we should pretend there aren't millions of people in America. Environmentalists are giving environmentalism a bad name."

Julie laughed. "Ya know, I never looked at it like that. But, when it comes down to it, I feel the same way. I don't litter. I recycle. Aren't I an environmentalist?"

Erika laughed. "Not in their minds. You're a heathen. You drive a car; actually, worse – a pickup. You live in a neighborhood." She gasped and cupped her hand over her mouth. "You eat meat, you sicko. And worst of all, you take hot showers with soap and scented shampoos, every day, sometimes multiple times a day. Don't you know that to be a true environmentalist you have to wear one of those dyed tee-shirts with weird colors, use a blue bandana to tie up your unwashed, uncombed hair, and let the hair grow out in your armpits and on your legs?" Erika wagged her finger. "No. You are not, and never will be, a true environmentalist."

Julie held up her arm and looked at her cleanly shaved armpit. "No, I guess not."

* * *

6:30 p.m. - Hoover Dam, outside Las Vegas, Nevada

Fred Grainger stood behind the computer technician in the control room at Hoover Dam. The control room was located on the downstream side of the dam just above river level. Fred, the site supervisor, had worked there for twenty-two years. At 53, he was the oldest guy at Hoover. Actually, that was only true if you counted the people who took care of the dam and were employed by the Bureau of Reclamation. There were many others, guides and even a few security guards that were older than Fred. But Fred considered them another group.

Jeremy Rottingham, the technician in front of Fred, stopped typing and turned around. "Just got a down request from California Edison. Want me to turn down Arizona or Nevada?"

Fred's group was responsible for monitoring power needs from locations throughout the western United States and adjusting electricity generation accordingly. Basically, all major dam controls at Hoover were his responsibility. There were two generation plants, one on the Nevada side of the river, and one on the Arizona side, hence Jeremy's question of which plant to throttle down.

"Which one is hotter?"

"Nevada, but not by much."

"Let's take it out of Arizona, then; she carried the load yesterday."

Jeremy made the necessary adjustments with the keyboard. The computer handled the rest of the job. Most of the controls at Hoover had been automated. The technicians set the amount of power that they wanted from each plant and the computer did the rest. The rest entailed adjusting water flow through the penstocks to each generator to determine power output. Penstocks were the huge tubes that carried water to each generator. At Hoover, each penstock was thirteen feet in diameter. Nine generators were housed in the Arizona plant and eight in the Nevada plant. Each generator rose over seven stories high and was capable of powering 100,000 homes. With all seventeen generators running, Hoover could power a respectable portion of the West.

"Aren't you out tomorrow?" Jeremy asked.

Fred shook his head. "No, that's next week."

Fred had scheduled a few days off. He had accrued too many days of vacation, and if he did not use them by the end of June, he would lose them. He had lost unused vacation days before, something that bothered his wife more than him.

"Where are you going?" Jeremy asked.

Fred moaned. "Nowhere special. The wife wants me to take her to see the inside of the new casinos. There are a couple of new ones that've been open for over a year that she still hasn't seen. The inside of one of them is supposed to be pretty cool. Least that's what she's heard. You been in 'em yet?"

Jeremy shook his head. "Nah, I spend all of my gambling time downtown. The odds are better in the smaller casinos."

"You gamble? I thought technical folks didn't gamble."

"I dabble. Craps is a statistics game. If you know the rules and when to bet, you can increase your odds."

Fred laughed. "You can increase your odds even more if you don't gamble."

Fred looked over Jeremy's shoulder at one of the readouts. "Did you turn down Parker?"

"Yeah, about an hour ago."

Parker and Davis Dams were downstream from Hoover, but Fred's group controlled both via microwave communication from the Hoover control center. Davis Dam, almost seventy miles downstream from Hoover, created Lake Mojave, and Parker Dam, another ninety miles farther, created Lake Havasu. Hoover of course, held back Lake Mead, the largest man-made lake in the United States. At over 110 miles long, with 9.3 trillion gallons, Lake Mead would cover the state of Pennsylvania with a foot of water. From the control room where they sat, Fred controlled the lion's share of the water in the lower Colorado River system.

"No adjustment requests for Davis yet this evening?" asked Fred.

"Not yet, but I expect one any minute," Jeremy replied.

Fred turned to go. "All right, I'm gonna take a break for dinner."

"Okay, boss."

Fred took his lunch box from his desk in the control room and ambled down two stories of stairs out of the central plant. Walking through a hallway deep in the heart of the dam, he came to the elevator. He used his personal key to call it, then waited for it to arrive. He would have dinner on top tonight. He needed some air and wanted to enjoy what was left of the sun. The elevator took a few minutes to cover the six hundred vertical feet to the top of the dam. Unlike elevators in high-rise office buildings, he could feel this one accelerate up to speed. He was glad his wife wasn't with him. It would have made her nauseous. When the doors opened, he shielded his eyes. He had forgotten his sunglasses. He stepped out of the elevator and made sure the elevator was locked.

Summers were always crowded at Hoover. Over a million people visited the dam annually. Since there were no major bridges across the Colorado River in the area, US-93 used Hoover as the bridge between Nevada and Arizona. The result was millions more people crossing the dam each year in cars.

Fred waited for a break in the traffic, and then crossed to the upstream side of the dam. He then headed west toward the Nevada shore, where the visitor center was located. His walk was on a slightly elevated sidewalk with a concrete rail to keep him from falling into the lake. The walk along the rail offered a spectacular view of Lake Mead. Every now and then, Fred had to step down off the sidewalk into the road to get around a family or groups of tourists looking over the handrail. As he walked, he passed a concrete walkway that went straight out into the lake on his right. The walkway, blocked by a chain, led to two huge column-shaped towers. The first tower was about one hundred feet away from the dam and the second another hundred feet beyond the first.

The two towers, and the two just like them on the Arizona side, were intake towers. Their purpose was to collect the water being routed to the turbines for generating electricity. The towers did not pull water from the surface, however. They pulled water from two inlets at depths of two hundred fifty feet and three hundred fifty feet. Pulling water from those depths avoided sucking fish and other debris into the turbines.

When Fred neared the west end of the dam, he followed the edge of the dam around to the right. The sidewalk now took him away from the bulk of the crowds and past the old visitor center on his left and the snack bar on his right. Walking through the employee parking lot, he was now headed upstream on the Nevada bank of Lake Mead. The Nevada intake towers were still on his right. Up in front of him on the other side of the parking lot was the Nevada spillway.

He found a bench that offered a good view of the spillway and the lake, then opened his lunchbox. He inspected the contents, wondering what kind of sandwich his wife had made, and was pleasantly surprised to find tuna. She must have run out of lunchmeat, the usual.

As Fred ate, he studied the spillway. The tops of the spillways were twenty-seven feet below the crest of the dam. Each spillway, one on the Nevada side and one on the Arizona side, fed enormous fifty-foot-diameter spillway tunnels that disappeared into the canyon walls and exited at river level downstream from the dam. In front of each spillway tunnel was a large trough or ditch about one hundred fifty feet long with concrete walls on both sides to keep water out until the levels rose high enough to flow over, or spill into the spillways. In fact, Hoover's spillways were equipped with metal gates that rose automatically with high water, forcing the water another sixteen feet higher before it was allowed to flow into the spillways.

Since the dam was built in 1935, only twice had the water been high enough to flow into the spillways: once, when the dam was first filled, and again in 1983, when high snowmelt in Utah and Colorado caused both Lake Powell and Lake Mead water levels to rise.

Fred had witnessed 1983. Lake Mead had risen high enough that four feet of water flowed over the metal gates into the spillways for 60 days. He remembered it as quite a spectacle. During that year the Nevada and Arizona spillways together dumped twenty eight thousand cubic feet per second of water, more than doubling the normal Hoover Dam output. This, however, was less than five percent of the capacity of the spillways, which together could theoretically handle about four hundred thousand cubic feet per second, although that had never been tested.

As Fred studied the spillways, he wondered what it would be like to see them perform to their potential. That was why he ate here. He liked to imagine seeing that much water blasting down the huge hole. Just thinking about it made him shiver. He wondered if he would dare stand so close, or whether he would feel inclined to stand back a little. Although he considered it unlikely, he wondered if Hoover's spillways would ever reach their potential. Maybe a huge flood in the Rocky Mountains would do it, but it would have to be a big one.

After Fred finished his sandwich, he stood and walked over to the fence. He looked right down the fifty-foot hole. He'd give anything to see the spillways at their full capacity. After staring for a few minutes, he blinked, then turned and walked away, back toward the dam. Unfortunately, it didn't matter how bad Fred wanted to see it, because there was no way it would ever happen in his lifetime.

CHAPTER 4

7:00 p.m. - Page, Arizona

As the man's car rounded the hill, the car in front slowed on the descent, forcing him to slow as well. As both cars drove onto the bridge, he glanced left and got his first good look at Glen Canyon Dam, his first look in the last several months anyway. It was always impressive, even though he couldn't see all six hundred feet down to the river from his angle on the bridge.

Although he hadn't been to the dam for several months, he had seen it many times before. He had spent almost a year studying it and for one three-month period, he had spent almost every weekend in Page, Arizona. He took the tours on and in the dam, he hiked up on the hills and looked at it, he bought books which he read and re-read, attended lectures, and talked to everyone he could about how the dam worked. He even rented a boat and motored down next to it, although a barricade of buoys prevented him from getting as close as he wanted.

As long as he could remember, he had always wished he could blow up the Glen Canyon Dam. But then, many others before him had wanted to do the same, yet the dam was still there. If it were easy, someone else would have already done it.

During the months of planning, he came up with numerous ideas to destroy it; unfortunately, none of them were practical or feasible. His favorite idea had been the one from Edward Abbey's "Monkey Wrench Gang", where houseboats were loaded with explosives, floated down toward the dam, and detonated on impact. The skinny man was no genius, but even he knew that wouldn't work. An explosion on the outside of the dam wouldn't be enough. Even an airliner crash, like September 11th, wouldn't work. There was just too much concrete: sixty feet thick at the top, and 300 feet thick at the base. The airliner would just splat on the concrete and then slide down to the river below. Most people thought of concrete dams as walls, but that wasn't really true. Most dams were built more like pyramids. One couldn't hope to topple a pyramid from the outside. If you were to have any chance at all, you needed to blow it up from the inside. Even Abbey knew that.

That led to all kinds of crazy ideas, like what if you sent a torpedo down one of the intake towers, so that it detonates inside the water works. But that would require an incredibly sophisticated bomb, tons of money, and, frankly, technology that he didn't understand. Besides, that level of sophistication would require that he work with others, something he was unwilling to do. He realized his lack of social skills, and his inability to include others without getting caught. No, if this were to be done, it would have to be done by him, alone.

So he kept coming to Page. He knew there was a good idea out there somewhere. He just hadn't figured it out yet. He continued to research and study. He spent hours up on the hills, staring at it. One week, while home in Las Vegas, he overheard someone talking about listening to the police using a scanner from Radio Shack. After that, every time he watched the dam, he listened to a scanner while he watched. He listened to the tour guides talking to each other. He listened to the operators and technicians at the dam. And most valuably, he listened to the security guards talk to each other.

He listened every weekend for almost a month. He learned all the guards' names, their interests, and their wives' and girlfriends' names. He actually started to feel like he knew them after a while. Then one night he heard something that gave him an idea, an idea that had grown with time. An idea that eventually had grown into a plan, a plan that tonight would be executed. Tonight would test both the worthiness of the idea, and his ability to execute it. A few hours from now, there would be no turning back.

After the slow car crossed the bridge, it turned left onto a lookout point. The skinny man had spent many hours at that lookout. But tonight he had other plans. He accelerated up the hill. The highway veered right, and he saw the city of Page on top of the knoll.

Suddenly, he wondered if his stuff had been discovered. What if the police were waiting? An ambush? When he turned left on Navajo Drive, he scanned the streets carefully. If he saw someone, he could just drive on, and hope they couldn't tie him to anything. Boat storage and repair shops lined the street. But, he saw no police cruisers, which allowed him to relax.

Almost a half mile down Navajo, he turned left onto a small unmarked street, then a hundred yards later he pulled up to a chain link gate and stopped. A rusted sign on the gate said "PETERSEN SELF-STORAGE – Authorized Access Only". The skinny man put the truck in park and climbed out. He stretched. The drive from the Grand Canyon had taken just over two and a half hours. He walked over to the gate and inserted a key from his key ring into the huge padlock. When he rented the garage in the facility, over six months before, the owner had apologized for the padlock, saying that he would install security cards and an electric gate. But he knew better, even then. The owner was filthy and the whole place looked ratty and run down. Any upgrades would have been out of character.

After unlocking the gate and swinging it out of the way, he pulled the truck inside and relocked the gate. Driving all the way to the back, past all the boats and motor homes to a row of rundown garages, he veered left at the end of the row, went another twenty yards, then parked in front of number seven.

As he jumped out of the truck, he instinctively scanned in all directions. He fingered through his keys again and found the one for the second padlock, which he inserted in the lock on number seven. What if they were waiting for him inside the compartment? The thought made him tense. But the lock was dusty, making an ambush from inside unlikely. Nevertheless, he carefully scanned inside as he rolled up the door, and let the evening sun shine into the contents of the compartment.

In contrast to the rest of Petersen Self-Storage, the inside of number seven was spotless. A large enclosed utility trailer was the only obvious occupant. The skinny man flipped on a light switch, lighting a single incandescent bulb, then pulled the door down behind him. Now completely secluded, he plugged a new orange extension cord into the outlet under the light switch and the whole compartment was bathed in fluorescent light from three separate fixtures, one above each side of the trailer, and one behind. The lights were his first improvement to the compartment. It was impossible to do precision work with bad light.

He walked behind the trailer and saw the motorcycle was still there, helmet, gloves and leather jacket still sitting on the seat. He wondered if he should start it up and make sure it still ran, but that could wait. He instead found a third key and inserted it in the lock on the back of the utility trailer. The utility trailer was top-of-the-line. The sides and top were white metal panels, connected at the corners by rounded aluminum. The front top corners were beveled, round silver pieces. After removing the padlock on the back, he rotated a cast handle at the bottom of each door, which in turn maneuvered large vertical brackets that went all the way to the top of the doors, just like on the back of every eighteen-wheeler on the road.

The inside of the trailer seemed much smaller than the outside. Like the garage, the inside of the trailer was immaculate. Black metal tool cabinets lined the left side, and on the right were a mixture of implements, including a small ladder, a stack of bright orange highway construction cones, a lab stool, a hard hat, a coiled extension cord, and a separate coiled utility light. Notably, each one of the items on the right had a special bracket or shelf designed to fit it exactly. Even the ladder slid into a long compartment along the bottom.

The man ignored the items on the right, and the black metal drawers on the left. Instead, he stepped immediately past them to a small, knee-high, white utility box. Carefully he bent down and looked closely at where the top left rear corner of the box met the wall. He craned his neck until his eyes were inches away, then slowly a smile broke across what had been a tense face. Nobody had disturbed it. He reached down and retrieved the single hair stuck between the utility box and the wall. They didn't know.

DAY TWO

Tuesday, June 22

CHAPTER 5

4:00 a.m. - Page, Arizona

The man turned off the alarm on his watch. It had been unnecessary because he was already awake and about. Sleep had been impossible, which was something he should have guessed before such a big day. However, he needed to perform flawlessly, in spite of the lack of sleep. Looking back, he should have considered sleeping pills, to guarantee he would be rested.

The fluorescent lights fully illuminated the storage compartment. He only had a few more things to do, the next of which was to put the stickers on the trailer. They were about the size of a soccer ball. He removed the adhesive backing, and then placed one sticker on each side of the trailer. He stepped back and studied his work. He considered it a perfect rendition. The logo was simple, and had not been difficult to re-create. The designer in Las Vegas told him that his picture taken with a telephoto lens was of adequate resolution, and that the company's logo was simple anyway. He had two additional logos for the sides of the truck, although they were bigger, more like the size of a basketball, and made of a magnetic material.

He looked around the compartment and decided everything was ready. He knew he should sit tight, but he felt too jittery to remain in the compartment any longer. Extinguishing the lights, he opened the garage's sliding door and looked out into the dark desert sky. In spite of the outdoor lights at the storage facility, the stars were clearly visible over the silhouettes of the boats and motor homes. The desert air was stifling even so early in the morning – between 85 and 90 degrees, he guessed. He placed the magnetic logos on the truck doors and was surprised at how hard they pulled when he held them close to the metal. He climbed in the truck, started the engine, and the headlights came on automatically. He would have preferred they had not, and hoped that no one else noticed.

He maneuvered the truck into a better position to hook up the trailer, and then turned off the engine to kill the lights. Rolling the trailer forward enough to line up the hitch was no easy matter. In fact, for a moment he panicked and thought he wasn't strong enough to do it. However, after he strained and got it moving, it lined up perfectly over the ball. He hooked up the trailer lights, but passed on the safety chain. It would be a short trip.

He jumped back in the truck and carefully pulled the trailer out of the garage. This time he left the truck running when he climbed out. He shut off the lights inside the storage compartment, which was now empty except for the motorcycle, and pulled down the door. He considered leaving it unlocked for later, but changed his mind and relocked the padlock. Back in the truck, he drove slowly up to the front gate. He left it running while he jumped out and opened the gate.

As he turned off Navajo Drive and headed down the hill, he could see the brightly-lit Glen Canyon Dam. Even from miles away, the sight of it stirred strong feelings in him. He hated the dam, how it had screwed up the Colorado River, and buried Glen Canyon. But in spite of his feelings, he had to admit the dam was an amazing structure, one of the most amazing he had ever seen. It made him doubt what he was about to do. How likely was it really, that he could blow it up? The nagging notion that he had little chance caused him to consider giving up, to just keep driving, all the way back to Las Vegas, back to his 8-5 job, and back to a life without such unrealistic goals. Who was he anyway, to think he could pull it off?

As he passed over the bridge, however, and looked down on the dam, the hatred resurfaced. After all, this wasn't the first time he had argued with himself over this issue. Yes, there was risk that his plan wouldn't work. In fact, he admitted it was a long shot. But he had to try. The upside was too good. Unleashing the Colorado River would be a historic event, something that would be talked about for generations. And when it came down to it, there was no other way. No one else was willing to take the risk. Besides, how could he live with himself if he did not even try?

He turned into the visitor center parking, and reached over on the seat and touched the clipboard, making sure it was still there. He drove past the visitor center, and then almost a hundred yards farther until he reached the west access road to the dam itself. A solitary guard walked out of the guard shack. He stopped the truck and rolled down his window.

The guard shined a flashlight in his eyes. "What are you doing here?"

He shoved the clipboard toward the guard. "I'm from Jensen Industrial Elevators in Denver. You know, to service the west elevator." He pointed toward the dam.

The guard skimmed through the pages of the work order. "Nobody said anything to me about—"

The skinny man interrupted. "When I talked to Dan last night, he told me to get here early, so I'd be gone before the visitor center opens at 8:00 a.m." He looked at the guard's badge and saw the name Brian. What a lucky break. He knew Brian was the graveyard shift supervisor.

He reached his hand out the window. "You're Brian, aren't you? Dan told me you'd be in charge when I got here."

He had learned all of the security personnel's names from the scanner radio. He lied, of course, about talking to Dan the night before, but if he could convince the guard that it was approved, he might have a chance.

The guard stared at the work order. "Well, Dan didn't say anything to me."

The skinny man was ready for this comment. "Call him," he said, although that was the last thing he wanted him to do.

The guard looked at his watch and grimaced.

The skinny man knew what was going through his head. The guard did not want to call his boss so early in the morning and wake him up, not for something routine like elevator maintenance.

He finally looked up. "When did you talk to Dan?"

"He called us yesterday morning. Said the west elevator wasn't lining up correctly at the top. Said people were tripping over it. He wondered if we could fix it before the tours started this morning. I drove straight through from Denver last night."

The guard shook his head and looked back down at the work order. "Yeah, but he usually tells us when to expect somebody."

He could tell the guard was weakening. "It's kinda weird he didn't tell you. Like I said, feel free to call him and verify it if you need to."

The guard looked around as if he hoped someone might walk up and make the decision for him. He glanced down at the work order again, then shook his head. "Naw. I ain't gonna wake him up over this. Everything looks legit." He took a pen out and noted a time on the work order then handed it back. "How sure are you that you can be done and outta here before eight?"

The skinny man felt goose bumps rise on his arms and he wanted to yell out in exhilaration, but kept his voice monotone. "I won't know for sure until I get down there, but I don't see any reason why not."

He watched the guard walk over and unlock the huge metal gate and swing it open. He then put the truck back into gear and started through.

"Hey, wait a minute," the guard said.

His heart skipped. What had he seen? He stopped the truck. "Yeah?"

"Didn't your company used to use vans?"

He relaxed. It was a question he had anticipated. "Yeah, we just got these rigs. Now we don't have to take the trailers on the small jobs. Besides, this truck does a lot better on long hauls. Those vans were gutless on the highway."

The guard looked skeptical but finally nodded and waved him through. "I'll be down in a minute to open the doors."

He started down the road again. In his mirror he saw the guard swing the gate back and lock it. He drove down the short access road and onto the dam itself. He turned left and headed toward the west elevator shaft. Looking east across the dam, he could see a gate blocking access to the east side of the dam, and about a half dozen cars parked on the dam itself. He knew that they used the east side of the dam and the east elevator shaft for workers and kept the west side accessible for tours from the visitor center. He didn't expect to encounter anyone else on the west side during off hours.

When he reached the west elevator tower, he drove past it, then backed the trailer right up to the door, leaving only enough room to open the trailer doors. He waited while the guard walked down to open the gate. So far, so good.

He was out of the truck and waiting when the guard arrived. The man rummaged through a huge key ring for the proper key, then opened the large metal door. The skinny man stepped forward and used a shim to block it open. Both men walked into a small room, where the elevator doors sat. Instead of a button to call the elevator, it required a key.

The guard looked back at him, at the same time twisting another key off the ring. "I'll leave this one with you. You'll probably need it. If you go down to the bottom, be sure to take it or you won't be able to get back up." He made a dismissive gesture with his hand. "I'm sure you know all about that."

When the security man opened the elevator, he looked down at the floor and ran his foot over the seam. "It looks fine to me."

"It might be intermittent. I'll run her up and down a couple of times and see. If not, I'll adjust the switches anyway. That should fix it." His research on elevator maintenance suggested that adjusting the switches was the answer to almost everything.

The guard nodded, then handed him the key. "All right, I gotta get back to my post. I'll come back to check on you occasionally." He started off, then stopped and turned. "By the way, what'd you say your name was?"

The skinny man froze. He forgot the name he was supposed to use. The name "George" floated through his head, and he almost popped it out, which would have been a disaster since it would not have matched what was on the work order. The name was not George, but it sounded similar – Jerry, John . . . He suddenly remembered and blurted it out. "Jim. Nice to meet you."

The security man didn't seem to notice anything strange. "Good luck, Jim. Let me know if it starts looking like you won't be done by eight."

He nodded, and watched the guard walk away. He clenched his hand around the elevator key. He was in. Now the hard part.

* * *

5:00 a.m. - Page, Arizona

By 5:00 a.m., he had the control panel open in the elevator, exposing the wires. He placed cones around the back of the trailer to discourage anyone from walking in. He hoped the guard wouldn't come back until he finished what he needed to do.

Out of the tool belt on his waist, he pulled a disassembled cell phone that had been wired into a small circuit board. He had already tested the phone back in Vegas, and he knew his modifications would work. He placed the phone up high, almost to the ceiling of the elevator, then duct taped it to the wall. He checked the signal strength and saw three bars, which was good enough, something he had worried about. Sorting through the wires from the control panel of the elevator, he found the two he was looking for. He bared some of the insulation from the two wires and then clipped a wire to each from the circuit board. He then quickly replaced the control panel. After close inspection, he saw that everything looked normal except for the two wires connected to the cell phone and circuit board. If anyone looked up, they would think it was a bomb. However, he had no intentions of letting anyone see it.

Now things would get exciting. He walked outside and peeked around the back of the trailer at the guard shack. He could see the guard was still in the shack. He knew he didn't have much time. He hustled back into the trailer, and removed the false wall, where the night before he had retrieved the single hair. Before, with the false wall in place, someone could have noticed that the inside wasn't even half the size of the outside. However, he had not intended to let anyone get a good look.

Now with the panels gone, a dozen white metal fifty-gallon barrels were exposed, stacked three wide, two high, and two deep. He used a special dolly with a lift jack to grab the first barrel off the top row. When he first tried to move the barrels back in Vegas he was surprised at how heavy they were, hence the expensive dolly. He wheeled the barrel down a metal ramp out of the trailer and right into the elevator. Laying it down on its side on the floor he shoved the barrel's bottom against the back of the elevator. A few minutes later a whole row of barrels were lying on their sides against the back of the elevator. He was on his way back to get the next barrel when he heard the security guard's voice.

"Everything all right in there?"

The sound made him freeze. He wiped sweat off his forehead, then poked his head out from behind the trailer. The security man had walked down the access road onto the dam, but headed west toward the visitor center door instead of toward the elevator.

He yelled out to him, "Yeah, I'm just checking everything right now."

The man waved and kept walking toward the visitor center.

He increased his pace on the remaining barrels. Fifteen minutes later he had all twelve barrels stacked, four wide and three high, against the back of the elevator. The elevator sagged slightly at the weight and no longer lined up perfectly with the floor. With the last barrel in place he removed the clamp off one of the top barrels and removed the metal lid. The inside was packed tight with what looked like dirty white crystals or pellets. The smell of diesel invaded his nostrils when the lid came off. He removed the remaining lids and tossed them in the small room outside the elevator shaft, the smell of fuel now strong in the elevator.

He hustled back into the trailer twice and retrieved the footlocker on one trip, and a car battery on the next. He set the car battery under the elevator control panel, and then opened the footlocker. He pulled a metal tube almost eighteen inches long and an inch in diameter out of the box. The tube had two wires hanging out of it. He forcefully rammed it in one of the barrels until only the wires were visible. The motion dislodged white pellets which trickled to the floor. He took no notice, continuing working until all twelve barrels had wires hanging out of them. He then spent the next few minutes wiring them together. He finished by connecting them to the circuit board and finally to the car battery. When he connected the car battery, a red LED illuminated on the circuit board.

He took a moment to check his work. The materials he used were all readily available. The white pellets were the hardest to get, and required that he make a purchase in Utah, using his grandfather's name for their farm in southern Utah. Even the farm stores wouldn't sell that much fertilizer to a city boy. The ammonium nitrate fertilizer was common enough, if you had a good reason to buy it. Of course his grandfather was too old to notice that it never made it onto the fields.

Although he had heard about ammonium nitrate being used for bombs, most notably the Oklahoma Federal Building, it had been a surprise to learn that ammonium nitrate was not the core of the bomb. The explosive part of the bomb was the diesel fuel itself. The ammonium nitrate only acted as an accelerant, providing an oxygen boost during the chemical reaction of the explosion. However, gasoline bombs, with and without the fertilizer, were not in the same league, as evidenced in Oklahoma, where the bomb sliced through ten stories of the Federal Building as if it were cut with a knife.

One of his biggest concerns for this bomb was channeling the explosive. Since the elevator shaft traveled down the downstream side of the dam, he needed the bulk of the explosion to be channeled upstream. That's why he pushed the barrels back against the back wall of the elevator, and left the fronts open. Explosions take the path of least resistance, and he hoped that the bomb would get plenty of upstream momentum before it hit the huge wall of concrete. It wouldn't do any good to blow the elevator shaft apart. He needed it focused upstream, to channel the explosion.

The detonators had been made using household chemicals and electronics. He had driven out in the desert one weekend and tried one and was surprised at how violent of an explosion the little suckers made. They needed to be pretty hot, to get the ammonium nitrate and diesel to react the way he needed it to.

Admiring what he had done in the elevator, he felt mixed emotions. On one hand it looked great. It had gone together exactly as he had envisioned it. On the other hand, he wondered if it would be enough. He needed to blast through nearly a hundred feet of concrete. Would any bomb be powerful enough to do that?

He reminded himself to keep moving, so he stepped out of the elevator and turned the key to let the door shut. He taped a strip of yellow stripping labeled CAUTION across the elevator door, although if anyone walked in, the smell of diesel would tip them off. He hustled out of the building and noticed that the security man was back in his shed. Walking around to the front of the trailer, he unhitched it. He wouldn't be needing it anymore.

The guard was waiting for him when he drove up the access road. But it wasn't Brian, it was someone else. His tag read "Jessie."

The new guard walked right up to the truck's window and looked inside. "What's wrong?"

He leaned out. "The good news is I found the lever that's starting to stick. That's probably why the thing was hit and miss. The bad news is I ran out of grease. I need to run into town for a second and get another tube of grease."

The guard checked his watch. "Everything's gonna be closed."

"I can get this grease at the gas station. I should be back in a few minutes."

The guard walked over to unlock the gate. "You gonna be done by eight?"

He responded out the window as he drove past. "Don't worry. I'll be miles down the road by eight. I guarantee it."

CHAPTER 6

6:00 a.m. - Lake Powell, Utah

"Okay, everybody ready?" Without waiting for an answer, Greg turned the key and fired up the Mastercraft.

Paul stood on the deck of the houseboat and unwound the rope from the two cleats. He tossed the rope into the water-ski boat, pushed off, and jumped in. He sat in the seat facing backwards from Greg. Julie sat in the other front seat next to her husband, and Erika sat facing backwards from her. Erika was rubbing her eyes, still half asleep. Greg shifted to forward and idled away from the houseboat.

Julie felt bad that Max and Darlene were staying behind, although spending the morning with just Paul and Erika would be fun. She felt the boat throttle up, and her body was pulled back into her seat. Julie watched her husband. He looked over at her and smiled. She relaxed and took in the majestic scenery all around them. The rising sun cast long shadows in the canyon. It had been hard to get going so early, but it was worth it. She loved being in these remote canyons. She grabbed the armrest on her seat as the boat banked in to a slow turn around a bend. She looked ahead and saw another curve. Every time they left the houseboat, she meant to count the number of twists and turns it took them to get to the main channel, but she never remembered until they were half way. This time she remembered but didn't feel like counting.

She turned and glanced back over her shoulder at Erika, who was gazing up at the red rock walls behind. Erika looked tired and had not spoken since they woke. Paul and Greg looked calm and happy. Julie changed her mind. Let Max and Darlene enjoy the morning alone. What difference did it make that they were separating for the day anyway?

* * *

6:05 a.m. - Page, Arizona

The man rode his motorcycle onto the Glen Canyon Bridge. The white truck was back on Navajo Street, safely parked inside the storage unit, away from curious eyes. After riding over the bridge, he continued slowly up the hill. He glanced in his mirrors to verify no one was behind him. The image of hundreds of police officers, sirens wailing, kept projecting into his subconscious mind. However, a quick scan of the road ahead and behind revealed that he was alone. Page, Arizona was not an early-bird town.

Approximately fifty yards up the hill, he pulled over to the side of the road. He put the bike on its kickstand and dismounted. He left the engine running. He pulled a cell phone from an inside pocket of his jacket. It seemed to tingle in his fingers. He walked across the street to the other side where he had a better view back toward the Glen Canyon Dam. Every movement seemed to be playing in slow motion in his head. The sun had just poked its head above the horizon. The effect left the rock walls on the opposite side of the canyon in darkness while sunning the ground under his feet. He focused on the huge concrete structure. Night lights still lit the top of the dam. Everything looked normal. No blinking police lights, no sirens.

He held the cell phone in front of him and dialed the nine-digit number from memory. Before he hit send, he hesitated. He thought about the Colorado River. He fantasized about it breaking through all the man-made chastity belts blocking it from where it wanted to go. Maybe the city dwellers, especially the greedy Californians, would finally have to conserve a little, turn down the sprinklers, turn off the water fountains, drain some of the pools and artificial lakes. He snickered as a scene floated through his head of a big fat guy diving into an empty swimming pool, the guy squishing head first into the bottom of the pool and tipping over, like in a cartoon.

He stopped the images. He'd come here for a reason. None of it would happen if he didn't press the button. In a moment of frustration, his head told his thumb to press, but it wouldn't obey. How could it all fall apart now, at the final moment? The thought made him angry. His brain sent the signal again, and this time he felt the small button click under the pressure. He stared at it for a second then cupped it to his ear. He heard two rings, then a connection, then nothing.

In the west elevator of the Glen Canyon Dam, another cell phone, this one with wires hanging out of it, rang twice and stopped. Electricity from the phone's ringer traveled onto a small circuit board, through a voltage relay, then down two wires into the elevator control panel. The elevator reacted immediately by starting down. Simultaneously a digital timer started a very quick countdown. Since the elevator was near capacity, stuffed with twelve barrels of ammonium nitrate soaked in diesel fuel, the downward motion began with a jerk. The elevator continued to descend into the dam. Exactly 18 seconds after the cell phone started its motion, the elevator had traveled approximately two hundred feet from the top of the dam. At that moment, the timer expired. A very small electrical current traveled from the timer to a voltage relay. This relay sent a much larger current from the car battery to the homemade detonation devices tucked into each barrel of ammonium nitrate. The result was immediate and forceful. Because of the way the explosives were packed in the elevator, the energy of the explosion was channeled horizontally upstream toward the lake side of the dam.

The skinny man timed the 18 seconds on his watch. It seemed like an eternity. For an instant, he thought something had gone wrong. Then directly below where the vertical elevator disappeared into the dam, a ball of fire and concrete exploded out of the face of the dam. Chunks of concrete fell to the river four hundred feet below. An instant later the top of the elevator shaft on the top of the dam exploded upwards, scattering debris in all directions. A crushing sound wave followed both explosions. The skinny man ducked instinctively.

Although the fireworks were impressive, they were less than he had expected and he felt certain the entire effort had been in vain. He strained to assess the damage, specifically if any water was leaking from the dam. Unfortunately, his view of the face of the dam was totally obstructed by a huge cloud of smoke. He stepped closer and craned his neck for a better look. The smoke swirled and for a moment he thought he saw something, then his view was blocked again. He needed to leave now, but he also needed to know.

Then he saw it: a single stream of water spraying from the small hole. It looked to be no more than two feet in diameter. He couldn't believe he hadn't seen it before. The pressure, 200 feet down in the reservoir, created a solid spray way out into the river, although because of his angle, it was impossible to tell the distance for sure. It was definitely far enough to clear the generation plants at the base of the dam.

As he watched, the water seemed to jerk, and change its trajectory. There was much more water now. He now estimated the column at least five feet in diameter. The jerking continued every couple of seconds, each time resulting in higher water flow. It reminded him of holding a frozen garden hose in the winter and feeling the water force the pieces of ice out the end of the hose.

He couldn't have hoped for a better result. The water tearing through the hole two hundred feet down in the dam was enough to continually carve at the dam. It would disintegrate rapidly. Not nearly as fast as an earth dam, but plenty fast enough. He had heard that if you could drill a small dime-sized hole through the face of a dam, the water rushing through the hole would eventually tear the dam apart. He would have loved to test that exact hypothesis, dangling from a rope from the top of the dam, but was fairly sure that the security people at Glen Canyon wouldn't have sponsored the experiment.

He watched for a moment longer. The water was now blasting. If only he could stay and watch it tear itself apart. He knew he could not. He needed to make St. George, Utah and I-15 before the cops figured out what happened and blocked the road, or the remainder of the week would be jeopardized. He turned and headed back toward the motorcycle. As he pulled back onto the highway, he glanced back at the rising sun. It was almost completely above the horizon. The LCD display of his digital watch showed 6:08 a.m. What a great day this was going to be.

CHAPTER 7

6:08 a.m. - Page, Arizona

Jim Nance heard the explosion while completing his security walk above the turbines in the base of the dam. Jim had worked graveyard security at the dam for three years without ever hearing anything that loud. He figured the sound came from the base of the dam and started running in that direction. When he arrived at the west end of the plant, he met Peter Hansen, a technician, running down the stairs from the control room.

The technician pointed toward the dam. "What was that? Something blow up?"

Jim nodded. "Sounded like it. From down there someplace." He pointed down the west elevator access hallway. "Is that where you were headed?"

Peter shrugged. "I don't know. I was just checking it out."

Jim continued jogging down the hall and Peter fell in behind.

They ran out the plant door, and across the walkway toward the dam. On their right a large expanse of grass had been planted on the roof of the structure to mitigate the dust. Jim reached for the glass door into the dam, and both men shot through. Jim led them down the long corridor. Up ahead, around the corner to their right, would be the west elevator. When the two men rounded the corner, they both stopped.

Water poured out of the west elevator shaft and smashed against the wall across the hallway. After hitting the wall, the water curled upwards ripping off ceiling tiles, and then headed down the hallway toward them. To Jim, it seemed like a dump truck had dumped a load of water at him, a dump truck with no end. Until now he had never understood why a deer would freeze in the headlights of an oncoming car. However, at that moment he understood the principle perfectly. He wanted to turn and run from this wall of water advancing toward him, but in spite of his desire, both he and Peter stood like statues while a large wave carrying a metal trashcan hit them head on. In the instant before the water hit, Jim heard his radio squawk, "The dam blew! Everybody get–"

Jim missed the rest when the wall of water hit him, but he could have guessed how the message ended anyway. The water knocked both men off their feet. In the fall, Jim dropped his radio and his head went under. He tried to secure footing to stand, but couldn't find traction on the wet tile. For a moment it felt like he was at the water park with his kids. The feeling of being carried, arms flailing and body thrashing, was similar. At a certain point, he realized the water had washed them around the corner and back down the long corridor, but he had no memory of going around the corner. He bumped into Peter several times, but not enough to hurt.

At that moment, Jim remembered the glass door at the end of the corridor, and he panicked at getting caught inside as the area filled with water. How would he open it? Then it hit him that the door opened out, and the water wouldn't have any trouble opening it. While he was thinking of just that, his head came up for long enough to see that they were almost at the door. He felt the water slow slightly, then suddenly accelerate again as he was sucked out the door.

Once outside, the water cascaded off both sides of the walkway to the plant, and Jim and Peter found their footing and stood up. Jim grasped the handrail.

Peter yelled to him. "You okay?"

Jim nodded. "I guess so, how 'bout you?"

"Yeah."

Jim motioned back in the plant. "Anybody else up there with you?"

"Yeah, two others."

Jim looked nervous. "We gotta tell them to get out of here."

"You want me to go back up?"

Jim felt for his radio, but it was gone. "Yeah. Why don't ya. I'll go back and clear the rest of the plant."

Both men took a second to look at the water coming out of the dam and running off the walkway. Because their view up was blocked by the canopy over their heads, neither could see the water spraying out of the face of the dam four hundred feet above them.

As they ran into the plant, Jim pointed east. "Take 'em down the east stairs."

* * *

6:15 a.m. - Page, Arizona

Overlooking the top of the dam in the security office, which was part of the Haden Visitor Center complex, Brian Thacker, graveyard supervisor, waited for a response from his radio alert. "Hello, is anybody there? Jim? Jessie? Mark?"

The radio squawked. "Jessie here." "Mark here." Jessie and Mark were stationed at the two access road gates, but Jim was down in the dam someplace.

Brian waited several seconds then pressed the button. "Jim? Do you read me?" Nothing.

He tried again. "Office calling Jim Nance, please respond."

His radio squawked again. The voice was much higher than Mark's usual tone. "I haven't heard him yet, Brian. You want me to go down and check on him?"

Brian knew something was wrong. Jim should have responded by now. He looked out the window again. The water was blasting out the hole. Every time he looked, there was more water. He felt sure that hole was close to twenty feet in diameter now. There was no way he could send anyone down there. It was too dangerous.

Mark's voice came from the radio again. "Brian, you want me to go down the east elevator?"

Brian looked at the water one more time. Jim was in trouble, but the dam was breaking apart. "Negative, Mark. Stay put. I'll try the control room and see if they know where he is."

He tried the radio one more time. "Jim, do you copy?"

He waited a moment, then dropped the radio and grabbed the phone. He dialed the control room first, letting it ring at least ten times. Next he tried the break room, then two different guard stations. Nothing from any of them. They were either dead or on the move. He prayed they were on the move. Walking to the windows, Brian tried to see down to the asphalt strip bordering the generation plant, but there was too much smoke to see down to river level.

He heard the radio again. "Brian, this is Jessie. You called anybody yet? Reported it?"

Brian picked up the radio. "When would I? I'm trying to figure out if everybody's okay."

Jessie's voice came back calm. "I know, Brian, but you need to call. Now. You can't help Jim from where you are. They can use the tunnel. Make the call."

Jessie was right. An access tunnel led down to the base of the dam from several miles away on the Page side. He needed to get the cops down there.

First he called 911. The phone rang three times. To Brian, it seemed like fifteen minutes. Finally, a calm voice answered, "What is your name, please?"

"There has been an explosion at the Glen Canyon Dam. The dam is leaking and might break up. I need you to—"

"Whoa," the woman interrupted. "One thing at a time. You say that you are at the Glen Canyon Dam? What is your name?"

Brian could hardly stand it. "Brian Thacker. The dam—"

"Okay, Brian, what is the problem?"

"The dam is failing. There is going to be a flood. A big one! Send a couple of police cars down the tunnel. I can't reach any of the crew on the radio. They might be hurt. Can you do that? I need to make some other calls."

"Hang on, Brian, I need you to stay on the line."

"I can't. Just tell the police to get over here." He knew he shouldn't, but he hung up the phone.

He walked over to a red clipboard hanging on the wall. The next calls would not be dialed from memory. The first call was to the Bureau of Reclamation in Denver. They built the dam and were responsible for it. He thought they would want to know it was falling apart. As it turned out, they were, in fact, very interested. The lady on the line took Brian's number and promised to have someone return the call in a few minutes.

The second call went to Hoover Dam, 300 miles downstream. He placed the third call to the National Parks Service, who would relay a message to the Grand Canyon. Both conversations were similar – short and to the point. Brian told them he was calling because there had been an explosion at Glen Canyon Dam. They asked if the dam had failed. He told them not yet. They asked how much water was flooding. He responded honestly and reported that the hole was about twenty feet in diameter. They both asked him to keep them updated. Brian left both calls with the same impression that they weren't going to do much unless he called back and said the dam failed completely. In fact, Brian wondered if they would even know what to do then.

CHAPTER 8

6:25 a.m. - Denver, Colorado

Grant Stevens burst out of the bathroom into his dark bedroom. The loud piercing beeps from his pager seemed to emanate from all four walls of the bedroom, making it impossible to zero in on it. He headed straight for the dresser, where he always left it. He held a towel around his waist with his left hand, while he swept back and forth with his right. His fingers found the small box and pressed a button to stop the noise. He looked at the luminescent readout and noted the seven-digit number had a '911' after it. He heard a clicking sound from behind, and the bedside lamp came on, illuminating the room.

"Who is it?" his wife mumbled from the bed. She shielded her eyes from the light.

"Somebody from work. I don't recognize the number."

"I thought they were all out of town," she said.

"Me too."

He walked over to the nightstand next to the bed and grabbed the cordless phone. His wife got up and went into the bathroom. Who could it be at this hour? Maybe someone headed to Kenya had forgotten something, some document or report. The fact that they would page him this early in the morning, with a 911, bugged him to no end, as if he didn't have anything more important to do. He walked back over by the dresser and considered for a while whether to delay calling back. However, a morbid curiosity of who was nervy enough to do it made him decide to make the call.

The number on the pager had timed out, so he pressed the button again to re-illuminate it. He keyed in the number and waited. In the process of holding the phone in one hand and the pager in the other, his towel fell to the floor. He had just bent over to pick it up when the person on the other end of the line answered on the first ring.

He propped the phone between his shoulder and ear while trying to position the towel. "Hello."

"Grant? This is Julia, you know, Roland's admin."

He knew who Julia was. She was the commissioner's new executive secretary. The consensus at the Bureau was that Roland had selected her because she looked like a model. Grant himself had never talked to her in his life. What could she possibly want? He wrapped the towel around his waist and tucked it in before he answered. For some reason he didn't feel right about talking to Julia when he was naked, even on the phone.

"Hi," he said.

"I'm so glad you're there. As you know, Roland and the other executives are on their way to Kenya. I can't get a hold of them."

Grant could tell she was nervous; she sounded like she might cry. "That's okay. What do you need?"

"I just got a call from the Glen Canyon Dam. There's been an explosion."

Grant sat down on the bed. "What?" The image returned from the day before of the concrete dam he had seen on TV.

She continued. "The guy who called's name is Brian. He's a night security guard."

The shock of the information waned enough to make Grant ask another question. "Julia, what is the Bureau doing?"

There was silence on the other end before she finally spoke again. "That's just it, Grant. Everybody's gone. That's why I called you."

He knew she wanted a response, but he couldn't speak.

"Grant, Roland told me he was leaving you in charge. You need to handle this." She continued, "I just called the pilots for the Gulfstream. They'll meet you at the airport."

Although the Bureau of Reclamation had an expensive corporate jet, only the commissioner and other executives used it. Grant had never flown in it.

"The Gulfstream?" Grant repeated.

"They'll get you down to the dam within the hour. I have Brian's number at Glen Canyon. Do you have a pencil?"

Grant realized his mouth was hanging open. They were sending him on the Gulfstream? He stood and moved back toward the dresser, subconsciously realizing the towel had dropped again. This time he made no effort to retrieve it. "Hang on a second." He grabbed a pen and one of his business cards, then flipped over the card to write on the back. "What's the guy's name again?"

"Brian," she repeated.

"Okay. Give me the number."

She read it to him and made him repeat it back to her.

"Is there anything you need from the office?" she asked.

Grant couldn't think. Then all of the sudden he wondered what would happen downstream if the Glen Canyon Dam failed. Lake Powell was huge, one of the largest reservoirs in the country. The damage downstream would be catastrophic. He remembered suddenly that the Grand Canyon was directly downstream from the dam.

"Julia, wait a minute. The Bureau did a study in the late nineties about what would happen if the dam failed. Can you get me a copy of the report? It's a Failure Inundation Study. I think Bruce's River Hydraulics Group did the analysis."

She responded slowly as if she had written it down. "Okay, but I won't be able to get it to you at the airport. I'll have to fax it to you on the plane."

"The plane has a fax machine?" He couldn't believe it.

"Sure."

Grant suddenly felt urgency. "What time should I–"

"They'll be ready for you as soon as you can get there," she interrupted. "I called them right after I paged you. How long will it take you to get to the airport?"

Grant looked at the alarm clock next to his bed. 6:27 a.m. What should he pack to supervise a dam failure in Arizona? A calculator? A measuring tape? Hip boots?

"How about seven? I'll try to get there a few minutes before. Wait, Julia! I've never been on the jet. Is it on the other side of the airport? How do I get there?"

She informed him that the Gulfstream was not at Denver International Airport, but at Denver Centennial, a smaller and closer airport. He knew the location, but she gave him specific instructions on how to get to the terminal. He wrote the information on the backs of two more of his business cards.

"What's your cell phone number?" she asked.

"I don't have one, the Bureau never thought . . ." He hesitated. "Wait, I'll take my wife's." He gave her the number and hung up the phone.

"What's going on?" his wife asked, now wide awake.

"There's been an explosion at the Glen Canyon Dam. They're worried it might fail. And everybody is out of town."

She looked puzzled. "So they're sending you?"

He nodded. "There's nobody else. The Bureau's jet is taking me to Arizona as soon as I get there. Can you help me pack?"

* * *

6:55 a.m. - Kanab, Utah

He slowed the motorcycle down to forty-five miles per hour as he approached the small city. He could not afford a traffic ticket. That would unravel everything. He scanned ahead for a roadblock. Although possible, he was fairly sure they wouldn't have one set up yet. He expected to hit one sooner or later. He imagined back at the dam they'd still be running around in circles and wondering what happened. He passed a sign that said "Entering the City of Kanab. Pop. 4492." Letting off the throttle, he allowed the motorcycle to coast down to thirty-five miles per hour, just five over the limit. You could usually go five over without getting noticed, even in these hick towns.

According to the signs, the run from the dam to Kanab, Utah, measured just less than seventy-five miles, all open road. He'd made it in just under an hour. He knew it was the most critical leg of his escape. At Kanab, he'd be joined by traffic from the north rim of the Grand Canyon and Zion National Park. After that, it would be easier to blend in. Another forty minutes and he'd pass through Zion National

Park, and traffic would be even heavier. Forty-five minutes beyond Zion and he would hit I-15 and St. George, Utah. After that he'd have to crash to get caught.

He cursed himself for not bringing a radio on the motorcycle. Would the news be carrying the story yet? Maybe not. And when they did, what would they say? There was a small explosion at the dam? The dam is failing? He was dying to know what was going on. When he last saw the water shooting out of the smoke, it had been maybe ten feet in diameter. It would certainly be way more than that by now. That was an hour ago. But how big, he had no idea. What if it had not gotten any bigger? What then?

Instinctively, he knew that the dam would tear itself apart. He had read that, but nothing said how long it would take. It could take days, for all he knew. His instincts told him it would take around eight hours. But he was not sure why. It just felt right.

As the motorcycle exited Kanab, he accelerated. It felt good. His hair stood up on the back of his neck. His arms felt stiff. He felt physically tired, although his mind raced. He had done it. He had blown up the Glen Canyon Dam. There was much more to do. But the big one was done. Even if they caught him now, which didn't seem likely, his name would be famous forever. The mightiest dam on the Colorado would soon be gone. The river wasn't free yet, but it would be soon.

* * *

7:00 a.m. - Lake Powell, Utah

Greg pointed at a rock wall on the east side of the channel. "That's it." He aimed the boat in that direction.

Julie saw only a rock wall. She saw no opening, or anything that looked like it might be a canyon. She wondered how it was possible for her husband to tell which canyon it was. All the rocks looked the same to her. But Greg seldom made a mistake, and if he did, he recognized it almost immediately.

Sure enough, as they approached the rock wall, an opening appeared. Greg steered in, and they passed through the gap into Forbidding Canyon. Once inside, the red sandstone walls rose vertically on both sides of the boat for hundreds of feet. Greg carved the boat back and forth along the winding channel. Not far in, they approached a fork, and Greg veered right without hesitation. How he remembered the way, she would never know. She had once heard a woman comedian joke that there were only two things where men were definitely better than women: navigating, and writing their name in the snow with urine. Julie agreed with both.

She held on to her seat as the boat carved back and forth around each bend of the rock walls. There was absolutely no traffic, a testament to Greg's decision to arrive early. By ten or eleven, traffic would be heavy around Rainbow Bridge.

She felt Erika touch her shoulder from behind. She turned and Erika's face was right there. Her eyes were sparkling.

"How far back in the canyon is it?" she asked.

"I think we are almost there. We should be able to see it in a few minutes."

At that, Erika came up and slid into the seat next to Julie. Julie made as much room as possible, but the seat was only meant for one person. The girls squished together, with Erika's bikinied rear end hanging off the edge of the seat. Julie laughed. Her friend always surprised her, no inhibitions. She saw Greg glance down at the girls and look back up, smiling.

Just when Julie thought straight ahead was the only way possible, Greg veered left into a narrow opening she had not even seen. She shook her head. No wonder explorers had spent months looking for it. After passing through this narrow cut, they finally saw their destination. Up ahead, a long line of floating docks wrapped around the bend.

Erika stood, holding on to the windshield of the boat. "Where is it?"

Greg pointed upstream. "It's around the corner." He slowed as they reached the first dock then pulled forward to the last available mooring.

There were no other boats. Paul jumped out and attached ropes to the cleat on the dock. Greg shut off the engine. Erika climbed out onto the dock and helped Julie up behind her.

Julie watched as her husband grabbed the cameras and a cooler that contained their breakfast. He climbed out of the boat. "Are we in a hurry?"

Greg looked at his watch. "Not really. If possible I'd like to leave before eight, but that still gives us an hour."

Erika pointed to where the docks disappeared around the bend. "Let's go already." She held out her hand for her husband. "Come on."

Julie took a camera bag from her husband and followed. "Why are you so excited anyway? You were just here last year."

"That was a year ago," Erika called out as she and Paul hurried along. "I love this place."

The two couples walked for a few minutes until Greg spoke. "There it is."

Erika, who was ahead of Greg, stopped and looked up. "Where? Oh. I see it."

The large rock bridge was barely exposed as it blended in perfectly with the cliffs on the right. The rising sun had not yet reached it in the deep canyon, further disguising it.

Erika stormed ahead. "Let's hurry and we can eat breakfast under the bridge before anyone else shows up."

"We can't," Julie called out. "It's sacred. The Indian tribes."

"That's bull and you know it. Besides, I don't see any Indians."

A sign mounted close to the rock bridge designated the area under Rainbow as sacred by six different Native American tribes. However, many considered it pretentious for the tribes to lay claim to the site, especially considering that when explorers first tried to find the arch in the early 1900s, most of the Indians had never seen it, and even with hired Indian guides it took months of trial and error to locate it. An early black and white photo showed a picture of an Indian sitting on a horse on top of the arch. Maybe it was only off limits to the white man. Julie generally avoided walking under it more to avert dirty looks from other visitors than any belief that the spot was sacred.

The closer the two couples got to the arch, the larger it became. Julie knew it was three hundred feet tall. She tried to imagine a football field standing on end under it, and agreed that it might fit. They were climbing now, but they stopped about a quarter mile away to rest and take a group picture. Julie glanced at her watch. They had plenty of time.

* * *

7:10 a.m. - Denver, Colorado

Grant gazed out the window of the Bureau of Reclamation's Gulfstream IV-SP. He was the sole passenger on the small jet – just him, two pilots, and a pretty flight attendant. The jet had already been running when he arrived. Supposedly the jet had just arrived from the east coast after dropping off the commissioner from his international connection the night before.

Before that morning, he had never seen the Bureau's jet. When he had approached it at the airport, the Gulfstream had glistened in the rising sun and looked brand new. He remembered hearing the scuttlebutt when the Bureau purchased it in the late nineties, replacing their older jet. Everyone at work was surprised that the government had funded it. And even now, riding in it, he wondered what kinds of shenanigans were performed to justify it. With federal deficits, how could the Bureau justify a 50-million-dollar-plane?

The story of how the Bureau of Reclamation had bought its first jet was legendary. In the 1960's, the haydays for building dams in America, Floyd Dominy, the most famous commissioner to ever serve in the Bureau, had asked for a jet and been denied. However, Dominy arranged for the cost of a jet to be buried in a dam appropriation bill in Congress. His bosses at the Department of Interior had been furious, but Dominy kept the plane. And over the years most of the other large government agencies had followed the Bureau and acquired jets. Since Dominy paved the way, commissioners of the Bureau of Reclamation, and whoever they wanted to schmooze, had flown in style, zipping back and forth between Denver and Washington DC at five hundred thirty miles per hour.

Grant repositioned himself into the comfortable leather seat, which felt infinitely better than a coach airline seat. Travel on commercial airlines would never be the same after this trip. The Gulfstream was even more luxurious than he imagined. The first thing he noticed was the huge oval windows along the sides. They were much larger than anything he had ever seen before. And they looked more like clear glass than the milky plastic of a commercial airliner. An expensive lever lowered an accordion blind between the panes. The cabin actually felt roomier than a full-sized plane, which Grant attributed to the lack of storage compartments overhead, and the large and well-spaced leather seats. Grant ran his hand along the polished wood grain hand rests below the windows. He stretched his legs out. No problem. A seven-footer could ride comfortably in this seat. The plane was beautiful as well as roomy. It made Grant envy the lifestyle of his bosses.

He knew that this particular trip was an anomaly. Normally he wouldn't be allowed within a hundred miles of this situation. He could guarantee the commissioner and his entourage would take over as soon as Julia could arrange their early exit from the symposium in Kenya. The remoteness of the location in Africa, however, would slow their return.

As the plane climbed out of Denver, Grant looked west over the Rocky Mountains separating Denver from Utah. A few cumulus clouds floated over endless mountains. The view from the valley floor in Denver was misleading, and gave the impression that one only needed to drive through a small mountain pass to arrive on the other side to another open valley. But the view from above told a different story. The range visible from the valley was only the beginning. The mountains continued, peak after peak, for what seemed like at least fifty miles. Grant knew that if someone tried to hike through, without a compass to point west, he would end up hopelessly lost in the range with no hope of ever finding Salt Lake and the Mormons.

The flight attendant tapped his shoulder. She held out a plate with a selection of bagels.

He nodded yes and selected one with onions on top.

She handed him a napkin, knife, and small package of cream cheese. "Would you like some orange juice?"

He nodded. "Sure."

He guessed she was in her thirties. She looked plain at first glance, but her smile changed everything. The perfect white teeth and sparkling brown eyes, in addition to her trim figure, made him wonder if she had been a model before. If not, it was only because she hadn't smiled enough.

She returned with a cup of orange juice, then sat on the arm of the chair next to him. "Hi. I'm Wendy."

"Grant Stevens," he replied.

When he first arrived, he was surprised to find a flight attendant at all. For some reason, he expected a big cooler on the floor, and executives tossing each other sodas and peanuts. Now the thought seemed absurd. When he cut open the bagel, it felt warm and fresh, making him wonder how Wendy could have had time to shop during the short layover.

"So how long are we going to be in Page?" she asked.

The question surprised him. It had never occurred to him that the plane would be waiting with him in Page. "I don't know. I'll have to figure that out when I get there."

The thought made him wonder what was happening at the dam. He looked out the window and decided the plane was at cruising altitude and he should probably make the call to Glen Canyon. He asked Wendy if the Gulfstream had a phone, and she pointed to a compartment by the window.

"What are you doing at the dam? Do you have an important meeting or something?" she asked.

He looked up at her and saw mild interest, but no fear whatsoever. "Julia didn't tell you?"

She shook her head. "No. She just said to be ready to fly somebody immediately. I just figured . . ." Her voice trailed off, then he saw her brows furrow. "Julia didn't tell me what? Why, what's going on?"

He opened his mouth to speak, but was interrupted by another phone in the rear of the plane.

"Excuse me, please," she said, then quickly stood and walked back toward the rear of the plane.

While she was gone, he figured he better make the call. He leaned forward in his seat and searched in his right rear pants pocket for the card he used to scribble the phone number. He found the crumpled card and straightened it enough to read the number. Grant took a bite out of the bagel, then punched in the nine digits. Someone picked up immediately.

"Hello, this is Brian."

"Brian, this is Grant Stevens from the Bureau of Reclamation. How bad is it down there?"

The man sounded nervous. "Well, there was an explosion about an hour ago. I didn't see it, but I heard it. It blew the top out of the elevator shaft and a hole in the dam."

Grant wondered what could blow up the elevator shaft. None of the turbines were even near there. "What blew up? Do you have any idea?"

"Heck, I don't know. It must have been somewhere down the elevator shaft. Something blew. It seemed like a bomb."

For the first time since the call from Julia, Grant considered that the explosion might have been intentionally set. Until then, he had considered it an equipment-related explosion, but, if it were intentionally caused, then why? "You said there was a hole in the dam, Brian. How big?"

Brian hesitated. "It looked pretty small when I first saw it, but now it's way bigger. It keeps growing. The water is really shooting out the hole."

Grant pictured water pouring over the top of the dam in a small cut, but Brian's description didn't make sense. "Where exactly is the hole?"

"It's in the west elevator shaft."

That wasn't what Grant meant by the question. "How far down?"

"About a third of the way, maybe two hundred feet."

The answer felt like a gut punch. Grant leaned back in the seat and rested his head against the cushion. Was it possible he misheard? "Sorry Brian, could you repeat that?"

"Two hundred, or maybe even two fifty."

Grant bent forward and put his head in his hands. This was much worse than he had imagined. The pressure that deep in the dam would—

Brian's voice rang in his ear. "Hello. Are you there?"

He rubbed his forehead. "Yeah Brian, I'm here." Grant hesitated at the next question, not too sure he wanted to know the answer. "You said the hole is much larger now, you said shooting out. Approximately how big is it?"

"You mean how big is the hole? I'd say let's see . . . maybe twenty-five or thirty-five feet."

Grant tried to picture the leak; he'd never seen a column of water that large. Actually, a thirty-foot column of water, no one on earth had, for that matter. How could there not be any casualties? "Did everyone get out of the plant?" he asked.

Brian's voice became low, almost a whisper. "I don't know, I couldn't contact them on the radio. I can only hope."

Grant pictured what amounted to tons of water falling another four hundred feet down onto the generation plants below. "Has the water destroyed the plant yet?"

Brian seemed to choose his words. "At first, the water shot out the hole so far that it cleared the plant completely. It didn't even touch it. By now, some of the water must be hitting the plant, but I can't really tell, there's too much mist down there."

Grant tried to picture the whole canyon filled with mist. "Are you alone?"

"I was alone in the visitor center, but there's a couple of my men at the upper access roads. Anyway, the cops showed up about a half hour ago."

Grant pictured a dozen police cars parked haphazardly. "What are they doing?"

"Mostly keeping people away, you know. But some of them are just looking themselves."

He imagined the spectacle and how temping it would be to just stand and stare. Grant wondered if he would be able to not stare after he arrived.

"Hey, I need to go." The security guard sounded anxious to get off the phone.

"Okay, Brian. I'll be there as soon as I can." Grant replaced the phone in the compartment.

Wendy was staring at him with wide eyes. "Is it bad?" she asked.

Grant sighed. "Oh yeah."

"The dam?"

Grant nodded. "Yeah. Looks like somebody blew it up. It's breaking apart."

Her eyes grew even bigger. "Will people die?"

Grant considered the question. How could people not die if the dam failed completely? "Luckily, the area downstream of the dam was the Grand Canyon, for three hundred miles. Not a lot of people. If someone could just warn them." He hesitated, then looked down. "I'm sure some people will get hurt."

Wendy just stared, then her demeanor changed as she remembered something. She offered Grant about twenty pages of paper. "This just came in on the fax machine. It's from Julia."

Grant took the pages and flipped them around. The title page read, "DAM FAILURE INUNDATION REPORT, Glen Canyon Dam, Arizona." He scanned the table of contents, then looked up.

"Wendy, how soon will we be there?"

"We should land in Page in about fifteen or twenty minutes."

Not enough time to read the entire document. He started reading. Out of the corner of his eye, he saw Wendy walk toward the back of the plane. After the second sentence, Grant skipped ahead, looking for paragraphs with numbers. Farther into the document he found tables that included flood depths and times

downstream at various places in the Grand Canyon. At some point he realized
he had been muttering. His stomach began to boil. He had to consciously stop
himself from rubbing his forehead. Near the back of the document, he found an
analysis of what would happen after all the floodwater from Lake Powell joined
with Lake Mead. It described theoretical water levels and their impact on Hoover
Dam. Grant swore under his breath.

* * *

7:15 a.m. - Lee's Ferry, Arizona (16 miles downstream from the Glen Canyon Dam)

Fifty-two-year-old Ted Johnson leaned upstream in the current and took a
step to his left. He felt with his toes to find a rock large enough to act as a perch,
but the rubber waders weren't the greatest for feeling around. He wiped sweat
off his forehead for the third time in what seemed like the last minute. He was
in serious trouble.

The morning had started out easy. He woke before the sun, and threw all his gear
in the back of the pickup. Then it was just a short drive to Lee's Ferry. He always
arrived early, before the rafters and other fishermen so he could be first down the
windy road and grab the best parking spot, the one next to the river. Although he
couldn't see the sun yet because of the steep canyon walls, Ted could always see the
light from the sunrise on the rocks high above. That put Ted in the river right when
those rainbow trout were just waking up and looking for their breakfast. And this
morning, just like every other morning, he waded right out into the shallow river,
staying close to the gravel strips. As usual, Ted had been overly careful to stay out
of deep places. Any fool knew that you couldn't swim with waders on.

And for the first hour everything had happened just like any other day. By then
he already had three big ones in his basket. But then, when he cast his bait over a
nice green hole that was sure to be a virtual trout condominium, he felt the cold
squeeze of the waders a little too high, up above his privates. It was a sure signal
that he was too deep.

The funny thing was, he didn't remember walking deeper. And when he tried
to climb back up the strip of gravel, he could have sworn the water had risen in
the last few minutes. It was at that moment that he looked around and knew
there was more water. He confirmed his suspicion by looking back at his pickup.
There was definitely more water between him and it, than when he arrived. After
climbing up to a higher point in the river, he looked back toward where he needed
to go. It was time for a big decision. He could either try to wade back, or strip off
the waders, shuck his clothes, and swim for it. He had taken a moment on the
decision, inspecting upstream and down, debating one route verses another, and
calculating the value of the gear he would be abandoning. It would be risky, but
he had decided to wade.

Ted Johnson now knew he had made the wrong decision. His feet were barely
holding against the strong current, and worse, even with water up to his waist, he
was fairly sure he was on a high point, meaning that any direction would take him

deeper. And nobody had to tell him he could not fight the current if the water levels got any higher, which Ted now knew was happening.

He scanned the bank to see if anyone was around to help, but saw no one. If only he could get out of the boots now. Unfortunately, the only way possible would be to first flood them, relieving the squeeze, and then try to swim out of them. It was a skill that he had heard of others practicing in a pool, in a controlled environment. At the time, he hadn't even considered practicing the skill. Now, however, he would pay anything for that knowledge. He would forfeit his favorite rod and reel for a quick lesson.

In fact, at that moment, the idea of his rod and reel meaning anything to him seemed absurd, even though an hour before, he would have chosen his graphite pole over his pickup. He looked down at the rod in his right hand, a few minutes ago his most prized possession, now a lead weight. He tossed it away and watched it disappear under the current. The basket over his arm was next, and then the hat with his best flies attached to it.

The motion of pulling off the basket upset his balance. He felt himself tipping. He reached with his left foot for the next toehold downstream. However, even a few feet downstream the water felt deeper. His foot slid in the gravel, finding no holds. To retain his balance, he let his other foot go. Now he was a passenger to the current. If he didn't find a hold in a second, it would be too late, although a part of Ted Johnson thought it already might be.

Suddenly, Ted felt himself drop into a hole. The feeling of water inside the waders was instantaneous. In spite of the feeling of panic, Ted knew what he had to do if he wanted to live. He could not survive with the waders on, and getting them off in deep water would be the most challenging feat of his life.

He tore the suspenders off his shoulders, and started peeling at the rubber material. During the motion his head went under. He let go of the waders and kicked upwards for air. Nothing. He frantically reached for the waist of the waders. His foot felt bottom. The waders were forgotten as he pushed hard off the bottom, flailing his arms for the surface of the water. Again nothing. He realized reaching the surface was impossible with the waders on. He bent and started pulling on them. His surroundings got darker, and Ted wondered if he was deeper, or if he was blacking out.

An intense pain in his chest told him that he needed air soon. A new pain in his ears meant something, but he didn't know what. His attempts to peel off the waders were not working. He gave up and decided to try to slither out of them. Moving quickly now, he straightened his body and a blurry feeling came over him, not in his vision, more in his mind. In spite of the blurry feeling, his heart was pumping furiously, and he lunged upward trying to shed the heavy rubber death boots. His movement did nothing to shed the waders, so he lunged harder, using energy he did not know he had.

The pain in his chest now spread through his body. He felt his motivation to struggle dissipate slightly, but not enough to make him quit. He resisted the impulse to gulp water. He lunged upward again, although he knew the motions were doing nothing to remove the waders. His last thoughts were of darkness, and pain in his chest, and a blurry drugged feeling that made it all bearable. He passed out without giving in to the urge to breath water, and became the first fatality on the Colorado River that morning.

* * *

7:25 a.m. - Lake Powell, Utah

The popping in Grant's ears told him the plane was descending. He looked out the window and noticed the landscape had changed dramatically; the mountain range was gone, replaced by endless red rock formations, canyons, and vertical walls. Down below he saw the blue of Lake Powell with its endless side canyons. It surprised him that Powell was so long and skinny. Although he had seen pictures before, his instinct kept painting the lake as much broader.

Wendy walked toward him and asked if he needed anything. "Are you done with that?" She reached for the empty cup and napkins.

He handed her the rest of the unfinished bagel. "Can you ask the pilot to fly low over the dam before he lands?"

"Sure." She turned and headed for the cockpit.

As the plane continued to descend, Grant looked down into some of the side canyons of Lake Powell. Many of the canyons stretched for miles away from the main channel. Occasionally a houseboat sat up on the shore, with what must have been either water ski boats or jet skis tied next to them; too small to know for sure. Here and there Grant spotted two or more houseboats in the same place. He tried to imagine the party that must have occurred the night before. "Get out of there," he whispered. "Turn on your radios." How on earth would they be able to warn everyone? They wouldn't. It would be impossible, he knew.

The right wing dropped as the plane began a gradual turn to the right. Grant could see the main channel of Lake Powell, a narrow expanse of water with rock islands rearing their heads out of the water. The Gulfstream had descended much lower and Grant could make out four people in a water-ski boat below them. The boat skimmed across the water below, headed for the other side of the channel, streaming a white elongated triangle behind, the wake stretching forever behind the boat.

Up ahead, Grant could see the end of Lake Powell. The water came to an abrupt end in a tight canyon, the abruptness bordered by a white structure, the Glen Canyon Dam. From this angle the dam seemed small, maybe twenty feet tall across the quarter mile canyon. However, Grant had looked over the downstream side of the dam just a few years before. The massive face of the dam dropped seven hundred and eighteen feet to the river below.

The pilot positioned the plane to finish its turn just downstream from the dam. The dam would be visible on Grant's right, directly out his window. Grant repositioned himself in the seat, to get a better view. Before he could see deep enough in the canyon to see the leak, he noticed the mist coming out of the canyon, rolling up over the canyon walls. Definitely not normal.

As the plane glided in at just over two hundred fifty miles an hour, he got the line of sight he needed. He heard Wendy gasp from the seat behind him. About one third of the way down the seven-hundred-foot dam, on the west side, a huge column of water poured out of the dam. Actually, pour wasn't the right word – it was pressurized, and shooting out of the concrete face, just as described by Brian. Grant estimated the column of water at seventy-five feet in diameter. He couldn't see it hit the river. There was too much mist. The canyon below would be radically re-arranged by the impact of that much water.

He considered that before when he had talked to the security guard, the water was only about thirty-five feet in diameter, and now it had grown to seventy-five. The diameter had doubled in a half hour. Additionally, since volume grew as the square of the radius, it meant the volume of water exiting the dam had quadrupled in that same half hour.

The plane completed its pass over the dam and banked left for the airport in Page. Grant lost sight of the jetting water. He leaned back in his seat, staring up at the ceiling of the plane in deep concentration. If the diameter continued to double every half hour, how long would it take? He pictured the dam, with a seventy-five-foot diameter circle on the left side. He then imagined a one hundred-fifty-foot circle, twice as big, on top of the smaller one, then a three-hundred-foot circle, then a six-hundred-foot circle. But the dam was only seven hundred feet high! Grant added up the half hours – four. His watch showed 7:28 a.m. local time. According to his rough estimate, the Glen Canyon Dam would be gone by 9:30 a.m. Grant closed his eyes and rubbed his fingers back and forth across his forehead.

CHAPTER 9

7:50 a.m. - Rainbow Bridge, Lake Powell, Utah

Julie climbed back in the boat. Greg had timed their trip perfectly. The two couples had been the only visitors at Rainbow for almost the entire duration of their visit, not encountering anyone else until they arrived back on the docks. At Erika's insistence, the two couples had in fact eaten in sacred territory under Rainbow Bridge. But, Julie made sure they didn't leave any trash or evidence of their trespass.

"How far is it up to Hole in the Rock?" Paul asked.

"A little over twenty miles," Greg answered off the top of his head.

Julie stored the cameras and the cooler and sat down. Everyone situated themselves and Greg fired up the engine. Paul pushed off.

"So about an hour, then?" Paul asked.

Greg nodded "If we hurry." He backed the boat around and headed back out the way they had come in.

Ten minutes later they exited Forbidding Canyon and headed north in the main channel toward Hole in the Rock.

* * *

7:55 a.m. - Glen Canyon Dam, Arizona

Grant arrived at the dam in a police car. The car had been waiting on the tarmac at the Page Airport. As soon as the Gulfstream taxied in, a cop rushed Grant into the police cruiser and sped off. When they drove down the hill and the dam became visible, Grant leaned forward in his seat for a better look. While driving across the Glen Canyon Bridge, clouds of mist floated over them and they actually had to turn on the windshield wipers. At the dam, an officer waved the cruiser through the barricade. They pulled right up to the door of the Hayden Visitor Center, a round building on the edge of the canyon. They parked in the red zone. When Grant opened the car door, he heard the rumble. It reminded him of Niagara Falls.

Before heading toward the building, Grant walked toward the rail, followed by the officer. Mist clouds rolled up over them and the entire canyon ledge. The handrail and sidewalk were sopping wet. Grant had looked over the rail before, but he had never seen anything like this.

He could clearly see the column of water exiting the dam in spite of the mist. The sound was deafening and Grant could feel the rumbling in his chest. He tried to grasp the amount of water exiting the dam and couldn't. The hole had grown to nearly a hundred feet now. It looked like it had dug farther down into the dam too. Hadn't Brian told him the original hole reached about two hundred feet down from the top of the dam? Grant now estimated it to be over two hundred seventy feet down. The width had expanded too. The hole was even wider than tall, almost reaching the center of the dam.

A man grabbed Grant's arm, yelling to be heard over the noise, "COME IN-SIDE WHERE WE CAN TALK." He pointed at the dam. "YOU CAN SEE EVEN BETTER INSIDE."

Grant waved a thank you to the police officer and followed the man into the visitor center. His clothes felt damp. As soon as the door shut behind them, the noise dissipated. He swallowed and his ears popped. The lobby was round with high ceilings. A curved wall shielded them from a wall of windows. Grant was pulled toward the windows in order to get a better view of what was happening below. As he approached, he noticed someone had set up a table and chairs next to the large windows.

The man who grabbed Grant's arm, obviously the security guard, shook Grant's hand. "Glad to see you."

Grant nodded. "Grant Stevens, Bureau of Reclamation. You must be Brian?"

The man nodded his head.

Brian's baby face made Grant wonder if he was old enough to be guarding anything. He had traces of fine blond peach fuzz on his face, which showed that he hadn't shaved for a while. He was shorter than Grant, maybe five foot six. Although his hands were small, when he shook, he gripped hard like a salesman.

"Yeah, I'm the one who called you. You sure got here quick."

Grant looked at his watch. "The Bureau has a small jet. It made a big difference."

There were four other men in the lobby besides Brian, three of whom wore the same security uniforms; the other wore Levi's and a polo shirt. Brian introduced the one without a uniform. "This is Dan Mumford. He's my boss in charge of se-curity for the dam. He just got here."

Grant nodded at the man, then turned back to Brian. "Did your guys get out of the plant okay?"

Brian nodded. "Yeah, they showed up after I talked to you on the plane. Every-body got out. It was a huge relief. As it turned out, the security guy down in the plant got hit by a wall of water and dropped his radio. That's why I couldn't con-tact them. They went out the access tunnel."

"Well, I'm glad they're all right."

Brian motioned toward the table by the windows. "I've set up a place over there where we can talk, a make-shift command center for lack of better

words. The light is better over there. We lost our power a few minutes before
you arrived."

Grant looked at the lights. "You lost power? So the water killed the turbines
in the dam already?"

Brian looked back. "Yeah, first the main power grids went down. Then a
few minutes later the small turbine that powers all the stuff in the dam itself
followed. I can only imagine the destruction happening below right now. Anyway,
the digital phone system went down with the power, but we found an old analog
phone in the back. It still works off the phone company's power; they must be on
backup or something. So at least we have a phone."

Grant heard the noise of the water again briefly as someone came in the door.
When the door shut, the noise disappeared. A police officer ambled across the
floor, seemingly in no hurry. He wore a khaki uniform, about the same color as a
boy scout. His face was covered with an extremely bushy moustache that hung
over his lips, completely concealing them, and rolling down on the sides of his
face to the sides of his chin. The brown facial hair was streaked with gray, giving
him a worn look. His eyes seemed to match – red and droopy. Grant couldn't
help wondering how the officer could feed himself without getting food stuck in
his mustache.

Brian motioned toward the man. "This is Earl Smith. He's the captain for the
Page police department."

"Nice to meet you," carried from somewhere beneath the mustache.

Grant didn't remember ever hearing such a raspy voice. He reached out his
hand. "Grant Stevens, Bureau of Reclamation."

Earl's hand was rough and cracked like a farmer or mechanic.

The group found chairs around the table and sat down. Grant chose a seat
that allowed a good view of the dam. Everybody looked at Grant, an unspoken
message that he was in charge. They all looked relieved to have someone new to
give orders, especially Brian.

Grant looked around the table before speaking. "Well, first things first. Has
everyone been notified, upstream and down?"

Brian nodded. "I called everyone in the red book. That includes the Grand
Canyon downstream and Lake Powell's water patrol." He pointed at Earl. "The
police closed all access to Lee's Ferry and other roads into the canyon."

"What about the dams upstream?" Grant asked.

Bran shook his head. "They weren't in the book."

Grant pointed at the phone. "Well, we should probably call them too, and
shut them down, like Flaming Gorge in Utah, it won't help us for a day or so, but
tomorrow, we're going to wish we had."

"How did the Grand Canyon folks react?" Earl asked.

Brian shrugged, glancing around as he answered "Well, that was one of the first
calls I made this morning. And to tell the truth, they didn't seem as worried as I
would have expected."

"You told them the dam was breaking apart, and they didn't seem concerned?"
Grant asked.

Brian looked around. "Well, like I said, that was a while ago, and I didn't want to say anything that wasn't true, so I just told them the facts, you know, that there had been an explosion, and that water was coming out of the dam."

Earl spoke from beneath the mustache. "Better call 'em back and update 'em."

Grant nodded. "So when the first calls were made, they were never told the dam was collapsing?"

Brian leaned forward. "When I made the calls, I didn't know—"

Grant waved his hand to silence him. "That's all right. You just gave them the facts." He stood and walked over to the large windows. He looked down into the canyon as he spoke. "Just in case you guys want an official statement from the Bureau, the Glen Canyon Dam is going to fail. My guess is it'll be gone before noon. Let's get back on the phones and update everyone. Maybe that'll wake up the rangers in the Grand Canyon."

Brian and his boss Dan stood to leave the table.

"Hang on," Grant said, pointing at Brian. "I need to ask you a few more questions. Can you get somebody else to make the calls?"

Brian's boss motioned to one of the guards who had been quiet up to that point and they walked a few feet away from the table and had a brief conversation. Afterwards the quiet guard left and Dan returned to the table.

Grant walked back from the window and sat down at the table. "All right, I want to start with what has happened so far, chronologically. Brian, can you tell us everything you remember? Try to include time estimates when possible."

Brian started, "Well, I was back in my office when I heard the explosion." He motioned down a hallway.

"Did you check the time?" Grant prompted.

"Sorry, no."

Grant coaxed, "The Bureau called me at 6:27 a.m. Arizona time. Try to estimate how long before that you heard the explosion."

Brian looked around nervously. "Wow, things were moving kinda fast around here. How about 20 minutes."

Dan, Brian's boss, spoke up. "Was it still dark?"

Brian shook his head. "No, the sun was coming up." He pointed to the window. "When I ran over here to look, the sun hit me right in the eyes."

Grant smiled, "You mean you saw the sun rising? A partial sun?"

"Yeah, I guess."

Grant nodded. "Good, we can estimate the time of the explosion based on sunrise. That'll give us a good approximation of the time. Let's use 6 a.m. as our estimate until we can check it against the 911 logs." Grant looked around the table. "Who's taking notes?"

Dan raised his hand.

Grant pointed to him. "Okay, Dan. You're elected." Grant turned back to Brian. "Now, you heard the sound at 6 a.m., then what happened?"

"When I looked out the windows, the first thing that caught my eye was the smoke on top of the west elevator tower. Then I noticed the water spraying out of the dam. There was smoke there too."

"When you first noticed the leak, how big was it?"

"I'd say about five feet in diameter, not too big," Brian shrugged.

"Did you see anybody around the elevator before it blew?" Grant asked.

"Sure, the elevator service guy was here working on the west elevator before the explosion."

Dan jumped up, "What elevator service guy? There wasn't any service scheduled last night!"

Brian looked nervous. He talked directly to his boss. "I know, but he showed me the work order and he said it needed to be done before we opened today, per you. He knew your name, first and last. I figured you forgot to tell me about it, so I let him in."

Dan yelled at him. "Why didn't you call me, I would have told you—"

Brian pushed his chair back and stood, yelling back at his boss. "It was 4:00 in the morning! Besides everything looked legit and it was the same company that always comes. I just thought . . ." He sat back down.

Dan remained standing, staring down at his employee. Brian put his head down.

Grant spoke to Earl, "Officer Smith, you want to ask any questions? I think we just figured out what caused the explosion."

Earl leaned toward Brian, "What did this guy look like?"

Brian gave a description of a slim, white guy in his early thirties wearing gray coveralls with a matching hat. He had a mustache, Brian remembered. He drove a white Chevy pickup, pulling an enclosed utility trailer behind. Brian responded to a question from Earl by stating that, no, they didn't usually watch when service guys were working.

"Did you guys write down the license plate?" asked Earl.

Brian nodded and handed a clipboard to the police officer, pointing to the number.

Earl barked orders to one of his officers. "Call our buddies in Utah and down south. We need roadblocks on all major highways. He looked at his watch and grimaced. "He's got almost a two-hour head start."

Everyone turned as Dan yelled from the windows. "Is that the trailer?" He pointed toward the dam.

The others hurried over to the window. A white enclosed utility trailer was parked on the dam, mostly hidden by the west elevator shaft. The lookers wondered why they hadn't noticed it before, possibly due to the more impressive sight of water blasting out of the dam.

Earl looked at Grant. "Mr. Stevens, I'd like to send a couple men out there to investigate. Does the Bureau consider it safe enough?"

Grant stood and walked to the window. Without looking back, he answered, "It's definitely going to collapse. The question is how soon."

"All we gotta do is run out there, look around, and get back. We got time for that?"

Grant turned and spoke directly to the officer, pointing toward the dam. "My assumption, based on how far down the hole is, is that the top of the dam will hold for a while, maybe an hour. I can't say for sure. However, my assumption is just a guess. The lawyers at the Bureau would never allow anyone on the dam."

Earl responded, "I ain't interested in what the lawyers think. I just need to understand how fast it's going to break up."

Grant continued, "How long do you think you need?"

"I'd just like to have my men look in the back of that trailer and see what they see. I'm bettin' that there are a few clues to what kinda bomb was used. Clues that could help us find out who did this."

Grant looked at Earl. "Officer Smith, obviously I can't authorize you to go out there. But I'm not going to say you can't, either. You make your own decision. However if you're going, go now. The longer we talk, the more dangerous it becomes."

Earl stood and headed for the door. This time his stride was hurried. He turned before he went outside. "We'll be ready in a few minutes." When Earl opened the doors, the sound of the water rumbled into the lobby again.

Grant wondered if he had made the wrong decision. If the dam collapsed while the cops were out on it, they would hold him responsible. He considered running outside and stopping Earl, telling him he had changed his mind. Although Grant still estimated it would be at least an hour before it collapsed, he could be wrong.

While he waited, Grant decided to do something he needed to do. There was a phone call to make. It'd been a mistake for Julia to send him alone. He knew that now. He needed someone here with him, to run calculations, and coordinate with the office in Denver. He had a feeling that the computers at the Bureau would be humming before too long, trying to analyze the flood implications downstream.

As he dialed, he hoped Shauna Kingsly would be at her desk. She was the one he wanted. She had worked for Grant for over five years now and although everyone considered her a little intense, Grant wanted her with him. She had the ability to organize data and make sense of it better than anyone in the group. She was tenacious at getting the support she needed from other groups, which would be essential to coordinate communication from the Denver office. She would definitely be overwhelmed. She was an introvert who thrived in a structured environment, and was terrified by change. She didn't have much of a personal life, seldom varying from the path between her parent's home and work. A trip to the field would freak her out, but do her good. Shake her up a little, in a positive way.

She picked up on the second ring. "Hello?"

"Shauna. It's Grant."

"Grant? Are you at Glen Canyon right now?" She sounded excited.

"Yup. What have you guys heard?" He'd wondered if the word had got around yet.

"Well, the news was all over the radio on the way to work. But I just thought you were late this morning. The rumor that you were there, at the dam, didn't come down until a few minutes ago."

"Well, I'm definitely here. And the radio doesn't do it justice. The Glen Canyon Dam is tearing itself apart by the minute."

"How big is the hole?"

"Just a second and I'll look." Grant carried the cell phone over and looked out the windows again. "I'd say about a hundred-fifty feet in diameter." He heard Shauna gasp. "And it's kind of hard to see, with all the mist, but the water is probably shooting out a couple of hundred feet before it hits the river below."

"Wow."

Grant got to the point. "I need you out here."

"What? Me?" she said softly.

"Yeah. I need somebody out here to run numbers and coordinate with the office. Bring your laptop. You'll need it. Get a cell phone too. Check one out. If they give you any crap, call Julia, Roland's admin. She'll help."

"When should I come?"

"I want you on the first plane out of Denver. You determine how much time it'll take to go home and pick up what you need. If travel gives you any guff or takes too long, bypass 'em and book your own ticket." Grant could tell she was writing while he talked.

"What airport do I fly into?"

"Page . . ." Grant suddenly realized that few commercial airlines flew into Page. She would have difficulty getting a flight. It would take her hours, maybe until late afternoon. He looked out at the dam. It would be history by then. She would never make it. "No. Don't fly here. By the time you get here, I'll be gone. Meet me at Hoover."

"Hoover?" She sounded surprised.

"Yeah. Fly into Las Vegas, then take a taxi to Hoover. That's where I'm headed after this."

He waited while she wrote, then continued. "If you beat me there, our contact is Fred Grainger; at least I hope he's there, not on vacation or something." Grant had worked with Fred before, definitely a good man. He needed to call him, as soon as he got a minute. "Hang on. Here's my cell phone number." Grant read her the number off his wife's phone.

"Anything else?" she asked.

"Yeah, before you leave, go tell Bruce that I have his Failure Inundation Report. You get a copy too. Tell him, if he has any updates, we need them now. I want the flood levels recalculated using this morning's water levels from Lake Powell and Lake Mead."

He waited again while she wrote.

"All right, what else?"

"That should be enough. You've got plenty to do. I'll see you at Hoover."

He hung up while she was still writing.

* * *

8:00 a.m. - Highway 59, East of Hurricane, Utah

Officer Leonard Smith waved the two old ladies through without making them stop. Although he had orders to stop every car, he felt safe in his assumption that the two gray haired grandmothers in a rusty Buick hadn't blown up the Glen Canyon Dam. However as they motored off, he wondered if maybe the man was hiding in the trunk or something. Leonard turned and watched the car go. What if somebody had a gun to their backs? He should have checked it. He decided not to make that mistake again.

The roadblock was set up about five miles past the city of Hurricane. Dispatch told him they would send another car to back him up as soon as they could find one. Supposedly, the Utah Highway Patrol was already en-route. Leonard had been alone for a half hour. So far, he was pretty sure that the bomber had not gotten past him. Not many cars had passed, and most of them had either been Utah or Arizona plates, and no white pickups.

He shielded his eyes and looked east under the morning sun. It looked like a motorcycle approaching. He could barely see the single illuminated headlight. He waited until the rider got closer, then walked to the middle of the road and held out his hand. As the motorcycle slowed, he saw that the single rider leaned back against a sleeping bag tied to a sissy bar. The bedroll was visible on both sides of the man's notably skinny body. The motorcycle pulled up next to Leonard and stopped, engine still running. Leonard walked behind and read the numbers of the Nevada license plate and wrote them down on his pad.

When Leonard returned to the side of the bike, the man spoke first. "Was I going too fast?"

Leonard ignored the question. "Where you coming from?"

"The Grand Canyon."

Leonard could have guessed as much. "You got your park pass?"

The rider probed the gearshift lever, finding neutral, and then released his hand from the clutch. Searching his pockets with both hands, he finally held up a National Parks ticket. Leonard grabbed it and saw that it was stamped the day before.

"You only stayed one night?" he asked.

The skinny rider nodded. "Got to be back to work tonight."

In Leonard's opinion, most of these bikers that rode in and out of the parks were hippies, and this guy didn't seem any different. He was going to ask to see the guy's driver's license when he spotted another car coming, a white one. He shielded his eyes again and saw that it was a pickup.

He waved abruptly at the motorcycle. "Okay. Go ahead."

"What's going on?" the motorcyclist asked.

Leonard yelled at him. "Get out of here!"

As the motorcycle sped off, Leonard touched the butt of his gun. He stood in the middle of the road with his hand out. This next one could be their man.

* * *

8:35 a.m. - Glen Canyon Dam, Arizona

Earl gave instructions to two police officers. The noise of the water made it impossible for Grant to hear what was said. They all stood outside on the west edge of the dam. Both of the officers had been rigged with a rappelling harness. Three hundred feet of rope was then snapped onto each officer. The rope was Earl's idea. Luckily, a couple of the police cars were equipped with repelling gear for rescues in the canyons. The rope would provide a safety margin, although the thought of trying to pull the two men back to safety as the dam collapsed made Grant uneasy.

Grant was surrounded by police officers. A group of them were dedicated to each of the two ropes. Each rope end was tied to a cement rail at the edge of the dam. A third rope, also tied off, was to be tied to the trailer, allowing the officers to pull it back across the dam. They wanted the trailer if they could get it. Earl finished his instructions to the two volunteers.

"OKAY. HURRY UP!" Earl shouted at his two harnessed investigators.

The two immediately set out across the top of the dam. Grant checked his watch, 8:35 a.m. The preparations had taken way too long.

The white trailer sat next to the west elevator shaft, about a football field away from the edge of the dam where the group was standing. Grant could see that some of the staff's cars were still parked over on the east side of the dam.

As the two officers hustled out to the trailer, they encountered pieces of concrete, metal, and other debris from the explosion of the elevator. Grant noticed the large metal door leading into the elevator was warped outwards. The door had held, a testament that the bulk of the explosion had been channeled vertically up the elevator shaft and out the top, taking all the concrete and framing with it.

Earl pointed at Grant, pulling him out of his thoughts. "YOU WATCH THE DAM! I'LL WATCH MY COPS," Earl shouted through the roar of rushing water.

Grant nodded and hurried over to the rail on his right so he could get a better view of the water shooting out of the face of the dam. As he arrived, he saw a chunk of concrete the size of a car break off and get carried down into the mist below. The air vibrated around him, buffeting his ears and rumbling into his chest. Watching that much water moving below him gave him the sense that he would be sucked in. The thought made him back up a half step. He glanced upstream of the dam and, for the first time, noticed a large whirlpool on the lakeside of the dam. He glanced back at the police officers and saw one was tying the third rope to the hitch on the trailer. The other had already gone behind it. When Grant looked back at the water, he saw another piece of concrete break off and get carried away. The dam was breaking faster than he had anticipated.

He turned and shouted to Earl, churning his hand in a circle. "TELL THEM TO HURRY."

Earl responded through a cupped hand. "YOU LET ME KNOW WHEN TO GET 'EM OFF."

Grant saw one of the officers reach down and scoop up something and put it in a zip lock bag while the other snapped a picture of the trailer with a camera. When Grant looked back down at the water, another block of concrete, this time the size of a tour bus, broke off and disappeared into the canyon. Grant estimated that the water was now within sixty-five feet of the top of the dam. A moment later, another huge piece broke loose and suddenly the water was less than fifty feet from the top.

"GET 'EM OFF!" Grant shouted. He waved his arms for emphasis.

Earl was on the radio immediately. The officers started moving back slowly, one snapping pictures as he moved the other reaching for something on the ground.

"NOW!" Grant yelled.

Earl talked in the radio, and the officers sped up slightly, but not as much as Grant wanted. He now regretted allowing them to go. He would be blamed if something went wrong. Grant saw another large piece break loose, this time followed by a large cracking sound, loud enough to make him cover his ears. The sound was just the motivation the two cops needed; they both sprinted for their lives back toward the edge of the dam.

As the two officers approached and slowed, Grant felt relieved they had made it. However, at that moment, with a loud sound like thunder, a fifty-foot section of the dam, including the elevator shaft itself, broke off and was dragged into the water, pulling the trailer with it. Before anyone could react, the third rope, tied to the trailer, tightened and swept suddenly to the right, taking the legs out from under both officers. The trailer dangled just above the water level on the downstream side of the dam. Grant heard a scream from behind and turned. The rope had pinned another policeman against the handrail, pinching his legs below the knees. His bulging eyes darted back and forth and his face contorted with the pain. Two other officers rushed over and tried to pull the rope away from the officer's legs. Even with both men pulling, they couldn't budge it. They wedged their legs against the concrete to get more leverage, but to no avail. The man screamed again as the rope cut into his legs. Then suddenly the rope disappeared. The previously trapped man collapsed, revealing Earl standing behind, a huge chrome hunting knife gleaming in his hand. Grant looked down and watched the trailer disappear into the Colorado River below.

CHAPTER 10

_____

9:00 a.m. - Glen Canyon Dam, Arizona

Two news helicopters hovered over the Glen Canyon Dam, cameramen hanging out open doors. The first one had arrived from Las Vegas twenty minutes before. The second arrived a few minutes after that from a television station in Phoenix.

The opening in the top of the dam stretched over two hundred feet across, and close to three hundred feet down. Grant knew that the amount of water draining out of Lake Powell was now more than the flow of the Mississippi. As he watched, a house-sized piece of concrete broke away and fell into the canyon, a sight that was becoming normal at Glen Canyon. The resulting splash could only be imagined, since the canyon bottom had long since disappeared in the clouds of mist.

Grant felt helpless. What could he do? The dam would disintegrate with or without him there. Maybe downstream, where all the floodwater was headed, there was still something to be done. He turned away from the windows. "Brian, who did you talk to at Hoover? What were they going to do?"

Brian shook his head. "I can't remember who I talked to. We didn't talk about what they should do. I just told them we had a hole in the dam."

Grant hoped Fred Grainger was at Hoover. He nodded to the phone, "I need to talk to them. Can you get me the number?"

Brian rustled through the papers on his desk and handed Grant a sheet while holding his finger under the number for Hoover Dam. Grant dialed the number and someone on the other end picked up.

"Hello, this is Grant Stevens from the Bureau of Reclamation. I'm calling from Glen Canyon Dam. Is Fred Grainger there?"

The man on the other end asked him to hold. While he waited, he wondered how long it would take to get to Hoover.

"Hello, this is Fred." He sounded tired.

"Fred, Grant Stevens calling from Glen Canyon."

Fred's voice seemed to cheer up slightly "Grant. How are things up there? Who's in charge?"

Grant shook his head, even though he was on the phone. "Like it or not, I'm in charge. I'm all the Bureau could muster for this one."

Fred was silent on the other end for a moment. "What about the commissioner, and the VP's? Where's Archibald?"

"They're all on their way to Kenya for the symposium," Grant explained.

"Holy crap. So they don't even know?"

"I don't know. They may have been reached by now. Commissioner Blackwell's admin sent me here this morning. I'm sure she's been trying to contact them ever since." The phone went silent for a moment, and then Grant spoke again. "What are you guys doing at Hoover?"

Fred spoke tentatively. "Well, we canceled all tours for the day. We're using some of the tour guides to work traffic to turn people back."

Grant couldn't respond. He hoped that they were doing a lot more than just canceling tours. "What about your water? Aren't you dumping any?"

"Not yet," answered Fred. "But we started notifying –"

"Why not?" Grant yelled into the phone.

Fred stumbled with his answer. "We're trying. But I had to notify the dams downstream first, and Laughlin, so they could, you know, prepare. I can't just flood 'em out."

Grant couldn't believe it. They were worried about flooding downstream. In reality, flooding downstream was a legitimate worry. The problem was, it was going to be unavoidable. And the longer they waited, the worse the flooding downstream would be. How could he make them understand? "Fred, we are having a catastrophic failure here! The Glen Canyon Dam is breaking apart. You are about to get Lake Powell in your lap. I suggest you start dumping water as fast as you can."

Fred hesitated on the other end. "I'm not sure I can authorize that. My boss is gone too. Besides, we're limited on how much water we can release downstream. If I let too much out, it'll cause problems."

Grant felt the muscles in his neck tighten. "You have to authorize it, Fred. You're all we've got. If you don't start dumping, you won't be able to handle all the water and Hoover'll get topped."

The phone went silent. Hopefully Fred understood that even Hoover, the king of the big dams in America, could not survive topping. Sustained topping, even of concrete dams, would tear them apart in no time.

After some silence, Fred responded, "I figured the two spillways could handle most of it."

Grant shook his head again. "Think about it, Fred. You think your spillways'll be able to dump two years of river flow in one day?"

Fred didn't respond.

Grant spoke slowly. "Open the gates, Fred. Now. Get rid of as much water as possible."

"I'm going to need some kind of authorization," Fred said.

"It's just us Fred. As crappy as it sounds, I'm in charge." He continued. "I hereby authorize you to dump water. Hell, Fred, if it'll help, I'll order you to. Blame me. Just start opening everything you got."

Finally, he responded. "All right. I'll open the gates."

"Good Fred. I'll be there as soon as I can. Let me give you my cell phone number." Grant read off the number. "You can't be a hero on this one, Fred, but you can definitely be the goat. Do what you have to do."

Fred seemed anxious to get off the phone. "I'd better go."

"Fred, you guys control the dams downstream too, don't you? You need to open the gates at Davis and Parker too."

The next two dams downstream from Hoover were Davis Dam, which created Lake Mojave, and Parker Dam, which held back Lake Havasu. All flow control at Davis and Parker was automated and initiated from the Hoover Dam control center.

"You want me to dump all three dams?" Fred asked, sounding more scared than before. "That'll flood everything downstream."

"You will absolutely cause flooding downstream, Fred. But that's nothing compared to the flood that'll occur if one of the dams fails."

"All right. I gotta go."

Grant felt uncomfortable hanging up, but he knew he had to. "Okay, Fred, keep me posted."

Grant hung up the phone. Brian was waiting.

He pointed to Earl. "Earl's got something to tell you."

Earl spoke in his raspy voice, "I just got a call from the Feds. The L.A. office of the FBI just landed in Page. They want a meeting with me and you as soon as they get here."

The FBI wanted to talk to him? What could he tell them? He had enough things to worry about without having to deal with them. On the other hand, maybe they knew something already. Maybe they knew who did it. He saw no way to avoid the meeting. He nodded to Earl. "Fine, I'll be waiting."

He walked to the windows. It was hard to believe how fast the sight changed when he was away for a few moments. During the phone call to Hoover, Grant estimated that the cut in the dam had grown by twenty or thirty percent. Now, watermarks were visible on the canyon wall just upstream from the dam. The water level next to the dam had dropped almost ten feet. Farther upstream, there were no marks yet, meaning the water was dropping ten feet in just over a hundred yards.

He turned back to the group at the table. "How are the safety warnings going?"

Dan answered, "Downstream, the police have closed all access to Lee's Ferry and other roads down into the canyon. The rangers at the Grand Canyon have called tour helicopters in Vegas and asked for their assistance in flying through the canyon to warn hikers to climb to higher ground. I need to check with them to see how it's going."

Grant pointed upstream into Lake Powell. "What about there?" he asked.

Dan nodded. "Yeah, we called 'em."

Grant continued. "How come I don't see anybody? What if some boater wants to motor down by the dam? If a boat enters this canyon upstream from the dam, he'll get sucked through the hole."

The group looked around at each other.

Earl spoke up, "I guess we could park a boat about a mile upstream to keep people away."

Grant smiled, his first smile in a while. "Better make it a fast one. We don't want to see a police boat get pulled over either."

* * *

9:10 a.m. - St. George, Utah

The man shut off the motorcycle and leaned it on its kickstand, then climbed off. Being an infrequent rider, nearly three hours on the road had taken its toll. His inner thighs and buttocks ached and his lower back wasn't much better. His fingers resisted straightening, preferring instead to remain in a gripped position. He fumbled while trying to unfasten his helmet strap; after removing his gloves, he was able to complete the task. He stuffed the gloves into the helmet, and left the helmet on the seat of the bike, unlocked. After all, this was St. George, Utah.

Entering the restaurant, he shucked the sunglasses and stuffed them in his pocket. Not waiting to be seated, he headed straight to the bar where the TV was located. Finding a bar with a TV in St. George had been no easy task, especially one open this early in the morning. On his previous trips, he had stopped at almost every restaurant on St. George Blvd. before finally settling on the small cafe just off the exit from I-15, which had a small bar and a television.

He climbed on a stool and looked up at the TV. He was glad to be alone at the bar. Unfortunately, the TV was tuned to a sports channel showing baseball highlights. A fifty-ish woman with gray hair, who looked like she would rather be anywhere else but waiting tables, walked up with a coffee pot.

"Coffee?" She laid a menu down in front of him.

He slid his cup toward her, an unspoken response to the question. While she poured, he pointed at the TV. "Can we put that on the news?"

She looked around the room, most likely to see if anyone else would care. After she verified the room was still empty, she nodded. "Sure. I'll get somebody to come in and change it for you." She left.

He picked up the menu and scanned it, but he was so anxious to see the news that he couldn't concentrate. Why couldn't she have changed the channel herself? He leaned over the bar and looked for a remote.

The waitress materialized beside him. "Ready to order?" Her voice sounded strange, as if she didn't approve of him leaning over the bar.

He dropped back in his seat and opened the menu again. There were pictures of omelets, eggs, French toast, and other breakfast specials. He didn't feel all that hungry. He just wanted to watch the news. "Is somebody gonna come in and change the channel?"

"Yeah. They'll be here in a minute. Do you need some more time?"

He scanned the pictures in the menu, not close to making a decision. "How about a couple of pancakes?" he said suddenly.

She pointed at a line in the menu. "Two or three?"

"Two," he said.

She wrote on her pad and continued talking without looking up. "Bacon, sausage, or ham?"

He didn't feel like any. "I'll take bacon."

She grabbed his menu. "Somebody'll be here in a minute to change the TV." She left.

He watched a highlight of someone hitting a home run, fans fighting in the grandstands for the ball. He hated baseball. What a boring sport – too much waiting. He looked at his watch. It had been three hours already. What if nothing else was happening at the dam? Maybe the news wasn't on to it yet. What if they figured out how to fix the leak?

"You want another channel?" A man in an apron, probably a cook, walked into the bar.

He pointed to the TV. "Can we see if there's anything on the news?"

"Sure." The man walked over to the TV, reached up, and started flipping channels. "Any one in particular?" he asked.

Which channel would be first to cover it? A local network, probably. He was about to say something when a picture of the Glen Canyon Dam, obscured in fog, appeared briefly then disappeared.

"Stop!" he yelled, holding out both of his hands. "Go back a couple."

The cook looked at him curiously, as if he was thinking he might pull a gun or something. The TV flipped back to the view of the dam.

"That's it." He stood and walked closer to the TV.

The view of the Glen Canyon Dam was taken from a helicopter. The whole area where the west elevator had been was gone. It had simply disappeared. Water poured from a football field-sized cut in the dam. His heart seemed to stop beating. This was better than his dreams. He couldn't stop a huge grin from stretching across his face.

The man in the apron stood next to him. "Is that the Glen Canyon Dam?" he asked, pointing toward the television.

The words "Glen Canyon Dam, Lake Powell" were written in bold across the bottom of the screen in bright yellow.

"Yeah," the man said, not taking his eyes off the TV. The camera panned downstream and showed the water rushing down the rock canyon. Brown water, obscured in mist, churned in constantly changing rapids, rapids that looked like they could swallow a whole house. He quickly estimated the water levels below the dam to be a hundred feet above normal.

"How did you know about this already?" The cook asked, without taking his eyes off the TV. "Did you hear about it on the radio or something?"

"Yeah," he answered, without thinking or looking at the man.

They both stared blankly at the television without saying anything. The camera showed the water line above the dam, and a close up of the water rushing through the break.

"What caused it?" the man in the apron asked. "Did they say on the radio?"

He heard the words, but at first he didn't realize they were directed toward him. He watched in amazement as a piece of concrete the size of a house broke off the dam and disappeared into the canyon below. He couldn't believe it. The scene seemed surreal, like a fantasy. He felt a large pit growing in his stomach.

The cook tugged at his arm. "Did they say what caused it? On the radio?"

He looked over at the man. "Huh?"

"What caused it? You said you heard about it on the radio."

He shook his head and motioned back toward the door, keeping his eyes on the TV. "I don't have a radio. I'm on a motorcycle."

The man gave him a funny look, making him realize he had just contradicted himself regarding the radio. In the depths of his consciousness he wondered if he should try to say something to cover up the contradiction, but his amazement of what was happening on the TV overrode the concern. The cook must have shared the same feeling, because he broke the stare and reached up and turned up the volume on the TV.

". . . no comment yet from law enforcement or the Bureau of Reclamation regarding the cause of this disaster. Additionally, we were unable to contact any-one downstream in the Grand Canyon."

"It's gonna drown everybody in the Grand Canyon," the cook said. "It'll kill a ton of people."

This comment bothered him. Hopefully the park would have enough time to warn everybody, and get them out. All they really needed to do was hike up a couple of hundred feet, to get above the water. He didn't want to see too many people die.

The trance was broken when the waitress delivered his plate of pancakes to the bar. He jumped when he heard the waitress behind him.

"Oh my gosh. What dam is that?" she said. The words "Glen Canyon Dam" were still painted across the bottom of the screen.

The man in the apron pointed at the screen. "Lake Powell."

The waitress held a hand in front of her mouth. "Oh my! What happened?"

He noticed that another waitress, this one much younger, appeared wearing the same dress. A man in regular clothes, not the restaurant uniforms, walked in. "What the . . ."

Over the next few moments, more people showed up, most of them other customers. The comments and questions became noisy enough that the cook had to turn up the TV again. The man watched for a few more minutes, until another enormous piece of concrete broke off the structure and fell into the water. He no longer had any desire to eat. And although the last thing he wanted was to pull his eyes off the images on the television, the group made him uncomfortable. And besides, Glen Canyon was only the first. He had much more to do. He pulled a ten out of his wallet, and tossed it near the untouched plate of pancakes. The waitress's eyes, like everyone else's, were still riveted to the television, so when he walked out the front door toward his motorcycle, no one noticed.

* * *

9:15 a.m. - Hole in the Rock, Lake Powell, Utah

Julie and Erika stopped for a rest. Paul and Greg were a hundred feet farther ahead. Erika took off her t-shirt and adjusted her bikini top. It was hot already, maybe ninety degrees. Julie unscrewed the lid on her canteen and took a long drink.

Fifteen minutes before, they had arrived at buoy 66, which meant they were sixty-six miles upstream from the Glen Canyon Dam. They turned into the small bay and tied off the boat on some rocks on the shore. There were three other boats parked and hikers were already spread out up and down the slope. Julie's first thought at seeing where they would be hiking was that you would have to be crazy to climb it. But, after a few minutes of complaining, she had reluctantly tightened the laces on her hiking boots, checked the canteens, and the two couples had started their hike.

Now, while Julie rested, she glanced back down and saw that another boat had arrived below and was preparing to hike. Julie wiped sweat off her brow and wished they had started earlier. "We should've done Rainbow Bridge on the way home."

Erika exhaled. "I don't think I would have felt like stopping anywhere on the way home."

Julie thought Erika had a good point. She looked up and saw the men still climbing. They looked strong, especially Paul, who had a springy step and looked like he could take off running at any moment. "Paul looks like he could go forever."

Erika looked up at her husband. "Yeah, and we were both stupid for not putting a rope around him so he could pull us with him."

Julie laughed. Now her imagination was going to be taunting her with that fantasy of a rope pulling her to the top.

Looking up the slope, Hole in the Rock was basically the intersection of two near-vertical cliffs, their merger creating a notch that climbed steeply upwards until it cut right into the rock and formed a steep 'V' shape. The climb up the notch was a minimum twenty-five percent grade, but sometimes increased to as much as forty-five. Julie's calves were burning already, even though they weren't even a quarter of the way up. Farther ahead the two men had stopped and were looking back down at their wives.

Erika pulled her black hair back and put a band around it. "You ready?"

Julie nodded. "Yeah. Let's go."

CHAPTER 11

Grant counted five representatives of the FBI walking in the door of the Glen Canyon Dam visitor center; two of them wore suits, the others navy blue coveralls with a yellow "FBI" insignia above the left pocket. All of them packed side arms. Brian had met them at the door, and then led them over toward the table.

A tall stocky guy in one of the suits spoke first. "Hi I'm—" He stopped when he got close to the window. "Wow!" He walked over to the glass and stared. The other four agents crowded up behind him. All five talked and pointed for what seemed like a minute.

When they finally broke away from the window, the stocky man spoke again. "Hi. I'm Phillip Sutherland. I'm a deputy field agent for the FBI. Who's in charge?"

Earl, still sitting at the table spoke from underneath his mustache. "You can be, if you want."

Grant laughed under his breath.

The agent took it in stride and smiled. "I'm sure you boys have had an interesting morning."

Grant reached out his hand. "Grant Stevens, Bureau of Reclamation. I flew in from Denver about an hour ago." Grant motioned around the table. "This is Brian; he was the security guard in charge last night."

Brian reached out and shook the agent's hand.

"This is Dan, head of security."

Dan nodded.

"And this is Earl Smith, Captain of the Page Police Department."

The policeman waved without standing up.

The agent looked at Grant. "Well, we have a lot of catching up to do, but we don't want to get in your way. Is now a good time to bring us up to speed?"

"Sure." Grant walked over to the windows overlooking the dam. Grant was getting used to the fact that every time he looked at the dam, the hole got a little bigger. "At approximately 6:00 a.m., an explosion occurred in the west elevator shaft. It used to look just like that one." Grant pointed to the east elevator shaft, still visible on the other side of the dam. "The explosion blew the top out of the elevator shaft and a small hole in the dam. According to Brian, the original hole in the face of the dam was about five feet in diameter and about two-hundred feet down."

Brian nodded approval of the description.

The agent wiped a hand across his forehead. "You mean at 6:00 a.m. the hole was only five feet wide, and now it's this big?" He looked astonished.

Grant nodded. "It only took a small hole to get it started. The water's doing the rest. Too much pressure. The dam'll be gone in less than an hour."

"How long before . . ." Phil stopped. "Go ahead. Continue."

Grant continued. "Last night an unscheduled elevator repairman showed up and worked on the west elevator. We assume he put a bomb in the elevator. He left his supply trailer on the dam when he left. Earl's guys got a look at it before that section of the dam collapsed."

Earl held up a zip lock bag with white pellets inside. One of the guys in coveralls snatched the bag from Earl and studied it. The agent opened it and used his hand to wave the scent under his nose without inhaling it directly.

"Ammonium nitrate fertilizer," said Earl, still sitting. "The same stuff that kook used to re-arrange the federal building in Oklahoma."

The FBI agent in coveralls nodded his head in agreement. "I think he's right."

"I assume that elevator repairmen do not normally use ammonium nitrate as part of their standard maintenance?" asked Phil.

The question was not intended to be answered, and no one tried.

The second agent in a suit spoke for the first time. "Are you guys searching for the perpetrator?"

Earl nodded. "There's a million ways out of Page, if you count all the dirt roads through the desert. But we setup roadblocks on all the highways a couple of hours ago. We're looking for any newer white pickups."

"And?" prompted Phil.

"And we ain't seen anybody suspicious in a new white pickup, Chevy or otherwise," Earl said unemotionally.

The questions then started to concentrate on what Earl's people found on their fact-finding episode on the dam. They were extremely excited when Earl showed them the camera and explained they had taken pictures of the trailer before it disappeared, then disappointed to find out that the pictures were not digital and would need to be developed. Obviously, things were done differently in the FBI. Grant told them about Brian's description of the sun peeking over the horizon, and one of the agents called someone on his cell phone for an exact time analysis. Overall, the number and detail of the questions was amazing.

At a certain point, when the discussions focused on Earl's officers and Dan's security team, Grant caught himself yawning. He stretched his arms and stood. He walked back over to the wall of windows. Since he had last looked, the water had carved another hundred feet across the dam. However, as the hole expanded east, it cut underneath the crest, leaving a huge section on top that had not broken off yet, an overhang of over a hundred feet. It just hung out there, defying the forces of water rushing around it. He expected it to break away any second. How long could it last? Then abruptly, the whole section let go and disappeared into the torrent below. An extremely loud crack, like thunder, followed a fraction of a second later. The group behind Grant stopped talking and looked at the dam, many standing up for a better view. Grant estimated to himself that about forty or fifty times more water than normal was heading down the Colorado River.

One of the agents in coveralls spoke first. "I'd hate to be downstream in the Grand Canyon right now."

CHAPTER 12

9:45 a.m. - Grand Canyon, Arizona

David looked at his watch and noted the time. The silver raft drifted silently along the smooth stretch. He was glad to be back on the river again. After gulping a big breakfast made of hash browns, eggs, bacon, and sausage, all scrambled together, which Keller called morning stew, the group had packed the silver rafts and pushed off.

David was falling in love with the leisurely pace of the river trip. They never rushed to do anything. After six days away from the grind at the office, routines were forgotten. Although the nagging feeling that a million things needed to be done was still perceptible, it had diminished to only an occasional passing thought, which he was learning to ignore. Sometimes in the past, after returning to work after a long vacation, David experienced a sense of re-orientation, where he had to try hard to remember how to do his job. He laughed to himself. After two weeks in the Grand Canyon he might just have to repeat the new employee orientation.

Judy, sitting just in front of him, turned and called back to the guide. "What have we got downstream today, Keller?"

"Ladies and gentlemen, today is an easy one. Probably the best rapids we're going to see are at Waltenburg."

Everybody turned around for the information. Afram asked the first question. "How big?"

"Class five at the best, nothing like the Jewels were yesterday. I'll have to take her in sideways just to cool you off."

The Jewel Rapids had been the best of the trip, especially Sapphire where they had lost Judy into the river. As they had passed through the jewels, they passed mile one hundred, meaning they were a hundred miles downstream from Lee's Ferry, and a hundred fifteen from the Glen Canyon Dam. David couldn't believe how fast the trip was slipping away.

Becky shook her head. "I'm plenty cool, Keller. You don't need to get us wet on purpose."

As the weekend had progressed, Becky and Sam had been acting more and more like an item. She tended to always need help or protection, and Sam was more than willing to fill the role. Sam had even asked Afram to switch places in the raft this morning, so he could sit next to her. David thought it was funny that they could work together every day and never even notice each other, then spend a few days camping with no showers or makeup and all of a sudden discover a little chemistry. Was it possible the outdoors stimulated their hormones? If so, why didn't Becky or Judy look any better to him? Or, more likely, the chemistry had always been there, buried and throttled by the office environment and politics. Sam generally gave his soul at work, and was one of those head-down workaholics. It was probably impossible for Sam to find love at work.

Keller had it figured out. "Why, girl? Sam's not going to let anything happen to you."

The group watched Sam to see what his reaction would be, but he didn't take the bait, showing only a poker face. Becky, on the other hand, couldn't conceal her smile. She obviously liked to be associated with Sam.

"If there are no rapids, then what's for lunch?" Afram asked with a very serious face.

Keller leaned forward. "Didn't I tell you? Today is YOYO day."

When Keller received the blank looks he expected, he continued. "Don't ya know what YOYO means?"

There were a few headshakes, but Judy was the one who asked, "No, Keller, what's YOYO day?"

"YOYO means: You're—On —Your — Own," he said, smiling.

They laughed and Afram elaborated. "You mean we can go through the supplies and take whatever we want for lunch?"

"No, what I mean is we'll pull the rafts over for lunch and you guys can eat whatever you find. Kinda like back to nature, environmentalism at its finest."

David looked up at the rock walls and felt glad that Keller was only kidding. He wondered how long he could survive on his own. Not long, he bet. He would wander around for days looking for food. In fact, he hadn't seen anything edible so far on the trip. There were fish in the river; he saw them jump occasionally, but without a pole and bait, he'd die of old age before he caught something.

David looked around. No one talked for a while, evidently having had their fill of sparring with Keller. Even Keller craned his neck and admired the canyon walls. Becky rested her hand on Sam's leg. A state of relaxation permeated. Even though the white-water was the primary reason they had come to the Grand Canyon, one day of smaller rapids would be a nice change.

* * *

9:55 a.m. - Glen Canyon Dam, Arizona

Grant stood at the windows overlooking the dam, or what was left of it. The water had torn almost all the way to the east side. Again, a section over a hundred feet long jutted out, ready to snap at any moment. This time the whole group stood watching, even the FBI agents.

"Why isn't it breaking off?" Phil asked.

"It will," said Grant. "Keep watching."

"Look at all the water down the canyon." Brian pointed downstream.

Grant looked and noticed that most of the mist was gone. He hadn't realized it until just now. The clear visibility allowed a good view into the canyon. The huge waterfall into the canyon had transformed, over the last hour, into a more gradual drop, gradual being a relative word describing a drop of over a hundred feet. With the water downstream four hundred feet above normal, the water didn't have to drop very far. Looking downstream at the new river, Grant saw an outcropping of rock break off and fall into the river.

"It's going," yelled one of the FBI agents in coveralls, pointing to the dam.

Grant turned in time to see the huge section of concrete falling into the river. The piece made a big splash and then it was gone. The loud sound followed a moment later. The only evidence of the break was the impact waves that dispersed quickly as they radiated downstream.

Grant looked around at the group. "The Glen Canyon Dam is no more." He checked his watch, 9:58 a.m. He thought to himself that he had only missed estimating the time by 28 minutes – not bad. No one said anything for a few moments.

"Guess I need to start looking for a new job," said Brian, the security guard.

His boss, Dan, looked at him. "Nobody said you were fired."

Brian looked back at his boss. "You better start looking too, boss. There ain't nothing left to guard here."

Dan's eyebrows came up as the realization sunk in.

Phil patted Brian on the back. "There's going to be a lot of Looky-Lou's for months. Somebody's got to guard this place. You guys'll be fine for a while."

The comment didn't seem to make them look any happier.

* * *

10:00 a.m. - Hole in the Rock, Lake Powell, Utah

Julie wanted to stop, but there were only a few steps more to go. She kept climbing and used her hand on the sheer rock wall on her left. Her husband and Paul watched her from above, and the breathing grunts and sounds of shoes on rock told her Erika was just behind. Her calves and thighs burned, but she tried to bury that thought or she knew she wouldn't make it. She had taken her t-shirt off as well, and she could feel her hair swishing through the slimy perspiration on her back.

"A few more steps, baby," Greg encouraged.

"Come on, Erika," Paul coaxed.

And then Julie reached the summit. She turned and held her hand out to Erika and pulled her up the last step. Both women stood and looked down the way they had come, breathing heavily. The notch seemed almost vertical back down to the boats and water below, forcing Julie to take a step backwards from the edge. The water looked inviting though, and made Julie wish she were already back at the bottom.

Her husband moved beside her. "Incredible view, isn't it?"

Julie agreed, but shook her head. "It wasn't worth it, though."

Her husband looked shocked, then put his arm around her. "Come on! You did great. We did it in less than an hour."

Erika spoke for the first time since reaching the top. "That was nuts. No wonder we never did this before."

Paul held out his hands. "It wasn't that bad."

Erika turned on her husband. "How would you know?" she shot back. "You're an animal."

Julie started to laugh. Erika's expression finally softened, then she and the men laughed as well.

Julie felt dizzy. "I need to sit down."

Greg led her over to a small rock ledge, which made a perfect bench. Julie sat, even though the rock was hot. Her legs trembled. Erika came over and sat next to her. The plateau was nothing but barren red rock hills for miles in every direction. A couple of hundred yards away was a small gravel parking lot for jeeps and other four-wheel drive vehicles that had driven to the spot. The lot was empty. The rock was burning Julie's legs so she stood and put her t-shirt under her and sat back down. She unscrewed the lid on her canteen and drank. She poured a small amount in her hair, and it felt wonderful. If only she had more, she would douse her whole body.

"How long do you want to stay up here?" Greg asked.

Julie wished again she were already back down in the water. "I don't want to stay here at all. But I'm not hiking back down until I rest for a while."

Paul pointed to something over by the parking lot. "There's a plaque over there that talks about how the Mormons got their oxen and stagecoaches down. We could go read it." He sounded hopeful.

"The Mormons were nuts, if they took wagons down there," Erika stated flatly.

Greg patted his wife on the back. "Well, I can see that we've got two pissed off women here. What's it gonna take to get you two in a good mood?"

Julie looked up at her husband. "Carry me back down."

He turned and crouched. "Okay, get on."

She cocked her head. "You're serious?"

He motioned onto his back with his thumb. "Get on!"

She decided to play along. She stood and climbed on her husband's back. Greg stood. Paul had done the same for Erika, and she climbed on his back.

"We're going down now?" Erika asked.

Greg brayed like a donkey. "Piggy back to the plaque. Piggy back to the plaque." He brayed again and started galloping roughly toward the parking lot. Paul followed. The girls spurred their husbands and giggled.

CHAPTER 13

10:05 a.m. - Glen Canyon Dam, Arizona

With the dam completely collapsed, Grant knew he needed to move on, downstream. They weren't doing all the things necessary downstream, he was sure of it. He looked down river and saw another outcropping of rock break off the canyon wall and fall into the river. The river was a raging menace. The canyon would look different after twenty-four hours of this river. It would tear it apart. He focused on the metal Glen Canyon Bridge, only a few hundred feet from the dam. Although the roadway of the seven-hundred-foot-high bridge was well out of the water, the latticework of steel girders under the arch reached hundreds of feet down and attached to the sandstone canyon walls. Grant could not see where they attached. They were underwater. He couldn't help but notice that many cars were stopped on the bridge. He could see people standing. The bridge was obviously a good viewpoint to watch the dam collapse.

Grant waved Earl over. He pointed down where the support structure disappeared underwater. "Check that out. The mounts and girders are in the water. That could bring it down."

Earl didn't need any more information. He pulled a radio off his belt. "Close the Glen Canyon Bridge. I need roadblocks on both sides. Get everybody off now. We might lose it."

Earl looked at the group, especially Phil from the FBI. "I need to leave for a while and make sure they get it cleared off. You know where to find me." He started walking toward the door.

One of the FBI guys in coveralls intercepted him. They both took out their radios and exchanged a couple of comments. The guy from the FBI wrote something down while Earl started back out the door. The agent punched something into his radio and then held it up to his face. "Earl, you copy?"

Grant heard the response. "Yup." Earl sounded even raspier on the radio.

The guy in coveralls went over to his briefcase and retrieved an earphone assembly. He plugged one end in a jack on his radio and the other in his ear. He then walked back over by the group as if nothing had happened.

Grant noticed one of the other guys in coveralls talking to Phil. Phil nodded and said to the group, "According to Brian's description of the sun rising, the explosion occurred somewhere between 6:05 and 6:30 a.m. this morning."

Grant remembered thinking the time of explosion seemed so important a couple of hours ago. Now with the dam gone and Lake Powell draining into the canyon, he wondered why it made any difference.

Phil came over to Grant. "Mr. Stevens, can we sit down and talk about a few things?" He motioned to Brian and the other security guys. "Can you guys join us?"

Grant looked at his watch. He needed to leave. "I guess I can talk for a few minutes." He sat down at the table.

"Our first suspicion on this kind of situation would be international terrorists, after all the problems with the World Trade Centers in New York and all, and we are proceeding with that investigation. However, a couple of things don't add up. The first being that Brian here described the elevator repairman as a white guy. We checked him out. The paperwork was fake, and the maintenance company has no employees that fit his description. We expected as much. It's still probable that he was a foreigner, but he could be an American or European working with them. There's a lot of sympathy for the Middle East and bad blood for Americans and what they are doing over there."

One of the agents in coveralls spoke to Brian. "Do you remember if he had any kind of noticeable accent?"

"I'm trying to remember what he sounded like." He shook his head. "I don't remember any accent. I just remember he was calm and confident. When I said we didn't have him scheduled, he showed me the paperwork and rattled off Dan's name and how it was already set up and all. No, I wouldn't say he had any accent. His speech was very professional, if nothing else."

Phil looked over at Grant. "Besides wanting to wreak havoc in America, why would anyone want to blow up this dam?"

Grant raised his eyebrows. "Are you kidding?"

The FBI man said nothing, obviously serious about his question.

Grant looked at the security guards for support, but everyone waited for him. He blurted the words at the FBI. "There are tons of people who wanted this dam blown up."

Phil seemed surprised. "Who?"

"There are whole organizations dedicated to having it decommissioned – the Sierra Club and Greenpeace, to name a few. There are web sites that talk about it. There is even one group, the Glen Canyon Institute, whose entire purpose is to decommission the dam. They hold debates and lectures at universities trying to get support. One time a group of whackos rolled a black piece of plastic down the face of the dam to make everyone think the dam was cracked. Gee, if you think about it, half of the Democratic Party probably wants it removed."

Phil shook his head. "You're talking about environmentalists?"

Grant looked around the room for support. "Absolutely. I'm not saying they did it. But they sure as hell wanted to." He pointed at one of the news helicopters. "They're definitely celebrating right now, while they watch it on TV."

Phil had not considered this perspective. "Why this dam, more than any of the other dams across the country?"

"There are lots of reasons they focus on this one. The biggest is the canyon itself." Grant pointed upstream to Lake Powell. "The area under the lake is called Glen Canyon. Less than a thousand people saw it before the dam was built. It was supposedly an incredible place, vertical carved rock walls on the sides, endless narrow side-canyons like Zion National Park, and some of the canyons had waterfalls and vegetation like rain forests."

Phil was amazed. "Why did the environmentalists let them build it in the first place? What about the environmental impact studies, the hearings . . .?"

Grant held out his arms. "When Glen Canyon Dam was approved in the late fifties, there weren't any environmentalists, at least not many, and they certainly weren't very powerful. There was only one salaried member of the Sierra Club. Environmental impact studies hadn't been invented yet. The Glen Canyon Dam is largely responsible for the changes. It pissed off the environmentalists and got them organized. They vowed never again. A couple of years later, they stopped the construction of two more dams downstream in the Grand Canyon."

Phil looked shocked. "They were going to dam up the Grand Canyon?"

"Yeah, in fact if you float down the Colorado River, you can still see the exploratory holes drilled in the canyon walls, where one of the dams was to be built."

"I still don't understand why the Democrats allowed it to happen."

Grant smiled. "The Democrats are the ones who built it. They ran the House and the Senate in those days. They wrote the bill and sent it to a moderate Republican president, Dwight Eisenhower, who signed it. In the late fifties, the Democrats were no more environmentally-minded than the Republicans. They were, however, adamant proponents of water projects – big projects that distributed water to cities and farmers, created electricity for homes and industry, and created jobs in the process. The water projects were big welfare, and the Democrats loved them."

While Phil was shaking his head, Grant's cell phone rang. "Hello, this is Grant."

"Grant, this is Julia. I got ahold of Roland in Paris. The flight to Africa had not taken off yet. I'll conference you in."

Crap. The last thing he wanted to do was talk to the commissioner. Grant looked out at where the dam used to be and wondered if they could blame him for it. He stood and walked away from the group. After he heard a series of clicks, he recognized the voice of the director of the Bureau of Reclamation.

"Stevens, this is Commissioner Blackwell, can you hear me?"

Grant thought it was arrogant of Roland to constantly refer to himself as commissioner. "Yeah, Roland, I can hear you fine."

"What the hell happened out there?"

Grant tried to organize his thoughts. "Looks like a guy posing as an elevator repairman planted a bomb in the west elevator. It blew a five-foot hole in the dam."

"Is that it? Only five feet?"

"That was four hours ago, Roland. The dam tore itself apart. It's gone."

There was silence on the line.

Roland voice was shaky. "You're saying the Glen Canyon Dam has completely collapsed? Lake Powell is gone?"

"Yes. The dam is gone. But no, Lake Powell is still there. It's draining now. It'll be gone by tomorrow, though."

Roland hesitated again. "Grant, I'm coming back. I'm trying to get a flight as we speak. I'm looking at all possible connection points. Julia, is the Gulfstream ready? I'll need it to meet me at whatever airport I can get to in the United States."

Julie hesitated. "It's in Page, Arizona. Grant used it to get down there."

The commissioner sounded shocked. "What? Stevens took the jet?"

Grant was amazed. The idiot was more worried about his plane than the situation at Glen Canyon.

Julia's voice was weak. "I thought under the circumstances . . ."

Grant jumped in. "Why not, Roland? It was a good idea. If I had tried to fly commercial, I'd still be waiting for connections. Then nobody from the Bureau would be here. Would that be better?" Grant realized he had gone too far.

The commissioner ignored him. "Julia, tell the pilot to stand by, as soon as I find out where my connection is. I'll call you back. Have them meet me."

"Okay. Let me know when you make your plans," Julia said.

Grant had other short-term plans for the Gulfstream, but he thought he should not bring them up right then with Roland.

The commissioner got back to the subject at hand. "Stevens, what are you doing right now?"

"The FBI is asking questions."

"What are you telling them?" He sounded scared. "Be careful what you say; you represent the Bureau."

Grant rolled his eyes. Why all the politics? Why couldn't anybody just communicate? "Don't worry, Roland."

"Oh, and Stevens, don't make any stupid decisions before I get there. In fact, avoid making any decisions at all if you can help it. Just do what's necessary."

Grant wanted to tell Roland to ram it, and then stopped himself. "Okay, Roland."

Roland sounded distracted like he wasn't speaking directly into the phone. "I gotta go. The ticket lady is waving at me."

Grant heard the phone click. "Julia, are you still there?"

"Yeah, I'm here."

"Call me before you take the Gulfstream. I need it for one more trip."

"But the commissioner said—"

"I know what he said. But there's plenty of time. It will take him a while to fly back across the ocean. Just call me first."

"Okay." Her voice sounded uncertain.

Grant thanked her and hung up.

* * *

10:15 a.m. - Glen Canyon Bridge, Arizona

Earl hustled out of the visitor center parking lot and over to where his officers were setting up the roadblock. A line of about ten cars was stopped at the sign. One officer was waving for the cars to turn around and go back the other way. The first car wasn't moving, however.

The driver was yelling out the window at an officer. "What about Navajo bridge downstream?"

"It's closed, too." The officer motioned up toward the lake. "You'll have to go around."

"That's almost three hundred miles around! It'll take five hours!"

"I'm sorry, sir," said the officer. "The bridge isn't safe right now."

"Bull. Look at all those people out there." He leaned out of his window and pointed at the bridge where four police cars were trying to move about fifteen parked cars and pedestrians off the bridge. Some cars were turning around. Others were boxed in by other cars or waiting for pedestrians to get out of the way.

Earl walked past the argument and the roadblock, and approached the edge of the bridge. He looked over the edge and down into the river. The water was only four hundred feet or so below him, far less than the normal eight-hundred-foot drop to the river. The water was hitting the steel girders in the arch that supported the bridge. Earl could feel the bridge moving like it was alive. He heard a loud creak from flexing metal. He picked up his radio.

"Get 'em off now. Turn on your sirens. This thing's gonna collapse."

He heard the sirens come on. He saw some of the pedestrians start running. Three cars drove past Earl off the bridge. The bulk of them, however, were going east toward Page. He saw about seven or eight cars get off the bridge on the other side. There were still three cars plus the four police cars. Two of the cars started to move. The third, a motor home, wasn't moving yet. A door opened and some idiot jumped out with a video camera. The PA on the police car roared, "GET BACK IN YOUR CAR." The guy kept filming.

Earl got on the radio. "All units get off the bridge now."

One of the police cars followed the two passenger cars toward the east side. The other two headed west toward Earl. The last one stayed with the motor home. The girders groaned and Earl felt the road move a little. He saw a crack open under his feet. He took five steps backwards off the bridge, keeping his eyes on the road. Two police cars flew passed him, slamming on their brakes once they were off the bridge. The cops jumped out of their cars and ran back to where Earl was standing. Earl took several more steps back from the bridge.

Earl saw that the motor home had started moving slowly toward him. The man with the video camera ran and jumped in the side door of the moving vehicle, but quickly re-emerged, hanging out the door with the camera rolling. The motor home was coming up to speed. The police car was right behind, siren still urging. As the motor home got within seventy-five feet of Earl, he could see the young male driver, shirtless and grinning from ear to ear.

While Earl was watching, the bridge let go with a screeching sound loud enough to hurt Earl's ears. The bottom of the west arch under Earl's feet broke loose and the road dropped and twisted, throwing the motor home and the police car off the bridge. Earl was still looking into the driver's eyes when it happened, and saw the grin replaced by an open-mouthed scream.

The asphalt in front of Earl disappeared just three steps in front of him. The motor home and the police car hit the water a hundred feet below. The police car knifed in and went under, but the motor home plopped in like a beach ball and bobbed on the surface. The west end of the bridge was pulled under immediately. The east end of the bridge, still attached, flexed downstream, then it broke loose and was gone too. The police car bobbed back up for a couple seconds, then back under. Earl watched the motor home floating along on the surface, front end down, the water twisting it around as it went. He saw the rear window, now on top, break open with unidentified debris exploding outwards. Without the window to trap air inside, the motor home sank like a rock.

The two officers, who barely escaped, ran up behind Earl. "How many did we lose?"

Earl responded, "One of our officers, and one motor home full of idiots."

* * *

10:25 a.m. - Glen Canyon Dam, Arizona

Grant saw the bridge collapse and two vehicles go into the river. The thought of being inside the car sickened him. He hoped it wasn't Earl in the police car. He turned and barked at the FBI agent with the radio. "Get ahold of Earl. Find out if he's okay. See if he knows how many people went in."

The agent walked away from the group while talking into his radio. He quickly gave a thumbs-up sign. "Earl's okay. There was one police officer in the car. They aren't sure how many civilians were in the motor home."

Phil looked at Grant. "What are you going to do now?"

"My job just moved three hundred miles downriver. After I talk to Earl, I'm flying downstream to the next dam to get ready to receive this water. Is that all right with the FBI?"

Grant spoke to the agent. "Tell Earl I need a police car immediately to take me back into Page to the airport."

There was a brief radio communication. "Earl says without the bridge, it's about five hours to Page," the agent relayed.

Grant forgot he needed the bridge to get to Page. He couldn't wait five hours. Suddenly, he was in a hurry to get back to the Gulfstream before the commissioner stole it from him. "Isn't there another way across? Do they have a helicopter?" He waited while the agent asked Earl the question.

"Earl says they don't have any choppers, but he might be able to talk one of those news teams into taking us across in their helicopter. They're still hovering around with cameras. He's going to try to get ahold of one on his radio. He'll let us know."

Fifteen minutes later, Grant was climbing into the green helicopter for KBXY out of Phoenix, Arizona. The chopper sat in the visitor center parking lot with its rotors idling. The network affiliate was more than happy to take Grant across, as long as they could ask a few questions.

Surprisingly, Earl climbed in the helicopter and sat next to Grant. "I DIDN'T WANT TO GO THE LONG WAY, EITHER," he yelled over the noise.

A cameraman climbed in next to Earl and shut the door. The helicopter became amazingly quiet. Grant felt the rotors accelerate. A head appeared around the seat in front of Grant. The guy shoved a microphone in his face.

"What caused the dam to break apart?"

"I'll answer a few questions, but no cameras or microphones."

The reporter showed displeasure, but pulled back the microphone. In an instant, a pad and pencil materialized out of nowhere. "Okay, why is the dam breaking apart?"

Grant felt the helicopter take off. "We think a bomb was placed in the west elevator shaft early this morning. The explosion caused a small hole deep in the dam. The force of the water then tore the dam apart in just under four hours."

"Has any group taken responsibility for the bomb?"

Grant didn't want to talk about that. "Law enforcement should answer questions about the perpetrator. The FBI is handling the criminal investigation."

"What kind of flood should be expected downstream?"

The helicopter was now above what used to be the Glen Canyon Dam. Grant paused to take a look. The water in the canyon was now flowing through the dam site as if it were not even there. The remaining dam only created what amounted to a fifty foot rapid in the river. Grant looked at the high water marks just upstream of the dam site and estimated the water had dropped more than fifty feet next to the dam.

Grant looked back at the reporter. "Could you repeat the question?"

"Flood. What kind of flood will this cause?"

"Luckily, downstream from here the Grand Canyon runs for almost three hundred miles, so not a lot of people or structures to worry about. There are efforts underway to evacuate the visitors from the canyon. Those efforts started almost three hours ago, long before the dam failed."

"Will the dam be rebuilt?"

"I don't know. That's a question for your congressman."

The reporter looked at his notes for a second. "Grant, what is your last name, and what do you do for the Bureau?"

"Last name is Stevens and I am a water resources manager."

"Why did the Bureau send you? Where is Roland Blackwell, the commissioner, or any of the vice presidents? Isn't this a big enough problem to warrant their presence?"

"Roland and most of his team are out of the country. They have been contacted and are arranging for return travel as we speak."

The helicopter had descended and was now landing on the road just past the roadblock on the opposite side of the river. The reporter pleaded with Grant.

"Mr. Stevens, can we get one camera shot of you answering a question? How about an easy one about the water downstream or the dam falling apart over a period of hours?"

Grant considered. He had heard that most of these people were not trustworthy, but this guy seemed okay. "No new questions, and no questions about who did it."

"Great! It will only take a minute."

The helicopter settled and the rotors began to slow down. Earl opened the door and the noise level rose considerably. When Grant climbed out of the chopper, the reporter was waiting for him.

In the noise, the reporter yelled through cupped hands. "LET'S GO OVER THERE WHERE WE CAN GET THE DAM SITE IN THE BACKROUND." He pointed to the river. They started walking away from the helicopter's noise.

Minutes later, the reporter was standing next to Grant, holding the microphone. The cameraman had the camera pointed at them. Grant had not expected the camera to be so close. He felt a sudden urge to straighten his hair, but resisted. The camera moved in close enough to see up his nose. The reporter asked Grant if he was ready.

He nodded. "One easy question," he reminded the reporter.

The reporter spoke into his microphone. "This is Kevin Scott with KBXY in Phoenix, Arizona. We are here at the site of what's left of the Glen Canyon Dam in Page, Arizona with Grant Stevens of the Bureau of Reclamation. The Bureau built this dam as well as most of the other dams in the country. Grant, give us a quick synopsis of what happened here this morning."

Grant felt like he had told this story a hundred times, but almost forgot everything with the camera in his face. He hesitated, which he knew would look awkward on TV. "Early this morning, an explosion went off in the west elevator of the dam. The original hole was small, approximately five feet in diameter. The water pressure then tore the dam apart over the next four hours." Grant stopped talking and looked back at the reporter.

The reporter didn't miss a beat. "As we speak, the FBI is on site investigating the cause of the explosion. As you can see behind us," the reporter turned and motioned to the dam site, "the Glen Canyon Dam has collapsed and Lake Powell is now draining into the Grand Canyon. That's all for now from Kevin Scott."

The light on the camera went out. The reporter looked at the cameraman. "How'd it look?"

"Great. I'll rewind it and you can check it out."

Grant dismissed himself and started walking to the waiting police car. The reporter called out his thanks, but was more concerned with the footage on the camera.

Earl joined in and walked next to Grant. "You're a natural. You oughta be in Hollywood."

"It'll probably get me fired."

"Why? You didn't say anything."

"Doesn't matter. The bosses will be jealous. It should come from them."

"Well, they ain't here."

"They will be." Grant reached out for the car door. "That's when the politics will start." He slid into the back of the squad car.

Earl climbed in the other side. The police car surged ahead and started up the hill toward Page. Grant felt funny leaving the scene, like he was leaving something undone. Part of him wanted to stay and stare. When they crested the top of the hill and entered the city, the car turned left.

He turned and looked at Earl. "What's going to happen here after I leave?"

"Don't worry. We'll baby-sit the tourists." Grant thought he saw a hint of a smile under the large mustache. "And the Feds," Earl added.

As before, the police car drove past the gate and out onto the airport tarmac. A moment later it stopped next to the Gulfstream. The high-pitched sound told him the jet engines were already turning. Grant climbed out of the cruiser and walked toward the plane.

Wendy, the flight attendant, met him at the base of the stairs. "Boulder, Nevada?"

Grant nodded. "Yeah." The mention of Boulder made him think about downstream. Would they lose Hoover too? He headed up the stairs.

Before he ducked into the plane, he turned and looked back at the captain of the Page police force, who was now leaning against the car. Grant cupped his hand and yelled at Earl. "Good luck. Don't let things get outta control."

Earl's response wasn't loud enough to hear, but three jabs from a pointed finger, and over-enunciation of the syllables sent the message loud and clear, "You already did."

Grant held up his cell phone and pointed to it, trying to send the message that Earl could call him if he needed.

Earl nodded and waved, then climbed back in the cruiser. Grant ducked into the Gulfstream that would take him to Hoover Dam.

Wendy shut the door behind him and the noise of the engines almost disappeared.

Although he could have picked any of the leather seats, he chose the second window seat on the right, the same one from his previous trip.

She interrupted him while he was fastening his seat belt. "Can I get you anything?"

He shook his head. "Not now." He touched her arm. "Could you ask the pilot if he could follow the river?"

CHAPTER 14

11:15 a.m. - Hole-in-the-Rock, Lake Powell, Utah

Julie didn't care if her feet were killing her. It had to be over a hundred degrees. She jogged the last few yards to the water, dropped the canteen, sun visor and crumpled t-shirt on the shore, and dove into the refreshing water of Lake Powell. She didn't even stop to take off her hiking boots. In the few seconds she glided underwater, Julie felt the water cool her face, arms, back, and legs, saving her from what felt like imminent heat stroke. She let her momentum and buoyancy bring her slowly back to the surface. When she turned, she saw the other three had stopped and were hastily unlacing their shoes. She stroked leisurely back to the shore.

"Aren't you going to take your shoes off?" her husband asked.

When she reached the rocks, she found a small ledge, just under the surface, where she could sit and get to her laces. "I couldn't wait. I was burning up."

Greg laughed. Paul had removed his shoes and had moved to Erika, who sat back and let her husband remove hers. She looked exhausted too, and Julie wanted to help her into the water so Erika could feel the same relief Julie was feeling. Even as Julie reached for her shoelaces, she heard first Greg, then Paul and Erika dive in the water around her.

"Oh, that feels so good." Erika purred.

Paul blew a small stream of lake water out of his mouth like a Roman statue.

Julie's laces released easily. As she struggled with the shoe, Greg swam over next to her and took over, pulling her right one off.

"Let me help you with that." He tossed it up on the bank, and then rolled her sock off, his fingers cleaning between her toes, then massaging her foot.

Greg's hands on her feet made her lean back on the rocks and sigh. She felt light headed. He repeated the service on her other foot, and she decided right then, she would never leave him.

After the foot massage, both couples frolicked in the water for a while. Julie took off her shorts and threw them up on the bank, leaving her only in her bikini. She wished the site were more remote and it were only she and Greg, because for the first time in her life she wanted to skinny dip. Even the small swimsuit felt too restricting.

Greg sat on a rock just out of the water. "How long do you want to stay?"

Erika floated on her back. "I'm never getting out of this water again."

Julie agreed. "What's the hurry?"

"We need to stop at Dangling Rope for gas on the way back."

Erika rolled over on her stomach and glided toward her husband. "Go ahead. My lover and I need some time alone. You can pick us up when you're done."

They all knew that Erika was joking because Dangling Rope Marina was miles downstream, almost to the houseboat. There was no way Greg was going to drive all the way there, then back up to Hole-in-the-Rock to pick them up.

Greg laughed. "No need, Erika. Julie and I will just wait here while you and Paul do what ever you need to do." He gestured to her with an open hand "Go ahead."

Julie laughed while she watched Erika swim after Paul who was staying just out of her reach, and splashing her. While the couple teased each other, Greg stood and stepped gingerly up the rocks to where they had left their possessions. When he reached their stuff, he turned and put his hands on his hips, scanning up and down the shoreline. Julie thought she could see a look of concern on his face.

"He pointed down by the edge of the water. "Doesn't it look like the water has gone down?"

Julie looked at the wet ring above the water. She saw Paul stop and look at it too. Erika took advantage, and grabbed her husband from behind. Paul shucked her like she was nothing and dunked her. Greg pointed at the Mastercraft. "Look at the boat."

Julie looked but did not see anything out of the ordinary. "What's wrong with it?"

Paul interjected. "The rope. We left some slack when we tied it off. Now it's tight."

Julie saw that the rope was in fact very tight and pulling the Mastercraft up against the rocks. "Maybe it came loose and somebody re-tied it."

"No, Julie. Look at the wet band around the lake." He motioned again with his hand and raised his voice. "The water has dropped, maybe five feet or more."

Julie wondered why the big deal.

"So?" Erika said. "Who cares if the water dropped a few feet?"

Greg crouched and chewed on his fingernail. It made Julie nervous. Generally Greg was very cool headed. She climbed up the rocks out of the water. Erika followed.

Greg started gathering shoes and socks. "Let's go. There must be something wrong. They must be dumping water like crazy or something."

"Who?" Paul asked.

Greg was already headed for the boat. "The people at the dam. I don't know. We can ask what's going on when we get to the Marina."

Julie gathered up her wet shoes and other possessions. Erika and Paul did the same. The three of them headed for the boat with their arms full. Greg was trying to pull the boat up enough to get slack in the rope with no success. Paul tossed his stuff on the ground and tried to help. Both men struggled, but the rope was already so tight that they would need to lift the boat to get enough slack.

"What are we going to do now?" Julie asked.

Greg fished through the glove box in the boat and retrieved his pocketknife. He freed the blade, cut the rope up close to where it was tied on the rock, and the Mastercraft settled into the water. He retrieved the remainder of the rope from the rock and threw it in the back. He climbed in while Paul held the boat away from the rocks. Greg reached for Julie and Erika's things, and then helped them both in. He was hurrying, which made Julie and Erika hurry too. When everyone else was in, Paul pushed off and jumped in himself. Greg started the engine immediately.

Julie sat in the other front seat and looked at her husband. His brow was furrowed as he scanned up and down the shore. He put the boat in gear and quickly accelerated as they headed out of the small bay into the main channel. Greg was very nervous, something that was very rare for Greg Crawford.

* * *

11:20 a.m. - Grand Canyon, Arizona

Sid followed his friend Ryan as they hiked east along the Escalante Trail. To their left, a couple hundred feet below flowed the Colorado River, which seemed to be running above normal. To their right the Grand Canyon rose gradually almost four thousand feet to the Navajo reservation, where they had left their car, but that was two days ago. Unlike the lightweights that rode mules up and down the tourist trails, Sid and Ryan considered themselves seasoned hikers. You had to be, to hike Tanner and Escalante, two trails which were not for the faint hearted, especially Tanner. Two days before, while descending the twelve-mile Tanner Trail, only two miles from the bottom they encountered the last obstacle, a steep climb nicknamed Asinine Hill. Two days later, Sid considered this whole hike to be asinine.

Over the years, he and Ryan had hiked most of the major trails in the Grand Canyon, some multiple times. Tanner, which was located almost 30 miles upstream from the major South Rim trails, had eluded them. And now Sid knew why. Tanner was a killer. Hiking down the trail had wiped him out. His left knee, which had never bothered him before, now screamed out with every step. And Escalante, comparatively, was the easy part. It only ran along the base of the canyon paralleling the river. The hard part, tomorrow, was yet to come, back up the twelve grueling miles of Tanner to the rim. Besides, this part of the canyon wasn't as narrow, and to be honest, wasn't as spectacular. In fact, when he lost sight of the river, Sid thought the landscape was downright ugly. Of course he grudgingly admitted that it might have something to do with the pain in his knee.

"Let's rest." Ryan said without looking back.

Sid didn't respond. But he immediately stopped and let Ryan help him out of his pack. With a sleeping bag, food, water, and stove, each pack weighed a ton. Sid leaned his pack against a rock then sat down and leaned back against it. He massaged his knee, but couldn't quite get his fingers deep enough to do any good.

"How much farther do you think it is?" he asked. Ryan always knew how far things were.

"Close. Maybe an hour." He looked at his watch. "We can have lunch at the trail head, filter some water, then head up Tanner. The farther we make it tonight, the better."

Sid closed his eyes and tried to wish himself a day into the future, up at the rim looking down, and the hike would be behind him. He opened his eyes to see if it worked, but saw he was still at river level. Maybe he was too greedy. He decided to try again, this time wishing only for a mule to carry him up the hill. Hanging from the mule, the knee would still hurt, but it would definitely felt better than hiking.

"Look at that helicopter!" Ryan said suddenly.

The mule disappeared. Sid opened his eyes. "Where?"

Ryan pointed upstream. "I didn't think they were allowed to fly that low."

The helicopter flew at an altitude of only a couple hundred feet above the water as it followed the river. Since the Escalante trail ran above the river, they were at almost the same level as the helicopter.

For a moment it looked like the chopper would fly right past the hikers, but it veered straight toward the two hikers. Ryan stood up defensively, something that Sid would have done too, if it weren't for the knee. Sid peered around the legs of his friend at the helicopter, which had stopped in the air and hovered less than a hundred feet away. They were close enough for Sid to see that both the Pilot and the other guy wore dark glasses and had dead serious looks on their faces. For a moment Sid wondered if the chopper had guns, because if it did, he and Ryan would be sitting ducks.

Not the pilot, but the other guy, spoke into a microphone. "The Glen Canyon Dam has collapsed upstream." The sound was so loud it made Sid want to cover his ears. "Hike immediately to higher ground. Try to get at least five hundred feet above the river, maybe more."

No one moved for a moment. The helicopter hovered. Ryan stood staring at it with his mouth open, and Sid sat peering around Ryan's leg. Was this a joke? He looked at the serious expressionless faces of the two men in the helicopter and decided it wasn't.

"Go now!" said the man. "The river is already rising and the water level will increase rapidly from here on out."

With that said, the helicopter veered off and dropped back into the canyon. They watched it go until it disappeared around the bend downstream. Sid had never seen the Glen Canyon Dam. He looked upstream and tried to imagine a wall of water. How tall was the dam? He couldn't remember, but something told him it was taller than two hundred, which meant he would be underwater if he didn't move. He noticed Ryan had turned and was pulling at the straps on his backpack. He untied the sleeping bag and tossed it aside.

"You just gonna leave that here?" Sid asked.

"Yeah. Screw it." Ryan responded. He tossed a frying pan and stove out as well. He stopped digging through his pack for a second and looked down at Sid. "Come On! Get up."

Sid argued. "Won't we need the bags tonight?"

Ryan pointed upstream. "Our first priority is to make Tanner without getting rimmed by the river. Sleeping in a warm bag is second priority."

Sid rolled over and stood, trying to ignore the knee, which didn't seem to understand the emergency. He reached for his pack, but Ryan grabbed it first and started tossing out anything that looked heavy, including his flashlight, pans, a coffee cup, sleeping bag, and ground cloth. The only thing safe was the water. Sid only watched. However, things had gone too far when Ryan readied to toss Sid's camping tool, the one that looked like needle-nose pliers except for all the accessories including straight blades, serrated blades, screw drivers, corkscrews, not to mention the black leather pouch. The tool had been a Christmas gift from his estranged father. Sid reached out and plucked it from Ryan's hands.

"No. I'll carry that." Sid clutched it close to his body with both hands.

Ryan looked at him for a second, then rolled his eyes. "All right, let's go."

Ryan grabbed Sid's pack and held it up for him, then pulled his own on. Ryan led and Sid followed. They were still buckling belts and straps as they walked. The knee hurt, but it felt much stronger carrying the lighter pack. Compared to before, the backpack seemed empty. Sid looked down at his knee and it thanked him. They walked quickly for almost five minutes before either spoke. Ryan actually jogged for a short stretch, but when he turned and looked back, Sid shook his head.

Ryan stopped and pointed ahead. "Look how high the river's getting."

Sid nodded, wondering if it had been that way for a while, and he hadn't noticed, or if it had increased in the last few minutes.

Ryan cocked his head and looked straight up the canyon walls, then back at the river, obviously agitated.

"What's a matter?" Sid asked.

"Before we get back to Tanner, Escalante goes right down by the river. It'll be underwater."

Sid remembered that. It would be impassable. He pointed at a ridge a few hundred feet ahead and above them. "What about that over there?"

Ryan hesitated and gritted his teeth. "Man I hate to go off trail. We could get rimmed, then what?"

Sid nodded. In the Grand Canyon, like any other steep rock canyon, it might look like you could just find your way back up, but in reality you would eventually get stopped by some vertical cliff that you just couldn't find a way around. There was a reason why the popular trails are so well used, and why there were so relatively few of them.

Sid shrugged. "We don't have any choice though, do we?"

Ryan grimaced. "Guess not." He started again, this time veering off trail and climbing upwards toward the ridge.

After a few moments of hiking over rocks, Sid's knee started to cry out again, making him wish he were back on the trail. Without slowing down, he reached down and rubbed it. Probably due to the combination of walking over rocks off trail, and rubbing his knee at the same time, Sid tripped. It wasn't a big fall. In fact he didn't actually go down. He caught himself with his hands. Unfortunately, he still held the pliers when his hand hit the rock. Which meant a nasty gash on two of the knuckles of his right hand.

"You okay?" Ryan asked.

Sid looked at his bloody hand, then at the pliers from his father, the ones that a few minutes before had been so important. He admired the way the leather pouch wrapped perfectly around it, and how the stitching gave it such a professional touch. He unclasped the top, and slid the pliers out, just a little, enough to feel the polished stainless steel handle. He glanced down at the river, then back at the ridge. "Yeah. Let's go."

Ryan turned and started walking.

Sid followed, tossing the pliers over his shoulder into the sagebrush.

* * *

11:25 a.m. - Las Vegas, Nevada

The man turned his motorcycle onto a street in the small neighborhood in East Las Vegas. Unlike the many newer developments around the outskirts of the city, this street felt neither clean nor organized. A dog, chained to the water spigot on the front of a neighbor's house, ran out and barked at the motorcycle. A worn semicircle area showed the reach of the dog's chain. A car up on blocks on the left side of the street, and a front yard enclosed in chain link fence on the right, told visitors that there was no homeowner's association in this neighborhood. No one was out in the street to wave at, not that he would have waved anyway.

The motorcyclist continued to the corner lot at the end of the street. He stopped in the driveway, found neutral, and put the bike on its stand. He let it run while he dismounted. His legs were stiff from the two-hour ride from Utah. After he stretched, he walked over and pulled up the garage door. Inside was another almost new white pickup. It looked almost identical to the one he left in Page. He returned to the motorcycle, mounted it, then drove it in the garage. After shutting off the engine and dismounting, he immediately pulled down the door to keep his neighbors from inspecting the contents of the garage.

He unbuckled his helmet and pulled it off. His hair was soaked in sweat from the long ride in the heat of the day. He ran his hands through the wet hair, and then scratched his scalp. He tossed the helmet on the seat and headed into the house, leaving the job of unpacking for later, or potentially never. He stripped off his shirt as he walked into the stifling house, and scratched his stomach and chest, which where also soaked in sweat. He walked through the kitchen, not noticing the clutter of unwashed dishes on the counters. He headed directly to a dusty television propped on what looked like a nightstand that belonged next to a bed.

He grabbed a remote control and hit the power button while he backed away a few steps for a better view. He remained standing. The channel showed a news reporter in studio with a picture of the Glen Canyon Dam behind, before it was blown up. He knew if he waited, the channel would eventually show what he wanted, but he flipped the channel anyway. The next channel showed a reporter interviewing what looked to be a park ranger. He flipped again. All the channels were running the story, but the third channel showed the view he wanted, an aerial view of where the dam used to be.

He caught his breath and backed up and sat on an old couch, not bothering to move the clutter aside. What he was looking at was even better than what he had seen in Utah two hours ago. Only the edges of the dam were still visible jutting from the rock walls. The water ripped through the opening, rolled over what looked like a fifty-foot drop, then raged down the canyon. It mesmerized him to watch it. It made goose bumps appear on his arms, in spite of the stifling heat. He smiled broadly and settled back into the couch.

He needed sleep after being awake most of the night. But at that moment, he couldn't imagine pulling himself away from the TV. The camera view panned upstream into Lake Powell, although he wasn't interested in that. He wanted to see downstream, where the water was going. He wanted to see the flooding in the Grand Canyon. He wanted to see how far the flood had traveled, and what the expected arrival times were at various places. He wanted computer rendered images of what would happen when the water reached Lake Mead and beyond. He wanted more information about downstream. That was where the action was headed. That was where he was headed.

* * *

11:30 a.m. - Grand Canyon, Arizona

Grant gazed out the large oval window of the Gulfstream. He could see the Grand Canyon stretch for miles ahead. He couldn't help but notice the thin yellow smog layer resting in the canyon, not completely blocking his vision, but partially obscuring it. He had heard about the phenomenon, where easterly winds blew air pollution from Los Angeles into the Grand Canyon, but had never actually seen it first hand. In spite of the smog, he had a great view of the canyon. The Colorado River snaked back and forth as if it didn't know where it was going. The water level looked normal, although it was impossible to tell from the plane's altitude.

Just after taking off in Page, at Grant's request, the plane had followed the river. Normally, the plane would have been required to follow traditional flight paths, but under the circumstances, since Grant was the lead government official in this emergency, the pilot had agreed to follow the river. For the first few miles the river had seemed completely full, almost overflowing. Where the canyon widened the river had widened, filling the space. There had been a few places where the canyon had intersected large side canyons. In these areas the floodwater had filled the side canyons as well. Gradually as the plane traveled at over 250 miles per hour down river, the levels subsided. The flood had not traveled this far into the canyon yet.

According to the computer modeling reports that Julia had faxed, allowing for varying friction coefficients of the canyon walls, the predicted water speed through the Grand Canyon would be between twenty and twenty-five miles per hour. The leading edge of the flood would reach the center of the Grand Canyon, Granite Narrows, between 4:00 p.m. and 6:00 p.m. It would exit the canyon at the end of Pierce Basin, which was the beginning of Lake Mead at between midnight and 2:00 a.m. Peak levels of the flood would lag the leading edge by five or six hours, ultimately reaching between four hundred and five hundred feet above normal in some places in the Grand Canyon. Since the numbers in Grant's report were based on a worst-case scenario, and since both Lake Powell and Mead were lower due to drought conditions, the flood levels would not be as bad. But how much difference could he count on really? Even with adjusted numbers, chances of survival for any human, beast, or structure below five hundred feet in the Grand Canyon was unlikely. Hopefully the Park Service's plan to send helicopters, warning all hikers and rafters to move to higher ground, would work, although Grant had yet to see any helicopters from the window of the plane.

Up ahead, at the end of the Grand Canyon, Grant saw a large body of water. That would be Lake Mead. When the Gulfstream flew over the lake, Grant looked straight down. The banks seemed flat, which would allow the water to spread out when it rose higher. That was good, although it was hard to tell how flat they really were from the sky.

Even without the extra floodwater, Lake Mead was the largest man-made lake in the US with a capacity of 9.2 trillion gallons. Someone had once calculated that the lake would cover Pennsylvania with over a foot of water. Right now Grant only hoped that the lake could handle all the water from Lake Powell. Lake Powell was the second largest, at 8.5 trillion gallons. But with the lower drought levels in both, there was a possibility. Grant looked at his watch. They had about eighteen hours to see if they could dump enough water out of Lake Mead to make room for the water from Lake Powell that was already on its way. While he·pondered that thought, the Gulfstream began its descent.

* * *

11:45 a.m. - Lake Powell, Utah

Greg pulled back on the throttle and the Mastercraft slowed, it's bow settling down in the water. The boat drifted in the main channel of Lake Powell just off the west shoreline. They had traveled south for almost a half hour since leaving Hole-in-the-Rock. Julie figured it would take another hour to reach the marina.

She didn't understand why Greg stopped. He looked agitated, scanning his head back and forth. Actually, he hadn't seemed himself since they'd left Hole-in-the-Rock.

"What's wrong now?" she said.

"Something isn't right." He pointed up and down the channel, "Look how many boats are on the lake. I've never seen this many. It's like everybody is heading out."

Julie had noticed the heavy traffic, but then again, she had never been to Hole-in-the-Rock. Some of this traffic could be attributed to Bullfrog Marina to the north. Julie pointed downstream. "Maybe there's something going on. Something at the marina or down by the dam, some kind of party or something."

Greg shook his head. "If that were the case, they'd be taking their water-ski boats, not their houseboats. This has something to do with the water level dropping. I'm sure of it."

"We could flag someone down and ask," Erika said. But there was no enthusiasm in the comment.

Paul spoke up. "We're stopping at Dangling Rope on our way back. We can ask there."

Erika was nodding. "Someone at the marina should know what's going on."

There seemed to be an unspoken consensus. Greg nodded and Erika turned back around in her seat. Greg pushed the throttle forward again and the Mastercraft accelerated back to speed. Julie looked out across the water. It did seem like everyone on the lake was heading out. Many seemed to be in a hurry. For a moment she wondered if something really was wrong. She looked at her watch. It would be lunchtime soon. She wondered what Max and Darlene were doing back at the houseboat.

* * *

11:50 a.m. - Houseboat, Lake Powell, Utah

Sitting on the roof of the houseboat, Max bent a page as a marker and tossed the paperback he was reading on the empty chair next to him. He glanced over at his wife, who was oblivious to the world, her face buried in her romance novel. The cover of the book showed a muscular man holding a woman by the waist, while the woman leaned back with a look of passion on her face. Max wished some of the passion from Darlene's books would translate into real life.

He stood and stretched, and then walked to the edge of the roof, scanning the water below and the small canyon where they were parked. He was glad he and Darlene had decided to stay alone today, but he had no intentions of wasting the whole day reading. He walked back to his wife and plucked the book from her hands.

She reached for it. "Hey."

"Enough reading for a while. Let's do something."

"Let me finish my chapter first."

He reached for her arm to help her up. "You can finish your chapter later. I'm bored. Let's eat or something."

She looked at her watch. "We just ate an hour ago."

"Fine, then lets do something else. We need to move around." He pulled her up until she was standing.

"Like what?"

He winked at her. "I don't know. How about we kayak up the canyon a ways?"

Her face showed skepticism. "It's too hot."

He pulled her away from her chair. "We'll be practically in the water. You can jump in whenever you need to." He pointed upstream. "The canyon might get really narrow up there. Maybe it's one of those cool places where you can reach from one side to the other."

"Can I bring my book?" She asked.

Max rolled his eyes. Unbelievable. But, he imagined her begging to come back after only a few minutes if she didn't have it. He gave in. "You can bring it, if you pack a few things for lunch to take with us."

She reached for the book, but he shook his head. "Not yet. Go get ready, and I'll put the kayak in the water."

A few minutes later, Max was dragging the kayak down the beach into the water. He noticed the sand was wet for at least ten or twelve feet above the waterline. He stood and looked at it for a moment. He didn't remember the wet band being so big before. Additionally, the ropes tying the houseboat to the rocky shore were tight, and Max thought he remembered them having slack before.

He was pondering whether the water had dropped when his wife walked out of the houseboat. She carried a paper bag with their lunch, and a full six-pack of sodas, and two large beach towels. More noticeable however, was that she had changed her swimsuit. Darlene was wearing one that Max had never seen before. The suit's lines were daring, and since Darlene was overweight, she rarely wore daring clothes.

Max gaped at her. She looked wonderful.

"You like it?" she asked, spinning so he could look.

He nodded.

She handed him some suntan lotion. "Here, rub this on me before we go. I don't want to get burned in this suit."

Max squirted some lotion in his hands, and forgot all about water levels and wet sand.

* * *

12:10 p.m. - Grand Canyon, Arizona

Sid and Ryan could see the bottom of the Tanner Trail, at least where it disappeared into the overflowing Colorado River. It was a hundred yards or so ahead. Until now, their decision to hike off trail above Escalante had been working. Actually, that was an understatement since the old Escalante ran somewhere along the original riverbank, which was now hundreds of feet underwater. So the decision to leave the trail had been genius.

Since the helicopter had warned them, Sid and Ryan couldn't believe how fast the water had risen. In total, Sid guessed the river was up three or four hundred feet. It was hard to tell. But he had never seen anything like it, even in the movies. As it rose, the river widened, and if possible, got dirtier than it already was. Before, there were rapids occasionally along the river. Now, the whole river was a rapid. This angry Colorado River was tearing apart the Grand Canyon. Every few moments, incredibly loud noises that sounded almost like explosions, echoed through the canyon as huge boulders and pieces of the rock walls broke off and rolled into the river. Rockslides were plentiful, and Sid was starting to worry that they'd get caught in one.

When they rounded the bend, the bottom of Tanner Trail was just up ahead. Well, it should have been just up ahead, instead it was underwater, swallowed by the swollen Colorado River. Something seemed surreal about the way the trail meandered back and forth down the hill then right into the brown frothy water. It was as if the two scenes didn't belong together. Ryan and Sid both stopped and stared. Although the Tanner Trail was less than a football field away, Sid had no idea how they were going to get to it. Their path was blocked. The ridge they were on led right into the river. They had almost made it. Sid looked at where the rocks led into the water. What if they just followed the path right into the water, and waded next to the rocks. They could even swim a little in the deep places.

Ryan must have been reading Sid's mind. He pointed at the scene, farther upstream than where Sid was looking. "Look how strong the current is up there."

Sid saw where the cliff jutted out into the river, and the current ripped past it. It would be impossible to get around that point. He held up his arms in frustration. "Now what?"

Ryan craned his head up at the small cliffs above them. "We need to get up there somehow."

The row of cliffs was only about twenty-five or thirty-feet tall in some places, and if they could find a way on top, the higher ridge would lead them the rest of the way over to Tanner.

The thought of scaling a rock wall made Sid's knee hurt even more. "I don't know if I can do it."

Ryan glared at him, angry. "What are you nuts? You want to die?"

Sid didn't answer. He was surprised at Ryan's anger. For a moment he felt more afraid of Ryan than the river itself. Something told him that Ryan wasn't going to let him quit.

Ryan continued to scan the cliffs above them for a way up. Sid joined in the search. However nothing looked plausible, especially with the knee. The rock ledges were almost vertical. A couple of places looked promising in spots, but then an overhang or some other obstacle made it too risky. Sid moved back along the ridge where they had come, to see if they had already passed something. However, if anything, the cliffs were even higher and steeper.

"Over here." Ryan yelled.

Sid turned and saw that Ryan was way down by the water, pointing up at a large cliff. Sid moved back down the trail toward him. He looked up at the rock wall where Ryan pointed. It was one of the taller parts of the ridge line, and the top was inverted and completely impassable, not to mention the bottom was in the water.

"You're kidding, right?" Sid pointed at the top. "How you gonna get over that?"

Ryan shook his head and pointed off to the left. "No. We cut across on that ledge about two thirds of the way up.

Sid hadn't seen the small ridge. It was too small. In fact it looked too small to traverse. "Are you sure?"

Ryan was already wading into the water. He was up to his armpits before he reached the base of the cliff. "Come on. The water's still rising."

Sid followed obediently. By the time he reached the base, Ryan was already twenty feet above him, climbing up the crease. The water was cold and Sid was already shivering even though only a moment ago he was burning up. The cold moved him and made him climb faster. The knee throbbed with every step, but the pain from the cold water was worse. When he had climbed high enough to be completely out of the water, he rested, and looked up. Ryan was grasping for a handhold.

"Are you stuck?" Sid asked.

"Nah. I'm okay. Come on."

Sid climbed on. What seemed like an eternity later, he reached the spot where Ryan had struggled to find a handhold. Like he'd seen Ryan do, Sid felt around with his left hand, trying to feel for something that offered a grip. He searched for what must have been a couple minutes, but he could not find anything.

"All right, how'd you get past this spot?" He asked, without looking up.

"I couldn't get a hold of anything." The sound came from the above, but also from the left.

Sid looked up, mostly with his eyes, not daring to move his head very far. Ryan was traversing across a split in the rock. He had almost made it.

"So how'd you get past this spot then?" Sid asked.

Ryan hesitated before answering. "It's kind of tricky. Put both your hands where you're holding on with your right. Then wedge your left foot against that rock over by your knee. Then you should be able to get high enough to grab on that ledge above you."

Sid glanced over and found the rock by his knee. Carefully, he slid his foot up until it found the foothold. He rested. The bad right knee started shaking, complaining about having to support the bulk of his weight.

"Now push with your left foot and pull yourself up to the ledge."

Sid looked up and saw that Ryan had made it. He was standing on a small ledge and looking down at Sid pointing. "It's right above you. See it?"

Sid saw the ledge, but he didn't think he could get to it. He considered it a risky maneuver, one that could end up in a fall. While he contemplated, an explosion accosted his ears. He let go instinctively with his left hand and covered his ear. He saw motion off to his left, something big. He looked over and watched a wall of rock fall into the river below, an avalanche of smaller rocks following behind. The rock, which could not have been more than fifty feet away, made him do something bad, something he had told himself he would not do, no matter what. He looked down. Sid looked down and saw the huge boulder swallowed by the river. One big splash and it was gone. The look down terrified him. First of all, he was much higher than he would have imagined. And the river, if possible, had risen even higher than when they started. It was as if it was chasing him up the cliff. Sid knew in an instant that if he fell, he'd be dead. The water was moving too fast, and churning too much. There was no way he could survive. He pulled his eyes back up, away from the danger below. But the momentary glance had done its damage. He instinctively pulled his body closer to the rock, hugging it. He had been climbing long enough to know that you can't climb if you are too close to the rock. It screws up your leverage. But he couldn't help himself.

"Sid. What are you doing?"

Sid heard Ryan, but he didn't look up. His face was touching the rock, and he felt sure if he moved, he would fall. "I don't think I can make it."

Ryan sounded angry. "What d'ya mean? You were doing fine a minute ago."

Sid didn't feel like telling Ryan the truth, that looking down had scared him. Ryan didn't seem in the mood for that. Besides, Ryan was already at the top. He'd made it. Ryan was angry because he wanted to leave, and Sid was holding him up. Would Ryan be happier if Sid fell? At least then he'd be free to go.

"Get your butt away from the rock." Ryan's voice wasn't angry anymore. It sounded sympathetic. "You can't climb like that."

Sid didn't move.

Ryan continued talking. His voice was patient and comforting. "Sid. You need to relax. That rock surprised me too. I almost jumped off the ledge."

That helped. The image of Ryan jumping in the river at the sound of the rock, made him laugh. "I'm a little freaked out here," he admitted.

"Take a couple slow deep breaths. Relax."

Sid did as he was told, and it helped. He had been too scared to breathe. "Now, let your butt go out a little, get some leverage."

Slowly, Sid stopped hugging the rock.

"That's it! Okay, now try to imagine you're practicing on a rock that's only a foot in the air."

It was an old climbing trick, a trick that had helped Sid before. Sometimes when a climber is stuck high on a rock, pretending the rock was only a practice rock, and not very high, made it easier to relax and climb when you were nervous. Sid however, used a variation of the trick. He instead imagined that the ground had risen behind him as he climbed, and that if he wanted, he could always just step off the rock, and rest. The trick had worked for him in the past. He had never tried it before while a flood was tearing boulders right out of the rock wall, but he did his best to put those thoughts out of his mind.

"Okay, now pull yourself up and down a couple times. Get a feeling for the handholds you got," Ryan ordered.

Sid did just that, and was surprised to feel that his arms still had a little strength left in them. Not as much as he wished, but more than he expected. He pulled up again, and took inventory on the knee. It had stiffened even more. He wondered how much more it could take.

"All right, you ready?"

Sid looked up this time. Ryan peered down at him from the rocks above, smiling. The sight made Sid relax even more. "Yeah, I guess so. Let's do it."

Ryan pointed at a ledge just out of Sid's reach. "Okay, that's your next handhold. You're going to need to push up with your left foot to get that high."

Sid put the rogue Colorado River out of his mind. He did the same for the memory of the cliff next to him breaking off and falling. He concentrated only on the ledge above. He stuck his butt out farther then pushed up, pulling at the same time with his hands. It worked. He slid his left hand up to the ridge and grabbed. The handhold was solid.

"Yeah! Good job." Ryan was clapping above him.

Once Sid climbed past the tricky part, the rest of the climb was uneventful. A few minutes later Sid was standing on the ledge next to Ryan. A part of him wanted to reach out and hug his friend, like a brother. After all, he would not have made it without the encouragement. But hugging his friend was unthinkable.

Sid looked out over the Colorado River. In his whole life, he'd never seen anything like it. He estimated it to be almost a half a mile across. And the level had probably risen four or five hundred feet. It was moving faster than a man could run, more like a bicyclist, maybe even faster than that. The water wasn't just flowing straight either, it churned and swirled like Sid had never seen before. The thought of falling in made him shiver. Even if he had a life jacket, which he did not, the river could easily pull him under and drag him along the bottom, propelling him up or down at its leisure. The thought reminded Sid of a guy, a SCUBA diver named Nelson, who he met in college. Nelson claimed that he and some other guys used to drift dive, wearing full SCUBA gear, down some river around Jackson Hole, Wyoming. And this river wasn't just a scenic tour either; it had rapids and white water. Anyway, Nelson used to say that only divers who could equalize their ears real fast could do it, because in one spot, the river pulled the divers down from the surface to eighty feet in a couple seconds, which would rupture ear drums if they weren't equalized. After that, he said it was like the center of a tornado, perfectly calm. However, seconds later, the river yanked the divers back up to the surface and back down the river. Sid wasn't sure if that story was true or not. But when he saw the swirling whirlpools and eddies, he remembered it. He thought it gave him a better perspective, as if from the victims point-of-view of what it would be like to be pulled under.

"Let's go." Sid said, but when he turned Ryan was already headed along the ridge.

A few minutes later they reached Tanner. An incredible feeling of relief washed over Sid. Back when he was hanging on the cliff, he would not have bet a dollar on making it. But here he was, and if the knee let go now, no big deal. Worst case they could send a mule down for him. Standing on the trail, they rested, looking down at where it disappeared in the swollen river. For a moment Sid thought he heard voices, but the Colorado River had become noisy as it grew. There were the constant sounds of water moving past the cliffs, and sporadic sounds of rocks rolling underwater, rock slides on the banks, and boulders breaking loose. The new noises came as the river carved into hillside it hadn't been able to reach for millions of years.

For the last hour, back when his life was in jeopardy, Sid saw the new river as something to be afraid of, but looking down on it from Tanner, it was different. It was spectacular, unbelievable, and breathtaking. Watching it on TV would not do it justice. Standing on the banks, he could feel it.

Sid heard the voices again and this time distinctively heard the words 'over there'. Ryan must have heard them too, because he cocked his head at the same time. Sid saw their heads first, but as the group crested the knoll, they became totally visible. Obviously, they were rafters not hikers. The men wore swim trunks, and the women bathing suits. One of the women still wore a life jacket. Another woman wore a green and white striped bikini.

A man pointed at Sid and Ryan. "Hang on!" He jogged toward them.

"Do you know where the trail out of here is?" The man asked, pointing up out of the canyon.

Ryan pointed at his feet. "We're standing on it."

The man looked down at the worn trail where Sid and Ryan stood. He turned toward the rest of his group, who had just reached the trail. "Thank God, we made it."

Another loud explosion rocked the canyon, making the group instinctively duck. Sid looked back where they had just come and saw another huge section of the cliff fall into the water and send waves across the river. Then just as quickly, while the sound still echoed through the canyon, the river swallowed the rock.

The rafters must have already seen boulders breaking off and fall in the river, because the man picked right up where he left off. "So how far up is it?" He pointed up the trail. "How long will it take?"

Sid looked down. The man wore aqua socks. They were coated with dust, except for wet spots where moisture squished up through them. One of the women wore platform flip-flops. Sid saw no hiking shoes, no tennis shoes, and absolutely no socks, none of them. He had a feeling if his knee went out and he had to stop, he wouldn't be alone.

"Three or four hours," Ryan answered. "If we keep moving."

Sid saw surprise and unbelief in the man's eyes. Many in the group cocked their heads back and forth, looking at each other.

"Three or four hours?" Mr. Aqua Socks asked in disbelief. "How far is it?"

"Eight miles." Sid answered. He reached down and rubbed his knee. "And they're not easy miles either."

"What happened to your boat?" Ryan asked.

Another man, wearing a yellow baseball hat stenciled with Los Angeles Lakers, stepped up by Mr. Aqua Socks. "We had already noticed the water rising before the helicopter warned us. We were looking for a spot to stop, but the water was moving too fast. Then after the helicopter, we found a sandy place where we could get out. As soon as we got out, the river took the raft. It's gone."

"Where's your guide?" Ryan asked.

Mr. Aqua Socks raised his hand. "I'm the guide, but I only know the river, not the trails. And this is my first year running the Grand Canyon. What about you two guys?"

Sid looked over at his friend, an unspoken message for Ryan to answer.

Ryan motioned up the trail. "We hiked down Tanner Trail from the rim two days ago. Then we spent a couple days hiking and camping along the Escalante trail." He pointed down at the river. "It's underwater now. Anyway, the rising water rimmed us on the way back to Tanner. We almost didn't make it."

No one spoke after Ryan's answer. They nodded politely, but Sid saw most of their eyes focused up Tanner Trail.

"Ready to head out?" Sid asked, already knowing the answer.

Mr. Aqua Socks nodded. "Sure." His comment was followed by nods from others in the group.

The group passed by Sid and Ryan and headed up the trail. However, neither Sid nor Ryan moved immediately. They stood for another few moments looking out over the swollen Colorado River. Something told Sid he would never see anything like this again in his life. He needed to try to burn it into his head, to remember it. Across the river, Sid saw a rock wall the size of a two-story building break off and fall in the water. The loud sound followed seconds later.

"Wow," Sid said. "This is amazing. Isn't it?"

"I wish I had a camera." Ryan added.

"Wouldn't do it justice."

Ryan nodded. "You're probably right."

They watched a moment longer in silence.

"Hey, you guys coming?" The question came from Mr. Aqua Socks.

"Your knee gonna make it?" Ryan asked.

Sid smiled. "As long as I'm following the one in the green bikini."

CHAPTER 15

___

12:15 p.m. - Boulder City, Nevada

Grant looked around as he walked down the steps from the Gulfstream. A small sign by the terminal announced Boulder City Airport. This airport looked even smaller than the one at Page. Aside from the Gulfstream, most of the other planes were small Cessnas, or Pipers and looked to be privately owned. Grant couldn't see any other jets. The Gulfstream stood out like a Ferrari in the ghetto. He knew that most visitors to Lake Mead didn't use this airport; they flew into Las Vegas, which was full of Lears, Gulfstreams, and other small jets.

As Grant walked down the stairs, a black & white police car drove up to the plane. The officer rolled down his window without getting out. "You the guy from the Bureau?"

Grant nodded and walked over to the passenger door. Before he jumped in, he waved back at the flight attendant. While they were en route from Page, the call had come in from Julia to send the jet to meet the Commissioner in Chicago where he would be connecting. The Gulfstream would be leaving immediately. Grant wondered if he would ever ride in it again.

He climbed into the police car and it took off immediately. After exiting the small airport, the policeman turned north, and headed into Boulder City. They sped down a small road, encountering little traffic. The south side of town, by the airport, was old and dirty. It gave a glimpse of the town's beginnings, when Boulder City was created in the late 1920s to house the five thousand workers needed to build Hoover Dam. Grant could see ahead on the bluffs a new and different Boulder City. Growing out of the hillsides were vacation homes and condos with views of the water.

The officer turned toward Grant. "You just came from Lake Powell?" He sounded curious and concerned.

"Yup. Things were pretty hairy up there. What have you heard?"

The officer kept his eyes on the road. "The news said the Glen Canyon Dam let go, a bomb or something. My wife says there's stuff on TV that shows water filling up the whole canyon. Real bad."

The car reached the intersection of US-93 just as the light turned green. Grant looked up and down the street and didn't see many other traffic lights. Without slowing, they merged onto US-93 heading down the hill. The road provided a great view of Lake Mead.

Grant was surprised to see some boats out on the water. He pointed. "Why are they still out there?"

The officer leaned forward and tried to look ahead of a car in front of them. "They've been trying to clear the lake all morning, since we got the news. But it's a big lake and there's not enough people to warn them." He took his eyes off the road for a second to look at Grant. "Why? How soon should we expect the water?"

Grant was happy the officer's eyes had returned to the road. "It won't get here until after midnight, but you need to get everybody off before it gets dark."

Grant tensed as the officer swerved into the passing lane and accelerated around an SUV pulling a water-ski boat. They passed the turnoff to Boulder Beach State Park and headed up a hill, losing sight of the lake. A casino sat perched at the top of the hill, the last opportunity to gamble for those leaving Nevada. The policeman keyed the mike on his radio.

"I've got your boy from the Bureau. We're just passing the casino."

After the casino, US-93 wound lazily for a mile through jagged rock ridges until dropping via a couple tight winding switchbacks to the dam. Ahead, he saw where the highway continued across the top of the dam into Arizona, and surprisingly, traffic was still being allowed across. Looking deep into the canyon, he could see the six outlets from the Arizona side of the dam were open, spraying huge columns of water across the canyon in a spectacular water show, a show not seen since the spring floods of 1983. However the six outlets on the Nevada side were still closed, a problem. All twelve outlets should've been open. It meant Hoover wasn't dumping as much water as they could. They hadn't followed his instructions.

A dozen orange cones blocked entry to the Visitor Center parking garage, which sat wedged into the cliffs. An officer stood next to a sign that read 'Hoover Dam Visitor Center CLOSED'. The visitors center itself, a modern oval building, hanging over the edge of the deep canyon, was similar to the one at Glen Canyon. The officer pulled right up next to the round building and stopped. A man waited outside for the police car. When the car stopped, the man reached for the door. Grant recognized him as Fred Grainger, the one he talked to from Glen Canyon.

Fred wore some slightly worn blue Dockers, a short sleeve button-down shirt, and a pair of walking shoes, and in general looked more comfortable than stylish. Fred was rumored to be in his early fifties. The one thing Grant knew was that Fred Grainger had been at Hoover Dam since before Grant joined the Bureau.

"Grant. We're glad you made it." Fred shook Grant's hand as he exited the car.

Grant couldn't stop the rebuke. "Why aren't the Nevada outlets dumping?"

Fred expected the question. "They won't let us yet. We're on hold. Come inside and I'll fill you in."

Grant wanted to argue, but instead followed Fred into the building. Fred led him down a set of stairs. As they descended, Fred started talking. "The mayor of Laughlin called the governor. So the governor came here and —"

"The governor of Nevada is here?" Grant asked.

Fred nodded "Yeah. And he's a jerk."

They walked into the main lobby lined with pictures of the dam's construction and facts about how the dam operated. They walked past a chart showing water levels over the past thirty years. The last time Grant had been in the lobby, it was filled with tourists and kids. Fred led them into a small movie theater with the words 'The Story of Hoover Dam' written above the doorway. Inside the theater, a large conference table and chairs had been set up on the floor in front of the screen. Beyond it, the room elevated to auditorium seating. At least fifteen people, mostly men, were talking when Grant and Fred entered. After they entered, the conversations stopped. All eyes met Grant's.

Fred broke the silence. "This is Grant Stevens, from the Bureau in Denver."

A large man in a suit sitting at the end of the table stood. "Where's Commissioner Blackwell?"

Grant knew immediately he must be the governor. He carried a visible aura of authority. Everyone else in the room deferred to him. The governor looked as if he'd played in the NFL before going into politics. His shoulders and chest were huge, and the suit, although obviously expensive and custom fit, seemed out of place on his body style. His hair didn't have a strand out of place, making Grant wonder if he was preparing for a press conference. His entourage contrasted with the Hoover Dam personnel. The governor's people were all in expensive suits; the Bureau people were casual. It was as if the party invitations had neglected to mention proper attire. Grant suddenly felt underdressed for the role he was playing in his slacks and polo shirt.

Grant tried to respond confidently, but his voice cracked. "The commissioner was on his way to Kenya for a dam building symposium on the Tana river. I talked with him this morning. He's made emergency flight plans to return. He's probably on his way here as we speak."

The governor shook his head in disgust. "How inconvenient." He pointed at Grant. "So who's speaking for the Bureau in the meantime, you?"

Grant had never liked guys like this, who tried to intimidate everyone they met. He felt emotion building up inside. He took a step toward the governor. "Yeah. I speak for the Bureau. And who are you?" although he already knew the answer.

The guy took a step forward, obviously unaccustomed to being challenged. The governor's attitude reminded him of the commissioner. The governor grasped both lapels of the expensive suit in a posture of authority. "The name is Rally Jenkins. I'm the governor of Nevada."

Grant nodded his head as if he had just figured it out. He felt himself stepping over the line. It was bad enough that this man had gotten in the way of what needed to be done at Hoover, but the pompous attitude was too much. Grant cleared his throat and then looked straight at the governor. "So are you the one getting in the way of what needs to be done, holding up dumping the water?"

The governor didn't hesitate. "Damn right. I got a call from the mayor in Laughlin early this morning, saying he was told to evacuate everybody around

Lake Mojave and Laughlin. He said you guys were going to open the gates and flood em out. When you started evacuating my cities without my permission, I had no choice but to get involved."

Grant nodded, then spoke as if he were talking to a child. "Do you happen to know why we need to open the gates Governor?"

"Sure, somebody blew up the Glen Canyon Dam. But that's over four hundred miles from here. My people need some time to —"

Grant slammed his fist on the table "There isn't any time!" He saw a few in the room jump at the outburst. The governor himself, showed a moment of apprehension, before his eyes narrowed. Grant brought his voice back to normal. "Sit down and let me explain a few things." He motioned for them to be seated, and some did, but not the governor.

"I know everything I need to know."

Grant started talking before he could stop himself. He pointed at the governor. "I highly doubt that, governor. If you understood the situation, you would understand why we need to open the gates. Since you don't understand, you obviously don't know everything."

The governor's eyes burned.

Grant lowered his voice and removed the hostility from his tone. "Please sit down governor, and I'll try to explain a few things that I think will make a difference in how you feel."

The governor looked around at the others and finally settled into his seat.

Grant looked around at the group. "The governor is correct, the Glen Canyon Dam was blown up this morning. I have in my hand a study completed in 1998 by the Bureau regarding what would happen in just such an event." Grant held up the report that Julia had faxed him in the Gulfstream. "Computer modeling was done to determine the speed of the floodwater, depths, etc. Before I get into the details governor, how about you telling me approximately how much water was in Lake Powell?"

The governor answered with only a touch of apprehension. "Well, I know it's not near as big as Mead."

"Partially true governor. Lake Mead holds 9.3 trillion gallons and Lake Powell holds only 8.5 trillion."

The governor's mouth dropped.

Grant continued. "To put it in perspective, Lake Mead holds just over 2 years of Colorado River flow, and Lake Powell just under. All of you who think there's enough room left behind Hoover to catch the water in Lake Powell, raise your hands." Grant paused for effect. No hands went up. "So, before I start reading from this report, I want to make sure we all agree that Hoover is not going to hold all that water?"

Fred Grainger asked a question. "How long does the report say it will take for the water to get here?"

Grant thumbed through the report until he found the table. "The water will reach the end of Pierce Basin—" He looked up at the group "That's the beginning of Lake Mead." He continued reading. "at approximately 14 hours after the dam failure. Peak levels will occur 20 hours after the break, and be approximately two hundred fifty feet above normal."

Grant looked up. No one spoke. A few persons had their heads down. The governor had a blank look on his face. Grant spoke directly to Fred Grainger. "Fred, do you remember ever using the spillways at Hoover?"

"Yeah, in 1983, the year of the big spring runoff. It was the only year we used the spillways since the dam was built."

"Do you remember how much water went down the spillways and the river?"

Fred nodded enthusiastically. "Yeah, peak was just over twenty eight thousand cubic feet per second. That was in addition to another seventy five thousand through the river works."

Grant shook his head. "So the worst flood since the dam was built netted just over a hundred thousand cubic feet per second." He looked directly at the governor. "Governor, were you around in 1983? Do you remember if there was any flooding downstream?" Grant already knew the answer.

The governor hesitated. "That was over twenty years ago, but I heard that there was quite a bit of flooding downstream. A lot of damage. Look, I'm not saying that—"

Grant interrupted him. "Fred, were the spillways running at capacity in 1983?"

Fred shook his head. "No, they'll handle over two hundred thousand cubic feet per second, each."

"Thanks Fred." Grant looked back at the governor. "So if the spillways were full, they'd handle over ten times more than in 1983?" He looked directly at the governor. "Does that sound like a disaster downstream governor?"

The governor stood. "Mr. Stevens, I'm not arguing there's not going to be a problem. I'm just making sure those people are allowed the proper time to evacuate."

Grant waved his hand. "Just a second, I'm not finished" He handed the report to Fred Grainger and pointed to a paragraph. "Fred, will you read this so everyone can hear?" Grant wanted to watch their eyes when they heard the words.

Fred took the report, and leaned forward against the table. "Overtopping of Hoover Dam would begin…"

Someone cut him off. "Water's going to go over the top of the dam?"

Grant glared at the person who spoke. "We already established that Hoover will not hold all the water." He lowered his voice and motioned to Fred. "Keep reading."

"Overtopping would begin approximately 25 hours after the failure at Glen Canyon and continue for 10 days before reaching a peak level of approximately 60 feet over the dam about 75 hours after the failure."

The governor's jaw dropped, as well as many of the others. A couple people who were standing sat down. The resistance in the governor's face drained away.

Fred continued reading. "Maximum discharges would be 75,000 cubic feet per second through the water works, 400,000 through the spillways and another 2,000,000 over the top of the dam, making a total of approximately 2.5 million cubic feet per second."

Grant paused then asked a question. "Fred, what would happen if sixty feet of water went over the top of Hoover Dam for ten days?"

Fred's answer was just above a whisper. "It would fail."

Grant repeated, "Hoover Dam would fail." He looked directly at the governor, then repeated it again. "Hoover Dam would fail and then the contents of both dams, which amounts to 4 years of river flow, would barrel down Black Canyon." He nodded at the governor of Nevada. "What do you think the mayor of Laughlin would think of that, governor?"

The governor spoke without looking up. He massaged his eyes with the thumb and index finger of his left hand. The arrogance was gone. "What does the Bureau suggest we do, Mr. Stevens?"

CHAPTER 16

12:30 p.m. - Lake Powell, Utah

It was exactly as Max would have hoped. They had kayaked for a half hour and then the canyons had narrowed. The kayak skimmed through a vertical rock canyon, narrow enough for Max to touch either side with his paddle. Max paddled slowly as Darlene leaned back, reading her book.

"Look at this honey."

She looked up from her book, then book-marked it and set it down. "Wow. This is cool."

"Now you see why I wanted to come up here?"

The canyon veered left, and when they came around the turn, the walls opened up to reveal a sunlit cavern with a sandy beach, very romantic, and very isolated.

Darlene sat up. "Look at that."

"Guess where we're having our picnic?" Max said.

Darlene smiled.

When Max pulled the boat up on the sandy beach, he noticed the sand was wet, as if it had been recently underwater. The walls were wet also, way above the waterline, maybe twenty-five or thirty feet. Max thought about that and decided it was strange, almost as if there were humidity in the canyons. However, he felt no humidity. If he didn't know better, he would have sworn that the water had dropped. But it was impossible for Lake Powell to drop twenty-five feet in such a short amount of time. Wasn't it?

* * *

12:45 p.m. - Hoover Dam, Nevada

Fred Grainger led them out of the visitor's center. The dry 110-degree heat hit Grant like a wave, then radiated into his body. He shielded his eyes and wished for a pair of sunglasses. Looking at Fred holding the door, who seemed to be unaffected by either the heat or the glare, he guessed the locals got used to it. Grant waited while the governor, his entourage, a couple of security guards, and a few Hoover Dam technicians came outside. Fred led them toward the crest of the dam. Since Grant's speech to the governor, US-93 had been closed, and the top of the dam was now devoid of vehicles. They followed Fred on the sidewalk that stretched along the edge of the dam. After walking several hundred feet, Fred stopped and they all looked down into Black Canyon. All twelve outlets were now open, six on each side, their spray crossing in the middle as they doused both sides of the canyon walls. With all outlets open, a wall of water covered the view farther down the river. After the governor's approval, Fred had radioed the command to open the gates and gradually the Nevada gates were opened.

"Okay, everything's open as you requested," said Fred, pointing downstream.

The tension in the group had dropped noticeably. Seeing the water spraying across the canyon created a magical feeling that made them forget about the reason for the show. Grant saw the governor point to where water was hitting the cliffs and dispersing in all directions.

While the group watched downstream, Grant glanced sideways toward the visitor center, and saw a petite woman with glasses walking toward them. He recognized her immediately as Shauna Kingsly, the employee he had sent for from the Bureau in Denver. She had made good time. He saw her eyes scan the group nervously. He walked away from the group to meet her and he saw her eyes light up when she recognized him.

The best description for Shauna Kingsly was plain. Her hair was straight and parted in the middle. The lack of makeup and the loose fitting clothes completed the impression of a librarian. However, the two pens in her shirt pocket suggested another image: a woman civil engineer, not that all female engineers look like nerds. They didn't, even at the Bureau. It was just a stereotype. But Shauna Kingsly fit the stereotype perfectly.

He met her on the sidewalk. "Any trouble getting here?"

She turned and pointed up the road. "The cops wouldn't let the taxi through. They ferried me down here themselves."

"Where are your bags?" he asked.

She pointed back to the visitor center. "I left them in there."

"Any trouble checking out a computer?"

She shook her head and smiled. "Not after I told them why I needed it."

That morning when he asked her to try to get a notebook computer, the thought hadn't occurred to him that for the moment he was the most important person at the Bureau of Reclamation. It was amazing how status helped cut through bureaucracy. No wonder the commissioner didn't seem as concerned with the red tape in the Bureau as the employees. He had probably never experienced it.

"Stevens!" Someone yelled from behind.

Grant turned and saw the governor approaching.

"Are you happy now?" the governor asked, pointing to the spray in the canyon. It seemed like the pompous attitude had melted away from Rally Jenkins, and that he held no animosity for the episode in the visitor center.

Grant looked at the spray, then across the dam to the Arizona side. The next recommendation would be a tough sell. "We're not done yet." He said. "Follow me."

Grant started walking back toward the visitor center, motioning for the governor to follow. The entire group followed, looking curious. Although vehicle traffic had been stopped across the dam, Grant looked both directions anyway before crossing US-93 to the upstream side of the dam. The group followed. He walked off the Nevada edge of the dam and right past the statue. They walked past the small tourist store on the left and a snack bar on the right. He continued walking through the employee parking lot until he reached the chain-link fence against the rock mountain. The fence prevented tourists from falling seventy feet into the trough leading to the Nevada spillway tunnel.

"Now we need to open these up." Grant pointed his left hand over the fence and into the Nevada spillway, and with his right across the river to the Arizona spillway.

Grant saw Fred wrinkle his brows and hesitate, then finally answer. It was a response Grant expected. "Grant, we can't open these. They don't have gates." Fred looked embarrassed at needing to explain why. "The water can only get in the spillway tunnels if it gets high enough to get over that spillway itself, over there." He pointed to a cement wall preventing Lake Mead from entering the trough. "We'll have to wait until the water rises another thirty or forty feet."

Grant nodded. "Oh they'll open all right. They just need a little help. We need to get some demolition guys in here."

The governor came back to life. "Let's get this straight, you want us to blow up the spillways?"

"That's exactly what I want to do governor."

He looked skeptical. "How much difference exactly would it make, Mr. Stevens? Are you sure that your boss, the commissioner, would make the same recommendation?"

Grant could see that attitude was as natural to Rally Jenkins, as breathing was to the general population. "Governor, I have no idea what the commissioner would recommend. I would hope that he would make the same recommendation, since it's the only possible strategy. As far as what difference, the report said sixty feet of water would breach this dam. We have two things going for us here. First, the report assumed the dam would be full as a worst case scenario, and second, we have a twenty four hour warning to dump water, of which we have already wasted almost three hours." Grant slowed down and tried to choose his words carefully. "Governor, if we can reduce the amount of water that ends up going over the dam by – let's say a few feet, it may be the difference between Hoover Dam failing or not."

Grant saw Fred walk over and peer into the spillways, then glance back at the wall holding the water from entering. He put one of his fingers in his mouth and looked like he was going to chew on his fingernail. Like waking from a trance, he straightened, bringing his hands back down, and looked at the governor. "He's right, Governor. I agree with Mr. Stevens."

The governor looked around the group for dissenting views. He also turned and looked at the concrete spillways. He spun and looked back at the crest of the Hoover Dam itself. Grant wondered if the governor might be visualizing sixty feet of water going over the top of the dam.

The governor held out his hands. "Anyone know any demolition guys?"

* * *

12:50 p.m. - Dangling Rope Marina, Lake Powell, Utah

As the Mastercraft rounded the bend in Dangling Rope Canyon, Julie saw the marina. It was unbelievable. She had never seen it that crowded before. Boats were stacked triple deep around the dock and there were at least a hundred people mulling around on the platform.

Dangling Rope Marina, which is accessible only by water, had limited resources. The floating docks were configured like a big cross, with a small grocery store, restrooms and a ranger station at the intersection, a sewage pump-out on the right, a repair facility on the left, a ramp to the shore on top, and the floating fuel station midway down the long bottom section. A state of the art photovoltaic power generation system on the hill powered the marina, with battery backup and propane generators for sunless days.

Greg pulled back the throttle and stood up in exasperation. "What's going on?"

Paul stood behind him. "This is crazy."

Julie touched her husband's arm. "Do we have enough gas to come back later when it's not so crowded?"

He shook his head. "No, Julie. Besides, something's wrong. We need to find out what it is."

He accelerated toward the frenzy of boats. When they approached the dock, Greg slowed to minimize the effect of the wake. Julie saw arms waving and she heard yelling as they approached. She heard someone say something about whose turn it was. Suddenly, a blue boat exited recklessly from the mass, and after seeing daylight, sped past them aiming for the main channel. The cluster of boats collapsed immediately, filling the previously occupied space. Julie guessed that the blue boat had either finally gotten his fuel, or had given up waiting.

When the Mastercraft pulled up next to the other boats, Greg called out to the driver of the boat next to them. "Where's the end of the line?"

"There isn't a line," the man said. He motioned at the mass. "It's every man for himself."

Greg grimaced. "What's going on anyway? Why the crowd?"

The man perked up. "You haven't heard about downstream?"

Greg shook his head. "No. We saw the water had dropped, but we didn't know why. What happened?"

"Somebody blew up the dam!"

Julie wondered if she had heard wrong. "What?"

"So the dam is leaking?" Paul asked.

The man exaggerated a nod. "The dam is more than leaking, it's gone."

"The Glen Canyon Dam is completely gone?" Greg asked.

"Yup. That's the word." The man motioned at the other boats. "And everybody is filling up and heading out before they get —" The man was interrupted and yelled at the boat behind. "Hey, watch it buddy."

Julie looked at her husband. "What does that mean? Should we just go?" She wondered if they had enough gas to get back to Wahweap where the truck was parked.

Greg checked the gas gauge and shook his head. "There's no way. We don't even have enough gas to make it back to the houseboat."

Paul interrupted. "Are you sure we should even try to leave?" Wouldn't it be safer to just wait it out?"

"Wait for what?" Greg asked. "To get stranded someplace up here on the rocks, fifty miles from civilization?"

"Yeah, but if we head down river, we could get pulled over the dam, couldn't we?

Julie didn't like the way that sounded. "Maybe he's right Greg."

Erika nodded.

Greg turned back to the man in the boat next to them, who had been listening to the argument. "What are you guys doing?"

The man pointed south. "As soon as we get some gas, we're heading home. We might not make it to Wahweap, but we're going to try to get as close as possible, Warm Creek maybe, Padre Bay for sure."

"Wouldn't it be safer to wait for help?" Paul asked.

"From who?" The man said. "Do you have any idea how many people will need rescuing? You could be waiting for weeks."

Greg looked at Julie. "He's right honey, we need to take care of ourselves."

Paul nodded as if he concurred.

Julie looked at the mob of boats waiting for gas. "Well, we better get in line then."

* * *

1:15 p.m. - Grand Canyon, Arizona

Keller told the rafters to paddle hard at the shore. David felt the raft nose up onto the sand. The landing had been small and a little tricky and they almost missed it. The rock cliffs and sandy beach looked enticing. Named Elves Chasm, the place featured a small stream that trickled through white and orange rock walls. According to the guidebook, Elves was located at Grand Canyon mile one hundred sixteen. A large waterfall, one of many at Elves, was visible just two hundred yards from the landing. The water seemed to flow right out of the rock then fall about twenty feet into a pool at the bottom. Half way up, there was a big cavern in the rock behind the fall, which Keller said they could climb up into. In the mist of the small waterfall, green plants covered the rock walls, more like a rain forest than a desert. It was one of the most incredible sites so far on the trip. Keller said that Elves Chasm continued above the lower fall with more falls and more small pools.

Judy expressed what David felt, "Wow, it's so beautiful."

They were all tempted to run toward the site, to explore it, but they were hungry. It was after one o'clock and they hadn't eaten since breakfast.

"Let's eat first," Keller said. "Then you guys can climb into that hole above the waterfall and I'll take a picture of you. We'll hang out here for a couple hours. There's more waterfalls and pools upstream from the main one." He looked directly at Becky and Sam. "It's very romantic up there."

Sam blushed enough to make the others laugh, but Becky showed no embarrassment.

"When are we going to meet up with the other raft?" asked Sam.

That morning, the group in the other raft, had decided to sleep in. They had seen Elves Chasm before and were feeling lazy. So the guides had agreed to separate.

Keller motioned upstream. "When they finally get up, they'll meet us here. It'll give you guys some time to explore Elves."

Afram popped the top on the cooler "All right. What's to eat?"

Keller looked confused. "I thought you guys were doing YOYO for lunch."

"Screw YOYO," Afram said smiling. "We'd all starve and you know it."

Keller gave in. "All right, who wants to make the sandwiches?"

No one actually volunteered, but everyone in the boat pitched in and helped. Why not? They were at an incredible spot and the mood was upbeat.

* * *

1:30 p.m. - Dangling Rope Marina, Lake Powell, Utah

Julie checked her watch. They had been waiting for gas at Dangling Rope for almost forty-five minutes and there was still a crowd of boats ahead of them. This was taking way too long. Additionally, the wind had started blowing, which was typical in the afternoons at Lake Powell. Patience was wearing thin in all the boats, and numerous arguments about who was next had taken place. The gas pumps had been operating non-stop since they arrived.

Dangling Rope's gas pumps were self-service with a slot to insert credit cards, and there were a total of eighteen pumps. On a big day, the marina pumped twenty thousand gallons, but Julie thought today might be a new record.

"What if they run out?" she asked.

Paul shook his head. "They better not."

While waiting, Greg had continued to nose the boat closer to the dock. Now they were pinched by boats that had arrived after them. They were committed to pump #11. A small yellow boat had just replaced the nozzle in the pump, and was trying to back out of the slip. The crowd of boats made his exit very difficult.

"Make room!" someone shouted.

Another man waved his arms at a red boat blocking the exit of the yellow boat. "Get out of the way!"

The man in the red boat looked uncomfortable, and when he tried to back his boat to make room he nudged a boat behind him.

"Watch it you moron!"

The small yellow boat took the opportunity to slip past. As soon as he was gone a large white boat pulled up to the pump. Instead of inserting a credit card, he started jogging down the docks toward the store.

A fat guy in an orange shirt in the boat next to Julie, yelled at him, "Where the hell are you going?"

The man's wife, who was still in the white boat, stood and faced the man in the orange shirt. "Sorry, but we only have cash."

"Then get out of the way, and let somebody else pump."

"It'll only take a couple minutes," she argued.

"We don't have a couple minutes, lady."

"Leave her alone," Greg said.

The yeller turned toward Greg. "Stay out of it. I don't have to wait for them. If you want to wait, you get behind them."

Julie wished that Greg would have stayed out of it, even though the lady needed somebody to support her.

The man in the orange shirt turned back to the white boat. "Move it out of the way lady."

She turned away and tried to ignore him.

"Lady, I'm talking to you."

Julie spoke before she could stop herself. "You're not helping."

"Like I said, if you guys want to wait, go ahead. But, they're not holding the rest of us up." He motioned at the other boats behind him as if everyone supported what he was doing. He turned back to the white boat. "Lady?"

Julie saw that the man from the white boat was now running back down the docks toward them. She pointed to him. "Here he comes."

The man in orange sat down and didn't say anything else.

While Julie watched the man take the nozzle and put it in his boat, she calculated that each boat took between ten and fifteen minutes to fill, and there were still four boats waiting for #11 ahead of them, including the man in the orange shirt. Counting their own boat, that was five boats total. She guessed they would be stuck at Dangling Rope for another hour.

While they were waiting, they overheard that at Dangling Rope, which was just over forty miles upstream from the dam, that water levels were dropping approximately ten feet per hour. Closer to the dam, levels were dropping even faster. At the upstream end of the lake, another hundred forty miles away, they hadn't noticed anything yet. Paul had pointed out a man adjusting cables on the floating docks to compensate for the changing levels.

Julie let her mind wander downstream to where the dam was supposed to be. She imagined boats getting sucked over the top, and people drowning. Maybe they were better off up here, miles away from the dam. But on the other hand,

Greg was right about getting stranded, and staying this far north would guarantee days or more before they were rescued. Julie wondered if they could save the Mastercraft. They had paid over twenty thousand dollars for it. She wondered if insurance would cover it, if they abandoned it someplace.

Hopefully, Max and Darlene would be waiting when Greg got them back to the houseboat. Julie wondered if Darlene would take the initiative to pack everything up in preparation. Then again, what if Darlene and Max didn't know. Maybe nobody had told them what was going on.

* * *

1:40 p.m. - Lake Powell, Utah

Max felt someone shaking him. He opened his eyes and saw Darlene's face.

"Wake up." She pointed at where they had kayaked through the slot canyon. "The water's gone."

"What water?" he mumbled. What was she talking about? He pulled himself up on his side and looked at where she was pointing. Then he sat bolt upright. "What the—"

"It's gone," she said.

Max saw that the water had dropped at least five feet since he fell asleep, because there was no water at all in the canyon, and the muddy bottom was at least five feet below where the water had been, when they paddled in.

After they had stopped an hour before, Darlene had spread out the two beach towels and they ate a quick picnic lunch. The romantic atmosphere of the private rock cavern interrupted their lunch, and well, one thing had led to another. Afterward, Max had taken a nap, while Darlene read her book. And obviously, while he was asleep, the water had disappeared.

Max stepped carefully over the rocks down into the wet streambed. His feet sunk up to his ankles in deep sticky mud. He moved forward with slow movements and wet sucking sounds, until he rounded the corner and could see into the narrow canyon. No water. He yelled for Darlene to wait, while he looked around. His movements were slow and awkward, but he managed to move all the way through the narrow portion, until it opened up and he could see. The water was now visible, about a hundred feet away.

Max tried to imagine what it had looked like when they kayaked through here. The water had been approximately ten feet deeper and had covered the bottom of the muddy canyon. Max looked at the shore, and the wet band, and cursed that he had ignored the signs. He realized now that he had noticed something even before they left the houseboat. In total, he guessed the water had dropped over thirty feet.

But, how could this happen? Lake Powell was a hundred eighty miles long. How could the water drop so fast? And then it hit him. There was only one answer. Something had happened to the dam. He turned back into the canyon.

"Darlene!" He tried to move quickly through the sticky mud. "Darlene!"

* * *

2:15 p.m. - Grand Canyon, Arizona

David looked at the rock ledge. Keller had said that the way to the upper falls at Elves Chasm was tricky, but he didn't think it'd be this bad. The ledge was only about a foot wide. If someone fell, they'd die. "I dunno," he said, shaking his head.

"Don't be ridiculous," Judy said as she slid past. "You desk jockeys are all chickens."

She stepped onto the narrow ledge and grabbed at the rock wall for hand holds. She shimmied carefully along the ledge without ever looking down and without hesitation. At the other end of the ledge, about fifteen feet away, she hopped onto the cliff and turned around. She motioned with her arm. "Come on, it's easy."

"Nothing like a girl to make ya feel like a complete wuss, huh?" Afram said, smiling.

David nodded. "Go ahead while I clean out my pants."

Afram started across, much slower and much more careful than Judy.

Although the ledge scared David, Elves Chasm had turned out to be a blast. After a leisurely lunch, they had hiked up to the lower falls and played for over a half hour. They climbed up behind the waterfall and maneuvered until they were all in the picture. Per Keller's promise, he played the photographer. Of course Becky and Sam had their arms around each other. It ended up being one of those screwy scenes where Keller had everybody's cameras around his neck and the group had to stay in place while he took a picture with each one. David's leg was stretched across a wet rock and it felt like it was going to slip. He needed to stand up and adjust it, but Keller kept yelling for them to hold still for a couple more.

After the pictures, Judy jumped down the waterfall into the pool at the bottom, something David had not even considered. After some amount of prodding from Judy and Keller, Afram followed, then Sam and Becky. David would never have done it, but after watching the girls and seeing that it was no big deal, he mustered up the courage and jumped in himself. After resurfacing from the cold water David realized that it had been no big deal after all. The entire group climbed back up and jumped again. Afram must have jumped five times, the last time holding one knee into his chest to splash everybody. At one point the whole group floated around in the pool under the waterfall. The weather was incredibly hot so the cold water felt good for short periods of time, but after a few minutes of sitting in the pool, the whole group felt hypothermic. Becky's teeth started chattering. Everyone climbed out and sprawled on the hot rocks to get warm.

Keller told the group how to get to the upper falls, then he headed back to the rafts. The group climbed higher. A short hike later they had arrived at the ledge where Sam and Becky had just made their way across, practically holding hands.

"Okay David," Afram called.

David approached the ledge, still nervous. However, watching the rest of the group go across without incident had convinced him that it was possible. His feet seemed heavy and unresponsive. When he gripped the rock with his hands, in spite of the great handholds, he kept imagining the rock breaking loose or his hand losing its grip, neither of which happened. He reached the other side and took what must have been his first breath since leaving. His heart was racing, but he'd done it.

Judy patted him on the back. "You need to get out more."

They continued up, hiking over and around some large boulders until they came around the bluff and could see some of the upper falls of Elves. The first thing they noticed was that they were not alone. A couple was lying next to the large pool completely naked. The group stopped when they saw the sunbathers, except for Judy who hadn't seen them yet.

"Hang on, Judy." Afram said in almost a whisper and Judy stopped.

David noticed that the sunbathers had noticed them too, but they didn't seem to mind, not even bothering to cover up. He had a better view than he wanted and even from thirty feet away got an instantaneous refresher on male and female anatomy. Aside from their lack of clothes, he noticed the almost white hair on the guy and the obviously non-shaven armpits on the girl. He guessed Europeans, which explained their comfort in lying around naked. Although he'd never actually been to Europe, he'd always heard about them hanging around without clothes in city parks, and beaches. Since there were no other rafts at the bottom, David at first wondered how the couple came to be at the site, and then he spotted the backpacks.

When the naked couple noticed them, the man stood and waved them over. "Come, we can share this place."

The accent seemed German to David. They were obviously friendly, but who wanted to walk up and shake hands with a naked guy? The girl must have figured it out, because she said something to the guy in another language. He nodded and they both retrieved some shorts and pulled them on. By then, the rafters had reached the pool. The man and the woman walked over to shake hands, neither of them wearing a shirt, which for the man was normal enough, but for the woman, well, not something you see every day.

"I am Ralph," the guy said, but it sounded more like Rolph. "This is Anna." He pointed to the smiling topless girl.

The groups shook hands. David had never shook hands with a topless girl before and although he was extremely nervous, she was not, and so he relaxed slightly. He tried to keep his eyes high. Each of the rafters introduced themselves. David happened to glance back while Sam was shaking hands with Anna, and he couldn't help notice the scowl on Becky's face in the background.

David waited until Ralph was looking, then pointed high on the cliffs. "You hiked down from above?" He over-enunciated to make sure he was understood."

"Yes, we hiked down from Royal Arch this morning." He pointed up above the falls. "There is a small cliff that requires a rope to descend. We left the canyon rim the day before that."

The English was near flawless and David regretted the way he had asked the question. He had heard that Germans spoke better English than most Americans and Ralph seemed to have driven the point home.

Afram asked the question that David wanted to. "Are you from Germany?"

They both smiled and nodded. David found his eyes drifting back to Anna and tried to control them, aiming them someplace safe.

"How far does this go?" Judy asked, pointing above the waterfall.

Ralph explained. "There are a few more small waterfalls and many pools above this one. If you haven't seen them, you should go. They are very beautiful. Anna and I will wait for you here. When you return, we can talk for a while. Yes?"

Judy answered, "Okay, we'll be back in a while," and she started heading up a trail.

David and the rest of the group followed. David consciously avoided taking a last glimpse toward Anna.

* * *

2:25 p.m. - Dangling Rope Marina, Lake Powell, Utah

Julie watched the gas pump count past fifteen gallons. "That's enough!"

Greg held the nozzle. "No. A little more, just in case."

Paul and Erika both stood and nervously watched as the gallon numbers counted higher.

Julie looked back at the boats behind them. There were even more than when they arrived an hour and a half before. She pitied the poor people who would be leaving hours from now.

Greg released the lever, climbed out of the boat and replaced it in the pump. He jumped back in the boat and fired up the engine. Julie noticed the gas gauge climb up to just over half full. The other boats made a space for them to back out of the slip, and Greg expertly backed the Mastercraft into the small spot. Immediately, another boat pulled into the space. Paul jumped up on the bow to prevent the boat from hitting anyone else, and Greg began a slow tedious meandering through the crowd of boats waiting to get fuel. Julie saw what looked like envious glances from other boaters.

When they finally passed the last boats and were out in open water, Greg pushed the throttle forward, ignoring the low speed buoys. The rangers had more important things to worry about than speeding tickets.

Julie cupped her hand so her husband could hear her. "How long to the houseboat?"

He shrugged. "We're close. Half hour, maybe less."

CHAPTER 17

2:30 p.m. - Hoover Dam, Nevada

A diesel four-wheel drive pickup with "Las Vegas – Demolition" on the door, led three industrial one-ton trucks with the same insignia down the switchbacks toward the dam. Grant saw the dam security guards wave them into the employee parking lot next to the Nevada spillway. The driver of the pickup jumped out of his truck and came over to where the group waited. He was a tall blond man in Levi's and a t-shirt. He wore lace up work boots. Grant guessed he was in his forties. The guy took off his hard hat with his left hand and reached out his right and Fred Grainger took it.

"Hi, I'm Todd Fisher." Seven other guys in hard hats crowded up behind Todd.

"Fred Grainger, site supervisor." Fred pointed to Grant. "And this is Grant Stevens from the Bureau of Reclamation in Denver."

The three shook hands.

Todd said, "I understand you have an emergency job for me."

Fred walked over to the fence by the spillways and pointed to the concrete wall holding back the water. "We need that wall blown as soon as possible."

Todd whistled for a second. "All that waters going to come charging through here after she blows, ain't it?"

"That's the whole point." Grant pointed to the other side of the dam. "Oh, and the spillway on the Arizona side will need to be blown too."

Todd looked at both Fred and Grant. "This is all related to the news on TV about the Glen Canyon Dam, isn't it?"

Fred nodded.

Todd looked back at the spillways. "I assume you want me to blow the wall as low as possible to allow the most water through?" He didn't wait for an answer. "Do you guys have any idea how thick the concrete is at the base of that wall?"

Fred responded. "We found the blue prints while we were waiting."

Fred turned and one of his employees handed him what looked like a rolled up poster. Fred unrolled it in one motion and Todd and Grant crowded around to get a look.

Todd spoke first "Wow, that thing is thirty feet high and over eighteen feet thick at the base. Plus the whole thing is full of rebar."

Fred looked over at Todd. "Can you do it?"

"Oh, we can break it up, no problem. But the rebar is going to hold all the pieces together. The water pressure might be able to tear it apart, but then again, you may need to get a crane in here to reach down and tear some of it out. We won't know until after the initial explosions."

Grant groaned. "It'll take hours to get a big crane in here."

Todd thought about it for a second, "Well, I can always increase the explosives. I won't be able to guarantee a precision job." He smiled. "I might blow the end of this parking lot off." It was said as if Todd blew up parking lots every day.

Grant and Fred's eyes met, both of their heads were nodding.

Fred looked back at Todd. "We'll risk the parking lot. How fast can your guys work?"

Todd turned and talked to one of the other guys in a hard hat. He motioned down into the trough leading to the Nevada spillway tunnel, and to the base of the concrete spillway itself. He pointed over to the Arizona spillway across the river. He walked back to Fred and Grant. "I think we'll be ready to detonate in less than an hour. However, I recommend we blow one spillway at a time, in case we need to make adjustments." Todd smiled.

* * *

2:50 p.m. - Lake Powell, Utah

Greg pointed at the canyon and slowed the boat down. "It's that one."

Julie looked around "Are you sure? It looks different."

The trip back from Dangling Rope Marina had been difficult. The amount of boat traffic was unbelievable and during some sections where the lake narrowed, the water was dangerously rough from waves trapped in the channel. They even saw a boat that had capsized. In a couple of places, the water was so low that rocks protruded into the normal boating channels, forcing the traffic to alter its course.

Greg motioned to Julie and Erika with his hand under his eyes. "Mask your view so you can only see above the water line. Then all the new exposed rock won't confuse you. See? Our houseboat is in the canyon with that big rock sitting in front of that wall of rock. We were just used to seeing it at water level, not forty feet up the slope."

Julie nodded, trusting her husband, although it didn't look anything like she remembered it.

As the Mastercraft entered the mouth of the canyon, Greg accelerated. The water was much smoother here than in the main channel. He looked over at Julie "Okay, no dilly-dallying at the houseboat. We get the necessities and get out."

Julie looked questioningly at her husband. "If we're going all the way up there, why wouldn't we bring the houseboat back with us? What about our deposit? That's thousands of dollars."

Greg answered immediately. "I'd love to, and I hope we can. But unless Max untied it, the houseboat is gonna be sitting high and dry on the rocks right now, thirty or forty feet above the water line. If so, we couldn't bring it back if we wanted too."

Julie looked over at Erika and Paul to see if they had heard the same thing. The look on Erika's face was as blank as Julie's. Julie had not thought about that. While she tried to imagine the scene, Greg accelerated again and she leaned back in her seat. Looking over her shoulder she noticed Erika staring behind in a trance. She now dreaded seeing the same houseboat that just a moment before she had been so anxious to see.

Julie marveled at how much the canyon had changed. Before, it felt more open. Now, with water forty feet lower, the canyon walls were higher and seemed to be closing in on her. The wet canyon walls were darker too.

The boat banked back and forth for a while as Greg carved deeper into the long canyon. A few times in the past, usually when she was sitting in one of the seats facing backwards, Julie's stomach had been affected by these long canyon excursions. She was all too familiar with the initial feelings of motion sickness, when butterflies started flapping around down there, the clammy skin, the dry mouth, and finally the apprehension that she needed to throw up, followed by relief after she finally did. But, that was not what she felt now. This feeling was worse, a deep pit, almost a pain, in her stomach, caused by heading farther into a canyon, which every bone in her body knew, was the wrong direction. She wanted to be back in the main channel, rough water and all, speeding downstream toward the marina, or better yet, back in the truck, on the road, headed home. She wanted to hug her children.

They rounded a bend and Greg swerved suddenly hard left. Julie wasn't ready and was thrown out of her seat onto the floor, hitting her head on Greg's hip. Julie rubbed her head and started to get up and she noticed Erika had also been knocked on the floor. The boat slowed quickly.

"Sorry." Greg reached down and grabbed her arm to help her up. "That was close."

"What was close?" said Erika from her hands and knees on the floor behind them.

Greg pointed directly behind the boat, where they had just been. "Look."

A large boulder was visible just under the surface of the water directly behind them in the exact area where they had swerved. Julie could only imagine what would have happened if Greg had not avoided it.

Greg grimaced. "I'm going to need to slow down a little."

There were no arguments from the passengers as they climbed back into their seats. As they rounded the next bend, much slower, Greg pulled the throttle all the way back and the boat coasted, settling back into the water. Julie saw many of the protruding boulders scattered around the channel.

Greg looked over at Paul. "Hey, can you climb up on the bow and keep an eye out. I don't want to tear up the prop and I can't see how deep it is in front of the boat.

Paul climbed up on the bow. Julie and Erika stood and watched over the side of the boat. Rocks were everywhere, especially ahead.

"Hang on," Paul said, pointing off to the right. "It gets too shallow up there. Go over that way." He pointed to the left.

Greg reversed the transmission, backing up a few feet, and then headed where Paul pointed. That worked for a while, as Paul guided him through a shallow channel. Greg had to back up a few more times, but they kept going. When they rounded the next bend however, Julie wanted to puke. There were rocks all over the place, but worst of all, the water ended completely about two hundred feet ahead of them on a rocky beach newly exposed by the dropping lake.

Greg cursed, which was something he never did. "We'll have to go the rest of the way on foot."

"How far are we?" Erika asked from behind, her voice cracking in mid sentence.

Greg looked around. "We've got to be close. It can't be more than a couple more bends up the canyon." He bit his lip when he finished talking, something Greg only did when he was nervous. "Why aren't Max and Darlene here, waiting for us?"

Paul shrugged. "They should be here, unless they got a ride with someone else."

"Or unless something's wrong," Julie added. "We better park the boat and get going." She had an overwhelming feeling that they needed to hurry.

Her husband turned and looked at her. "We can't leave the boat Julie. Somebody's going to need to stay with it."

"Why?" Erika asked.

"The water's dropping too fast," Greg answered. "We'd get back here and find the boat high and dry. Then we'd never get out of here."

Julie looked back and forth between the other three. "Then who's staying? You want me or Erika to stay?"

Erika pointed back toward where they came. "I can't drive the boat back through that."

Julie realized immediately that she couldn't either. She was great with the boat out in the open, but in close proximity to anything, Greg always had to maneuver it. "It'll get trickier as the water drops." She looked at her husband. "You better stay with the boat."

Greg looked unhappy, but he nodded, having come to the same conclusion. She could tell he was worried, and that was enough for now.

"Besides Max and Darlene, what do we need to bring back?" Julie asked.

Greg counted on his fingers. "Truck keys, my wallet, your purse –"

"What about clothes?" Julie asked her husband.

He shrugged. "Don't try to carry too much."

She looked around the boat for a second, wishing she had a list.

He pointed back the way they had come. "I need to move the boat back out of here before the water gets any lower. You're going to need your shoes." He pointed at the rocks.

The comment made perfect sense. Julie reached down and grabbed her sandals. Not great for hiking, but they would have to do. She looked at Erika and Paul who both wore flip-flops.

"You guys be careful," Greg said. "And hurry."

She kissed him on the cheek then slid over the side into the water, holding her sandals up so they'd stay dry. Erika and Paul followed. As soon as they were away from the boat, Greg backed it away from them. Julie swam a few strokes toward a rocky strip poking out of the water, then climbed up on it and started walking toward the shoreline in front of them. When she looked back, the boat was already pointed the other direction, Greg was standing on the seat looking at the water in front, steering the boat with his left hand. She waved but he wasn't looking.

* * *

3:10 p.m. - Grand Canyon, Arizona

David decided he liked Ralph. They'd been talking about ten minutes since the rafters returned to where the Germans were sunbathing. He was extremely friendly. Not like the stereotype of stiffness and arrogance he'd expected. Then again David didn't know why he'd expected Germans to act any different anyway. After all, how many had he actually met? He liked Anna too, even after she put her shirt on. She was much quieter than Ralph though, speaking only when spoken to. At first David guessed she didn't speak very much English, but after hearing her speak, she proved she was as fluent as Ralph.

Ralph had been asking questions about the rafting expedition. "So what will be the total duration of your river trip?"

"Thirteen days," said Afram.

"And where do you sleep?"

"There are campgrounds all along the river. We stop, setup camp, and sleep on the sand in our sleeping bags."

"Do you recommend the river trip?" Ralph wanted to know.

Afram looked around at the other rafters. "Yeah, it's great. Real relaxing. But if you want to go, you have to get reservations early, like a year in advance."

"How did you determine —"

"The internet." Afram interrupted. "We searched around until we found the deal we wanted."

David started to get up. "Why don't you and Anna come down to the rafts and we'll introduce you to Keller. Maybe he has a business card he can give you."

Ralph and Anna both agreed enthusiastically and the group, including their new friends, started back down toward the river.

* * *

3:15 p.m. - Hoover Dam, Nevada

The sound of jackhammers echoed off the canyon walls upstream from Hoover Dam. Todd's crews, one on the Nevada side and one on the Arizona side, wasted no time before cranking up the air compressors in the industrial trucks, tossing air hoses down into the spillways, and starting work. They used jackhammers and impact drills to drill the deep holes into the concrete walls. Todd was down in the spillway pointing to where each hole should be drilled. If there was a science to where Todd had them drilling, Grant didn't recognize it. The holes seemed fairly random. They were focused around the bottom and sides of the wall, with a few vertical lines of holes in the middle, which Grant assumed, were to break up the big wall segments. Each hole was drilled at a slightly downward angle.

After forty-five minutes of the noise, the sounds stopped. The workers climbed a ladder out of the spillway. They unloaded boxes marked with a yellow triangle on the side of each box and the words "Danger – Explosives." Grant noticed the workers jockeyed the boxes around as if they were just normal building materials.

He pointed the boxes out to Todd. "Aren't you afraid that stuff will blow up when you throw it around like that?"

"Nah, this stuff is completely stable, even after we add the propellant, it doesn't get dangerous until you detonate it."

"So why the big warning labels?"

"Government mandates it. Some desk pilot that didn't know anything about explosives decided we better handle them like eggshells." Todd smiled at Grant. "The markings do tend to keep people away and make the psychos trying to steal it a little more visible."

The men handed the boxes down into the spillway. Then one by one they opened the corner of each box and poured what looked like a coarse white powder in each of the holes on the wall. Grant now understood the drilling had been aimed downward so the powder would go into the hole; it would have been harder to fill horizontal holes. It took over ten minutes to fill all the holes with explosives.

When the holes were full, they passed the remaining boxes up the ladder. The hard hats immediately passed down a few five-gallon gas cans and began pouring the liquid in the holes.

Grant again approached Todd. "Is that just gasoline?"

He shook his head. "Kerosene. It burns hotter than normal gas."

"What else do you put in there?"

"That's it. Just the detonators and we're done."

The workers passed the cans up and Todd passed one box, again marked as explosives, down into the spillway. The workers took the detonators and stuffed them in the holes. One guy worked behind them, linking the wires coming out of the detonators together. A longer wire was used to extend from the last detonator up the ladder to where Todd was standing. The box was passed up the ladder, the workers followed, and the ladder was pulled out of the spillway. The workers loaded the remaining materials in the truck and drove the truck out of the parking lot. Todd stood holding what looked like a transistor radio in one hand and the wires in the other.

"This is where you can blow yourself up if you don't know what you are doing. I suggest you guys clear out of here."

Grant didn't need any more encouragement. Fred and the other staff from the dam started walking across the parking lot to where the hard hats were waiting. Grant walked over to one of them.

"What's he doing now?"

The man pointed. "That little unit in his hand is the receiver for the detonator. First he'll hook it up to the big battery by his feet. It will make some lights illuminate. He'll verify that the detonation light is not illuminated, that would be bad. If it's not, he'll hook up the wires and flip a switch to activate the receiver."

As the explanation was finishing, Grant saw Todd set the box down walk over to where they were standing.

Todd nodded. "Okay. We're ready on this side." He reached down and unclipped his radio. "Steve, how're things in Arizona? You guys about ready?"

The radio responded. "Yeah we're just waiting for you."

"Okay, I'm gonna blow this side and see if it works, I'll give you the word."

"We'll be waiting."

Todd took another black box out of his pocket and flipped a switch. Grant saw a green light illuminate. Todd pressed another button and a red light started blinking. Without looking back Todd yelled, "Cover your ears." He waited a couple seconds and pressed another button.

Grant saw gray and black dust shoot high in the air in multiple directions. A fraction of a second later, the sound of the explosion reached them. The dull noise offended Grant's ears even though they were covered. He felt the impact of the explosion over his entire body, especially in his chest. As he dropped his hands he heard a sparkling sound like crystals and looked to his right and noticed that some windows were broken in the snack bar. While Grant was still verifying that he was alive, the workers jostled past him, jogging toward the spillway, led by Todd. Grant followed.

When he reached the spillway, he could hear the water and loud banging noises like rocks hitting each other. Most of the wall had been opened up. Rebar was hanging from the walls on both sides. The water was dragging and rolling concrete remnants of the wall into the huge spillway. The moving water seemed to be clearing out most of the concrete dust in the air. The water level appeared to be about half of the way up the culvert. But even that was an amazing amount of water to behold as it crashed down into the spillway. Each Hoover spillway was capable of almost 200,000 cubic feet per second, about the same as Niagara Falls, and he guessed it was currently running at about half, which was more than the total amount of all Hoover's turbines combined, plus the twelve outlets spraying across the canyon. He estimated the spillway, plus all the other gates that were open, had increased the normal downstream flow from Hoover by a factor of ten. Looking down the spillway, he couldn't help but feel that the water was going to suck him, and the parking lot as well, down its fifty-foot hole.

Todd walked a few steps away from the spillway and lifted his radio to his ear. "There were a few big pieces of wall that didn't break up, but they fell over. The water will do the rest. Go ahead and blow your side."

A few seconds later Grant saw the dust shoot into the air on the other side. Todd headed for the diesel pickup "Come on, let's go see how that one looks." The workers piled into the back of the truck, while Grant and Fred squeezed into the front.

The hole on the Arizona side wasn't as clean. The left side was broken, but still hanging on by the rebar. There was a big piece in the middle also, with water rushing around it from both sides. But, Grant guessed the two obstructions were only impeding about twenty percent of the flow. Besides, the water pressure would eventually finish the job.

With the water flow on this side only slightly less than the other, and adding the two together, plus the twelve outlets in the canyon, Grant came up with a little over 250,000 cubic feet per second being dumped. He walked over to the hood of Todd's truck and took out a piece of paper. He borrowed a calculator from Todd. He multiplied the number by 60 twice to get cubic feet per hour, then divided it by a conversion factor to get acre-feet/hour. By this time, Fred, Todd and the workers had huddled around to see the result. He then divided the number by the total acreage of Lake Mead, 161,000 acres, which he got from Fred, then multiplied it by 18, the approximate number of hours until the flood arrived. He looked up.

"A little over two feet, maybe closer to three feet when you consider that the spillways will double as the water starts to rise." Grant got a couple blank looks from the huddle, so he continued. "The level of the lake, I was trying to figure out how many feet we are going to drop the lake before the flood arrives."

Grant saw that the group was largely unimpressed. They didn't get it. He completed the explanation, while looking straight into their eyes. "When a wall of water flows over the top of the dam for ten days straight, it will be three feet smaller because of what we just did. It might save the dam."

Many of them turned their heads toward to crest of the dam. Grant knew they were trying to visualize water flowing over it. When they turned back, a couple of them had mouths hanging open. He thought that they now understood.

CHAPTER 18

3:30 p.m. - Grand Canyon, Arizona

As the rafters and the two Germans approached the Colorado River, David noticed the second raft had just arrived. George was transferring his stuff from the other raft into Keller's. Keller was holding onto the ropes for his raft. As they walked closer, David could see that most of the sandy landing was now covered with water.

When Keller caught sight of the group, he called out to them. "Get over here. We gotta go." He seemed edgy.

The group came to life and started loading into the raft.

"What's up Keller?" said Judy.

"The water's rising fast. It must have risen almost ten feet in the last hour. I've never seen it rise this fast. We gotta get downstream and find a high campground." Keller's voice communicated near panic.

The other raft pushed off. They also seemed edgy. As David climbed into the boat, he remembered Ralph and Anna who were standing on what was left of the shore, staring at the now panicky rafters. "Keller, these two hikers we met at Elves are interested in one of your trips. Do you have a card or a flyer or something with a phone number?"

Keller didn't even look up at them. "coloradoriverfoam.com. All one word. The number's on the web site." He pushed off and the river current grabbed the raft and pulled it downstream.

David looked back at the Germans and waved. "Bye." Not the kind of goodbye he would have liked.

Ralph and Anna waved at them from the shore as the raft drifted downstream.

"Right side paddle. Left side paddle." Keller called out from behind.

* * *

3:35 p.m. - Lake Powell, Utah

Julie's feet were killing her. After forty-five minutes of hiking on wet rocks, they ached all the way up to her ankles. Erika was suffering too; you could see it in her face. Both grimaced as they walked. Both had slipped on the wet rocks countless times, but neither complained. It wouldn't have helped. Julie vowed she would buy differently in the future when shopping for shoes. To hell with fashion. And most maddening was that Paul had not slipped or had any problems, even though he had the same flip-flops.

Julie was also nervous that they had not reached the houseboat yet. She could not help wondering if they were in the wrong canyon, or if Max and Darlene, had already moved the houseboat. What if they had already taken it downstream?

"There it is," Erika called from behind.

Julie looked up. She saw the houseboat still tied to the shoreline, resting on a steep patch of rocky ground about forty feet above the bottom of the canyon. It hung downward at a steep angle. There was no sign of Max or Darlene anywhere.

Paul cupped his hands "MAX? DARLENE?" but no one responded. "Where are they? I hope they're okay."

Julie was worried. Where were they? Darlene was not the type to wander. "MAX?"

Erika pointed at the houseboat. "Come on."

After a somewhat difficult climb up the steep muddy hillside, Julie reached out and pulled herself up next to the houseboat using one of the ropes dangling off the back. She felt the houseboat give slightly at her pull and immediately released the rope. It wasn't stable. Erika climbed up behind her and grabbed her arm. She was panting. Paul passed them both, climbing up to where the boat had been tied to the shore.

Julie and Erika maneuvered upwards to where Paul was standing. When they reached the top, Julie sat down in the shade caused by the front deck and looked back down in the muddy canyon. Erika sat next to her. Julie looked downstream and up, even up on the cliffs surrounding the small canyon, but saw no signs of the other couple.

"Where are they?" Julie asked.

Paul shrugged. "I wonder if someone already picked them up."

"Maybe they left a note or something," Julie said hopefully.

Paul motioned to the two women. "Let's climb up and start gathering everything together. We can look around and see if there's a note or something."

Erika nodded.

Paul grabbed one of the lines tied to the shore and hoisted himself up. The houseboat shifted with a loud groan. He dropped back to the ground and backed up a few steps. "That's not going to work. How bad do we need that stuff anyway?"

"My wedding ring is in there," Erika argued. "I'll climb up."

Paul looked at her apprehensively. "Don't be stupid Erika, it's not safe."

Erika walked over and tested the ropes that held the houseboat to shore. The first rope was tight enough to not budge when she pulled on it, the second almost the same. She crouched down and looked under the boat, where the two pontoons sat on the rocky ledge. "I think it's okay."

Paul walked behind her. "You're not going. If anyone is going I'll do it."

Erika walked over to the side of the boat and put her hands on it, dug her feet, and shoved. The boat didn't move. She wedged herself against it and shoved again. Nothing. She glanced at her husband. "I'm lighter, I'm going to do it."

Julie protested. "Wait. Let's think about this for a second."

Erika shook her head. "It'll be okay. I'm the lightest. And we have to look for a note from Max or Darlene. We can't just leave them."

Paul nodded reluctantly. "Okay, but if something happens, be ready to jump off."

Paul clasped his hands together to make a step for Erika. She put her foot in and climbed onto the deck. The houseboat creaked loudly, which made Julie's heart stop, but the vessel didn't move. Erika stood, ready to dive off if necessary. They all hesitated for an instant, before Erika headed inside.

"Leave the door open while you're in there," Paul yelled. "Actually, try to leave all the doors open. Leave yourself an escape route, and be ready to jump if it starts to move."

Julie called out a list of all the things they needed, starting with car keys, wallets, a cell phone, and a few pieces of clothing. Based on the hike up the canyon, they needed better shoes for the hike down. Since there was some probability of spending the night outside, they needed blankets. Julie tried to describe as best as she could the location of each item on her list, based on what she could remember.

"I can't find your truck keys."

Julie looked up. "Did you try Greg's shorts?"

"Yeah."

"And on the hutch next to the bed?"

"Hang on. I found them. They were on the floor next to the hutch."

Erika appeared and handed both sets of keys, wallets, purses, an armload of clothes, and Julie's tennis shoes to them. She then went back into the boat.

Paul yelled inside. "That's enough. Get out of there."

Erika returned with an armload of blankets and pillows. She dropped them to Paul, then went back into the boat. "I'm looking for some shoes for me. I'm not going to—"

The houseboat shifted slightly with a loud screeching noise from the metal pontoons on the rocks. Julie heard Erika scream from inside and a thud that sounded like her falling down. One of the ropes holding the boat snapped and fell slack.

"Get out of there!" Paul screamed.

No response.

"Erika? Are you okay?" Julie called out.

The last rope vibrated with tension. The houseboat shifted again with another loud screech. It wouldn't last much longer.

"ERIKA!" Paul screamed.

The second rope let go. The houseboat started to slide. Through her scream, Julie saw a motion through the door of the houseboat. The houseboat fell, but a running Erika dove headfirst off the boat onto the sand like a baseball player sliding into second. She hit the ground hard completely stretched out on her front side. Julie heard a loud groan when Erika landed.

The houseboat picked up speed fast and fifteen feet down, one of the metal pontoons dug in and the momentum caused the houseboat to roll over in one swift motion. After that, it rolled a few more times, leaving small pieces along the way. It hit a rock outcropping and lost one of the pontoons. It hit the next rock dead-on and the whole thing disintegrated, debris shooting in all directions. The pieces all came to a stop at the bottom.

Stunned, Julie stared at the rubble for a second before kneeling by her friend. "Are you okay?"

Erika lay on her stomach. She pulled one of her arms out from under her and lifted herself up. She had a bloody splotch on her forehead and her cheek. In spite of her condition, she smiled. Her voice came out broken and soft like someone who had the breath knocked out of her. "I got 'em," she said, and she held up her tennis shoes.

A sound came from behind them "Hello!"

All three of them looked up the canyon to see where the sound had come from. They saw Max and Darlene running toward them.

* * *

4:00 p.m. - Grand Canyon, Arizona

After two days on the river, David had learned that water levels varied daily. Supposedly, these changes were caused by adjustments at the Glen Canyon Dam, even though it was over a hundred-thirty miles upstream. Some mornings when they awoke, the water could be as much as five feet higher than the night before. However, David had never seen Keller nervous like he was at Elves Chasm. Keller said he didn't remember ever seeing it rise that fast. After that, Keller hadn't spoken much since they pushed off. He kept scanning the banks of the river as if he were looking for something. In all the days on the river, David had seen many emotions from Keller, but never fear.

As the raft came around the next bend, they could see white water ahead. Judy pointed at it. "Keller, what's this one called?"

Keller craned his neck around. "There aren't supposed to be any rapids here. Something must have . . ." Keller then yelled to the guide in the other raft. "What happened here?"

The other guide yelled back, "Nothing. The water is just way higher."

Keller looked at Judy. "I've never seen this much water in the river. Usually, this section is calm." He looked upstream nervously. "They must be doing some kind of experimental dump up at the dam."

"What do you mean experimental dump?" asked Afram.

Keller motioned upstream. "In the early nineties, a politician from Arizona, think his name was Babbitt or something, made 'em open the gates at Glen Canyon for a couple weeks to stir up the silt in the river. They were trying to restore the sand on the banks. Maybe they're doing it again." He shook his head. "Although, you'd think they'd have said something." He looked confused. "It's going to make it tough to find a camp site."

Judy got an excited look on her face. "You've never seen it this high, right? So if this experimental dump lasts for a few days, does that mean we're going to have the best white water you have ever done Keller?"

All eyes were on Keller.

"Yeah, I guess so. This is higher than I've ever seen it." He shrugged. "It'll definitely make for good whitewater, but right now we need to find a campsite."

David wasn't good at reading Keller, but he didn't need to read minds to see that Keller was nervous.

* * *

4:30 p.m. - Hoover Dam, Boulder, Nevada

Back inside the visitor center, Grant, Fred, and Shauna sat over by the large windows looking over the canyon. They could hear the governor talking on his cell phone. Shauna stood, and asked Fred where the restrooms were. He motioned down the hall. Fred and Grant waited in silence for a moment before Grant spoke.

"What's going on at Davis and Parker Dams?"

Fred looked nervous. "Not enough. I told them what you told me, to open everything, but they wouldn't hear it. They wanted more time."

Grant looked pleadingly at Fred. "Look, I've never been to Davis, so I'm not too familiar with it. What's the flow capacity of its spillways?"

Fred looked at his watch, as it if the answer were inscribed on it, then looked back up "I'm not exactly sure, but I think Davis can handle around the same as Hoover, 75,000 cubic feet per second through the water works and another 400,000 through the spillways."

Grant furrowed his brows. "That's not enough." He hesitated for a moment. "It won't be able to keep up. It needs to be more than Hoover. When water starts going over the top of Hoover, Davis won't be able to dump fast enough. Lake Mojave's water level is going to rise like crazy."

Fred held out his hands. "What can we do about that?"

"Well there's going to be some flooding on the banks. The water will definitely go over the dam. We'll just have to hope she holds."

Fred got a terrified look on his face. He spoke so softly that Grant barely understood. "Davis is a landfill."

"What?" That didn't jive with what Grant remembered. "I've never been there, but I've seen pictures of the structure. I thought —"

Fred shook his head. "It's definitely a landfill. The water works are concrete, and so are the spillways, but the levy creating the dam is rock and dirt. It definitely can't be breached. Overtopping would break it in five minutes. It'd drain Lake Mojave."

Grant remembered an aerial picture, taken at night, of Davis Dam and the Casinos downstream. The concrete waterworks were off to the side of the earth dam. "Damn! What about Parker downstream, it's definitely concrete, right?" Grant remembered Parker Dam. Parker was a semi-circle shaped concrete arch dam wedged into a tight canyon.

Fred nodded. "Parker is concrete, not a landfill."

"That's good, but it probably doesn't matter. It wouldn't hold if Davis busted upstream, and Lake Mojave drained into Lake Havasu. Would it?"

Fred rubbed his eyes. "Lake Mojave is almost three times bigger than Lake Havasu. The flood would definitely bust Parker."

Grant sat back in the chair and looked up at the ceiling. According to simple math, Davis Dam could not keep up with the water coming out of Hoover, even if only a foot of water went over the top of Hoover Dam. The water flow would overwhelm the output capacity of Davis Dam. He slowly looked up at Fred and held out his hands. "We can't save Davis, can we?"

Fred shook his head. He had obviously come to the same conclusion.

Grant slouched back into his chair. "How big is Lake Mojave?" Grant's voice was lifeless.

"Just over a half a trillion gallons. A little over five percent the size of Lake Mead."

"And Lake Havasu is only a third of that?"

Fred answered without hesitation. "Yeah, only a couple hundred billion gallons."

Grant thought it over. "Well according to the report from the Bureau, the water probably won't breach Hoover until tomorrow morning. Figure a couple more hours after that before Lake Mojave rises high enough to bust Davis. I'd say by noon tomorrow, we're looking at the second biggest flood in North America since the ice age."

Fred stared at Grant with a confused look. "What's the biggest?"

Grant pointed out at Lake Mead. "The one that's already headed our way from Glen Canyon."

Fred's eyes glazed over. "Oh yeah. I forgot about that one."

Grant sat up. "Hang on." He stood and looked downstream as if he could see all the way to Davis Dam. "If Davis is going to collapse anyway, why don't we turn it loose early, before the water gets down here?"

Fred wasn't following. "What do you mean?"

"We could get a couple bulldozers up on the dike and dig a little trench. All we'd have to do is get it started. The water would finish it"

Fred caught up. "You mean bust Davis ourselves? Break open the dam? What good will that do?"

"It'll spread out the damage a little. The water we let go, will be a lot less than Lake Mojave tomorrow at noon when it's ready to overflow."

Fred waved his hands back and forth. "I don't see what difference it'll make. It's still going to flood all the houses in Laughlin and Bullhead City, and bust through Parker Dam. Plus it'll leave even less time to evacuate the area."

Grant couldn't deny Fred's logic. "Is there anyway to drain Havasu at the same time? I wonder if we can blow Parker Dam and drain some of the water out of Havasu before we bust Davis?"

Fred didn't respond. He looked around as if he was afraid somebody else was listening.

Grant got back to basics. "Look, let's go get the governor and at least get him to make the calls to get Davis and Parker to open the gates."

Fred held his hands out in front of him. "You're not going to say anything about busting the other two dams yet are you?"

Grant shook his head. "No, we'll wait to bring that up until after we get the gates open."

Fred stood and they both went to find the governor.

* * *

4:55 p.m. - Lake Powell, Utah

Julie stopped to wait. Paul set down his armload of blankets on a clean rock. Erika sat down on a muddy rock, too tired to worry about getting dirty. Erika had been limping slightly and she showed Julie what was going to be an awful bruise on her hip from her leap from the houseboat. They waited for Max and Darlene. Darlene was traveling very slowly and was holding the group up.

Julie guessed they had started hiking down from the remains of the houseboat more than a half hour before. Julie's ankles and feet were aching even with the tennis shoes. She was also thirsty, and hungry. She realized now, that they should have searched through the remains of the houseboat for some food. Too bad she had not thought of that until it was too late.

As soon as Darlene and Max reached them, Paul started walking again. "Let's keep moving."

Julie helped Erika up. She had mud on her legs from the rock. As they walked Julie thought about brushing it off, but decided to ignore it. She was too tired to care and felt sure that Erika felt the same. Darlene and Max followed behind.

After they walked for a few minutes, Paul stopped and turned around, facing the girls. "Is this the section where Greg dropped us off?"

Julie looked around. "I don't think so. It looks completely different."

Erika nodded. "Yeah, it is. It just looks different because all this was underwater." She pointed at some rocks. "See, that's the ridge over there we walked along after we got out of the boat."

Julie stared for a moment before her eyes confirmed it. "Wow. Good thing we didn't leave the boat here like I wanted to, huh?" She managed a small smile. There were only a couple pools left with trapped water, none very large. The pool she and Erika had swum through was empty.

"The water is dropping that fast?" Max asked. "You guys were just here a while ago weren't you?"

Darlene stared at her husband. "Well, that's about how fast the water dropped while you were asleep."

Paul started off again. "We should be close, let's keep moving." The others followed.

Around the next bend was the section where Greg had swerved and both girls were thrown out of their seats. The water had drained this section too. Julie wondered if Mars would look similar. She had seen pictures of Mars and its rocks. The orange rocky landscape seemed exactly the same.

When they passed the boulder, they could see around the next bend. Although most of this section had also drained, a hundred feet away was the receding shore of the lake. Julie looked back and guessed in total the water had dropped twenty-five feet since they had left Greg. The sight of water ahead gave all five hikers a boost of energy and they picked up the pace. When Paul reached the water, he walked around it along the left shore. The canyon continued for another hundred feet before the next bend.

"Where is he?" Erika asked.

Paul cupped his hands. "GREG."

They listened, hoping he was just around the corner. No answer.

They continued hiking until they reached the bend. Vertical cliffs down to the water prevented them from avoiding getting wet.

"I'll swim around this bend and see if I can see him." Paul said.

"Crap." Erika sat down on another muddy rock. "I thought he'd be down here."

"He's probably just around the corner a little bit," Julie said, although she felt as disappointed as Erika.

Darlene sat down on a rock. By this time Paul had waded into the water. He waded out until the water was up to his chest then put his head in the water and started swimming. The bend wasn't too far and Paul reached it in a few minutes. He stopped for a second, treading water. He turned and started swimming back. He walked up the bank and ran his hand back through his hair. He motioned at the expanse of water they had just walked around. "This is just a hole." His voice came out winded from the swim. "The water has drained on the other side. We'll have to swim through, then hike again for a while."

"What?" Julie said. "This is just a pond?"

"Yeah. I saw more wet rocks around the bend.

Julie wanted to complain, but she knew it wouldn't help. Darlene groaned.

Paul started rolling the blankets tight like a sleeping bag. Julie realized they would need to swim while holding their possessions over their heads to keep them dry. She motioned to Erika that they should get ready too.

She spread out two shirts and rolled everything else into them. Julie tied her car keys to the strings on her swimsuit.

Paul tried to keep the group focused. "Are you ready?" He held the roll of blankets over his head and waded into the water.

The others followed. By the time Julie got to the other side, the muscles in her arms were burning from holding the clothes above her head while swimming. Paul came down and took the clothes from her, and helped her up.

"Thanks," she said.

He helped Erika and Max, then Max held Darlene's hand as she climbed out. They were off again. Paul picked up the pace slightly which Julie didn't mind. She felt anxious to find Greg again. They had been gone a long time. She hoped nothing else had gone wrong. The thought of him not being there when they arrived kept popping back into her head. She tried to push it out, knowing that he would be waiting, but she kept picturing an image of him screaming as the Mastercraft floated over the Glen Canyon Dam. In the image, she was looking over the edge of the dam and the boat kept falling and falling until she lost sight of Greg in the mist of the waterfall.

Paul had put a little bit of distance between himself and the group. He turned and yelled for the others. "We made it. I see him."

The tired feeling seemed to subside as Julie covered the distance. As she rounded the next bend in the river, she saw a pool of water that this time seemed to go on forever. Greg was floating about a hundred feet from the edge. He apparently hadn't seen them yet.

"GREG, WE MADE IT."

His head cocked and he smiled. "About time." He fired up the boat and idled it over to where all five hikers were now standing. "I was beginning to wonder if you guys were ever coming back."

Julie saw Greg look them over, especially Erika and Darlene. Erika was starting to look like a ghost. She didn't have any color in her face except for the red dirt and dried blood. Her eyes were lifeless. Darlene was breathing heavy. Julie looked down at herself and decided she didn't look very good either. She had the red dirt on her legs and swimsuit. Paul, on the other hand, looked fine.

"What happened to Erika?" Greg asked.

While Max handed bundles of clothes and blankets to Greg in the boat, Julie gave a brief description of the events at the houseboat including Erika's last second jump to safety. Erika didn't peep for the whole conversation. Max then gave a short explanation of his and Darlene's aborted kayak trip. When finished, Julie reached up to climb in the boat. Greg raised his eyebrows, and told her to rinse off first, a testament to how dirty she was. The other four followed Julie's example, cleaning and refreshing themselves in the water, before climbing in the boat.

A few moments later they were under way. The padded seats and the breeze felt wonderful. Julie took a long swig from the water jug and passed it back to the others. She had a clear view back at Erika. She was falling asleep, the poor girl.

* * *

5:00 p.m. - Grand Canyon, Arizona

"Right side paddle. Left side paddle. COME ON. Becky, don't give up."

David was exhausted. "We're trying Keller."

"One last burst. NOW. Paddle. Right side. Left."

The current moved them quickly along a rocky shore toward a sandy canyon inlet just up ahead. They needed to be in perfect position or they would miss it, and they were going too fast. Keller had tried to maneuver the raft so they could land in the big campground. But the current was pulling them away from the beach, out into the river.

Becky started to cry, "We're not going to make it."

Keller stood. "WE ARE GOING TO MAKE IT! Come on folks. Give me all you got. NOW!"

All six rafters dug in with the paddles and pulled as fast as they could. David's arms were burning. If anything, the raft seemed to be a few feet farther from the shore. The beach swept by at an alarming speed. Then the beach was gone, replaced by rocks.

"Damn it!" Keller sat down. "Okay, right side paddle a little and let's get away from these rocks."

The rafters gasped for breath. Becky sobbed in slow convulsions. Sam put his hand on her shoulder.

The beach was the raft's second failed attempt at a campground in the last fifteen minutes. Keller kept commenting that the speed of the water was increasing dramatically as it rose. David didn't think the group needed Keller to keep reminding them. It was obvious. It made timing the landings much more difficult. Three other campgrounds Keller wanted to stop at had been completely underwater when they passed. David was beginning to wonder if they would be able to land the raft at all.

Afram swiveled and looked at Keller. "How far's the next one?"

Keller looked around, rubbing his forehead. "Forster Canyon is the next big one, but it's on the other side of the river." He stood up in the raft and looked across. "But it's only about a half a mile. We'll never make it in time." Keller sat down as the raft slid through a rapid splashing the left side of the boat.

"What about past Forster?" Afram asked.

"There's a couple small ones around the bend, but I bet they're under water too."

Becky turned around still sobbing. "Well what're . . . we . . . gonna do?"

"There's a small canyon about a mile down on our right. It's too rocky to make a good campsite, but maybe we can land there and find some shelter in the canyon until the water subsides a little."

"Can we rest for a minute?" David asked.

"Yeah. Good idea. Everybody rest," Keller said.

* * *

5:15 p.m. - Hoover Dam, Nevada

After an hour of phone calls, conference calls, explanations, arguments, persuasion, and coercion, the gates were finally opening at Davis and Parker Dams. The decisions would not have been made without Rally Jenkins, the governor of Nevada. His clout made the difference, especially when the governors of Arizona and California got involved. With a break in the action, Fred motioned for Grant to follow him.

"How long since you ate anything?"

Grant looked at his watch. "Not since I got here."

"I thought so. I sent one of my guys out to get us some sandwiches. Let's take a little walk and clear our minds a bit."

Fred led him up the stairs and out the glass doors into the hot, dry Nevada air. Grant shielded his eyes from the sun until they adjusted. The stifling air immediately sapped the energy from his body.

Fred started walking away from the visitor center, out onto Hoover Dam. Grant followed. Fred walked on the sidewalk, even though the road was closed. As they walked, Grant looked down the downstream side of the dam to the river below. Fred stopped in a five by five foot viewpoint jutting out from the top of the dam. He leaned over the rail, which was actually an eighteen-inch thick concrete wall, and looked straight down the face of the dam.

"I wanted to get you out here before you talked to the governor about your idea of intentionally breaching Davis Dam."

Grant put his head down and kicked at a candy wrapper on the ground. "Yeah, I can only imagine how he'll react to that."

"Are you absolutely sure that it's going to fail?"

"Of course, based on the report from the –"

"How do you know the report is right? Didn't they make lots of assumptions when they put it together?"

Grant looked up. "Fred, the computer modeling is all we've got. The engineers spent months putting the report together. Even if it's not perfectly accurate, it's predictions could be worse just as easy as they could be better. Besides, the report is based on facts, numbers, and calculations. You want us to make decisions on feelings instead?"

They were both silent for a moment. Then Fred continued. "You said that the water is thirty feet lower in Lake Mead than the report assumed. Plus, blowing the two spillways should drop it another three feet." Fred turned and looked across the crest of the dam. "So what's your guess as to how much water's going to go over the top?"

Grant looked across the dam too, as if the answer was painted on the cliffs on the other side. "We have a couple other things going for us. The study assumed that both Lake Mead and Lake Powell would be full, as a worst case. Lake Powell is lower than normal due to this drought. With both lakes lower, it'll make a big difference. That's what I've got Shauna doing. She's trying to adjust the numbers based on the lower levels. My guess is that when it's all said and done, ten to fifteen feet of water is going to go over this dam, but twenty is not out of the question."

"Well that's better than the seventy you told the governor."

"Yeah, but even if it were only five feet, it would still take out Davis and Parker Dams. I don't see anyway possible to prevent it."

Fred looked over the face of the dam again, seemingly mesmerized. He looked depressed. When he finally raised his head, his face seemed lifeless. "So what you're saying is that seventy years ago, five thousand men spent five years building this dam seven hundred and twenty six feet high, and it needed to be fifteen feet higher."

The reality of Fred's observation hit Grant in the gut. His heart skipped two beats. He looked across the dam, then ran out into the middle of US-93 to get a better look. He looked right down the yellow line across the dam. He mentally calculated the distance between the handrails on both sides.

"That's it Fred!" He looked at his watch. "You're a genius."

"What is it?" Fred joined him in the middle of the street. "What did I say?"

Grant turned and started running back toward the visitor center with Fred right behind. He called over his shoulder. "We'll make the dam twenty feet higher! Let's go talk to the governor."

CHAPTER 19

5:30 p.m. - Lake Powell, Utah

Julie couldn't help but marvel at the height of the watermarks on the rock walls. She guessed the water levels had dropped over seventy feet. The crowd of boats heading south had grown too. There were literally hundreds of boats, and they could be divided into two groups, the sane, and the insane. The sane meandered down the center of the channel at a steady pace; this group included many houseboats. The second group, the insane, swerved back and forth recklessly in between and around the others; this group included the faster crafts including smaller water-ski boats and all types of personal water craft. When Greg merged the Mastercraft in with the other boats, part of Julie was glad that he chose the steady pace of the sane, but a small part of her understood the other group, and wanted him to gas it.

At one point, the canyon had narrowed at a bend in the river, forcing every-one to slow, including the insane. Boats funneled together, bumper-to-bumper, through the tight turn caused by the much lower river. Paul had moved to the bow, and with his feet, kept the boat from banging into the boats in front of them. After the delay, and the river widened again, the boats were able to accelerate back to speed.

They had continued that way for a while, when Greg slowed the Mastercraft again. Julie stood and looked at what must be five hundred boats crammed together, all of them snaking around a huge red rock butte directly in front of them. The butte, which appeared as if someone had placed it right in the middle of the channel to block traffic, was vaguely familiar, yet something looked out of place.

"Where are we?" Julie asked.

Greg pointed at the rock. "That's Gregory Butte. And over on the right is Last Chance Bay."

Julie looked around. "Wait. I thought Gregory . . ."

Greg pointed to the left of the huge rock structure. "Normally, we pass through over there. All that . . ." He motioned across a rock plateau from Gregory to the left shore. ". . . is usually underwater."

Julie saw that the exposed rock left of Gregory Butte was dark and wet, something she should have noticed before. She tried to imagine what the area would look like if it were still underwater. She decided that if the water level had been higher, she might have recognized the butte, if not by name, at least by sight.

As the Mastercraft fell in line with the other boats, they again drifted almost to a complete stop. Paul flipped the boat's bumpers over the side and climbed back on the bow. A boat nudged the Mastercraft gently from behind.

Exhaust from so many boats in close proximity made it hard to breathe. Since the line wasn't moving at all, Greg shut off the engine. Many of the other boats followed. Within minutes of stopping, other boats filled in behind them until Julie could barely see water. Although they drifted slowly downstream, Julie was sure walking would have been faster.

They heard a radio squawk in an old red boat that had pulled up next to them. Julie and Greg's boat did not have a radio. There had been one in the houseboat, but they never used it because it did not work when they were in the canyons.

Greg motioned to a bearded man in the red boat. "What's happening on the radio?"

The bearded man with tattoos on both arms took a swig from a can of Coors. By the glazed look in his eyes, it wasn't his first. A woman stood up next to him, and although she didn't have a beer in her hand, she had the same lazy look in her eyes as the bearded man.

The man motioned downstream. "The Castle Rock Pass is officially closed. The water's already too low to get through to Wahweap".

Julie didn't like the sound of what she heard. Wahweap was the largest of the three primary marinas, and the only one on the south end of the lake for fifty miles. It was where the Crawford's car and boat trailer was parked.

"What does that mean?" Julie asked her husband.

"Well, it's bad, but we knew that would happen. It means if we want to go back to Wahweap, we have to go all the way around Antelope Island, right past the dam," He grimaced. "what's left of it."

Julie shivered at the thought. Wahweap Marina was not built on the edge of the river, but on a large bay named Wahweap Bay that branched off of the river. To travel up lake from Wahweap, boaters avoided the main channel, instead taking a shortcut through a shallow gap next to Castle Rock Butte into Warm Creek Bay. Whenever the water in Lake Powell dropped low enough, Castle Rock became impassable, and everyone was forced to go the long way, an additional twenty miles down the windy main river channel, around Antelope Island, and then back into Wahweap Bay. The entrance to Wahweap Bay was only a mile from the Glen Canyon Dam.

Greg had told her that in the early days, while the lake was still filling, the only possible route was the long way around Antelope. But after the lake filled and flooded between the two bays, a shortcut was born, and Antelope Peninsula became Antelope Island, and all traffic immediately diverted, leaving the main river channel and the backside of Antelope largely unused. Exceptions occurred in the late summers of dry years, when the water dropped low enough to force everyone around again. In these years, the park service sometimes dredged Castle Rock Channel to delay the inevitable detour as long as possible.

Although Julie was concerned about the time that would be lost on the detour, the danger of passing so close to the dam was her main concern.

She questioned her husband. "Won't that be dangerous? Aren't you afraid we'll get sucked over the dam if we get that close?"

Greg nodded. "Yeah, sure." He turned back to the bearded guy. "How fast is the water moving down there, aren't they afraid some of these boats are going to go over the dam?"

The man motioned with his beer can. "Well, first of all, the rangers ain't sayin nothin on the radio. I'm getting my info from other boaters. But yeah, for a while they were making all the houseboats divert into Warm Springs Bay. Course nobody wanted to just wait in the bay till they got grounded, so it sounds like they stormed the ranger boats or something, cause now the rangers aren't tryin to stop em no more."

Paul stood up on the bow. "Did you hear whether any boats went over the dam?"

He shrugged. "Nah, I ain't heard of any. Course I imagine that they wouldn't be talkin on the radio much if they was getting sucked over the dam." The guy chuckled at his own humor.

Greg seemed perplexed. "So you say that for all practical purposes, the radio is silent from the rangers?"

The bearded man motioned with his beer again, causing some to spill out. "This morning, they was all over the radio, telling folks the dam broke, but to stay put, ya know, not rush back to the marinas. But every time they said to stay put, about a million people would try to talk to 'em at once. You couldn't understand nothin. Everybody wanted to know when they'd get rescued and everything. Finally, I bet most started worryin how they was going to get their boats up seven hundred feet up sheer rock onto their trailers to go home. They figured the rangers didn't have a plan for that yet. And they was right. You sit around too long and your boat is gonna be high and dry. Then if ya ever get out alive, you're gonna hafta hike fifty miles back to visit your boat next year. Cause if you don't move it now, it'll be there forever, and the Indians'll be painting teepees and deer on the side of it."

Julie grimaced at the comment.

He continued and motioned around at the mass of boats with his beer can. "Just like me, all these people said to hell with the rangers. If ya want to get out a this bathtub before it drains, ya gotta get out now, while the gettin's good."

Julie noticed that while he had been talking, his red boat had been creeping forward in relation to the Mastercraft, and another boat was sliding forward to replace it. Ironically, Julie had a knack for always picking the wrong line at the grocery store, the bank, or even on the freeway, but why did it have to happen here? At this rate, it could take over an hour to get around the bend, and then how many more bends would there be beyond this one?

Somebody from another boat asked the bearded man a question that Julie couldn't hear and he walked to the other side of his boat to answer. Julie glanced back at the people in the boat that replaced him. The guy driving the new boat tipped a blue hat stenciled with the letters 'BYU.'

"Where you guys from?" he asked.

Greg pointed at Paul. "They're from Southern California." He pointed at himself and Julie. "And we're from Phoenix." He pointed to Max and Darlene. "And they're from Las Vegas. How about you?"

The man didn't have to answer for Julie to know they were from Utah. The friendly looking guy's t-shirt was also stenciled with 'BYU.' A very petite wife, who's skin looked so white and pasty that it was obvious she never got out in the sun, sat in the other front seat, and five kids, including a couple of teenagers, were sitting on a pile of bags and suitcases stacked in the back of the boat. The teenagers were unusually clean-cut with no goofy hair, tattoos, or piercings.

The man pointed north. "We're from Provo, just south of Salt Lake. We come down here every year for a week. At least we used too. Doesn't sound like we'll be back next year."

"You guys have a houseboat?" Paul asked.

"Had one. It's grounded upstream in one of the canyons. We came back from water-skiing and found it sitting on some rocks. We tried to pull it back in the water with the boat and a water ski rope. All we accomplished was to break the rope. How about you guys?"

Greg explained. "We were headed back from Hole in the Rock this morning, when we figured out something was wrong. We had to get gas at Dangling Rope, and then we had to hike a couple miles up the canyon to find our houseboat. We were trying to get some stuff out of it when it slid down the hill and broke to pieces. We're a little bit worried about the deposit."

"Thank heavens for insurance." The man grinned.

Julie wondered if the Utah man was an insurance salesman.

Paul continued. "We just hope it's covered. This is one sequence of events we didn't count on when we signed the waiver."

As they talked to the Utah man, she noticed that they were drifting ahead of him. Maybe they picked the right line after all.

* * *

5:45 p.m. - Grand Canyon, Arizona

David and Afram were positioned on the front of the raft. Both had coils of rope in their hands.

"Get Ready!" said Keller.

Since they had been unsuccessful at beaching the raft, the plan was for David and Afram to try to jump onto the beach and pull the boat in by the ropes. It had been Afram's idea. Keller had initially resisted, but had finally caved when they missed two more potential landing spots.

"Right side paddle. Left side paddle," Keller yelled, as he tried to position the raft close enough to the shore for them to jump.

"We're down two paddlers," Sam complained. "and our arms are dead."

David looked back at Sam. It was unusual to hear him complain, but his face looked pale and sweat ran down his forehead. Becky looked even worse.

"Get ready." Keller said. "Paddle! Come on."

David could see the transition from rocks to sand up ahead. It looked like they might be close enough this time. He adjusted the rope in his hands and re-checked the bottom fastener on his life jacket, just in case.

"Okay, everybody paddle hard. Let's get em as close as possible," Keller encouraged.

David watched the sand approach, faster than he wanted.

"Ready . . ." Keller called out. "Set . . ."

David put his foot up on the edge of the rubber boat, ready to jump.

"GO!"

David thought he was ready, but Afram jumped an instant before, which jostled the boat just enough to make David's foot slip on the slick rubber. The result was a pitiful head first plunge off the front of the raft which immediately ran over him. The cold water shocked him, and he resisted the impulse to gasp for air. When he popped up, he was under the raft and rammed his head into the bottom. However, while he was under the raft his feet found sand. It was shallow. He let the boat pass over him and he tried to stand, but the current was too strong. He pushed toward shore with his feet. He saw that Afram was up on the shore now, trying to pull the rope. Everyone in the raft was looking at Afram.

David pushed toward shore until he could stand. Then he quickly ran through the shallow water up onto the beach.

"Pull, David. Help him." It was Keller's voice.

David pulled as hard as he could, but he realized immediately that he and Afram would never be able to pull the boat against the strong current. It was pulling both of them at a fast walk toward the rocks at the other end of the beach.

"Dig in when I tell you." Afram said over his shoulder.

David leaned back even more and prepared to dig in.

"Now!" Afram said.

David dug in his heels and saw Afram do the same, but they were both pulled vertical immediately. David saw large rocks ahead and knew that the whole effort had been in vain. He wondered how he and Afram would get back in the boat. Then while looking at the rocks he saw something. He stopped pulling, letting his rope go slack.

"Hey, what are you –"

David crossed under Afram's rope and ran toward the rocks. "Come on," he said.

Afram figured out what he was doing and followed.

When David reached the rocks, he wrapped the rope around a large rock twice. Afram did the same on another rock. Not a second later both ropes were pulled tight, but they held. In the water, the raft stopped with a jerk and slid quickly over against the rocks. The others in the group yelled their approval and climbed out of the raft onto the rocks. A moment later Keller and Sam reached them. Together the four men were able to pull the now empty raft back upstream and onto the sandy beach. David collapsed on his back in the sand.

"You kinda did that the hard way, didn't you?" Judy smiled at him from above. "That whole under the boat thing was planned, right?"

David laughed. "At least we made it, and we're safe."

Not if the water gets any higher." Keller said. He pointed at the beach where they had just landed. They all looked. If the water rose another twenty feet, the sand would be underwater, and then they would be floating in a small canyon with vertical rock walls on all sides.

* * *

5:50 p.m. - Hoover Dam, Arizona

"You want to do what?" The governor put his hands on his hips.

"We want to extend the height of the dam another twenty feet." Grant pointed out at the concrete dam.

"What good is that gonna do?"

Grant tried to choose his words carefully. "Governor, we're in a dry year. Luckily both Lake Mead and Lake Powell are lower than usual. The Bureau's study in 1998 assumed both lakes would be full, as a worst case. We've run some new numbers based on the newly opened spillways and the extra capacity available in Lake Mead. If we're right, only about ten or fifteen feet of water will end up going over the top of Hoover."

The governor's eyebrows furrowed as he tried to understand the reasoning. "That's good, isn't it?"

"Yeah. It means that the overtopping won't be as bad as I originally told you."

"Then why do we need to do anything?"

Grant started ticking off his fingers. "Two reasons, governor. First, even ten feet going over Hoover could still break it apart. Second, even ten feet would definitely take out Davis Dam downstream, and Parker too."

The governor's face lost some color and he wiped his hand across his forehead. "If the water breaks though Davis Dam, Lake Mojave's going to drain out and flood Laughlin?" He didn't wait for an answer. "Hell, most of the casinos are below the lake. It'd wipe em out. Laughlin would be obliterated."

Grant knew Laughlin's casinos were going to be destroyed either way with all the water that would be going downstream, whether or not Davis Dam failed. But, he didn't want the governor to worry about that yet. "Exactly, governor."

"That's billions of dollars." He looked at Grant and his voice changed from bewildered to harsh. "What makes you think Davis's gonna break? How can you be sure?"

"It's a landfill dam, governor. It can't withstand overtopping."

The governor looked as if his home had just fallen into the ocean. "So what are you guys suggesting?"

Grant jumped back into the conversation. "We think if we can build up the top of Hoover Dam by another twenty feet, we can hold the flood water in Mead. And save Davis and Parker." The tone came out almost pleading.

The governor looked confused. "Is there enough time? The concrete wouldn't even have time to set."

"We're not going to build it with concrete. We're going to build a landfill dike on top of Hoover."

Fred looked at Grant with a questioning expression. "Landfill, do we have enough space?"

Grant grabbed a piece of paper off the table and turned it over so he had a blank sheet. He drew a cross section of a dike. When he graduated in civil engineering and joined the Bureau over fifteen years ago, he'd had high hopes of designing huge engineering marvels like Hoover and Glen Canyon Dams. Finally he would build his first dam. With the governor and Fred looking over his shoulders, he estimated that he would have at least thirty seconds to perfect his design. "Okay. The standard formula for a land fill dam is a three to one ratio of substrate to the height of water you want to contain."

"So to hold ten feet of water it needs to be thirty feet wide?" The governor pointed at Grant's picture.

Grant smiled. "Kind of. I'd like a little bit of a safety margin. In case the water is over ten feet."

Fred nodded. "The dam is about forty feet wide at the top."

"Then let's use it all. We can build it twenty feet high and forty feet wide. Then we'd be able to contain almost fifteen feet of water. If it gets any higher than that, we'll be in trouble." Grant looked up for approval.

All three men looked at each other, waiting to see if there were any arguments.

The governor looked at his watch. "Is there enough time? It's already 6:00."

Grant's stomach felt like something was boiling inside. They expected the water to rise above the top of Hoover early the next morning. According to Shauna's latest calculations, they had roughly twelve hours to build the dike. "There's only one way to find out."

CHAPTER 20

6:15 p.m. - Hoover Dam, Boulder, Nevada

It'd taken only fifteen minutes to persuade the governor, although Governor Jenkins still didn't think they could build it fast enough. In the end he had convinced himself that even if they didn't finish building up the dam in time, whatever they did finish would delay the floods downstream. Grant, Shauna, and Fred stood in the hallway of the visitor center and plotted how to accomplish their task.

Shauna shook her head. "It won't work."

"It has to," Grant said.

"But Grant, when you build a land fill dike, you have to build it slowly, and wet it, and you have to use non-permeable soil. If we rush it, it'll leak."

Grant knew she was right. They couldn't just throw it together, even if they compressed it with bulldozers. If the soil allowed water to seep through, it would wash out. He wondered if they would find the right kind of soil around Las Vegas, where as far as he knew, everything was sand. And everyone knows you can't build a dam with sand.

Grant held out his hands. "How do they build those dikes around the Mississippi River when it floods? It seems like they're always trying to protect some town from getting flooded by the river. Don't they need to be built fast?" He felt helpless. He had convinced the governor, but now he wasn't convinced himself.

"Seems like all the ones I see on the rivers in the Midwest are built out of sand bags," Fred said.

Grant and Shauna both looked up at him. Sandbags? It just might work. Heaven knew there was certainly plenty of sand around Las Vegas. Besides, building a dam out of sand bags would be faster since the layers would not need to be meticulously compressed with heavy equipment. The more he thought about it the more excited he became. A sandbag dike might even hold up if it were overtopped by a foot or two. It could even hold water while it was being built. The question was, where would they get enough bags, and the labor to fill them?

* * *

6:20 p.m. - Lake Powell, Arizona

Julie guessed they had been in the traffic jam at Gregory Butte for almost an hour. They were almost out. The narrowest point had only enough room for ten boats to go through the turn at a time. Unfortunately, about 50 lines were merging into the small space. And after living in California, Julie knew what happened during rush hour when cars needed to merge. Boats were even worse. It was like a herd of sheep trying to get through an open gate. Julie was glad the bumpers were out because the Mastercraft had been bumping other boats for an hour. Finally they were only a few boats away. Greg let the boat on his left go past.

"We're next," Greg said. "Everybody sit down."

Paul climbed down off the bow and started pulling in the bumper pads from both sides. As the boat on their right pulled out, Greg pulled in behind it. They idled slowly at first around the bend with the boat almost touching on both sides. As the canyon turned straight again, it widened. As a result, the boats were able to spread out and speed up. Greg gave the boat some throttle.

Julie had been on many crowded lakes before, but nothing compared to this. There were probably between 15 and 20 rows of boats, all going as fast as possible. Greg tried to stay in the wake behind the boat in front of him, but many others were swerving back and forth passing each other. That many boats, traveling that fast, made for rough water. Julie saw Darlene and Max hanging on tight as the boat jarred up and down, sometimes with loud banging noises. Personal watercraft darted between the boats. It reminded her of the motorcyclists in southern California that dart between the cars on the freeways. Even though it was perfectly legal in California, she was always afraid one would go down in front of her and she would run over it.

Julie felt Greg swerve hard right and looked up in time to see a stalled boat in front of them. A family with kids was standing up waving their arms to be seen. She guessed Greg had missed the boat by less than ten feet. The family would be lucky if they lasted another five minutes before they got hit. When Julie looked back, the stranded boat had disappeared, lost in the chaos behind them. Julie offered a silent prayer for the small family.

* * *

6:30 p.m. - Grand Canyon, Arizona

David looked around. The sandy beach where they had landed was now completely underwater. David and Keller were standing in waist-high water while holding the raft. Everyone else had already climbed in, not because they wanted to go anywhere in the rubber boat, but because they couldn't stand the cold water. David could feel the cold swirling around his thighs and felt it sapping the heat out of his body. He sensed his teeth were close to chattering.

For the last few moments he had been thinking about the final scenes of the movie Titanic, when thousands of passengers froze to death in only a few minutes in the icy water. How ironic was it that this could happen in hundred-degree desert air? Although David could see no ice floating in this water, he knew most of it came from the bottom of the Glen Canyon Dam, and was probably in the forties. He wouldn't freeze to death as fast as the victims on the Titanic, but he would die of hypothermia just the same if he stayed in the water long enough. As he felt the water creep up around his waist, he wondered how long he could last. 45 minutes? An hour?

Afram peered down at him. "You want to switch?"

David shook his head. "Wait 'til my teeth start chattering."

Afram nodded, but nobody laughed at David's attempt at humor, not even David.

"We're not going to be able to do this much longer anyway," Sam pointed out. "The water'll be too high in a few minutes."

Judy pointed toward the main channel of the river. It was running even swifter than before, and new rapids had emerged where the river had been smooth. "Well, we can't go out there, either."

Becky sobbed, "Why is the water doing this?" Sam put his arm around her.

David agreed. "They should have warned us if they were going to let this much water out of the dam."

When Keller spoke his teeth chattered. "I don't think this is a controlled release."

"What do you mean?" Judy asked.

Keller continued, "The water must be 50 feet above normal, and we are more than a hundred miles downstream. Opening a few head gates wouldn't have done that."

"Then what could it be?" Afram asked.

Keller looked reluctant to speak, and his teeth continued to chatter. "I wonder if the dam broke."

"What?" David heard himself say.

Everybody talked at once and no one could understand.

Finally, Afram spoke. "If the Glen Canyon Dam failed, then we haven't seen the worst yet. The water will get a lot deeper, won't it?" The question seemed to be aimed at Keller.

Keller nodded. "Keep looking for handholds, or places we can climb. If the dam really broke we'll need to climb out of here."

The group craned their necks upward looking for anything.

Afram pointed about twenty feet above. "If we could just get up there. It looks like we might be able to hike a little from that ledge."

Sam stood up in the raft. "Yeah, I think he's right."

David and Keller, with their backs against the rocks, could not see where the others were looking.

"Unfortunately, these two can't hold the boat while it rises another 20 feet." Judy said angrily.

Afram pointed at something above them. "See that rock outcropping up there? What if I get the rope around it? We could tie up the boat, then everybody could get in."

"Try it," Becky said, wiping tears from her eyes.

David's teeth chattered while he watched Afram make a loop in the end of the rope. Afram secured the loop with a square knot. David was no Eagle Scout, but he felt pretty sure that there was a better knot than a square knot for the situation. Afram must have been thinking the same, because he added a double knot to make sure. Nobody spoke while he coiled the rope, hesitated, then tossed it underhand. David knew Afram had missed without seeing it; he could see it in Judy's face, which contorted before the rope fell back down in the raft. Afram picked it up and tried again. Same result. Sam wanted a turn, and Afram gladly conceded the rope. The water had risen above David's waist, and his teeth were chattering uncontrollably now, but no one noticed. He hoped one of these cowboys learned to lasso quickly, because he didn't think he or Keller would be able to hold the boat much longer.

* * *

6:50 p.m. - Lake Powell, Utah

Julie looked up at the vertical rock walls on both sides of them. After clearing the traffic jam at Gregory Butte, they had been able to go fast for a while before traffic thickened and the water became rougher, forcing Greg to slow again. But the landscape was changing. Just south of Gregory was Padre Bay, the largest open area of water at Lake Powell. Normally, Padre Bay by itself would be a huge lake, but with the water levels so low, most of it had disappeared. The main river channel, normally too far underwater to be visible in the bay, now cut back and forth like a snake. Access to what was left of the bay had been reduced to numerous channels. Most of these channels were impassable, however, since the amount of water draining from Padre into the river was so great. Attempting passage would be like running upstream through rapids.

Greg slowed slightly as they rounded a bend. Up ahead on the left, a waterfall about ten feet high flowed from a side canyon into the main channel. The volume of the waterfall was staggering, and the boats ahead were steering as far to the right as possible to avoid getting sucked under the falls and capsized. Julie cupped her hand over her mouth in horror as she saw a boat upside down next to the falls. She couldn't see anyone in the water, but if they were not wearing life jackets, she wouldn't be able see them, would she? She tried to imagine the Mastercraft being pulled under the falls and taking the brunt of the water. She suddenly knew that the people in the boat were dead.

As they pulled alongside the capsized boat, Greg had to actually accelerate to pull away from the current that pulled them toward the falls. Julie saw what looked like a life jacket bobbing. Her first thought was that somebody was still stuck in there, being bobbed like a toy up and down under the falls. But then she saw the life jacket was empty. She wasn't sure whether it was good or bad. Where were the people?

"Man, that's amazing," Paul said.

Greg nodded. He pointed to the hull of the boat floating upside down. "It looks like it's at least a twenty-footer."

Paul shook his head. "Wonder why they let it get too close."

Greg shrugged. "Maybe they stalled it or something. Without an engine, it would suck you in."

Julie thought of the family they had passed, the one whose boat had stalled in the middle of the channel and Greg had swerved to miss. What would happen to them when they drifted down here? She thought of the little girl clutching her mother. Julie suddenly realized this would not be the last waterfall. All the bays, canyons and side chutes off the river would eventually have to drain into the main channel. Over the next several hours, the Lake Powell channel would become a gauntlet of waterfalls.

CHAPTER 21

7:00 p.m. - Hoover Dam, Boulder, Nevada

Grant looked at his watch. This was taking way too long. After everyone agreed a dike made out of sandbags would work, the calls had gone out all over Las Vegas. They expected trucks to start rolling in any minute, but so far nothing. Based on quick estimates from the construction companies, there were somewhere between 75,000 and a 150,000 bags available in the Las Vegas area, although only a small fraction were already full. The remainder would need to be filled. Even if they were full, Grant knew that wasn't nearly enough. A few more calls located a distributor in Los Angeles and a manufacturer in Salt Lake City. The manufacturer was already closed, but the owner had been located on a cell phone and he was arranging to get enough staff to ship his entire inventory. Between the two companies, Grant figured they could get another million bags. Speed was a big issue, but cargo planes would be used from both locations. Grant went out on a limb and said the Bureau would pay, and Governor Jenkins pulled a few strings to make it happen.

In the meantime, the construction companies didn't think they could possibly fill a million bags before 5:00 a.m., which was the goal Grant gave them. They estimated they would be lucky to fill a tenth of that. The problem had then become how to fill a million bags in the next ten hours, bags that probably wouldn't be in Las Vegas for a few hours.

"Why don't we ask for volunteers?" asked Shauna. "Anybody with a shovel."

Grant shrugged. "Where are we gonna get enough volunteers on this short notice?"

"They're all watching the news. All we'd have to do is make an announcement on the ten o'clock news."

Grant scoffed. "That would be chaos. What are we gonna do, just tell them to bring their shovels and come on down?"

"Why not?" Fred said, moving over next to Shauna. "Everybody's got a shovel, and right now we need all the help we can get."

Grant shook his head and glared at his friend. "You can't be serious, Fred."

"I am serious. Every time those guys in the Midwest get flooded out, it's always the people themselves that are sandbagging to protect their cities. Don't underestimate the people – they care more than you think."

Grant looked at the two of them while they waited for his response. Actually, Shauna's volunteer idea would probably work if they just had more time. He felt bad for snapping at both of them. He wondered how many volunteers they would need to fill a million sand bags. What if each person filled a hundred bags? That would be 10,000 people. But, a hundred bags seemed like too many for one person; maybe 20,000 people would be better. What about loading and carrying? Better double it again. Grant guessed, to be safe, they would need at least 50,000 volunteers.

Grant held out his hands as if to say slow down. "All right, let's think out loud for a second. What if we asked for volunteers and we got 'em? Where do we want them to go? We'd need to have multiple locations; we can't just have them digging on the side of Boulder Highway. And who is gonna supervise them, and distribute the bags? What about light? It's gonna be dark, right? And what about moving the bags when they're full? We're gonna need trucks. We can't have a thousand pickups driving down to the dam to unload their bags. This is a big enough deal that we are going to need somebody to organize it, somebody who can focus specifically on this task."

Shauna and Fred both smiled at Grant. Grant could tell they were both happy he was at least considering it.

"Didn't the governor say the mayor of Las Vegas was here at Hoover?" Fred asked.

"Politicians need to get re-elected," said Shauna. "And politicians are usually great at delegating. The mayor could appoint a bunch of his buddies to head up other groups."

Grant didn't like the way it sounded, but he wondered if there were other types of people who could handle thousands of volunteers better. "What about cops, or firemen? What if we had about 50 cops team up with each group of politicians? Would that be enough supervision for a couple thousand volunteers?"

Fred nodded. "Yeah. That would be good, or even the National Guard. As long as they had uniforms. Then the volunteers would know where to go to ask questions."

"Okay, where do we tell them to go?" Shauna asked.

Grant considered that. He cringed at the thought of 50,000 volunteers scattered along the highway. Their cars would block the road and cause a horrific traffic jam that wouldn't allow the sand bag trucks through to the dam. But where else could they go? The best plan would include numerous locations scattered around the desert. Then they wouldn't conflict with each other; the crowds would be separated and not blocking anything. Unfortunately, Grant didn't know any locations. He wasn't from Las Vegas.

"We'll need some help from the mayor," Grant said. "We'll recommend that he and his staff choose ten or twenty places around Las Vegas with lots of sand and gravel where we can have the volunteers go. We can list the sites on TV. We can have a politician or two head up each spot, with a bunch of police and firemen to support them."

"This could work," Fred said, smiling.

Grant looked at his watch; they were running out of time. "All right, let's go talk to the mayor of Las Vegas. We'll find out what he's made of, see how he handles responsibility."

* * *

7:15 p.m. - Grand Canyon, Arizona

David couldn't believe how far the water had risen in the last hour. Could it be a hundred feet? He thought so. It seemed like ages ago when Afram and Sam were trying to lasso the rock outcropping. Thankfully, they succeeded, but the rope hold had only lasted maybe ten or fifteen minutes before the raft had risen up to the same level of the outcropping. Luckily, by then they found other handholds, and were able to hold the boat without anyone in the cold water. Over the past few minutes the water seemed to be rising a foot or two per minute.

Although the sun was still a few hours from going down, it was already getting dark deep in the Grand Canyon, and David had to look up to see where the setting sun still shown on the east rock faces high above them. Meanwhile the dark water of the Colorado River was making more noise as it rose. David thought he could hear a waterfall somewhere downstream, although that seemed unlikely. Either way, just looking out at the main channel scared him. The water was traveling so fast.

"Look how smooth the water is," David said. "It looks like a lake."

"Except it's moving." Judy motioned with her arm.

Afram pointed to the other side. "David's right. It's perfectly flat and spread out. If I didn't know better, I would think there was a dam just downstream."

Keller spoke. "There is, kind of."

Afram looked perplexed. "What do you mean?"

"Well, Granite Narrows is at mile 135, and we are probably a mile or less from there."

"What is Granite Narrows?" Judy asked.

David knew the answer. He had read about it. "It's where the Grand Canyon squeezes to less than a hundred feet wide. It's by far the narrowest place in the whole canyon."

"76 feet to be exact," Keller said.

"How is that a dam?" Becky asked.

"Think about it," Afram explained. He pointed to the other side. "The river is almost a half mile wide, and yet it all needs to fit through the narrows. It's like a dam."

Becky furrowed her brows. "But wouldn't the water just go faster through the notch?"

Keller nodded. "No question. The water has got to be blasting through the gap. But it would still back up, which is what we are seeing here."

Sam spoke for the first time. "The water level would be lower on the other side. It would be like a waterfall."

David cupped his hand to his ear. "That must be the sound I can hear."

"You know what this means?" Afram asked the group.

"What?" Becky said nervously.

"It means that we're lucky that we found this spot when we did. I don't want to even think about what would happen if we had tried to drift toward Granite Narrows."

David imagined the raft getting sucked through the gap and spit over a hundred-foot waterfall.

The group sat silent for a moment. An explosion echoed through the darkening canyon, making them turn their heads.

"There goes another one," Afram said, craning his head around.

Becky whipped her head around. "Was it upstream or down?" Becky had evolved from jittery to frantic over the last hour. Her voice was now a few notches higher than normal.

The explosive sounds of the rock breaking off and falling in the river was starting to occur every few minutes. Although they couldn't see most of them, one had broken off just across the river about a half hour before in an earsplitting bang that had reverberated off the canyon walls.

"I think that one was way upstream someplace," Keller said reassuringly. "It sounded like it was a long ways away."

"Not to me!" Becky argued, near tears.

Sam put his arm around her, a maneuver that seemed unnatural to David under the circumstances. David would have been more apt to slide away from her while she was being so hostile, and give her some space.

David considered their situation: water rising a hundred feet an hour, getting dark, raft being held by people's hands grasping the cliff in precarious holds, with no place to stand or hike in a rimmed canyon. David wondered again if they were going to make it.

"Heads up," Keller yelled. He grasped the rock for a better hold.

David felt the raft pulling away from the rocks and he renewed his grip. He thought about Granite Narrows downstream and gripped harder. Every now and then the current swirled under their raft and tried to pull it out into the channel and downstream. Sometimes these currents lasted a few seconds, and sometimes a few minutes. David's hands ached. He didn't think he could last much longer. After a while, the current let up and David relaxed his hold slightly. He looked up at the sky. Was there a God? He had always believed it, but now he wondered. If there was a God, would he help? David wasn't sure. But there was one thing for sure – it didn't hurt to ask. Without anyone else seeing what he was doing, David nodded his head slightly, then without making a sound he talked to his God. He thanked him that they were still safe, and then he pleaded with him to spare them through the rest of the night.

* * *

7:40 p.m. - Lake Powell, Utah

Greg pulled back on the throttle in response to a large houseboat cutting in front of them. He veered to the right and passed it.

"Look up ahead." He pointed off to the right.

Castle Rock could be seen miles in the distance. Julie noticed they were passing Padre Point on the left, which signified they were beyond the remains of Padre Bay, and were entering the narrows. The narrows did not look much different from before except now the walls were much higher. The waves in this stretch of the lake had always radiated back and forth between the cliffs, which sometimes capsized smaller boats. But, Julie had never seen it this rough and she held on as the Mastercraft rocked violently.

The narrows, from Padre Point to Antelope Island, was a four-mile straight shot with Antelope Island dead ahead. There were two choices at Antelope Island: the narrows veered left and wound for another 11 miles to the dam, or Warm Creek Bay, which opened to the right. Logically, the only decision would be to turn right into the safety of Warm Creek. As the water dropped, the boat would be stranded, but that was infinitely safer than continuing down the narrows, which would take them within a mile of the Glen Canyon Dam site.

"We need to talk," Greg said.

Julie faced her husband. "About what?"

Greg rotated so the other four passengers could hear him. "What do we do up there?" He motioned in front of the boat.

Julie felt confused. "What are you talking about?"

"Which way are we going? Right or left?" Greg was biting his lip.

Julie couldn't believe it. "I thought it was settled. We're going into Warm Creek." Julie saw nervousness on the two other couples' faces, as if this were her and Greg's argument.

Greg shook his head. "We haven't even talked about it."

Paul spoke up. "Going into Warm Creek would essentially be writing off your boat."

"Couldn't you come back and retrieve it later?" Darlene asked.

Max put his hand over Darlene's. "If the dam is gone, the lake will eventually drop another three or four hundred feet. By then, Warm Creek will be just a muddy wash. It would be basically inaccessible as far as retrieving a boat was concerned."

Darlene eyes bulged as the realization set in.

"I wouldn't abandon this boat if it was mine!" Erika said.

Julie was shocked that they were all talking this way. "So all of you are willing to risk your lives for this boat?"

Greg shook his head. "I never said we all have to go. I could drop the rest of you off at Warm Creek."

Julie pictured Greg leaving the five of them on the rocks someplace and taking the Mastercraft down past the dam by himself. She didn't like that idea any better. She remembered what she had felt like earlier in the day when they had been separated, and she didn't want to be separated again.

Paul leaned forward in his seat. "I'll go with you, Greg."

"Paul, the boat isn't worth you dying over," Greg responded.

Julie pointed her finger at her husband. "Then why are you going?"

Erika spoke directly to Julie. "If Greg thought he was going to die, he wouldn't go."

"I don't think he's thinking that far ahead," Julie responded. "Or we wouldn't be having this conversation."

Max motioned at Greg. "Is Julie right? Have you thought it out?"

Greg chose his words carefully. He glanced at Julie, then pointed to the shore of the narrows. "Look, you can see how fast the water is moving here. It's reasonable to assume that it's traveling about the same down by the dam, or possibly a little faster."

With all the traffic in the channel, Julie hadn't even noticed the strong current carrying them down the narrows. She looked at the rock walls moving past on the shore and realized they were already being pulled toward the Glen Canyon Dam. It scared her.

Greg continued. "But, at full speed, the Mastercraft can do almost 30 knots, which is way more than enough to overcome this current."

"How do you know it's not way stronger down there?" Darlene challenged.

"The width of the narrows is relatively constant," Greg answered, "and it's the same water down there as it is here."

"Isn't the spot where the dam was built the skinniest part of the canyon?" Paul asked.

Greg shrugged. "Well, yeah, but it's much wider where I would be turning into Wahweap." He motioned at the shore. "It's at least this wide."

"What if you ran out of gas?" Julie argued.

Greg pointed at the gas gauge. "We have plenty of gas. That's why we stopped at Dangling Rope."

"What if the engine stalls?" Darlene asked.

"It hasn't stalled all week."

"But what if it does? You'll die!" Julie said.

Greg stared into his wife's eyes. "Julie, if I thought I was going to die, I wouldn't do it. The engine is running great. I'll be fine."

No one said anything.

Greg continued. "I don't think insurance is going to cover it, if we just abandon it. I think I should try."

Julie knew that Greg would not be able to afford to replace the Mastercraft for years without insurance money. And there was still the issue of the houseboat, for which hopefully, they would not be held financially responsible. But Julie still didn't feel it was worth risking a life. "The problem, Greg, is that there is no trying. Once you go left toward the dam, there's no turning back."

"That's not completely true," Paul inserted. "There's that new marina in the narrows."

"Antelope Point," Greg said, remembering.

"Yeah, you could get off there if you were in trouble," Paul said.

"If we can get to Antelope Point, why are we even talking about Wahweap?" Julie asked.

Paul shook his head. "Antelope Point was never designed to launch boats with the lake this low. You would basically be looking a hundred-feet up the cliffs at the launch ramp."

"Wouldn't Wahweap's ramp be the same?" Max asked.

"No." Greg said. "They used to launch boats at Wahweap while the dam was filling. The ramp goes hundreds of feet down."

"But it would be covered with moss and slimy stuff, wouldn't it?" Paul said.

Greg shrugged. "Probably. But all you'd need is a power washer to clean it off. Then you could drive right down and grab your boat."

Max leaned forward. "So is that your plan? Just park the boat next to the ramp at Wahweap, and retrieve it after they clean the ramp?"

Greg nodded.

The three couples looked back and forth between themselves.

"And you're dropping us off first?" Max asked.

Greg nodded. "Yes, both for your safety, and the lighter the boat, the better."

Erika spoke for the first time in a while. "But that means you'll be back to the marina tonight, and the rest of us will be stuck on the shore through the night."

Greg smiled. "That's the upside."

"I want to go with Greg," Erika said teasingly. "I'd willingly risk my life to avoid a night out on the rocks."

Julie could see that ahead they were quickly approaching the landmass of Antelope Island. The island loomed huge, much larger than Julie ever remembered it before. Judging from the height of the wet marks, she estimated the water levels had dropped over a hundred feet at this spot in the lake. On the left side of the channel Julie saw a ranger boat tied to a rock, its lights blinking. The boat was broadcasting some sort of message that she could not quite decipher at first. But as they got closer, she could understand.

"Danger. Danger. Currents downstream near the dam site are hazardous. All boats must detour right, into Warm Creek Bay, especially houseboats and other slow-moving watercraft. Repeat. Danger. Danger."

Slightly past the first ranger boat, another one on the right side of the channel broadcasted a similar message. She could see that ahead most boats were veering right, but a small number were ignoring the warnings and turning left. The sight gave her the chills. When their turn came, Greg turned right with the larger group.

As they passed into Warm Creek Bay, they could see that it was littered with boats, many of them stranded high and dry around the edges of the bay. Hoards of people were standing around the beached boats. There were trails of people hiking up the hillsides toward Castle Rock. Julie guessed that many had decided to try to hike to Wahweap Marina tonight, a journey she estimated at almost ten miles.

When the boats parted in the large bay, Greg accelerated toward Castle Rock. Julie was nervous about the separation that would occur in a few minutes. A million arguments were running through her mind. Too soon, Greg slowed and brought the Mastercraft up to the shore. He shut off the engine. Without saying anything, Max, Darlene, and Erika started gathering their clothes and blankets.

Paul walked up behind Greg. "I'll go with you."

"Not necessary."

Paul nodded, not waging much of a fight.

Max had jumped into the waist-deep water, and was helping Darlene down. Julie handed the pile of blankets to Max. Erika followed, then Paul. Julie handed Erika's and Paul's shoes to Erika. Greg moved to help Julie, but instead, she sat down in the front seat next to her husband.

"What are you doing, Julie?" he asked.

"I'm going with you."

He looked concerned.

"Are you going to die, Greg?"

"No, but—"

"Then, I'm staying with you." She could see she was making him re-think his decision.

"Honey, there's no reason for both of us to risk—"

She stood and raised her voice. "We both go, or we both stay."

He backed off, considering her statement. "Are you okay going?"

She nodded. "We can always ditch at Antelope Marina, right?"

He smiled. "Yeah. And you're not mad?"

She shook her head. "I want to go with you."

He nodded and turned to the others, who had been quietly watching the argument. "Okay, if everything works the way I think it will – and it will!" he emphasized, "—then I'll pick you guys up on the other side of Castle Rock in a half hour. Then I can motor you back to the marina and you won't have to sleep on the rocks." He winked at Erika.

Julie hadn't considered that option. That was better for them. Paul pushed the Mastercraft out into deeper water, and then both couples wished Greg and Julie good luck.

CHAPTER 22

8:00 p.m. - Hoover Dam, Nevada

Standing on the Arizona side of Hoover Dam, Grant watched as a line of trucks formed on the winding road from the Nevada side. The trucks, loaded with sand bags from construction companies all around Las Vegas, had started arriving 20 minutes before. The logistical nightmare was beginning to sort itself out. The original plan was to direct the trucks to turn around, and then back all the way across the dam to unload their sandbags. It was Shauna who had suggested the alternative. Plan B called for the trucks to drive across the dam, turn around on a small access road on the Arizona side, then pull back onto the dam. The sandbags from many trucks could then be offloaded simultaneously by a swarm of volunteers and National Guardsmen. After the trucks were all unloaded, they pulled out at the same time, making room for the next group waiting on the hill. The plan meant that sandbags were to be stacked only on the upstream side of the dam, leaving the downstream side open for vehicles. Starting on the Arizona side where the east side of the dam abutted into the cliff, and all along the upstream side, a ten-foot wall of sand bags was being erected. Plan B ended up being a huge time saver, since the sandbag dike could be built all the way from Arizona to Nevada at the same time.

Only after the first phase was done, sometime in the middle of the night, would they go back and extend the dike to its planned twenty-foot height and widen the base to the full width of the dam. And by building the dike in two phases, it gave them much more time, almost a day, before the water rose above the eight-foot first phase dike.

A man with a bullhorn moved along the dam, barking orders. "Overlap that one, soldier. That's it. Right to left. Yeah you." He pointed to someone placing a bag below him. "Butt it right up against the others or it'll be a weak spot. Yeah, pick it up and move it over. That's it. The stagger gives the dike strength."

Originally, Grant had expected to be in charge of the construction of the wall of sandbags, something he was not confident about, especially since he had never worked with sandbags before. However, the mayor told them about the man with the bullhorn, a retired engineer named Steve Alby, who lived in Las Vegas. Before he retired, Alby had actually been in charge of building sandbag dikes along the Mississippi for the Army Corp of Engineers. Grant had been more than willing to concede the responsibility to the old engineer who had arrived just before the trucks.

Grant watched as the old man trained the soldiers. He was incredible. He watched the placement of every sand bag. He barked orders through the bullhorn like an auctioneer. When the cops found him at his house a few miles south of the strip, he was working in his yard. They hadn't allowed him to change. So he was still dressed in denim shorts, a grimy white t-shirt, black tennis shoes with contrasting white socks, and a green camouflage hat, which he hadn't been wearing when he arrived. Grant guessed he had been given the hat by one of the soldiers.

When Grant first saw Alby, he wondered if they had made a mistake. The man seemed feeble in his movements and speech. Grant guessed the man was in his mid-sixties. He had short gray hair, bird legs, and a potbelly that peeked out from under his t-shirt. However, after they explained to Alby the goal of the next 24 hours, the man went right to work. The National Guard gave Alby a bullhorn, and as soon as the trucks started to arrive, he transformed from a lamb into a lion. It was obvious he had done this before. When Grant looked at him, he thought he could imagine a much younger Alby, dressed in a raincoat in pouring rain, helping farmers build dikes along the Mississippi to protect their farms and homes. Grant wanted to talk to him, to ask him some questions about the dike, but to interrupt him now would be like trying to talk to a conductor during a symphony.

When Grant looked back at the incoming trucks, he wondered if everything could happen in time. These bags came from the construction companies. The bags from the volunteers would come later. The empty bags being flown in were not expected to arrive in Las Vegas for an hour or more. To avoid needless chaos, a TV announcement calling for volunteers would not be made until after 9:00 p.m. In the meantime, eighteen sandbag locations had been chosen around the area, and police crews were roping off parking areas, making signs, ordering portable toilets, and generally making whatever other preparations they could think of before they were mobbed by thousands of volunteers.

So much could still go wrong. The extra bags could be late. It could take longer than planned to fill them. Traffic could affect their delivery to the dam. And what if the call for volunteers went unheeded? Grant worried more about the opposite: that they would be bombarded by crowds too large to manage. Even if the plan for sand bags worked, what if the Bureau's numbers were wrong? What if the water rose more than fifteen feet over Hoover? What if the water arrived early, before the dike was completed? Grant stared upstream. He tried to imagine the water coming toward him. He imagined a tidal wave roaring across Lake Mead. But that wasn't logical. No, there would be no waves on the lake. It was too big and would dissipate the flood. If anything went wrong, it would happen gradually, as the water rose inch by inch until it breached the dam. All violent waves, currents, or flooding would be limited to the Grand Canyon.

* * *

8:15 p.m. - Lake Powell, Utah

Julie saw Greg look at his watch. They had made good time from Warm Creek. Since most of the boats had gone the safer route, the lower canyon had not been nearly as crowded. The boats had taken advantage, spreading out and going full blast. The water was rough, but not unbearable. Greg had even leaned over at one point and commented to Julie that if they weren't in danger, it could have been fun, going full bore, racing other boats down through the narrows. Julie was still nervous, but she was glad she had come.

When they approached Antelope Point Marina, Greg slowed and pointed at the docks. "Do you want to stop?"

Julie noticed that the ramp was in fact isolated high on the rock wall, well out of reach of the boats. The current was moving very fast in the channel, but she was comfortable they could overcome the current and make the turn into Wahweap Bay. This wasn't as bad as she had feared. She shook her head and Greg accelerated back to speed and they continued.

The jaunt continued and after a while Julie wondered how far it would be. Finally, they rounded a bend and they could see a mile ahead to where the Colorado River split, the right being Wahweap, and the left, the dam. Julie watched nervously.

As they approached the fork, the water became rougher, and the Mastercraft jarred up and down loudly. Then Julie saw something that made her heart stop. A small green and white striped boat was running on the left edge of the pack of speeding boats. A man and a woman were in the boat. Julie saw the small boat was having trouble with the waves, actually coming clear of the water a couple of times. Then the driver lost control and the boat veered sharply to the left and rolled twice before stopping on its side. It filled with water. Julie scanned the surface for the two passengers and held her breath until both their heads bobbed to the surface. They looked to be at least thirty feet from their boat. Instantly, Julie knew that without intervention, they would both be sucked over the dam, and killed. But the risk to anyone who tried to help would be too great. Greg had seen it too and looked over at Julie.

Julie made the decision. She nodded vigorously.

Greg didn't hesitate. He weaved through the boats to the left of them, and headed for the two people in the water. The current was already dragging them around the corner and when Julie caught sight of them, she could see the Glen Canyon Dam visitor center on the hill behind them. Although it was almost a mile away, it didn't look far enough. At the rate of the current, they would be pulled past the dam in a minute. Greg looped behind the two, and drove right between them.

"Throw them something!" he yelled.

Julie, now panicky, ran to the back of the boat and started pulling the water-ski rope out of a small compartment. She looked downstream and saw what remained of the Glen Canyon Dam, the broken concrete protruding from the cliffs on both sides. She willed herself to ignore it, and threw the tangled rope toward the woman. The coils of rope landed right on her head. The woman began pulling herself hand over hand toward the Mastercraft. Julie pulled on the other end. In the meantime the man had swum to the back of the boat and was trying to climb in. He had difficulty with the ladder before finally climbing up and falling awkwardly into the boat. Julie had pulled the woman to the back, but the woman made no move to climb in.

"My leg," she said, her face showing intense pain.

"Hurry!" Greg urged.

Julie lunged toward the man on the floor who was trying to stand up. She grabbed his arm and yanked him to his feet. She looked at the woman again, then at Greg. "Her leg is hurt. We're going to have to lift her." Greg left the steering wheel for a second to look at the woman, then returned quickly to the controls.

"Flip her around so her back is against the boat. It's easier."

Julie remembered once when she was too tired to climb in the boat after water-skiing. Greg and Paul had lifted her in that way.

She and the man climbed out on the platform on the rear deck and they each grabbed an arm. Julie saw that the dam was approaching much too quickly.

"Ready?" the man said.

Julie nodded and they both pulled. The lady was heavier than Julie expected and Julie lost her balance. She had no choice but release her grip. The woman slipped back in the water.

"Can you do this?" the man asked nervously.

Julie nodded. She had just underestimated. As she prepared for the next pull, she saw what looked like a group of policeman up on the right shore, near the dam. They were waving frantically at the boaters.

Julie braced herself and looked at the man. He nodded and they both pulled hard. The lady came up out of the water, and all three of them fell into the boat. She felt the Mastercraft accelerate immediately. She pulled herself up to her knees.

Greg had the boat going full blast and was heading up the river, but they were only gaining ground slowly. When Julie looked back, she saw that they had been close enough that the wake was now rolling over the remnants of the dam. She looked up on the canyon walls and saw that the policemen were clapping and thrusting their fists into the air. Julie crawled forward and hugged her husband's leg.

* * *

8:30 p.m. - Grand Canyon, Arizona

David was out of the raft again. They all were. The water had risen to where the canyon spread out. There were finally flat places to stand. That was the good news. The bad news was that where they had been in a protected canyon before, if the water rose any higher, they would now be exposed. And it was very dark. Deep in the canyon, the sun had set long ago. The last remaining rays touched the west-facing rocks thousands of feet above them. The river, which an hour before had been expanding from its channel, now enjoyed free rein to flow where it wanted. Although it was getting too dark to be sure, David guessed the big, black expanse of water to be a half mile across.

* * *

8:40 p.m. - Lake Powell, Utah

The Mastercraft merged back with the other boats entering Wahweap Canyon. Julie glanced back at the couple still sitting on the floor. The lady was sobbing uncontrollably and clutching her leg. Julie guessed the tears were not for the leg, but for how close they had come to losing their lives. The man sensed Julie's eyes and looked up. His eyes were also misty. He nodded thanks at Julie, and turned back to his wife. Julie looked back at the remains of the Glen Canyon Dam again. That had been too close.

With the water down over a hundred feet, the entrance to Wahweap felt like a canyon. The walls were narrow and steep, and Greg and the other boats had to slow to get through safely. Wahweap Bay was draining into the channel, and creating a current, but not nearly as strong as in the Narrows.

Only a few minutes later, the canyon opened into the wide expanse of Wahweap Bay. The water here was wide and calm. Greg and many of the other boats slowed and took a breather. Up ahead on the left were the buildings and docks of Wahweap Marina. On the right was Castle Rock, and even in the setting sun, Julie could see crowds of stranded boaters cresting the pass and hiking around the bay toward the marina.

CHAPTER 23

Back in the visitor center, Grant felt like sleeping. If he hadn't known better, he would have sworn he left Denver a week ago. He checked his watch and added an hour for the time change. It was already 10:15 p.m. in Denver – past his bedtime. He imagined his wife getting ready for bed and putting on her worn flannel pajamas, which she wore year round, even in the summer. He detested those pajamas. They were the least sexy things he could imagine. But right now, he decided, they wouldn't bother him at all.

He walked over to the wall of windows in the visitor center and looked out at Hoover Dam. The lights on the canyon walls lit up the dam like daylight. The dam itself was buzzing with action. The trucks kept coming. The sandbag dike had grown steadily along the upstream side of the dam, now reaching almost ten feet high in some sections. At the current rate, they were on target to finish the upstream portion by 3 or 4 a.m. – just in time, based on the projection that the water would rise above the concrete dam somewhere between 6:00 and 9:00. But it would be close. Then the slower and more difficult task of building it up to fifteen feet would begin. Grant could not see the old man with the bullhorn on the dike, and guessed that he must have taken a break. Hopefully the stackers had learned something and a sandbag wouldn't be misplaced in his absence.

Fred walked up behind Grant while he was gazing out the window. "You look beat."

"Yeah, I think it just caught up to me."

"You want me to find you a room for a couple hours? That casino between here and Boulder City is only a few minutes away."

"There's no way I could sleep tonight, but thanks anyway."

It was quiet for a minute, while both men watched the action on the dam. Grant broke the trance and looked over at Fred. "You think it'll work?"

"What? The dam?" Fred hesitated, and rubbed his chin. "I guess that depends on your girl's estimates. If she's right about the water levels, sure, I think it'll hold. The old man definitely knows what he's doing with the sand bags."

They were both silent for a few moments, staring out the windows, before Fred smiled and spoke again. "They're calling it 'Hoover-Two', you know."

Grant turned, raising his eyebrows. "What, the dike? Who is?"

Fred pointed down at the dam. "I think the soldiers started it. But I heard 'Hoover-Two' in the visitor center a few minutes ago. It seems to be catching on."

Grant looked back at the dam. Hoover-Two. It seemed appropriate. A small dam built on top of the famous one below. He wondered why he hadn't thought of it himself. He looked back at Fred. "Hoover-Two." He felt the words roll off his tongue. "I like it. Let's just hope Hoover-Two's legacy will be a success."

Fred nodded. "Yup. There's a lot riding on it, that's for sure."

Grant changed the subject. "What's been happening downstream?"

Fred glanced up. "Nothing yet. We know Lake Mojave has been rising about nine inches an hour since we blew the two spillways. Davis Dam's internal gates are open, but that won't keep up with the water we're dumping. They're supposed to open the spillways at Davis, but just like here, they won't run at full capacity until the water level rises. According to Shauna's calculations, that won't happen until a little after midnight."

Grant pondered the data. "Once her spillways are running at full tilt, Mojave should be able to hold her level, right?"

"Yeah. Theoretically."

Grant pursed his lips, trying to imagine the spillways at Davis Dam. "They've never been tested at full capacity, have they?"

Fred smiled. "Course not."

Grant smirked. "That would be too good to be true."

Fred shrugged. "We have to trust them. They were designed specifically to keep up with Hoover. The problem is, even assuming they work, the trouble will just move downstream. Lake Havasu will have to rise high enough for the water to reach the top of Parker Dam's spillways. Its internal gates aren't going to be able to keep up either. Both dams, Davis and Parker, will need their spillways flowing at full capacity to keep up with all the water we're dumping."

A thought kept nagging Grant. "How certain are we that Parker's spillways can really handle it? Isn't that just theoretical too?"

Fred rubbed his forehead. "Same story. None of the spillways have ever been tested at capacity." Fred turned toward Grant. "Why are you asking me all these questions? You work for the Bureau too."

Grant nodded. "My guys in Denver are all desk jockeys. You're out here in the real world. I was just curious what you think."

Fred showed a hint of satisfaction at Grant's remark. "If I were betting, and I am from Vegas, I'd bet on the Bureau's numbers. They may be desk jockeys today, but these three dams were all designed over fifty years ago. Those boys got out in the sun and got their hands dirty. They ran their calculations on slide rules. They checked their numbers, then checked them again. Yeah, I trust them."

Grant smiled. It had not occurred to him that the calculations were done by hand. Over the last fifteen years the Bureau had not done anything without modeling it on a computer first. If someone took all the computers away today, the Bureau would stop dead. They wouldn't know what to do. Grant had seen slide rules, but he didn't even know how to work one. Actually, Grant wasn't sure he could balance his checkbook anymore without a computer.

Fred looked at him. "What are you thinking?"

Grant shrugged. "Just that we're sitting here racking our brains, and the flood's not even here yet." Grant looked back out at the action on the dam and kept talking without looking at Fred. "If we're able to contain all this water in my little dam extension project – Hoover-Two," he corrected himself, "then all three sets of spillways will be running at full capacity for weeks. None of the three dam's spillways have ever been tested at full capacity for a minute, let alone weeks."

Fred spoke from behind Grant. "In 1983 when the water was high, only two feet of water went over the spillways at Hoover for sixty days – less than five percent of capacity. Even that almost ruined the spillways. I can't imagine what this is going to do."

Grant smiled. "Compared to what would happen if the water breaches Hoover, they're going to be happy to re-build the spillways after it's over."

Grant's cell phone rang. He picked it up. "Hello."

"Grant, it's Howard."

Grant recognized the voice of his boss. His stomach turned. His boss was the last person he wanted to talk to. "Oh, hi Howard. How's Yellowstone?"

Howard spoke fast, obviously excited. "We've been driving around in the park all day, then we went out and ate. I hadn't heard any news. I flicked on the TV and . . . the Glen Canyon Dam – unbelievable. I called Cindy at home and she forwarded me to Julia. Julia told me that you're there handling it. I can't believe . . ." His voice tapered off.

Grant silently cursed the two secretaries for giving Howard his phone number. "Yeah, that about sums it up."

"Where are you? Page? Why didn't you call me?"

Grant hesitated. Actually, the thought of calling Howard had never occurred to him. Howard would have no idea what to do, and of course Grant didn't want the bureaucratic interference. He felt like he had plenty of obstacles without his boss questioning everything. "I'm at Hoover Dam in Veg–"

"I know where Hoover is. Why aren't you at Glen Canyon? Isn't that where the problem is?" Grant could already detect the condescending attitude.

Grant couldn't stop the defensiveness in his voice. "What'd you want me to do at Glen Canyon? The dam's gone."

"Well, what are you doing at Hoover?"

"We're getting ready for the flood; we're dumping as much water as possible to lower the lake." Grant decided not to bring up the part about dynamiting Hoover's spillways. "And we're building a dike on top of the dam to try to prevent overtopping." The phone went silent for a moment.

"Overtopping – you think that might happen?"

Grant talked down to him. "Yes, Howard, Hoover is going to get overtopped."

"How do you know that for sure?"

It never ceased to amaze Grant how some people could argue with so much conviction when they were completely wrong. "Howard, Lake Powell holds almost two years of river flow. You think Mead has that much extra capacity?"

There was silence on the line before Howard continued. "Well, then, what makes you think a dike on top of Hoover will hold it? Two years of flow held by a dike?"

Grant willed himself to not lose his temper.

Howard continued. "And besides, who approved building a dike on top of the dam anyway? That's going to cost a fortune."

Grant gritted his teeth. "The governor of Nevada approved it."

There was silence on the other end of the phone for a moment. Even though Howard was a little behind, it didn't prevent him from saying something stupid. "You got him involved? What the hell were you thinking?"

Grant spat the words out. "He was here when I got here. I didn't call him. Besides, I needed him to get things done."

Howard switched his line of questioning. "How high is the dike you're building?"

Grant knew where this was going. "Twenty feet."

"Twenty feet, what's that gonna do? How'd you come up with that number?"

Grant got angry and yelled into the phone. "We calculated the height we'd need based on the water levels at both dams. Why, how high do you think I should build it, Howard? Do you have a better number in mind? Or, do you want me to tell the governor to stop the dike? You want to make the decisions now? Go ahead."

Howard hesitated. "Well, it's just that . . ."

Grant couldn't stop himself. "It's just that you're great at complaining, but you don't have a clue what to do." Grant realized he had gone too far.

The retort came, but Howard's voice was weak. "Hey, I'm just thinking out loud here."

Grant resisted the urge to tell his boss he shouldn't think out loud – it tended to make him look like an idiot.

Howard changed the subject. "What did Roland say when he called?"

"He told me not to make any decisions."

Howard laughed. "Well, it sounds like you screwed that up."

Grant agreed, "I didn't have any choice. Something had to be done."

Howard's tone changed to consolatory. "Well, you better hope your ideas work, 'cause we both know what'll happen if they don't."

Grant summed it up. "Yeah. I'm screwed if I do, and screwed if I don't."

"When's Roland going to be back in the country?"

Grant wished he knew. "I have no idea. When I talked to him around 10 a.m., he was still trying to find a flight back from Paris."

"He hasn't called since?" Howard asked.

"No, he didn't call back, which I'm assuming means they're in the air. I figure he could be arriving somewhere between midnight and noon tomorrow."

"You think the dike will be done by then?"

"It better be. We expect overtopping before 6:00 a.m."

Howard asked a question that must have hurt. "How did you figure out when the water would arrive?"

Grant answered. "The bureau put together a failure study in the nineties for Glen Canyon. They modeled the whole thing. I have a table showing when the flood arrives at each location."

The phone went silent. Howard had finally run out of questions. Grant asked his boss a question he was afraid of. "What are you going to do? Are you coming here?"

Howard hesitated. "Well, we're here in Yellowstone. We drove from Denver. I'd hate to leave my wife and the kids. She doesn't like to drive. It's a long drive home with the kids."

Grant felt elated. Reading between the lines, it seemed like Howard was a little scared to come. Somebody might figure out he was over his head.

Howard continued. "But I guess I'd better at least check on some flights. Y'know with Roland coming and all. I – don't know. Do you need me?"

Grant shook his head. He wanted to laugh, but didn't. "You'll have to make that decision yourself, Howard."

His boss went silent for a moment. "All right, I'll look into some flights, and talk to my family. I'll call you later."

"Okay," Grant responded.

"Call me if anything changes."

Grant knew he wouldn't call, and he thought Howard knew that too. "Yeah. Okay, Howard."

"All right, I'll call you later." The line went dead.

Grant hung up the cell phone. He wondered how these guys with attitudes ever get anywhere. Wasn't it obvious to everyone? Yet there seemed to be at least one of these guys in every organization. And somebody had to have been stupid enough to promote them to a powerful position. The thought was mind-boggling.

Fred had been listening to the whole call. "That your boss?"

Grant nodded. "He's new at the bureau."

Fred raised his eyebrows. "New? Sounds like it. But he's your boss?"

Grant smiled. "It's a long story. He's not an engineer. He's a lawyer. Some congressman stuck him in our organization to look us over. He's a plant."

Fred shook his head. "You're kidding, right?"

Grant just shook his head.

Fred looked at his watch and then motioned to the door. "Come on. Let's go up to the casino and eat. You need to get out of here for a while."

Grant took one last look out at Hoover Dam and the partially constructed dike.

Fred grabbed his arm and pulled him. "Come on. This can take care of itself for a while. They can call us if they need us."

Grant felt wrong about leaving. What if something came up?

* * *

9:20 p.m. - Grand Canyon, Arizona

David wondered how much higher the water could rise. It had to already be four or five hundred feet above normal. There was no question in David's mind that the Glen Canyon Dam had broken. There was just too much water for any other explanation.

The canyon was now completely dark. Only the stars were visible. The entire group had retrieved their flashlights from their packs, but Keller had forced everyone to take turns to save battery power. David wore a headset light on his forehead, but it was currently not illuminated. At the moment, Sam was shining his up and down the rock walls, searching for handholds higher up.

They were close to getting rimmed again. The rising water had forced them against a vertical rock wall and it was David and Afram's turn to hold the raft. The two of them stood in waist-deep water, while everyone else sat inside. David felt the raft trying to pull him deeper into the water.

"It's too deep," Afram complained. "I can't hold it much longer."

Judy illuminated her flashlight. "Sam, look over there." She pointed her light at a small rock outcropping at eye level, off to the left of the raft.

Sam pointed his light at the same spot.

"Couldn't somebody climb up there?" she asked.

"Then what?"

She motioned upwards with her light. "You might be able to traverse up that ledge."

Sam shook his head. "I don't think you could make it. It's too narrow."

David's teeth chattered. "Try it! We can't hold on much longer." The water was almost to his waist and he had no leverage.

Keller helped Judy climb onto the outcropping. As soon as she found a place to grab, she pulled herself up. Like a spider, she clung to the rock and tried to traverse higher.

"It works," she said. "Somebody else come up."

Keller motioned for Sam to climb, then maneuvered to give him a leg up. Sam handed his light to Becky. Then with a boost from Keller, he reached for the wall as Judy had. But he missed the handhold. The action of Sam leaning against the rock was pushing the raft away from the cliff. David felt Afram stumble and lose his footing.

"I can't hold it!" Afram screamed.

But it was too late. Afram slipped into water over his head, and David couldn't hold the raft himself. It had almost pulled him deep before he let go. With the raft moving away, Sam fell into the boat and Becky screamed. Afram came up from underwater and stroked back to the rock wall.

Keller, Sam, and Becky were in the raft, and David, Afram, and Judy were on the rocks. And then the raft was gone into the darkness. Becky was screaming. There was no time to do anything. The beam from the flashlight hit David once more before the raft disappeared around the bend.

David wanted, needed, to yell out something, to scream at the top of his lungs. But nothing seemed appropriate. What could you say? Goodbye? Good luck? He heard Judy sob.

They were enveloped in darkness. Becky's screams eerily tapered off as the raft moved quickly downstream. David knew his friends would be dead in minutes, and the shock of that knowledge paralyzed him. After a while, they could no longer hear Becky screaming.

* * *

9:25 p.m. - Grand Canyon, Arizona

Keller regained his senses and took inventory. Only he and the couple were in the raft. The other three were behind on the rocks. He waited a few seconds for Becky to stop screaming, and then he barked out orders. "Find the paddles!"

She sobbed. "What good is that going to do?"

"FIND THEM!" he ordered. "If I die, I'm going to die paddling."

The girl shined her light on the floor and Keller saw paddles scattered around the boat. He grabbed one and made sure that Sam got another one. The girl was worthless. Keller straddled the right side of the raft. "Sam, you take that side," he ordered. Sam took his position.

"Shine the light out there and find someplace for us to land," he told Becky.

She obeyed. They drifted through the darkness. The sound of the waterfall was getting much louder.

Becky pointed the flashlight downstream toward the noise. "Is that —"

"FORGET THAT!" he yelled. "Shine the light at the shore. Try to find us someplace."

Keller expected Sam to defend her. He had been protecting her for the whole trip. But Sam said nothing.

"What was that over there?" It was Sam's voice.

Keller had seen it too. "Back to the right."

Becky moved the light and found a rock outcropping, jutting from the shore. "We can make it!" Sam called out. "Paddle!"

Keller paddled, but he knew it was too far away. When they passed, they were more than three boat lengths from reaching it.

The waterfall noise had become much louder, and Keller knew the struggle was over for them. The currents were moving the raft farther into the middle of the channel. "Tighten your life jackets!"

The right side of the boat lagged slightly and he stroked twice to straighten it. He yelled to be heard over the water. "Okay, Becky, shine the light straight ahead!"

She did as instructed, and Keller saw the V shape of Granite Narrows less than fifty feet ahead. He yelled loudly to be heard. "RIGHT SIDE PADDLE! LEFT SIDE PADDLE!"

Keller felt the water accelerate the raft as they were sucked into the narrows. Shooting through the entrance, he knew it was the fastest speed he had ever achieved in a raft. Becky was screaming again. Keller felt the wind on his face and the water on his feet. His hair blew back. He yelled at the top of his lungs and paddled harder. The raft bucked, but stayed in shape.

Suddenly, there was nothing. They were falling. The raft pitched backwards and Keller fell out. He felt mist in the air. He felt fear. He felt exhilaration. He felt peace when he hit the water. Then he felt nothing.

* * *

9:30 p.m. - Las Vegas, Nevada

Like a million other Las Vegas residents, the Van Buren family was glued to the TV. Just like when the war started, or the Los Angeles riots broke out, or even the O.J. verdict, this was a time when all the networks had abandoned their sitcoms and concentrated on the news. To the people of Las Vegas, this was not just any news, either; it was their news. It concerned their river, the Colorado, the one that provided their electricity and their water. It also concerned their dam, Hoover, which could potentially fail under the onslaught of floodwater en route toward it.

The Van Burens were not what you would call an ideal family unit. They consisted of a dad and three boys. No mom – she had run out on them fifteen years before. The two older boys and their father worked security at the casinos. Like his older brothers before him, the youngest boy played linebacker on his high school football team. The Van Burens were big. And they were pissed off that a bunch of terrorists thought they could get away with what they had done to the Colorado River.

When the news showed another camera shot of the floodwater in the Grand Canyon, Jeremy, the oldest son, set down his Budweiser. "If only I could get my hands on those towel-heads." He clenched his hands around an imaginary neck, and pretended to violently strangle the life out of the poor dumb sucker.

Milt, the father, tilted his beer at his son. "And we would do it for free, wouldn't we boys?"

All three boys nodded enthusiastically.

The TV then showed an aerial view of Hoover Dam, zooming in on the sand bag dike being constructed. The Van Burens had already talked at length about this dike, and whether it would work or not.

The TV switched to the mayor of Las Vegas. "Citizens of Las Vegas and neighboring communities, we need your help."

All four Van Burens stopped talking about strangling terrorists and listened closely.

The mayor continued. "Engineers estimate that we will need close to a million sandbags to build up Hoover Dam high enough to retain the floodwater. That is more than construction companies in the area can manage, so I am calling on you, the people of the great city of Las Vegas, to help us. We need all able-bodied men and women to bring your shovels and help us fill sandbags. We have set up a dozen locations around the city."

A list of locations showed up on the screen. The Van Buren boys noticed that the second spot on the list was a huge sandy hillside only a couple of miles down the road.

"So if you can help, please come prepared to work. We ask that all volunteers bring their own drinking—"

Milt shut off the television. "Come on, boys." He finished his Budweiser and tossed the can on the floor. "We got work to do."

CHAPTER 24

9:35 p.m. - Davis Dam, Laughlin, Nevada

The skinny man drove his other white pickup truck up to the police roadblock at Davis Dam and stopped behind a sport utility vehicle. The emblems on this second truck were not from Jensen Industrial Elevator like he used at the Glen Canyon Dam. Instead, the truck had the official blue oval logos of the Bureau of Reclamation, including the images of a mountain range. The large emblems made the truck look very official.

Although the highway normally continued up over the crest of the dam, the police roadblock now stopped traffic a half mile from the dam itself. The combination of police cars blocking the road, wood barriers, and orange cones set in a semicircular pattern left no doubt that they were not allowing traffic over the dam, but instead wanted them to follow the cones around in a small semi-circle and head back the way they had come.

He saw a policeman approach an SUV in front of the truck and motion around the cones. The driver of the SUV rolled down her window and pointed up over the dam. The skinny man cracked his window to see if he could overhear the conversation. Even through the small opening, he felt the stifling hot air outside. He could hear the policeman clearly.

"Sorry ma'am, but the road is closed." The policeman pointed down the hill. "The other bridge is only a few miles down the road."

The lady responded with animated motions from her hands, but the skinny man could not quite hear what she was saying.

"Ma'am, I understand it's an emergency, but all evacuations are being routed over the other bridge. We're not allowing any traffic over the dam." The policeman stepped back to end the conversation and motioned the SUV to continue back down the hill.

The SUV moved forward abruptly, the driver obviously unhappy, but the vehicle followed the cones around and headed back down the hill.

The skinny man's heart pounded as he pulled the truck up to the policeman and stopped.

The policeman tried to wave him around, but he didn't move, instead rolling his window all the way down and leaning out. The policeman reluctantly approached the window. "Sir, you can't stop here. All traffic–"

The skinny man pointed down at the door emblem. "I'm with the Bureau. They sent me down here to run some tests."

The officer hesitated, and then motioned for him to pull the truck forward and off the side of the road. When he stopped, a second man wearing a generic security uniform approached him. He noticed that the security man had a small Bureau of Reclamation patch above the pocket of his uniform. It was show time.

The Bureau's security guard was a short black man who looked like he was trying to grow a beard but failing. He leaned in the window of the truck. "About damn time somebody showed up. We were beginning to think nobody cared."

This surprised the skinny man. They were actually happy to see him. He stumbled slightly with his words. "Well, uh . . . I've been up at Hoover. They sent me down here to run some moisture tests." He reached for the fake Bureau ID in his pocket.

The guard perked up. "What's going on at Hoover? We ain't heard nothin' down here except on the radio."

He retrieved his identification, but this guy didn't seem like he cared, so he held it closed in his hand. No sense showing it if he didn't need to. The question about Hoover needed answering, although the skinny man hadn't really been there. Fortunately Hoover had been all over the television all day. "Well, you probably know they've been scrambling to get ready for the flood water. They dynamited the spillways this afternoon." He had heard about the spillways on the news. That had been a brilliant idea to save Hoover, one he never would have thought of. The possibility that Hoover might survive could screw up his whole plan. Hoover's collapse was an important domino in the chain.

The guard continued, motioning with his hand at nothing in particular. "They told us about the spillways. Our water level's been rising ever since. What about the floodwater coming down the Grand Canyon? When do they expect it to get to Hoover? And what about that thing they're building on top of the dam? Do they really expect that to hold anything?"

The skinny man had been glued to the TV and had the same questions. When would the floodwater arrive? Would the sandbag dike hold? Building the dam higher with sandbags was another thing he hadn't thought of. He could not imagine it actually working, not with all the water headed toward it from Lake Powell. But what if it did?

He realized he was wasting too much time. "I know you have a ton of questions, but I'm kinda in a hurry. They want me to make some moisture measurements up on the crest." He pointed up. "This dam is gonna get a workout tonight and we don't want it to leak."

The guard stepped back away from the window. "How long you gonna be up there?"

He thought about it. "I don't know. A half hour, forty five minutes." He started to roll up his window, then lowered it again. "Hey, just so you guys know, to take my measurements, I'm gonna be drilling a couple of holes in the top of the dam. I need to make sure they're not seeping."

The guard smiled. "You the boss."

He put the truck back in gear and headed up the road. That had been too easy. He couldn't believe it. They had actually been hungry for news and interaction. That had worked to his advantage. He had not even needed the fake ID.

As the road wound its way to the top of the dam, he looked across and saw how well the dam was lit up. Too well, he thought. He was going to be out in the open. If somebody watched too closely, they'd figure out what he was doing. The road reached the crest of the dam and he drove across it.

Lights along the dam spilled out over the water and gave him a view of the water level. It had risen much higher than he remembered from his scouting missions. For the level to rise this fast, Hoover must be dumping an incredible amount of water. It didn't matter, though. It all worked into his plan. He needed Hoover to dump enough water to rupture the gravel dam he was standing on. Not that he could count on the water itself to do the trick. No, he was going to give it a little head start.

He drove to the middle of the dam and stopped in an area between two of the floodlights. The area wasn't dark, but it was the best he could do. He had already shut off the engine before he looked around, and had another idea. He fired the truck up again, and turned it around so it faced the other direction; the truck bed was now hidden from the security guards below. He opened the door and let the wave of hot desert air envelop him. He hopped out of the cab and stood for a moment staring out over the water of Lake Mojave. The black water stretched beyond the reach of the dam's floodlights until it disappeared somewhere in the distance. He couldn't help but think about upstream at Hoover Dam, and the imminent flood. To him, the thought of the water coming was good. It was a satisfying feeling. In fact, he wanted the flood to hurry.

In preparation, just like when he scouted Glen Canyon, he'd listened for hours on a scanner to determine who was who and how they expected legitimate visitors to check in. And, like Glen Canyon, if you knew the right words, submitted the right paperwork, and dropped the right names, they let you in. That would change in the near future after they analyzed the events of the next couple of days. In fact, the policy would no doubt change after this particular visit. This would be his last freebie and he needed to make the best of it.

He walked to the back of the truck and opened the tailgate. He grabbed a long tool shaped much like a jackhammer, which he dragged from the truck. The tool had an auger where the bit on a jackhammer would be. Holding the tool by both handles, at about eye level, the auger could drill a six-inch hole five feet deep. He'd told the guard that he'd need to drill several holes in the dike to do the moisture absorption tests, so he didn't expect to raise any suspicion with the tool.

He pulled the crank on a small compressor in the back of the pickup and it came to life. He plugged the huge drill into the compressor and lugged it over to the waterside of the dam. He had to lift the tool over a waist-high cinder block wall that bordered the upstream side of the dam. He chose a spot as far from the boulders as possible, braced and pulled the trigger. The auger spun against the hard ground before finally biting in and began its slow drop into the roadbed. Gravel piled up around where the auger spun in. A couple of times the tool jarred his arms, almost tearing the handles out of his hands, but he was braced for it, and it caused him no problems. He had already practiced with the tool and knew what to expect when the drill hit rocks.

The oversized drill chugged deeper until the auger buried itself and the handles almost rested on the ground. He released the trigger, flipped a switch to reverse the auger, depressed the trigger again, and the drill climbed back out of the hole. Shutting it off, he lifted it carefully away, so as to not knock gravel back in the opening. He admired his work for a moment, but didn't tarry, knowing full well the first one was the easiest. He hefted the drill back over the wall onto the asphalt road. He lined it up with the previous hole, so he would have a line of holes from the wet side of the dam to the dry side. He pulled the trigger again, hoping there wasn't a concrete pad under the asphalt. The drill spun harmlessly for several seconds on the hard road before it finally grabbed and started sinking.

When he rented the tool, they had told him that highway construction teams used the same tool to bore through pavement all the time, and that he could dig through asphalt all day long as long as he didn't hit any concrete. He watched closely as the black debris came up out of the opening around the bit. Suddenly the debris changed to gray dust and gravel and he knew he was past the asphalt. No concrete pad. He had just relaxed his hold on the drill when it jammed, jerking his arms savagely before an override shut it off. Maybe there was concrete down there. He pushed the reset button and pulled the trigger again, but it jammed again. He reversed it, then tried once more. Same result. A feeling of failure washed over him and he wondered if this whole exercise had been in vain. What had ever made him believe he could succeed?

He gave up on that spot and reversed the drill, letting it climb out of the hole. He picked a different spot only two feet away. He let it rip again, and waited while the drill did its thing. He wondered if he would have the same result, but this time the auger kept spinning. It jerked hard a couple of times, but kept going until the hole was done. He wiped sweat off his brow. Working in the intense heat was suffocating. He looked out at the water of Lake Mojave and briefly considered taking a dip to cool off, but instead he moved the drill to the next target. He repeated the process three more times, until a line of five holes stretched across the dike.

With his arms now shaking, he lifted the tool back into the truck and used his shirt to wipe more sweat off his face and neck. But the motion was a waste of time since his shirt was soaked too. He rummaged in the truck and grabbed another gadget, one he'd designed himself. It included a two-foot-long plastic tube, with a bucket on the top. At the top of the tube, right under the bucket, he'd mounted a ball valve. He opened another bucket and poured white pellets into his tool, filling the bucket on top. The substance, ammonium nitrate fertilizer, was the same as he had used at Glen Canyon. He carried the gadget over to the first hole, put the bottom of the tube in the hole, opened the ball valve, and felt the fertilizer drop into the hole. He shook it to get it all out. It took four more trips before all five holes were filled. Next he used the same tool to put diesel fuel into all five holes. He was almost finished.

He looked past the pickup toward the police roadblock, but the police were busy with a line of almost ten cars. Opening the truck's passenger door and reaching behind the seat, he retrieved five small cylinder-shaped devices with wires hanging out of them. He had designed these detonators himself, just like the ones he used at Glen Canyon. With a converted broom handle, he tucked a detonator in each hole with the wires hanging out. Holding the wires, he kicked the loose gravel back in the hole, stopping occasionally to use the broom handle to tamp the gravel. With all five holes done, he took a roll of wire out of the truck and connected all five sets of wires together. A small motorcycle battery and a timer completed the project.

He loaded the truck and shut the tailgate. He checked the guard shack one more time, and seeing nothing, bent down to set the timer. He'd planned on ten minutes, scripting the whole scenario, but his subconscious kept nagging him to do fifteen. He compromised at twelve. He pressed the button and a small red light illuminated while the digital timer started counting down from twelve. He immediately stood and walked around the truck. As he came around the back, he tripped on something. He looked down and saw the wires. Damn! With the timer still running, he quickly checked the connections between the five holes, making sure all five sets of wires were still connected. They looked fine.

He jumped in the truck, hoping it would start. Thankfully, it did, and he drove back along the dike. It took all his self-control to resist the urge to floor it and speed down the hill. When he finally pulled up to the roadblock, he could feel the hair standing up on the back of his neck. The Bureau guard stepped over to talk. The man had hoped to get waved through.

"What'd ya find out?" the guard said, looking in the back of the truck.

"Dry as a bone, just as I expected."

This seemed to relieve the guard. "I guess that's good news. This dam's likely to get a good work out for the next couple days with all the water headed our way."

The skinny man had a hard time not rushing his words. "Yeah. You know it."

"So ya think it'll hold?" asked the guard.

For some reason, the question caught him off guard. No, it wasn't going to hold. It would explode in eight and a half minutes and counting. For a moment his brain told him to warn the guy, tell him to get away as fast as he could, to not look back. He felt like screaming, "There's a bomb, you idiot! It's going to blow! Get out of here!" But he didn't. Instead, he responded in a calm, clear voice that surprised even him. "Yeah, it'll hold. No problem. But there's going to be a ton of water barreling out of those spillways."

"Unbelievable," said the guard, looking over at the dam itself. "Unbelievable."

The skinny man nodded. "You said it. Things are going to get a little crazy around here."

The guard smiled and stepped back, an unspoken signal that he was free to leave.

* * *

10:10 p.m. - Davis Dam, Nevada

Blaine Roberts leaned against a police car and sipped his coffee. They had been turning cars away from the dam for three hours straight and finally they caught a break. Maybe the word was finally getting around that they had closed the road across the dam.

What a night. He'd worked night shift security at Davis Dam for almost three years now. Nothing ever happened during the night shift. Then the disaster a few hundred miles upstream had changed everything. When he arrived at work at 8:30 p.m., the whole place buzzed like a stirred-up hornet's nest. They told him when he arrived that Hoover Dam, just sixty-five miles upstream, was going to try to catch all of the floodwater. Unfortunately for Davis Dam, that meant Hoover was dumping a ton of water, the most in its history – 250,000 cubic feet per second, ten times normal. It was going to get worse, too; when the water started to rise at Hoover, the flow would increase to almost 500,000 cubic feet per second. He summed it up to himself. Unbelievable.

They had told him that in reaction to what Hoover was doing, this afternoon they had opened all the water works at Davis Dam. Unfortunately that wasn't enough. The water in Lake Mojave was still rising over eight inches per hour, targeted to reach the top of the spillways a little after midnight. With full spillways, theoretically Davis Dam should be able to match Hoover Dam's 500,000 cubic feet per second, and the water in the lake would stop rising. None of that had ever been tested however. Unbelievable.

In spite of everyone running around like chickens with their heads cut off, the guy from the Bureau had been the first official visitor they'd had at Davis Dam today. Blaine was more than happy for the guy to go up on the dam and take some moisture measurements. Hell, he could measure all damn night if he wanted to, as long as he gave Blaine a heads-up if the dam was going to bust so he could get the hell out of here. It'd never bothered him earlier in the evening, but Blaine now wished the roadblock wasn't right below the earth dam. He'd prefer a place a little higher or maybe farther downstream.

When the guy from the Bureau returned from his inspection and his measurements, he had seemed calm and cool. He said the moisture tests went well, whatever that meant. The guy had acted like the whole thing was routine, as if he drove around taking moisture measurements every day in the face of dam failures. Blaine wondered if the guy would return later, when the spillways were going full blast. That was when the moisture measurements would mean something. The guy hadn't said anything about returning and Blaine hadn't thought to ask.

He stood and walked behind the police car to see if there were any more good donuts. The pink box sat on the hood of a second police car. He liked chocolate, but the only chocolate one left had coconut sprinkled on top, and Blaine was no fan of coconut. He grabbed it anyway because the sprinkles were easy to pick off.

He leaned on the other car and looked up at the dam. He had never seen water in the spillways, not in his three years working here.

He glanced up at the gravel dike, holding back all the water in Lake Mojave, just in time to see the explosion, a gray and black cloud shooting high into the air over the middle of the dike. Blaine instinctively ducked for cover. Looking back out to the dam he could make out rocks and other large clumps of material in the cloud. While Blaine watched, mesmerized, the sound wave hit him like a hammer, knocking him backwards. He dropped the donut. The intense pain in his ears caused him to drop the coffee as well in an attempt to cover them to protect them. He heard one of the policemen swear. He looked up at the dike again and saw that most of the debris had fallen, but a large cloud remained. He looked down at the ground and saw his spilled coffee and donut.

He articulated his feelings. "What the hell happened?" His ears were still ringing so loudly that ambient sounds were muffled.

Blaine looked around. He knew the techs were over by the spillways someplace and he'd seen Billy, the other guard, walk over there too. Ears still ringing, he pulled his radio from his belt and looked at the display, half expecting the thing to be busted. The radio blasted before he tried to talk into it. It was Billy. "Blaine, you okay?"

Blaine heard it, but just barely over the ringing in his ears. He turned up the volume and responded. "Roger, I'm okay, but my ears are ringing like a church bell. What happened?"

The radio squawked again. "We don't know what blew. From the control center, we heard it, but we couldn't see anything."

Blaine looked back up on the dike where the dust had mostly settled and now he saw a thirty-foot-deep, thirty-foot-wide notch in the dike. He keyed the mike. "Unfreakin believable, there's a big hole blown out of the top of the dam."

There was silence after Blaine's description before Billy asked another question. "Blaine, the techs wanna know if there's any water, you know, coming out of the notch."

Blaine looked hard, trying to see through the remaining cloud of dust. "It don't look like it."

There was silence again. Blaine guessed that Billy was talking to the techs.

Finally Billy said, "Blaine, the guys are going up to check it out. You'd better call Hoover and report it." The radio went silent for a second, then, "Maybe you'd better call the cops too."

Blaine looked over at the two cops working the roadblock with him. They both stared up at the dam with they're mouths hanging open. Blaine didn't think he would need to call them. But the call to Hoover was a great idea.

* * *

10:15 p.m. - Boulder City, Nevada

A waitress, probably in her fifties, far beyond the age to wear such a short, revealing cocktail dress, took their menus, then turned and headed back to the kitchen. Grant wondered how the casinos persuaded older ladies to wear those dresses. You'd think they'd go on strike or something. They were unionized, weren't they? Yet you saw it in almost all the casinos, especially the older ones.

At Fred's request, she had seated them where they could look out over the casino floor. An infinite number of lights blinked on and off, while the sounds of clinking coins and the distinctive cycling sounds of slot machines permeated the large room. Grant watched a fat woman on a stool between two slot machines feed coins into one, pull the handle, then feed coins into the other, while waiting for the three windows to sequence and stop.

The Hacienda Hotel & Casino sat on top of a hill offering a spectacular view of Lake Mead, just minutes from Hoover Dam. Fred told him that although listed in Boulder City, the Hacienda was technically just outside the city limits, on county property, necessitated by an anti-gambling ordinance in Boulder City, the only such ordinance in Nevada.

In the 1930s, in the midst of the depression, Boulder City had been a private community, built to house workers and their families employed in the construction of Hoover Dam. When the construction companies ran the town, they outlawed booze, gambling, and prostitution. In fact, to discourage bad habits, the workers were paid with special Boulder money, only accepted in grocery and clothing stores in Boulder.

Fred laughed when he pointed out that it hadn't taken long for the casinos in Vegas to react, and accept the Boulder money. Consequently, citizens of Las Vegas, including prostitutes, casino workers, and liquor storeowners, often came to shop in Boulder for groceries or clothes, and spend the Boulder money. Once the dam was completed, Boulder City transformed into a normal city, governed by elected officials, but the anti-gambling laws remained, something the citizens of Boulder were proud of.

As Grant scanned the casino floor, looking at the people mulling through the slots, video games, and card tables, he tried to discern their level of anxiety. The gamblers did not seem overly concerned about the impending flood on the Colorado River, or about Hoover Dam being closed. Because of the Hacienda's location, he guessed that many of the casino's occupants lived in Arizona. This was their state-line casino. However, they didn't seem panicky or even nervous, trapped in Nevada with their only bridge closed. They acted more like skiers, snowed in at the ski resort, forced to call their boss and request a couple more days off due to an unfortunate turn of events that ended up forcing them to extend their vacations.

When Grant looked back at Fred, Fred was smiling.

"What?" Grant said.

"You. What are you thinking?"

"Just that all these people . . ." Grant motioned at the gamblers, "They seem oblivious to everything that's going on."

"You jealous?"

"Nah. It's just hard to believe, with all that's going on less than two miles away. Most of these people look more concerned with whether or not they're going to lose five bucks in the slots." Grant took a sip of ice water. "It's just amazing."

Fred sipped his drink. "So how'd you get roped into this, anyway?"

Grant smiled. "I almost didn't. I was supposed to be in Africa with the rest of them. It was a last-minute thing to leave me in charge. Believe me, if they had an idea something like this was going to happen, they would have sent me to Siberia. They wouldn't have wanted me within a hundred miles of this thing."

Fred's brows furrowed. "Why not? You're doing a great job. Everything you've done has been right on."

The day had been such a whirlwind that Grant hadn't thought much about it. He did feel good about himself, though. He had made more decisions today than in the last fifteen years at the Bureau. It felt like a different job. When he joined the Bureau as a new civil engineer, he had dreamed about this life. Not the crisis management, but the offsite assignments at construction projects scattered around the country. He had always felt he would be in charge of a big dam, making the necessary decisions. But the 80's and 90's bore few new construction projects for the Bureau of Reclamation. For the last few years, Grant struggled to fit in. He wasn't good at politics. He'd even considered leaving. But today had been different, more like he envisioned fifteen years before.

Grant considered Fred's compliment. "I think it's a little early to say everything's going to work. Roland is never going to understand me blowing the spillways. Besides, if the Hoover-Two fails, I'll be the goat."

Ever since coming up with the dam extension idea, Grant kept imagining the rising water breaking through his sandbag dam. He thought it would work, but the image of it failing kept playing over and over in his mind.

Fred shook his head. "It's not going to fail. Besides, when it holds, you'll be hailed as a genius."

Neither of them said anything for a moment.

Fred finally broke the ice. "You're married, right? You got kids in Denver?"

Grant looked abruptly at his watch. He had forgotten all about his family. He glanced at Fred apologetically. "You know, I've been so busy, I never even called my wife. I should probably take a moment and give her a call. With the news and all, she's probably wondering what's going on."

Fred motioned away with his hand. "Sure. Take as long as you want."

Grant stood and walked over to a quieter place in the restaurant where the casino noise was muffled before punching his home number into the cell phone. She was probably already asleep. The phone rang twice before his wife picked it up.

"Hello?" Her voice sounded energetic, not sleepy.

"Hi honey."

"Grant!" she said, excited. "I wondered if you were going to call. We saw you on TV. The kids couldn't believe it. All the neighbors called. The news channels have been showing the dam breaking up all night. Wow, it's terrible."

The image of the Glen Canyon Dam breaking apart seemed like a lifetime ago. Grant had actually forgotten about the TV interview. The thought of his face being broadcast around the country was incomprehensible. He tried to remember what he'd said, but couldn't. It really didn't matter anyway; Roland wouldn't like it.

His wife continued, "I almost called you, but I wasn't sure it'd be okay. What are you doing now that the dam's gone?"

"I'm not in Arizona anymore. I flew to Hoover Dam this morning, right after the interview."

"Hoover? Isn't that where we went when we were in Vegas?"

He remembered the trip.

"Yeah, Vegas is about forty minutes away."

"What are you doing there? Did something happen there too?"

He laughed to himself that most people viewed a dam failure as an isolated event, not considering the inevitable destruction downstream from all the floodwater. "No, but it will. All the water from Lake Powell is headed our way. We're doing everything we can to get ready for it. It's pretty hairy, actually. We're doing all kinds of crazy stuff."

His wife hesitated for a second. "Are you in danger?"

"No. Not really," he replied.

"How does it feel to be in charge?"

He thought about the question. The pressure had been intense but exhilarating. Even the governor of Nevada had acted on his decisions.

"A lot different than normal, that's for sure," he said. It was all he could think of.

She spoke boldly. "Well it's about time. You're smarter than those morons you work for anyway. They're just brown-nosers." She hesitated. "Have you heard from them?"

Grant realized he was nodding. "Yeah. Roland called this morning and Howard called an hour ago."

"Are they coming back?"

"Roland never made it to Africa. He's trying to get back here now. I expect him sometime tomorrow morning. Howard is still deciding." Grant laughed. "He's afraid to abandon his wife in Yellowstone. But I expect him, too. You know him, he can't stand being out of the loop, especially with Roland coming here."

"He's a creep, Grant."

"Yeah, I know."

The phone went silent again. Grant looked back at the table and he saw the waitress setting the dinner plates on the table. He didn't know what else to say. "Hey, I better let you go so you can get to sleep."

"When are you coming home?"

He wondered the same thing himself. Realistically, he might get stuck out here cleaning up messes for weeks or even months. "I don't know, honey. I'll call you tomorrow when I get a better idea."

"I love you," she said.

Her comment caught him off guard. The "love" words were not often verbalized in their marriage. "I love you too," he mumbled uncomfortably.

He hung up and wandered back to the table. Fred, already cutting into his steak, looked up and smiled when Grant returned.

"What'd she say?"

"She said all the neighbors saw me on TV."

Fred grinned and stuffed some steak in his mouth and responded while still chewing. "Can I wait and get your autograph after dinner?"

Grant laughed. "Yeah. Sure." He sat down and grabbed his steak knife and started to slice his steak when the cell phone rang. He looked at Fred apologetically. "Probably my wife again." However, when he saw the display, the number showed 702, a Nevada number.

He answered, "Hello?"

"Mr. Stevens?" the voice asked. It was a woman's voice that Grant didn't recognize.

"Yeah. I'm Grant Stevens."

The person on the other end sounded nervous. "You guys better get back here. There's been another bomb."

Grant dropped his knife on the plate. Fred looked up and stopped chewing.

"At Hoover?" Grant asked.

"No, Mr. Stevens. Downstream at Lake Mojave. Davis Dam."

The information made no sense. Grant stood. "We'll get back as fast as we can."

Grant hung up the phone and looked over at Fred. "They blew up Davis Dam." Grant waited for Fred to stand, then turned to leave before remembering the check, which the waitress hadn't left on the table yet.

Fred, one step ahead of him, pulled his wallet from his pocket and pulled a twenty out and tossed it on the table, more than enough to cover the casino steaks.

At the last minute while standing and ready to go, Grant looked back at the steak and felt a huge regret, finally noticing how hungry he was. He reached down and cut a large slice and stuffed it in his mouth. Fred nodded and grabbed the rolls out of the basket in the middle of the table.

"Back to Hoover?" Fred asked, more a statement than a question.

Grant nodded.

CHAPTER 25

———

10:20 p.m. - Hoover Dam, Nevada

As soon as Grant and Fred walked back into the Hoover Dam visitor center, they tracked down the person who had taken the call from Davis Dam. The call had been taken by one of Fred's technicians. The woman explained that the guy at Davis was a security guard named Blaine. Grant dialed the number, and Blaine picked right up.

"Davis Dam. Blaine."

"This is Grant Stevens from the Bureau of Reclamation. I'm calling from Hoover Dam. What happened there, Blaine?"

"He blew the place up. Up on the dike. There's a big hole in it now."

He? The reference threw Grant for a loop, making him abandon his previous questions. "Who, Blaine? You said 'he' blew it up?"

Blaine's answer came back as if everyone should know. "The guy from the Bureau. He was just up there drilling holes in the spot where it exploded. He's the one that must've done it."

Grant was confused. "Bureau guy?"

"Yeah. He drove up here in a Bureau truck, logo and everything. Said he needed to take moisture tests and that he would be drilling into the dam."

Grant wanted to ask a million more questions about the perpetrator, now possibly an insider, but forced himself to focus on the damage. "Blaine, I'll come back to him later. What about the dam? You said something about a big hole. How bad is it?" He was afraid of the answer.

"It's big. About thirty feet deep and forty feet wide."

Grant concluded that the amount of water already flowing through must be incredible. "How fast is it washing out, Blaine?"

There was silence. "Whaddya mean?"

Grant explained. "Water. How much water is going through the hole and how fast is it growing?"

There was a moment of hesitation from the guard. "None. There ain't no water coming out yet, just a big notch in the dam. Hell, you think I'd be standin' here answerin' the phones if the dam was falling apart?"

This confused Grant. How could there not be any water? At the same time, he felt like he had just won the lottery. They might still be able to save Davis, something he hadn't even dared to consider since he first received the news of the explosion. "I'm confused, Blaine. You said there's an opening in the dam thirty feet deep, yet there's no water. That doesn't make sense. How could the water not be pouring out? The dam's almost full, isn't it?"

"I don't know Mr. . . . What'd you say your name was?"

"Stevens. Grant Stevens." Grant could sense the guy's excitement and forgave him for not remembering his name. "Blaine, has anyone gone up there and inspected it yet?"

"They're up there right now, Mr. Stevens."

"Can you connect me with one of them?"

* * *

10:30 p.m. - Davis Dam, Nevada

Billy Watkins walked up to the edge of the crater on top of Davis Dam. His nostrils flared at the smell of something he didn't recognize. It reminded him of the air after a thunderstorm, only this air didn't smell as clean. It had the same charged quality, but it was mixed with dust and a chemical smell, some of which still floated in the air. Billy stood tall and lanky in his security uniform. He had ratty, unkempt blond hair that wandered out from under his security hat, and he sported a thin mustache. Billy tried to make up for the thinness by letting it grow longer, but this only resulted in the hairs tending to mat together and highlight rather than cover up the thinness.

He peered down into the hole, bracing himself, not knowing how stable the bank might be. He jumped when his cell phone rang. He saw the others, Dennis the night shift technician and the two day-shift techs, glance over at his ringing phone. He picked it up. "Hello?"

The man introduced himself as a Grant Stevens from the Bureau of Reclamation. He said he was calling from Hoover and that Blaine had given him Billy's cell phone number.

"What can I do for you, Mr. Stevens?"

"Blaine told me that you are inspecting the dam. What can you tell me about the damage?"

Billy looked around, noticing that the crater was concentrated on the dry side of the dam. The notch didn't go all the way through to the wet side, which would have been a disaster. "We just got up here," he said. He described, as best he could, the huge crater and how it didn't reach to the wet side of the dam. While he explained the situation to the guy on the phone, he saw Dennis run over and pick up something. Dennis waved to him, motioning him over to look at what he had just found.

"Hang on, Mr. Stevens. Looks like Dennis found something." Still clutching the phone to his ear, he skirted the perimeter of the crater over to where the notch would have extended to the wet side. Dennis held the ends of two green wires that stuck out of the ground. Billy relayed the find to Grant.

"So one of his bombs didn't detonate?" Billy heard Grant ask into the phone, a conclusion Billy had reached independently.

"Yeah, I'd say that's what happened," he responded.

"Is the dam stable? Does it need to be reinforced?" Grant asked.

Billy looked around. He was just a security guard. How was he supposed to know? He brought the phone down and asked Dennis, "Hey, this guy wants to know if the dam needs shoring up. He's wondering if it might be weak enough to fail as the water rises."

Dennis shrugged, looking down at the water. "Gee, I don't know. Then again, it wouldn't hurt anything to shore it up, would it?"

Billy relayed the message to Grant. "Mr. Stevens, none of us are qualified to make that decision, but why not shore it up?"

Grant responded immediately. "You're right, Billy. Let's do it. I'm coming down there. I'll be in touch." He gave Billy his cell phone number in case anything changed and hung up.

Billy looked back at the crater, and imagined for a moment what might have happened if the bomb had worked as planned. He looked down at the dry riverbed below the gravel dike holding back Lake Mojave. He tried to picture the potential destruction. He glanced downstream toward Laughlin. He knew the water would wipe out all of the buildings within his view. They had been lucky, very lucky.

* * *

10:45 p.m. - Hoover Dam, Nevada

Grant hung up the phone. Fred sat looking at him, having patiently listened to Grant's side of the phone conversation.

"So you're gonna go down there?" Fred asked.

"Yeah. We need to shore it up. We can't have it breaking when the water rises."

Fred pointed at him. "But what can you do?"

"That's where I need your help. Since Davis Dam is managed from here, where do you guys get the construction equipment, operators, and gravel?"

Fred sat back in his chair and shook his head. "Grant, that dam's old. I don't remember anybody messing with the dike for years. The biggest projects have probably been moving gravel around in the parking lot."

"Fine. Who'd you use to do the parking lot?"

Fred held out his hands. "Like I said, I don't know; probably some private company."

"All right, call the biggest construction company in Laughlin. Track 'em down and get 'em out of bed. Call the cops if you need to. Let's get them to the dam site as fast as possible. If you're not sure if there's any fill material available at the site, then tell 'em to bring some in dump trucks." Grant wondered if he'd missed anything. "Oh, and I need you to find a helicopter to fly me down there."

Fred took a moment and wrote down a few notes. "I know someone with a helicopter who can fly you down. When do you want to leave?"

Grant looked at his watch. "Immediately." Then he had another thought. "Wait, make that ten minutes. I have another phone call I need to make."

Fred hurried away, and Grant dialed the number from a note in his pocket. When the man answered, Grant spoke into the phone. "Hello, I'm trying to find Phil, of the FBI."

The special agent responded immediately. "Yes. This is Phil. Who's speaking, please?"

"Grant Stevens from the Bureau. I met you at the Glen Canyon Dam."

"Grant Stevens. Long time no talk. It has been a long day, hasn't it? How are things at Hoover, anyway? Did you think of something for my investigation?" The lifeless tone in Phil's voice told Grant that he hadn't rested either since it began.

"Let me guess – you guys haven't caught the bad guys yet, have you?"

"No, but we are working on a few leads." The agent didn't sound nearly as confident as his words.

"Well, I have another lead for you. They struck again at Davis Dam. Maybe twenty minutes ago."

The agent came to life, almost shouting in the phone. "How do you know it was him?"

Grant hadn't even considered it might be unrelated. "I don't. I just assumed."

Phil interrupted. "Where is Davis Dam anyway? How bad is this one?"

Grant was surprised Phil didn't know where Davis was. He was from California. "Davis Dam holds back Lake Mojave. It's just downstream of Hoover Dam. You know – Laughlin, Nevada."

"How bad is it?" Phil asked again.

"As far as the damage goes, we got lucky. They found two wires sticking out of the ground, next to the main crater. Looks like at least one of the bombs didn't detonate. If it had, we'd have another dam gone, another big flood."

The phone went silent for a moment. Grant guessed that Phil took a second to process the information. "Grant, where are you going to be? I'd like my men to look over the un-detonated bomb, before it gets disturbed."

"A helicopter's flying me down to Davis Dam in a few minutes. We're trying to arrange for some construction guys with some front loaders and bulldozers. We need to shore it up, before it really does fail. I haven't seen the site yet, so I can't promise that we'll be able to do our stuff without disturbing it."

Phil sounded desperate. "Look, I just need a few minutes with it. How soon are your guys going to be ready?"

Grant knew he couldn't risk it. "Phil, we're just trying to round up the machinery as we speak. It'll probably be an hour before anything happens. But, I can't hold 'em. If you want to see it, then get one of your men out of Vegas and helicopter him down there now. The risk is too great if I wait." Grant was amazed at the way he was bossing around the FBI.

"Okay, that's fair. I'll try to get a special agent out of Vegas, pronto." Phil took a second, then continued. "Oh, and Grant, thanks for the call. I think I'll leave a few agents here and move the investigation your way, where the trail's still warm. Are you going to be at Davis for long?"

"No. I'll only be there for a couple of hours, until I feel the dam's safe. Then I'm coming back here. We've got a lot of water heading our way, and I'm setting up a science experiment to see if we can contain it."

"All right Grant, we'll see you soon."

Grant heard the connection drop.

Fred was waiting. "The helicopter's on it's way here. Are you ready?"

Grant looked around and considered the question. "Ready as I'll ever be."

CHAPTER 26

11:15 p.m. - Hoover Dam, Nevada

Grant felt his stomach turn as the helicopter lifted. It wasn't that he was overly susceptible to motion sickness. But he felt strange just the same. It had been a long time since he'd flown in a helicopter, maybe ten years, and never in a work capacity for the Bureau of Reclamation.

As they gained altitude, the left seat offered a great view of Hoover Dam and the frantic construction project underway. He could see that progress on the sandbag dike continued unabated. The top of the dam was a beehive of activity. If nothing went wrong, it should be completed in time. Again, he had to fight the image of Hoover-Two not being high enough, the floodwater spilling over the top, washing away the sandbags. But he did feel it would be high enough. They'd done the math multiple times. Nevertheless, the image kept coming, tormenting his thoughts.

The helicopter banked and the view of Hoover Dam rotated behind him, lost from sight. Up ahead, the clear night and partial moon allowed a haunting view into the dark chasm below of Black Canyon. Occasional sparkles of light reflected off the Colorado River deep down in the canyon and showed the path carved by the river millions of years before. Eventually, as they passed the canyons and surrounding hills, the landscape opened up and began to flatten out. From here to the Gulf of California was all flat desert. Up ahead, far in the distance, Grant could make out a grouping of lights. He and the pilot both wore a set of headphones with a microphone extending from the left side. Grant shouted into his headset microphone, "Is that Laughlin?" He could hear his loud voice in the headphones at the same time.

The pilot, who had not yet spoken, responded, "Yeah, the first set of lights are from North Laughlin. The lights behind are from South Laughlin and Bullhead City, Arizona, which is below the dam; those casinos are on the banks of the Colorado River."

Grant quickly determined that if the Davis Dam broke, he would not want to be staying in South Laughlin.

The pilot and helicopter had come from one of the many Las Vegas tour companies, which were available for charter twenty-four hours a day. They flew Las Vegas visitors to a multitude of places including the Vegas skyline, Hoover Dam, Laughlin, and even the Grand Canyon. Fred said they were extremely flexible and would fly you almost anywhere you would pay them to go. For a little extra, negotiated by Fred, they had agreed to pick Grant up at Hoover and drop him right in the parking lot at Davis Dam.

Although it was too dark to tell, Grant wondered how much flooding would be occurring right now in the upper reaches of Lake Mojave. With all the gates and spillways open at Hoover, the flow down the Colorado into Lake Mojave dwarfed anything in the history of the lake.

For a moment Grant's thoughts wandered randomly, not dwelling on any one subject. Then he thought about the perpetrators of the two bombings, something he had been too busy to think much about. The bomb at Glen Canyon Dam this morning had been easy enough to explain. The dam had been considered a foreign terrorist target for years by the federal government due to its massive size and social prominence. Additionally, the environmentalists hated it passionately, mostly due to Glen Canyon being buried under Lake Powell. Others claimed the Glen Canyon Dam was not financially feasible, and accused the Bureau of cooking the books to get it approved in the first place.

But why Davis Dam? Most people had never even heard of it, including FBI Phil who was from Southern California. It certainly didn't seem prominent enough to attract foreign terrorists. Why then would they want to blow up something no one had ever heard of? And as far as he knew, Lake Mojave didn't bury any environmental treasures like Lake Powell did.

He wondered briefly about whether they would blow Davis to kill someone downstream in Laughlin, but if that were the case, why Glen Canyon earlier that morning? Theoretically, it was possible that the casino owners in Las Vegas would want to destroy the casinos in Laughlin to reduce competition, but the idea seemed far-fetched. In his estimation, blowing up the Glen Canyon Dam would be much more difficult than Davis, even though the attempt at Davis hadn't been successful. No, Davis had to be part of a bigger overall plan. And if so, what could be their primary goal? If Grant were a terrorist, and had succeeded in taking out the Glen Canyon Dam, he would have celebrated and retired. Glen Canyon was the mother-lode of controversial dams. What more could they want?

Grant concluded that he did not have all the pieces to the puzzle, which simultaneously convinced him that more puzzle pieces would be forthcoming. In other words, more dams would be blown. He was now certain of it. They were now dealing with a serial bomber. A heightened level of anxiety settled over him. This wasn't over yet. Where would the next strike occur? He hoped that Phil and his FBI team arrived at Davis soon. They needed to talk. In fact, they needed to do more than investigate. They needed to beef up the security at more potential targets. If only he knew what those targets were.

The pilot pulled Grant out of his thoughts. "You can see the dam right up there."

Normally a statement like that was accompanied by a pointed finger or motion of the hand, but the pilot's hands were busy on the controls. Grant couldn't miss the dam a couple of miles away, completely lit up with strong lights, just as Hoover was.

* * *

11:50 p.m. - Davis Dam, Nevada

The construction guy stood waiting for Grant when the helicopter landed. Blaine, the security man, stood next to him. The construction guy introduced himself as Reese Burke and drove a four-door, four-wheel-drive pickup that looked remarkably like the one driven by the demolition guy at Hoover earlier in the day. Reese had a gut that wouldn't quit, making it impossible to tuck in the front of his shirt, and his pants hung very low, making Grant wonder how they stayed up at all. Grant made a mental note to look away if Reese bent over.

The construction man Reese accused the Laughlin cops of scaring him to death, waking him by banging on his front door. It had taken him another twenty minutes to gather his senses, decide what to do, and raise enough men to get things moving. Five dump trucks were loaded and en route, as well as two bulldozers and a front loader. The five trucks were expected any minute.

Grant looked around and saw that generally things looked normal at Davis Dam. To an unsuspecting eye, the dike looked normal and unharmed. The concrete waterworks gave no hint of the water building up behind them. He was anxious to get up on the dam and inspect the damage, but was delayed again when another helicopter approached and landed in the parking lot. Covering his eyes to shield the dust stirred up by the chopper, Grant saw a woman wearing blue FBI coveralls jump out, crouch, and run toward them. She carried a large briefcase. The helicopter, from another Las Vegas tour company, took off immediately, climbing back into the night sky.

After waiting a second for the noise to abate from the retreating chopper, Grant stuck out his hand and introduced himself.

"Special Agent Susan Williams," she responded. Grant noticed that her handshake felt firm, like a man's, which was surprising since her features were noticeably feminine. She had a plain but pretty face without blemish, long brown hair, and probably barely tipped the scales at a hundred pounds.

"You're the explosives specialist that Phil talked about?"

She nodded.

He glanced at his watch. "Wow. You got here quick."

Her gritted teeth showed her disapproval. "Phil told me you wouldn't wait for us, and that if I wanted to see the bomb site, I needed to get here before you. That didn't give me much time."

Grant felt the resentment and took note to walk on eggshells with her. "Well, I appreciate the effort." He pointed up at the crater on Davis dam. "Let's get up there and look around. We probably have about a half hour before Reese here," He motioned toward the construction man who was smiling broadly at the FBI woman. "will have bulldozers and trucks trampling the whole area."

The agent nodded anxiously. Grant turned toward the dam and had actually taken a couple of uncertain steps before he heard the security guard, Blaine, from behind.

"You can drive up over there."

Grant turned back in time to see Blaine point at where the highway climbed the west side of the dam.

Reese motioned toward his pickup. "Hop in. I'll take you and the girl up."

Grant thought he detected a brief look of resentment in the agent's expression at Reese addressing her as a girl, but it was gone before he could be sure.

Before she walked to the truck, she turned to Blaine. "Which one of you saw the bomber?"

Blaine's eyes went down as if he might be in trouble. "It was me. But he looked pretty official when . . ." His words trailed off.

"Come up there with us," she told him forcefully. "I need to ask you some questions."

Blaine nodded. "Sure."

Grant and Special Agent Williams reached Reese's truck at the same time and Grant went out of his way to offer her the front seat. She acted slightly irritated, but Grant thought he also detected a touch of appreciation as she consented and climbed in the front. The security guard climbed in the back with Grant. Reese had no sooner started the truck when she turned abruptly.

"Wait." She was looking in the back seat toward the security guard. "I need a shovel."

Reese slammed the truck in gear and took off, ignoring her. "Relax. I got shovels in the back." Grant didn't think Reese's mannerisms were earning him any points with the FBI.

When the truck leveled onto the crest of Davis Dam, Grant saw the water level was alarmingly high. The huge spotlights lit up the water for a hundred feet or so from the dam. Grant couldn't help thinking about Hoover Dam, just sixty-five miles upstream, dumping water at record levels. He looked out the other window, down the 200-foot-high gravel embankment. Although he knew the dike's height, looking down it at night made it seem much taller. He straightened up and looked ahead between Reese and Agent Williams and saw the large crater, just ahead.

"You see it, right?" he said to Reese.

"See what?" Reese joked, although none of the passengers laughed.

Agent Williams leaned forward, grasping the dashboard to get a better look. "Don't get too close. Stop about here." She didn't look at Reese, but kept her eyes on the crater.

Reese eased the truck to a halt. "Here?"

"Yeah, that's fine," she said.

Reese shut off the truck and all four of them hopped out.

The agent looked at Blaine. "How many people have been over the site since the explosion?"

Blaine responded, "Billy and two technicians."

"Did they drive up here or walk?"

"They walked. They came over from the generation plant. " He pointed toward the concrete structure that housed the turbines.

"So no other vehicles have been up here since the explosion?"

Blaine shook his head. "No. We're the first."

"Did they touch the wires?" she asked. Her presence was much more powerful than Grant would have guessed when he first saw her.

Blaine hesitated. "Yeah, I think Billy said they picked up the wires when they saw them." He looked around at Grant and Reese for support. "Sorry," he added.

Grant thought he saw her grit her teeth again.

"Don't worry," she said. "Hopefully we can still get a few good prints off the wires."

She started off toward the crater and stopped abruptly, turning around to face them. Although none of them had yet moved, she told them to stay put and give her a few moments alone on the site.

After she walked out of earshot, Reese spoke up. "Bossy little thing, ain't she?"

Grant guessed that in Reese's line of work, he seldom ran into women in powerful positions. He defended her. "At least she seems competent. Let's hope she gets some fingerprints or something else to catch our bad guy."

Reese lowered his voice. "Is this the same guy that wiped out Lake Powell's dam this morning?"

The question surprised Grant. He shrugged his shoulders. "Hey, I'm not the FBI. I'm just a guy that works on the dams. But yeah, that's the speculation."

"Unbelievable," Blaine said from behind.

DAY THREE

Wednesday, June 23

CHAPTER 27

12:02 a.m. - Davis Dam, Nevada

Grant, Reese, and Blaine watched the FBI woman meticulously walk the area around the crater. She stopped occasionally, and with a huge set of tweezers, retrieved small objects and placed them in zip-lock bags. After she had spent a few minutes covering the area, she stood straight and glanced back at the men.

"Can we come over there yet?" Grant yelled.

She scanned the area under her feet, then looked back up and waved them over. "Bring the shovels," she yelled.

Reese grabbed two shovels out of the back of his truck, then the three men walked toward the crater and the waiting agent. The crest of the dam had been just over fifty feet wide. However, the explosion had carved over thirty feet away on the downstream side. At first glance, Grant guessed that there had been a line of explosive devices, and that one had not detonated. When they reached Agent Williams, she crouched, holding something. Grant saw two green wires sticking out of the ground, which the agent had wrapped in plastic to prevent further contamination. She asked for one of the shovels and immediately started trying to dig next to where the wires came out of the ground. The wires extruded from a hole drilled into the asphalt road, and the shovel made no progress. She swiveled around the wires, looking for a better angle, but the asphalt wouldn't give. Grant wondered what she would do next.

Reese walked up behind her. "That ain't gonna work."

She glared at him and Grant could tell she resented the man, but she stopped digging. "What do you suggest?"

Reese lifted his hat and swept his hand over his balding head. "I have some other tools, chisels and stuff that would work to widen the hole a little, but it'd take too long." He pointed from Grant to the crater. "We can't wait around for a couple of hours while you bring up a spoonful at a time." She glared at him, but he continued. "Why don't we just pull the thing out of the hole?"

She looked at Reese and frowned. "It's an intact detonator. I don't want to pull the wires out of it or I might damage it."

The comment made the construction man hesitate. "It ain't gonna blow up, is it?"

She shook her head. "No, but I need to get the detonator undisturbed if possible, especially if it's homemade, and we need to get a clean sample of the explosive material, which I'm assuming is ammonium nitrate fertilizer. That's what they used at Glen Canyon."

"Assuming it's the same guys," Grant added from behind.

Agent Williams and Reese both looked at Grant, but neither said anything.

Reese motioned toward the hole. "I got some long screw drivers and stuff that we can poke down there. If we can loosen all that stuff on top, you might be able to pull the detonator out without screwing it up too bad."

She gave in and nodded.

Reese scrounged around in the back of his truck and returned with the tools and a section of galvanized pipe. Reese knelt down to dig, but the agent handed him the wires, took the long screwdriver and began the excavation herself. In order to see better, she pulled a long metal flashlight out of her case, and shined it down the hole. She dug only a few inches, before she became excited.

"Definitely ammonium nitrate," she said enthusiastically. She carefully scooped small amounts into another zip-lock bag.

Reese watched her zip a bag closed. "You need that for evidence?"

She resumed digging. "We should be able to get a chemical signature off these samples. It could show whether it was the same batch as Glen Canyon." She glanced at him for a second. "We might even be able to figure out where it was manufactured."

Reese turned around and winked at Grant. "If I was married to her, I don't think I'd be sneaking around behind her back."

Grant noticed Agent Williams grunt a small laugh. It was the first sign that she might actually have a sense of humor. Somewhere behind, he heard a rumbling sound. He turned to see a large flatbed semi coming through the security gate with a huge bulldozer on the back. He saw two more trucks behind, one carrying a second smaller bulldozer, and the third with the front loader. He wondered how much longer Agent Williams would need.

"Hold it." She stopped Reese who was scooping debris away from the whole with his hand. She took the wires from him and gently tugged in various directions. "It's coming." She jostled it again, then carefully withdrew a black metal tube from the hole.

"Got it," she said and they all watched as she carefully coiled the wire and the detonator into a large plastic bag, trying not to handle it any more than necessary.

"Unbelievable," Blaine whispered from behind.

She retrieved a small dipper out of her case and scooped up more of the white pellets. These she put in a smaller plastic bag. She went down for two more scoops before she felt satisfied. She started packing the two bags back in the case when Reese interrupted her.

"Is that it?"

She looked up, obviously not as stressed as when she arrived. "Yeah, sure." She hesitated, staring at what she had in her hands, then looked up at Grant. "You guys can go ahead."

Reese walked back to his pickup to radio the truck drivers below. Special Agent Williams spent a moment measuring the hole with a small ruler, then retrieved a camera from her briefcase and shuffled around the hole taking multiple pictures.

With the explosive issue taken care of, Grant turned and studied the crater for the first time. At thirty feet wide, it covered most of the width of the top of the dam, leaving only twenty feet where they had dug up the explosives. It made him hesitate to step too close to the edge, afraid the bank would collapse and he'd fall into the crater. A glance upstream where the still, black water inched higher by the minute more than convinced him to count his lucky stars that the bomb in question had not detonated. If the explosion had gone as planned, water would be flowing over the dam and they would have lost Davis Dam.

Reese approached. "I'm going back down to talk to my boys that just showed up." He motioned to the truck. "You staying up here or you want a ride?"

Blaine spoke to Special Agent Williams. "If you don't need me, I'll go with him."

The special agent shook her head at Blaine. "No, you can go. I'll catch up with you later." She looked at Reese and motioned around the ground. "I'll look around some more, see if I can find any more evidence before you guys trample it."

Grant didn't think there was anything he could accomplish below. "I'll stay up here too."

Reese nodded and he and Blaine headed for the pickup. Before they reached it, Grant heard the truck engines below shut off. In the absence of the sound of the engines, he heard a rumbling that he didn't remember from before. He turned his head to isolate the sound without any luck.

Grant cupped his hands and called out to the others. "Hey, what's that rumbling sound?"

He saw them turn and look around. Blaine pointed back toward the dam's concrete water works. "The spillways!" Blaine yelled. "They're opening them."

Grant turned. Three huge square head gates situated at the top of the concrete structure, each the width of three cars, were being slowly opened. An amazing amount of water was now sliding down the face of them and crashing into the pool at the bottom. The rumbling noise, similar to a waterfall, had come from there. They had waited as long as possible to open them, allowing more preparation time for the casinos and homes downstream. But Grant had warned the governor that they could only delay opening the spillways until Lake Mojave was full, which it now was.

When he looked back, Reese and Blaine were already in the truck and backing away from him along the crest of the dam. He saw Agent Williams walking around the crater, stopping occasionally to kick her feet in the loose debris from the explosion. He listened again to the rumbling water behind him, and then walked carefully over to the reservoir. He crouched down and looked at where the water met the dike. He watched it ripple onto the shore. After a few moments he gave up. It wasn't rising fast enough to see. However, the bank of Lake Mojave was dry less than six inches above the water line. He didn't remember ever seeing a wet band that small around any lake. That alone was enough evidence of how fast the water was rising.

In the meantime, the dump trucks had arrived, and one was already headed up the dam. A wave of tiredness rolled through him and made him look at his watch: 12:25 a.m., 1:25 a.m. in Denver. No wonder he was so tired. He considered sitting down somewhere and resting. He wiped sweat off his brow and thought about slipping under the covers with his wife in his air-conditioned bedroom back in Colorado.

The first dump truck reached the crest of the dam, made a three-point turn, then began backing across the dam toward the crater. The first bulldozer had climbed about halfway up the dam. Grant saw below that they were already unloading the second bulldozer, and the second dump truck had started up the hill. When the first truck had backed up to the crater, it stopped, engine running, and the driver climbed out of the truck and walked over next to Grant.

The man wore a stained cowboy hat and smiled broadly. "Where do you want this?" he pointed at the truck.

Grant fumbled for a response.

"Just kidding," said the truck driver. "Reese already told me to dump it next to the hole." The man tilted his head toward the spot. "Then the 'dozers can push it where they need it." The man looked down in the crater while he took off his cowboy hat and wiped his brow with his arm. "Looks like somebody almost drained the lake."

While they were both staring in the hole, they heard Reese honk the horn of his truck from below. Grant wondered what Reese meant for them to do.

The man donned his hat again. "That's the boss telling me to shut up, dump, and go get another load." He glanced down at the crater again, then trotted back to his truck.

The engine revved as the hoist tilted the bed of the truck. Grant stepped back a few steps. When the dirt began to slide out, the man pulled the truck forward slightly to spread the drop. When it was empty, he kept moving as the hoist lowered back to the normal position. As the truck headed back toward the west access road, Grant noticed the first bulldozer had crested the dam and was pivoting toward him.

Grant took the moment to inspect the pile of dirt that came out of the dump truck. He grabbed a handful and let some of it slip through his fingers. He squeezed and it compressed nicely in his hand. Reese had done a good job and got the right stuff. You put the wrong material in a dam, and you might as well not bother. Satisfied with the material, Grant walked over to the edge of the crater. He looked down, wondering again what might have been if the bomb had been slightly more successful. And then he saw it.

It couldn't be. He stood as close to the edge as possible. The glistening in the bottom of the crater had caught his eye. He needed a better look. He looked back and forth to find an easier way down, finally settling on a slightly more gradual slope on his right. The first step would be just over six feet, then a steep incline to the bottom.

He didn't have the right shoes for it, but he jumped anyway, spinning so that he was facing the bank and his toes, not his heels, would dig in and stop him. The bank wasn't as soft as he'd estimated and instead of digging in, his shoes slid down the embankment, throwing his upper body forward where the underside of his forearms caught much of his fall, scraping against the rocky dirt which tore at the soft skin. A yell escaped him before he rolled to his back and slid the final portion on his back, coming to rest near the bottom, dirty from head to foot with both arms bleeding.

Disregarding the pain, he moved quickly over to where he'd seen it, hoping even then that it'd been a mistake, a shadow maybe, or a darker clump of dirt. But it wasn't. No, it was a shallow wet puddle, a slow leak through the remaining portion of the dam. He stuck his fingers into the small puddle, hoping his eyes were deceiving him, but they weren't. Using both hands, he scooped away mud. He needed to see where the water was coming from and how much. He continued to dig with his hands, and at first he thought he had plugged it, but the dry dirt turned wet and a small stream of brown dirty water sprinkled down out of the hill.

Agent Williams called from above. "Hey, what happened? Did you fall?"

He didn't know what to say. "It's leaking," was all that came out.

And as he said it, he noticed the small stream had grown in the last few seconds. He bent over to make sure his eyes hadn't misled him and the flow increased noticeably again. He looked up at the twenty-foot section of remaining dike between him and the water and realized it wasn't wide enough. While he looked up, a clump of earth broke away and fell into the crater close to where he stood. Simultaneously he felt the unmistakable feeling of water on his right foot. When he looked down he saw his right foot in a new puddle. He could now hear the water trickling, even with the noise of the bulldozer's diesel engine and the rumbling spillways in the background. He wondered if the dike would hold until the bulldozer arrived, and decided suddenly that it wouldn't.

"Start waving your arms at them!" he yelled at the FBI agent who was still staring at him. "Wave them over here now. Tell them to hurry up."

He remembered the cell phone and frantically searched through his recently used numbers for the guard. Finding the number, he called and waited for the answer. While it rang, he felt water around his feet again.

Billy, the second guard, answered.

"Billy, this is Grant up on the dam." He waved so the guard could see him. "There's a leak in the crater. I don't know how long it's going to last. Tell Reese to get his equipment up here fast."

He saw Billy run out of the guard shack and yell to them. He saw a radio go up to Reese's mouth. Grant looked over at the bulldozer coming toward him along the crest of the dam. He waved frantically at the man, pointing into the crater. The driver must have seen him because he craned his neck, then pushed a lever. Simultaneously, black smoke poured from the exhaust pipe and the bulldozer accelerated.

Grant turned and ran back toward the puddle, only to find himself in water up to his shins. He slogged through it toward the source, but when he arrived the water reached almost to his crotch and he had to reach underwater to feel the spring. With his hand he felt the water gushing out of the dam, but it felt different than spring water; it felt gritty and occasionally Grant felt small rocks wash past his hand.

"He's almost here," Agent Williams shouted from above. "Get out of there or he'll bury you!"

A much larger block of dirt caved off of the upstream side of the crater. Grant saw it out of the corner of his eye, but with both feet in the water, he couldn't move fast enough to evade it. He put up his arms and the dirt hit him head on, knocking him back into the water. He went under. When he tried to stand up, he realized his right leg was partially buried and he had to pull hard to get it out. He lost the shoe in the process.

The thought of getting buried alive by the bulldozer motivated him that he needed to climb out, but looking up at the sides of the crater and remembering his descent, he wondered how. Then he looked downstream and realized that was the answer. He slogged toward where the dirty water was now washing out onto the face of the dam. Grant felt a gush of water take his feet out from under him. Before he went under he saw another section of the dike between him and Lake Mojave start to drop and he heard the female agent scream. For the next few moments he wasn't driving; he was just along for the ride. After he got his head back above water, he tried to grab with his hands and dig with his feet. He felt the water carry him along from the crater onto the outside face of the dam. He was dragged down the steep slope. For a moment he felt like he was on a waterslide, then he banged his arms on some rocks. He felt his big toenail tear out on the shoeless right foot. The thing that saved him was the water spreading out on the face of the dam. He stopped himself by grabbing a large rock with his right hand. Ignoring the pain now radiating out from multiple body parts, he quickly traversed across the stream to the dry incline and collapsed.

"Oh my! Are you okay?" Agent Williams had hurried down to where he lay.

He looked up at her. "Yeah," he said, although he really didn't feel okay.

She grabbed his hand. "You're a mess. We need to get you out of here." And to punctuate the statement, Grant felt water flow over his left foot as the stream expanded.

The ground vibrated and the diesel engine screamed as the bulldozer approached the flowing crater. The operator wasted no time, dropping the blade and pushing a swath in. Not waiting for the result, the machine reversed, backing up for another load. The bulldozer went back and forth multiple times until all the material from the truck was in the crater. Grant saw that the operator was getting the upper hand, as the stream diminished and finally stopped. Meanwhile, the second truck had arrived and the bulldozer waited while he dumped. The bulldozer then shoved it into the hole. When that material was in the hole, he started carving into the original dike, and pushing that into the hole. Before long the operator had built up the crater enough to drive into it and compress it, which he spent a while doing.

Grant lifted himself up, and felt what were going to be bruises. Agent Williams held his arm and they started the steep hike back to the crest. The operator stopped the bulldozer, left it idling, and jumped down and jogged over to where Grant and Agent Williams stood. "Wow, that was close. You okay, buddy?"

Grant nodded. "Just a little banged up." He pointed at the partially filled crater. "For a while there I didn't think you were going to be able to stop it."

The operator smiled. "For a while there I almost didn't. A few more seconds and it would have beat us. We'd be evacuating this place."

While they talked, Reese pulled his pickup behind the idling bulldozer and walked over. "Thanks for the heads up, Mr. Stevens. Good save." His eyes gave Grant a once over. "By the way, you look terrible."

Grant looked down and saw that his clothes were filthy. There was blood on both his arms and on his foot where he lost the toenail. "Thanks," Grant responded, managing a small smile in spite of the pain.

They were interrupted by the sound of diesel engines again and Grant noted that two more dump trucks had finally appeared below.

Reese looked over at Grant. "I'm gonna drive back down there and give my boys their marching orders. We're going to need more material than I thought. You want a ride, or you gonna slide down the face of the dam again?"

Grant couldn't imagine anything better than sitting back in the leather seats of Reese's truck. "I think I'll ride this time."

* * *

1:20 a.m. - Grand Canyon, Arizona

More than anything, David wanted to sleep. He wanted to crawl into his sleeping bag and get into the fetal position. Only then would it be possible to wake up and find that this all had been a bad dream. Besides, he was freezing. Even though he and Afram had been up on the ledge with Judy and out of the water for more than an hour, their clothes were still wet, and the night temperature in the Grand Canyon was cold.

As Judy had first anticipated, the outcropping enabled them to traverse upward to a small ledge where all three could sit down. Originally they had worried that the water would rise and rim them again, but that had not happened. The water had only risen about five feet farther after they lost the raft, and since then had actually receded slightly.

During the last hour, they had talked sporadically about their friends in the raft. All three agreed that their friends' chance of survival was minimal. Could they have survived going over the falls? Potentially, yes. Realistically, no. Could they have landed the raft someplace before they went through the narrows? Potentially, yes. Realistically, no. The logic had depressed them too much to allow long conversations on the subject.

David shivered and his teeth started chattering again. "I'm real cold. I don't know how I can make it through the night."

Afram agreed. "Me too."

Judy reached over David and motioned for him to move over so she could crawl in between the two men. "I'm cold too." She snuggled close to David. "We're going to have to share body heat to avoid hypothermia."

David embraced her and felt Afram do the same from the other side. The spot they were on was small and jagged and they were uncomfortable.

"And don't either of you try anything," Judy said jokingly.

David felt himself smile slightly for the first time since his friends died.

* * *

1:25 a.m. - Lake Powell, Utah

Julie cuddled Greg, draping her arm over him. Although the seats on the Mastercraft could be reconfigured into a comfortable bed, tonight she did not feel comfortable. It was not the seats; it was the way the boat was leaning. Gravity kept reminding her that her body was not level, which made her imagine they were on the verge of falling.

In the last three hours since they arrived in Wahweap Bay, they had been busy. First they had dropped off the rescued couple at the marina. Then they had retrieved Paul, Erika, Max, and Darlene from Castle Rock, and motored them over to the marina.

The marina itself was chaos. All of the docks were sitting on the ground. Although Wahweap's docks were capable of being adjusted for changing water levels, the water had dropped too fast, and they couldn't keep up. There were probably five hundred boats in the bay. Many sat high and dry on the banks below the marina; many more were crowded together on the water, and some motored around in the bay or parked on the shore. Just like in Warm Creek Bay, trails of people hiked around the rocky shore toward the marina.

After an hour of talking to other boaters and deciding what to do, Greg had finally beached the Mastercraft at about 10:30 p.m. He parked it right next to the launch ramp for easier access. The Crawford's boat was one of many boats that had been parked nose-to-tail on both sides of the ramp. Since the water was now dropping almost twelve feet per hour, it was now stranded on the slope over thirty feet out of the water, with many boats parked behind it; hence the lean.

Greg had been right about the Wahweap launch ramp. It continued down with the receding water. He had also been right about the mossy growth. The ramp was covered in a thin film of slimy plant life that made the ramp slippery to walk on. The general consensus of all the boaters was that someone would clean the ramp in the morning, and everyone could begin retrieving their boats. The details of how everyone would get their boats up off the ground and onto their trailers was still being discussed. A crane had been suggested.

After Greg parked the Mastercraft and the water had abandoned it, the three couples discussed what would happen the next morning. It quickly became evident that it was not necessary for everyone to remain at the lake. Max and Darlene elected to head home. Although Greg argued it was not necessary, Paul and Erika decided to stay, primarily because Paul did not want to leave and miss out on the action of retrieving boats the next day. When sleeping arrangements were discussed, Erika had insisted that she and Paul sleep in the back of their van, which was at least oriented horizontally in the parking lot above.

Julie whispered to her husband. "Are you asleep?"

He rolled onto his back and looked at her. "No. It's too noisy."

She laughed. "I keep feeling like the boat is going to slide down the hill."

In the night air, they could hear conversations all around them from other boats. It seemed like no one could sleep. Julie's mind kept returning to the scene at the dam where they had rescued the other couple. In her head, the results were not always the same. Sometimes the boat stalled, or the water just pulled faster than the Mastercraft would go. Julie would be standing in the boat, drifting closer and closer to the edge.

"We could be here for days," Greg said. "There's no guarantee we'll get out tomorrow."

"At least we're here," Julie responded. "We could have been stuck at the houseboat, or at Warm Creek, or dead below the dam. There are a lot of people worse off than us. I'll take our predicament."

Greg spoke carefully. "It wasn't too smart. I can see that now. We could have died. I wasn't thinking."

Julie hugged her husband. "Maybe it wasn't smart. But we made it. And we're way better off, and that other couple is alive because of us. It might not have been smart, but it worked." She kissed her husband on the cheek. "It's behind us now, so try to get some sleep."

"I don't think I'm going to be able to sleep tonight."

"Then let's just snuggle."

* * *

1:30 a.m. - Davis Dam, Nevada

Grant stepped out the door of Davis Dam's generation plant into the night air. He felt much better. He had bandages on his arms and he was wearing dry clothes, albeit work coveralls that did not fit. Special Agent Williams and Blaine had bandaged him up from a first-aid kit in the plant. They dressed the deep scrapes on his arm with antibiotic ointment and wrapped them in large gauze pads. Blaine found a pair of running shoes in one of the offices upstairs. They were a size too big, but that actually worked in Grant's favor with the bandage on his big toe. Wearing the coveralls with running shoes looked a little strange, but Grant didn't plan on giving any more interviews, especially before he returned to Hoover and changed into his other clothes.

He looked back up to the crest and saw another truck dumping. Reese's men had already rebuilt most of the dike.

"Grant." A voice came from behind.

Grant turned and saw Phil, the FBI agent he'd met at Glen Canyon. "Special Agent Williams tells me that you saved the dam, but got beat up a little in the process." Phil reached out to shake his hand while Agent Williams and two other agents stood behind him. Grant thought he recognized the two men from Arizona the previous morning, but he wasn't sure.

"I'm a little sorer than yesterday, but I think I'll be okay," Grant responded.

Phil put his hands in his pockets. "Look, I know you said you'd be heading back to Hoover once things settled, but I wondered if we could sit down and talk before you leave."

Grant looked at his watch. He figured the floodwaters from Glen Canyon would have reached Lake Mead by now. The lake was probably rising by the minute behind Hoover Dam. He definitely needed to get back. However, it would be many more hours before the water rose above the concrete dam. And he wanted to talk to the FBI anyway. "Sure, I can give you a few minutes."

Phil pointed back at the metal door. "Special Agent Williams found a room in the building where she thought we could talk. With a conference table," he added.

They moved back into the building with Grant limping to keep up. As soon as they reached the room and sat down, Phil started firing questions. "I'm going to ask you the same question I asked at Glen Canyon this morning. Why would anyone want to blow up this dam?"

Grant scratched his head. "I don't know on this one, Phil. Glen Canyon has always been considered a target. The government even closed it to all tourists for over a year after September 11th. Plus, the environmentalists all hated it. But this dam . . ." Grant hesitated. "Most people haven't even heard of it."

"Then why Davis?" Phil pleaded.

"I was just thinking on the way down here – Davis Dam itself probably isn't the target. Not if you believe that the same guy blew both dams."

Agent Williams interjected, "Both dams were blown with ammonium nitrate fertilizer. Both dams were blown by a white guy in a white pickup. Both guys posed as if they should be allowed inside."

Grant glanced over at Agent Williams. It sounded pretty convincing when she said it like that. He nodded and looked back at Phil. "So, assuming it's the same group, with similar point men, then I don't believe that the two puzzle pieces fit yet."

"What do you mean 'yet'?" said Phil.

"I mean that the two, Glen Canyon and Davis, don't fit together by themselves, meaning I can't think of any one reason to blow those two dams. I have a sneaking feeling that we haven't seen all the pieces of the puzzle yet. I think there's going to be more bombings." Grant looked up to see their reactions. He didn't think any of them were surprised by his comment, although he'd made Phil hesitate before asking his next question.

Phil held out the palms of his hands. "What if Davis was an afterthought, a reaction because blowing Glen Canyon didn't achieve the goal the bomber intended?"

Grant didn't understand. "Gee, guys, I don't know about you, but if I were the bomber, I'd consider the bombing of Glen Canyon Dam a raging success. It's gone. Lake Powell's draining." He looked at his watch. "Actually, 'mostly drained' is probably a better term for it."

Phil pointed at Grant. "What if you hadn't done anything at Hoover? What if the floodwater from Lake Powell had breached Hoover as anticipated? What if Hoover had failed too? Your dam extension project at Hoover is all over the news. Maybe you stopped him from achieving his goals. What if his ultimate goal was Hoover?"

Grant hadn't considered that line of reasoning, but he still didn't think it fit. "If that were the case, why bomb Davis? That won't do a thing to Hoover." He hesitated. "But I see your point. Davis would've collapsed from all the floodwater spilling over Hoover. Although I have some issues, like the way he bluffed his way in here with Bureau credentials and everything. Normally, that would take days of preparation. I'm not sure he could come up with the ID's at the last minute like that. This feels more like part of his overall plan." Grant let the words settle, and he thought Phil looked as if he at least partially agreed.

Phil changed the subject. "You said that you think there will be more bombings. Why?"

Grant knew he'd have trouble explaining this. "Well, like I said, these two dams don't have much in common. One is huge and well known; the other small and unknown. One buried an archeological wonder and the other only raised the water in an obscure canyon." He hesitated, then looked straight into Phil's eyes. "Look, I admit that it's more like a feeling than logic, but I'm almost certain he hasn't shown all his cards yet. What we have now just doesn't add up."

Phil continued. "What do you think the results would have been if the bomber had successfully destroyed Davis Dam?"

Grant shrugged. "Well, it would've wiped out all the Casinos in Laughlin. There would be tons of flooding and damage in Bullhead City and around Lake Havasu. And most of the water would go right over the top of the next dam downstream, Parker."

"Who would be affected the most by that?" said Phil.

Grant looked around. "Boaters, I guess; water-skiers and vacationers, and everyone who owns a house on the banks of the Colorado River."

Phil grinned. "Exactly. And who was most adversely affected by draining Lake Powell?"

Grant rubbed his chin skeptically. "So you think this guy's blowing up the dams because he hates boaters?"

Phil leaned forward. "Why not? It's something that both dams have in common. If you added up all the boaters on Powell, Mojave, and Havasu, you'd have a hard time finding three other lakes in the country with more boats."

Grant looked into Phil's pleading expression and understood immediately that Phil wanted to believe it, in a bad way. "I dunno, Phil."

Phil pleaded. "What if the guy's wife and kids were killed in a boating accident, Grant? What if a boat trailer came unhooked on the freeway and killed his mother?"

Grant could see the logic. A part of him wanted to embrace the theory, if for no other reason than to believe that the bombings were finally over. "Well, that should be easy to investigate. You should be able to get a list of boating related fatalities, right?"

Phil nodded. "I got a bunch of agents checking into it already. They were isolating the search around Lake Powell. I just need to expand the search to Lake Havasu and Lake Mojave."

"Better add Lake Mead," said Grant, with no enthusiasm.

"Good point." Phil jotted down some notes.

Grant hesitated to bring it up. "What about securing other likely sites?"

Phil was disappointed. "You mean if he tries to bomb other dams? Sure, we can do that. Where would you suggest?"

Grant started counting across his fingers. "Well, definitely all the dams on the lower Colorado, starting with Parker just downstream, Head Gate Rock, Palo Verde, and Imperial. But why not send a bulletin out to all dams, reservoirs, and lakes in the western United States? We could tell them to beef up security and watch out for persons masquerading as repairmen, Bureau of Reclamation, Fish & Game or anybody else who gets VIP access." Phil didn't seem that interested, so Grant continued. "Keep in mind that even if we accept the water-skier theory, his attempt at Davis has failed. He may need to strike again." Grant saw that putting it that way had gotten Phil's attention.

Phil instructed one of the other agents to write down Grant's suggestions. The agent asked Grant to repeat the names of the lower Colorado Dams, which he did. Phil asked if Grant could facilitate getting the information out to the dams via the Bureau of Reclamation. Grant gave Phil a contact at the Bureau to help him.

Grant asked another question nervously. "What about the whole international terrorist theory? Did you give up on that?"

Phil shrugged. "I have a whole team still investigating that scenario just in case. But it's not holding water." He smiled quickly as he realized the innuendo. "Solitary white guys at both dams, fertilizer bombs, big dam, little dam. It just doesn't fit."

Grant looked at his watch again and felt anxious. He needed to get back to Hoover. In spite of Phil's satisfaction with the anti-boater theory, Grant was sure more bombings were coming. He hoped that it was just paranoia, and that the destruction was over. The FBI, after all, was experienced at this kind of thing. Grant vowed to let them do their thing, their way. He had plenty to worry about already at Hoover. He stood, gingerly putting weight on his right foot, and reached out his hand to Phil. "I gotta go. I have to get back to Hoover. We've got a big morning ahead of us."

Phil nodded, also standing. "Well, we know how to get ahold of you."

Grant reached down to his hip for the cell, but it wasn't there. He looked back up at the FBI agents. "Actually, you won't be able to get ahold of me for a while. I lost my phone during my little accident." He motioned up toward the dike. "I'll try to get another one when I get to Hoover."

Phil nodded to one of the agents in coveralls, who unclipped his cell phone and handed it to Grant. Grant looked strangely at it, not knowing what to do. He was just about to hand it back when Phil held up both of his hands. "Hey, we can't afford to not be able to get in touch with you. Consider it a gift from the FBI. You can send it back to us when all this is over."

The agent who'd given it to him wrote down the phone number for him and made sure Grant knew how to work it. Phil turned and engaged one of his agents in conversation. Grant took the opportunity to sit back down and use the new phone to call Fred at Hoover to schedule the helicopter for his return flight. When Fred answered, he sounded like he had been asleep, but said he would arrange the helicopter and call back with the flight details. While Grant waited, Special Agent Susan Williams sat down next to him.

She checked the bandages on his arms and tugged at the wrapping on his left arm that was slipping down. "Good luck at Hoover," she said.

"Thanks, we'll need it." He held up his arms. "Thanks for bandaging me up. You went far beyond the call of duty for an FBI agent."

She stood and smiled down at him. "Not a problem. The government needs you at Hoover so it doesn't collapse. I was just doing my part."

Grant's eyes drifted to the black semi-automatic gun strapped on her hip. He remembered how rigid and tough she had acted when she first arrived, and how precise and meticulous she had done her job at the bombsite. But underneath the FBI façade, she had turned out to be personable, something he never would have guessed two hours earlier.

Grant checked his watch again. It was time to move on. He had forgotten to get an update from Fred about what had happened at Hoover since he left. Hopefully, no news was good news. Regardless, Grant was anxious to get back as soon as possible.

CHAPTER 28

2:45 a.m. - Davis Dam, Nevada

When the helicopter touched down in the parking lot, Grant shook hands with the FBI agents and the security guards, then hurried to climb in and sit down. His bandaged toe was throbbing. He would need Advil or something even stronger as soon as he reached Hoover. He buckled in when the pilot handed him his seat belt. When he pulled the door shut and put on the headphones, quiet enveloped him.

After the rotors accelerated, the helicopter rose gently and Grant felt himself relax into his seat. The altitude gave him a great view of Davis Dam. Down below he saw Reese leaning against his truck, talking to someone on a radio, and the bulldozers sweeping back and forth over the damaged section created by the explosion. They were past the critical stage. Grant relaxed for the first time in many hours. He closed his eyes to savor the feeling, and had difficulty re-opening them.

He pried open his eyes when he felt the helicopter lean forward and accelerate. By then they were headed north across the glimmering black surface of Lake Mojave. He stared at the blackness ahead and rested his eyes again. The rhythmic thump of the rotors felt so relaxing. This time when he closed his eyes, Grant Stevens slept.

* * *

3:00 a.m. - Mohave Desert, California

The truck cut through the desert air at 70 mph and the radio blasted George Thorogood's "Bad to the Bone." The skinny man sang along enthusiastically, " . . . I'm here to tell ya honey, that I'm bad to the bone. B-B-B-B-Bad, B-B-B-Bad, B-B-B-Bad to the bone." When the song ended, he laughed out loud. He slapped the dashboard and yelled as loud as he could. His neck and shoulders tingled so he shrugged them a few times. He didn't remember ever feeling this much energy. It felt wonderful. A road sign shot past on the side of the road. He was getting close. Reluctantly, he turned off the radio and tried to relax. He didn't want to miss the turnoff.

Since he had planted the bomb at Davis Dam, he had traveled back to Vegas for more supplies before heading south again. His ammonium nitrate supply was almost depleted, but then again, who would have ever thought he would be able to accomplish so much with so little. Back in Vegas, it had taken only forty minutes to restock the truck. He almost stopped at McDonalds before realizing that this could possibly be his last meal. So he drove on, and instead chose an all-night restaurant, with a steak and jumbo shrimp, the big ones, not those little dinky ones they give you on the all-you-can-eat special. He put the whole thing on the card. Why not?

By the time he gassed up the truck and bought a Big Gulp for the road, it had been almost 1:00 a.m. After driving south for several hours, he had turned west away from the Colorado River on Highway 62. That had been almost twenty minutes before. If he continued that way, he would eventually end up in Palm Springs, but for now, he had another destination in mind.

Ideally, he would have loved to stop and blow up Parker Dam, but he figured by then it would be heavily guarded, along with all the other dams on the Colorado River. They would be on to him by now, and a little less trusting of white pickups with explosives.

On the desert highway, with no traffic, he drove with the brights on, and easily spotted the gravel road on his right. He slowed and turned onto the bumpy road and headed up a slight incline for a quarter mile. Up ahead, barely visible in the night, was a string of four large culverts stretched across the top of the road, causing the road to dip to get under them. He slowed, turned off the gravel road, and pulled up alongside the culverts and shut off the truck. He opened the door and climbed out into the desert air. When the door light extinguished, it was just him, the moon, and the stars. He took a few steps away from the truck, unzipped, and drained his radiator while his eyes adjusted. By the time he was done and had zipped up, his eyes were more dilated, and with a little help from the moon he saw the outline of the hills clearly, and could even pick out sagebrush on the hillside. He spun and looked back toward the Colorado River and Lake Havasu, over fifty miles away, and scanned for lights. But he saw nothing, which was not surprising since there were hills in between.

He took a few minutes and looked around, allowing his eyes to further adjust. He could just make out Highway 62 as it carved through the small valley. Finally, after he procrastinated as long as he could, he walked to the back of the pickup and grabbed a shovel and his cowhide gloves. He pulled on the gloves and carried the shovel over to the first of the four large metal culverts. The culverts were eight feet in diameter each and carried the water from the huge canal over the gravel road. If he had continued driving straight, he would have driven under them. Each one was almost thirty feet long.

He moved under the culverts, until he found a spot where the dirt angled down enough to give him a couple of feet of clearance to dig. When he dropped the shovel head to start digging, he heard a distinct buzzing sound. He jumped back, but after his nerves settled, he returned, bending down for a better look. The moon and the stars did not provide enough light under the culvert, so he reached the shovel where the sound seemed to be coming from and swept it out. He got it on the third sweep. Without a flashlight, he couldn't be sure it wasn't a Mojave Rattlesnake, but considering the location and the size of the snake, he felt confident he was looking at a Western Diamondback, almost a four-footer. Shaken from getting dragged out of its hiding place, the snake took a moment to coil again and resumed rattling. With the gentleness of a mother, he carefully scooped up the snake in his shovel, carried him over to the sagebrush in front of the truck, and let him go. No sense killing the poor thing.

He returned to the spot and started digging a hole under the culvert. When the hole was approximately two feet in diameter and eighteen inches deep, he moved to the second one. This hole ended up being slightly more difficult, the dirt being harder for some reason. He continued working and finally, with all four holes dug, he walked back to the truck and drank some of the melted ice and water in his Big Gulp. He took off his t-shirt and wiped sweat off his face. In the distance, he saw the lights of a car coming down Highway 62. He rested a moment while he watched the car get closer and finally pass by. They would never be able to see him up here on the hill, he knew, unless he turned on a light.

He carried two of the white buckets over to the culverts, uncapped them, and dumped a bucket of ammonium nitrate in each of the first two holes. A second trip for two more buckets and all four holes were done. A blue bucket of diesel was next. He poured it on top of the ammonium nitrate. The one bucket was enough to douse all four holes. He put all the buckets and lids back in the truck. He returned and poked one of his detonators in each hole, and wired them together with strands from his spool of wire. Finally, he hooked up the batteries and the small timer. Again, he felt tempted to set the timer short so he could witness the destruction, but Davis Dam had been too close for comfort. He stuck with the plan and set it to twenty minutes, enough time to get miles down the road. Long before anyone figured out what happened, he would be deep into California.

He pushed the button, causing the red light to illuminate and the timer to start counting backwards from 20:00. He walked quickly back to the truck and was just about to jump in when he saw car lights in the distance. He knew if he opened the car door and jumped in, the lights would give him away, so he had no choice but to wait. Unlike the car he had watched earlier, this one seemed to take forever. When the car finally passed, he considered jumping into the truck immediately; maybe they wouldn't be watching their mirrors. He felt glad he didn't, however, because he saw another car behind. This time his heart raced as he watched it slowly get nearer. He thought about stopping the timer, but he didn't. His heart beat loudly when the car appeared to slow in preparation to turn onto the gravel road. But when the car passed, he realized it had only been his imagination.

He only waited until the car was a few miles down the road before jumping in the truck. Let them watch their mirrors. He started the truck and slammed it in reverse, backing it under the culverts. He pulled it into drive and sprayed rocks everywhere as he accelerated back down the gravel road. The truck jarred as he bounced onto the highway and headed west toward Los Angeles. They would be watching for him if he stayed too close to the Colorado River. His plan was to take the long way through L.A. down to San Diego, then back east to the river.

He was miles down the road when he saw the next car, and he was miles farther when his watch told him the explosion had occurred.

* * *

3:15 a.m. - Hoover Dam, Nevada

Grant awoke at the slight jar of the helicopter landing. He had wanted to inspect the progress of Hoover-Two from the air, to get a better perspective of the progress. But, unfortunately, he slept through the whole thing. Grant had never been a night owl, preferring to be in bed snoring long before 11:00 p.m. In fact, his wife and kids complained every year when he insisted on celebrating New Year's Eve at 10:00 p.m. with New York, and then going to bed. He hadn't made it to midnight on New Year's Eve for years. He had never gone an entire night without sleep and he tried to ignore his body's desire for more. Hopefully the short nap would help. When he tried to step out of the chopper, the throbbing pain in his foot reminded him of the ordeal at Davis Dam. After the helicopter departed, he headed down the stairs from the top of the visitor center parking structure.

After being waved past security in the visitor center, Grant walked straight to the big windows looking out over Hoover Dam. The first ten-foot phase of the dike looked complete. It stretched all the way across the dam from the Arizona side and butted into the cliffs on the Nevada side. The manner in which the artificial light cast shadows on the sandbag dike gave Grant the impression that the dike was not an addition, but part of the structure itself. The texture of the sand bags from a distance reminded him of scales on a lizard. As he stared outside, Fred and Shauna arrived and joined him at the windows.

"The progress is amazing," he said excitedly to Fred and Shauna. "It looks incredible."

Fred nodded. "Yeah, I think we're going to make it."

"What happened to you?" Shauna's eyes were large and filled with concern.

Grant glanced down at the bandages on his arms, the coveralls, and the oversized tennis shoes. "Ah, well, I had an accident down at Davis."

She interrupted him. "I can see that. What'd you do?"

He took a few minutes to explain to Shauna and Fred the sequence of events at Davis Dam. Shauna cupped her hands over her mouth when he explained how close the dam had been to breaking, and how he was swept out over the rocks by the water.

"So what's wrong with you?" Fred asked, pointing at the bandages.

Grant held up his arms. "Oh, they're just scraped up. It's not as bad as it looks." He pointed at his shoes. "It's my foot that hurts, where the toenail was ripped off. Do you have anything? You know, Advil or something?"

Fred nodded. "We'll find you something."

Grant looked over the dike to the water. "The water's way up, isn't it?" He turned and looked at Shauna.

"It's risen about ten feet in the last three hours," she said.

Grant returned his gaze to the ongoing construction. "Is that within our projections?"

"It's close. We actually expected it to be a few feet higher by now. I think we'll be okay."

"Are the spillways at capacity?" asked Grant.

Fred answered. "Not yet, not for another hour or so." All three sat silent for a few moments before Fred spoke up. "You know, I haven't checked them for over an hour. You wanna go look?"

"Absolutely," Grant said, moving away from the windows.

"You guys go ahead," Shauna said. "I need to finish my downstream calculations."

The two men headed out the door, Grant limping on his sore toe. As they walked out of the visitor center, Grant saw a truck had just unloaded sandbags and a group of National Guardsmen scurried to place them on the dike. The old man was still on the dike with the bullhorn, and barked instructions when somebody placed a bag incorrectly.

Fred detoured around an empty truck and found a spot of partially constructed wall where they could climb sandbags to get over Hoover-Two. As they crested the dike, Grant heard it. It reminded him of a gigantic waterfall. After they descended the other side, the rumbling increased with each step. Grant felt his excitement build as they walked past the snack bar. When they came around the rock cliff and looked over the fence, Grant had to catch his breath.

The water was still ten feet from the top of the fifty-foot-diameter spillway tunnel, but the amount of water moving into it was staggering. The tunnel's steep fall, coupled with the sheer volume of water, created a strong suction, and the sound of air being pulled into the hole alternated with loud "wuf" noises as air pressure occasionally pushed spray back up the hole. Part of Grant wanted to turn and run to save himself from getting sucked in. The other part wanted to stay and stare for hours.

Fred cupped his hands and yelled to be heard. "Impressive?"

Grant only nodded and returned his eyes to the water. They both stared, not saying anything, knowing that they were both witness to something never before seen at Hoover Dam. In 1983, the only other year the water reached the spillways at Hoover, it had only been one tenth of what they were seeing now. The spillways had never been full.

They remained standing, unable to move, mesmerized by the scene. Finally, Fred touched him on the shoulder to get his attention, and motioned with his thumb. "You ready?"

Grant nodded and reluctantly pulled his eyes from the spectacle. Neither spoke as they walked back toward the visitor center. When they climbed over the wall of sandbags, they stopped to admire the work in progress. Grant followed

Fred over to a National Guardsman who looked like he was in some sort of supervisory role. The three men shook hands.

"How much longer for this phase?" Fred raised his voice to be heard over the trucks.

The guy looked at his watch. "Probably less than an hour." He looked at Fred. "Will that be soon enough?" Grant could see the concern in the man's face.

Fred filled in the details. "Yeah, that will be fine. The leading edge of the floodwater hit us a couple of hours ago, so we expect the water level to start rising very fast now." He pointed over at the parking lot and the snack bar by the spillways. "It'll probably flood the concrete by 6:30 or 7:00 a.m. Peak flow into Lake Mead will be a few hours after that. That's when the water will be rising the fastest."

The guardsman cupped his hand by his mouth to be heard. "What about the ten-foot dike? When will the water go over that? When do we need to have the second phase of sandbags done?"

Fred deferred to Grant who answered the question. "We don't expect peak levels until late this evening. But the levels should be almost as high as the current phase of the dike by noon. Is that a problem?"

The man looked at his watch, then smiled nervously, obviously not completely comfortable. "It'll be hard to estimate until this phase is done and we start building the taller dike. We'll have to see how fast that goes."

The man hesitated before asking the next question. "You think it'll hold?"

Grant responded, "It'll hold as long as the water doesn't get too much higher than fourteen or fifteen feet over the original dam." He smiled and put his palms together as if in prayer. "And our calculations say it shouldn't."

The soldier laughed. "I just hope your math is better than mine."

* * *

4:15 a.m. - Mohave Desert, California

The red Chevy Cavalier barreled down Highway 62 at almost 90 m.p.h. Milton Jessop was in big trouble. He told his wife he would be home before she went to bed, and now it was almost 4:30 in the morning. Home for Milton was Palm Springs, and he guessed he had another hour to go. She would be mad enough that he had been gambling, but when she found out about the two hundred bucks he lost on the blackjack table, she just might kill him. He floored the Cavalier to see if he could get it over ninety. He figured he was unlikely to encounter a cop on this stretch at night. At this hour cops were more likely to be snoozing in their cars or sampling the merchandise in some all-night donut store.

Milton looked ahead and saw something glistening across the road. It almost looked like water. Milton had lived in the desert his whole life and he knew a mirage when he saw one. When heat waves radiated out of the desert, it looked just like water. However, Milton could not remember ever seeing a mirage at night. He wondered if the alcohol in those complimentary drinks at the casino was playing with his mind. One strange thing he noticed about this mirage, besides it being at night, was that usually they moved away from you as you approached them, kind of like rainbows, but this one seemed to stay put.

Suddenly, Milton wondered if it wasn't a mirage at all, but real water. But where would enough water come from to create a lake in the middle of the Mojave Desert? He had no idea.

When Milton finally realized it was real water, it was too late. He slammed on the brakes. The car skidded a few feet before it hit the water. At almost ninety, the small Cavalier hydroplaned easily, shooting across the top of the water. The back end came around on Milton and he tried to steer out of it; however, the effort seemed to backfire as the small car swapped ends. At least he hadn't hit anything. But then the car left the road and the tires dug into the deeper water. The motion flipped the car and it rolled twice before sliding to a stop upside down and sinking into waist deep water.

Upside down, Milton touched himself to make sure he was still alive. The left side of his head hurt. He must have hit it during the roll. As the car sank, water poured through the broken right window. Milton decided he'd better get out or he would drown. When he reached for the seatbelt release his head went underwater. He found the latch and when it released he fell on his head. The Cavalier was cramped and he gulped water and almost drowned before he turned upright. Finding the door release, he pulled. Nothing. He braced himself and pushed with his feet while pulling the lever and finally the door released with a loud screeching noise.

Milton stumbled onto his feet and found himself standing in three feet of water. He saw lights coming toward him from another car and he sloshed farther away from the road in case there was another crash. This car slowed, however, and stopped. Once Milton decided he was in no danger, he found the submerged road and waded back to where the vehicle had stopped.

"Are you okay, buddy?" the man asked, walking in front of a black SUV with its hazard lights blinking.

Milton put his hand up to the left side of his head. "Yeah, I think so."

"Didn't you see the water?"

"Not until it was too late." He looked around and saw water in all directions, illuminated by the lights of the SUV. "Where'd all this come from?"

"The aqueduct probably broke," said the man.

"Aqueduct?"

"Yeah. The California Aqueduct runs right along the hill over there." The man pointed up on the hill.

Milton should have known. He knew about the California Aqueduct. It was one of the main sources of water for Los Angeles from the Colorado River. Without it, Palm Springs would be even more of a desert than it already was. It's just that his head was a little foggy. Milton wondered what they should do. "Should we report it?"

"Definitely." The man headed back toward his car. "I've got a cell phone. Looks like we're the first ones here."

Milton looked around again. He tried to see the other side of the water, but the SUV's lights were not bright enough to reach. He wondered briefly if his wife would go easy on him now that he was hurt, then decided not. He was lucky to be alive, but his wife would not see it that way. She might still kill him. And another thing – Milton had thought about it for a while now and he was pretty sure there were no mirages at night.

CHAPTER 29

4:30 a.m. - Hoover Dam, Nevada

After Grant returned to the visitor center, he found his suitcase and changed out of the coveralls into a clean pair of slacks and a polo shirt with the Bureau of Reclamation's logo on the breast pocket. He ran a brush through his hair and adjusted the bandages on his arms. He tried his shoes, but they fit too tight on the swollen toe, so he put the oversized jogging shoes back on.

When Grant walked back into the lobby, he saw the governor had returned, surrounded by his entourage. The group huddled around someone that, at first, Grant didn't recognize. However, as he and Fred walked toward the group, Grant saw that the man shaking hands with the governor was his boss Roland Blackwell, the commissioner of the Bureau of Reclamation. Grant felt a knot in his stomach. He hadn't expected the commissioner for another hour or more. The flights and connections from Paris must have gone well. While still shaking hands, the governor led the commissioner over to the large windows. Grant thought they looked good together, Roland and the governor, both wearing suits, and both completely comfortable rubbing elbows with other politicians. Grant saw the commissioner's eyes pass over his with recognition. The commissioner looked slightly angry. Grant knew immediately that was a bad sign.

The governor swept his arm across the panoramic view of the dam. "As you can see, my boys have almost completed the first phase of your dam extension project." He paused for effect.

Roland looked at the sandbags stacked across the top of Hoover Dam as if he were seeing a ghost. He hesitated, then reacted angrily. "Dam extension? Who authorized that?"

The governor's eyebrows furrowed. "Uh . . . the Bureau did." He spotted Grant and Fred, motioning toward them. "Mr. Stevens, come over—"

The commissioner cut him off and took a couple of steps toward Grant. "You authorized this?"

Grant looked up into his boss's eyes. "Yes, sir. It was the only thing we—"

"You're fired," the commissioner said quickly.

Grant heard the words, but couldn't believe it. "What?" he said.

"You heard me. You're done. I remembered specifically telling you not to make any big decisions until I got here." He turned to walk, then faced Grant again. "And you go off and come up with this crazy scheme. Unbelievable." Roland turned and started walking.

The governor watched in disbelief, then quickly grabbed Roland's arm. "Whoa, hang on a second there commissioner." Roland turned to face him. "Am I hearing that you don't approve of Mr. Steven's dam extension idea?"

"I'd call that an understatement. I've been in the Bureau for twenty five years and I've never seen anything so stupid." One of Roland's sidekicks nodded to reinforce.

The governor looked briefly at Grant, then back at the commissioner. "What should he have done?"

"Well, not that!" spat Roland, pointing again at the dike.

The governor's lips formed a sinister smile. "That's not what I asked, Mr. Commissioner." He paused for effect. "What would you have done, if you would've been here?"

The commissioner stammered, "Well, I uh –"

The governor, sensing the vulnerability, piled on. "Commissioner, as the governor of Nevada, I am formally requesting instructions from the Bureau of Reclamation. I have the bulk of Lake Powell, which I am told . . ." He looked briefly at Grant. ". . . constitutes almost two full years of Colorado River flow, barreling my way as we speak. I need your organization's expertise to tell me how to save my communities, here and farther downstream. You have just insinuated that your employee gave us bad instructions. Please tell us, commissioner, what should we do instead?"

While waiting for an answer he knew wasn't coming, the governor motioned toward Grant and Fred. "Can I assume that you do not trust the calculations of your team here? If not, then how long do we have until the flood water peaks?"

Roland Blackwell looked around confused for a second, then glared at Grant. "When did you tell them the flood would arrive?"

Grant's mouth still hung open from being fired. He looked at his watch and tried to get his brain moving again. "Uh, in the next few hours, I think."

"You think?" the commissioner bellowed.

The governor raised his voice. "Commissioner Blackwell, we have two or three hours to high levels. What are your instructions? Do you wish me to halt construction on the dike we are building?"

Commissioner Roland Blackwell looked scared. "There's not enough time to make any intelligent –"

The governor raised his voice. "Do you want me to halt construction?"

Roland must have realized the hole he'd dug himself into. "I need to confer with my team for a few minutes."

The governor folded his arms as if he were waiting.

"In private!" said the commissioner. He looked around. "Don't you have a room someplace?"

Fred motioned to the small theater they'd been using as a conference room. Roland and his two sidekicks started walking. Grant stood still. The three men had barely disappeared into the theater before one of them stuck his head back out.

"Stevens, get in here!" he said.

The governor held out his arm to block Grant. "I thought you just fired this man?"

The Bureau man's head disappeared for a moment, and then reappeared. "You're not fired Stevens. Now get in here."

Grant walked into the small conference room to find them all sitting, Roland massaging his temples with both hands. Grant shut the door behind him and one of Roland's men motioned him to a seat. In spite of the way he'd been treated, Grant understood how the commissioner felt. He was in over his head. The modern Bureau focused on politics, budgets, and schmoozing, not flood dynamics and disaster mitigation. However, compassion or not, the commissioner had already jettisoned him with little concern for Grant's well-being. Grant knew he had to tread very carefully for the next few minutes.

The commissioner started talking without looking up. "You've put me in a difficult situation here, Stevens."

Grant wanted to point out that he felt like he was in an even worse situation, but thought better.

Roland looked up at him. "What the hell is that dike out there? How did you come up with that crazy scheme?"

Grant tried to choose his words carefully. "I used the Bureau's research from the late nineties. According to the report, over sixty feet of water would breech Hoover, or about two million cubic feet per second."

Grant saw Roland's jaw drop, but he kept going. "As you know, that would wipe out Hoover, and most of the dams downstream." He paused in case the group had any comments, but they remained silent. "We knew that water levels in both Mead and Powell were below maximum due to the drought, so we had to estimate the new flood levels compared to the research. With the lower levels, we calculated just over fifteen feet would still overtop, which I reduced a few feet by blowing the spillways." Grant hadn't meant to talk about the spillways yet.

The commissioner's head came up. "What? What do you mean 'blowing the spillways?'"

Grant wanted to get the subject back to Hoover-Two, but didn't know how. "When I arrived here yesterday, they weren't dumping as much water as I told them to. I'd called them from Glen Canyon and told them to open everything, all the gates. But when I arrived, the governor was here, preventing them from opening the gates. They wanted more time to evacuate downstream."

"Yeah?" Roland prompted.

"Well, I had to explain to the governor what would happen if he didn't start dumping immediately." Grant smiled a little. "I had to scare him. I asked him if he wanted to take responsibility if Hoover failed and wiped out everything downstream."

"Go on." The commissioner looked perplexed. "What about the spillways?"

"Well, after we convinced the governor to open all the gates, we were still only dumping about 75,000 cubic feet per second. And I knew that the spillways could handle almost 400,000 between them, but by the time the floodwater arrived and rose high enough to spill, it'd be too late. So I convinced the governor to bring in a demolition team and open 'em up."

Stuart Jaconi, one of Roland's sidekicks, shook his head. "How many dollars worth of damage do you think you caused?"

Grant tore into him. "Less than what it would've cost to rebuild Hoover and the other dams downstream."

"You don't know Hoover would have failed. We don't even know if your numbers are right."

Roland held out his hand to call off Jaconi then looked back at Grant. "Did anyone check your numbers?"

Grant nodded. "Of course. Bruce's team checked 'em. We're within a couple of feet."

"What difference did you say blowing the spillways will make?" Roland asked hesitantly.

"We figure that by the time the water is high enough to go over the dam, we will have dropped the lake almost three feet."

Roland surprised Grant by his next comment, and judging by their expressions, he surprised his men also. "I'm not sure I would have done it, but I understand your logic in opening the spillways." He pointed out of the room. "Now I want to hear about that sandbag circus out there."

Grant continued. "Well, we still expected between ten and fifteen feet of water to spill over the top of Hoover, and even that, we knew, would take out Davis Dam downstream and cause millions of dollars worth of damage to Hoover, especially the generation plants. We felt that even ten feet topping Hoover could potentially break it, especially since it will be topped for almost two months."

Jaconi interrupted. "How could you be sure Davis would fail?"

Grant talked down to him like he would to a child. "Davis Dam is a land fill. It's made of dirt. How much water over the top do you think it could stand?"

"I know what a land fill is," he retorted, but he immediately shut up.

"Go on, Stevens," the commissioner urged.

"We knew that Davis was a goner, but I was surprised to find out that Davis held over three times as much water as Lake Havasu downstream. Therefore, when Davis failed, it would definitely take out Parker Dam downstream with it."

"What about the dams downstream from Parker?" asked the commissioner.

"Oh, we'll lose them regardless," Grant stated unemotionally.

Jaconi stood. "How can you be sure of that?

Grant faced him. "Easy math, Stuart. Their spillways aren't nearly as big as Hoover, Davis, and Parker. Since the big spillways will be running at capacity, the smaller dams will definitely get topped."

Roland put his hand over Jaconi's, an unspoken command to shut up. "Please continue, Stevens."

"Anyway, we were fairly certain that we couldn't save Davis and Parker. We were concentrating mostly on how to mitigate the damage. It was frustrating. Finally, in desperation, we concluded that if Hoover were only fifteen feet higher . . . and . . ." Grant motioned toward the dam. "In fact, the more we thought about it, the more we realized we might be able to save all three dams with a twenty foot dike."

The commissioner thought about it. He looked around at the others who were silent, then looked back at Grant. "What if the sandbags don't hold?"

Grant shrugged. "Then ten feet of water would spill, the same as if we hadn't built it." Grant stood on his feet, sucked up the pain from the sore toe, and walked over close to the commissioner and leaned down close. "But what if it does hold, Commissioner?"

Roland turned and scanned the eyes of his men, then looked back at Grant, hesitating for a few moments. "Stevens, I'm going to let you keep working on the dike." He rubbed his temples again. "Things aren't as bad as they seemed when I first arrived. I'll tell the governor we are proceeding." He looked directly at Grant. "But make sure it doesn't fail. I don't have to tell you that the Bureau can't win in this deal. The publicity from Glen Canyon and the other dams downstream that we're going to lose is going to kill us."

Grant nodded.

The commissioner stood and walked toward the door, then stopped and turned. "Stevens, you should probably know that the Bureau could have done much worse than what you've done here."

"Thank you, Commissioner." Grant marveled that the conversation had gone so well.

* * *

5:30 a.m. - Hoover Dam, Nevada

When Grant walked out of the conference room, Fred was waiting for him. He looked nervous. He immediately walked over and grabbed Grant's arm. "He blew up the California Aqueduct."

"What?"

"They called right after you guys went in the conference room. I've been waiting for you to come out. There's been another explosion. Somebody blew up the aqueduct."

Grant felt confused. "Where did this happen? Do we know if it's the same guy?"

"It happened about fifty miles west of Lake Havasu. Out in the desert. There's water all over the place out there."

Grant considered the repercussions. "How does this affect us? The dams downstream?"

Fred hesitated. "Well, they obviously had to shut the pumps off in Havasu. I'm not sure what you're getting at."

What did this have to do with the other bombings? He had the next piece of the puzzle, but he wasn't sure where or if it fit. "I'm not sure I know what I'm getting at either. I'm just trying to figure out why. What does this have to do with the other explosions?"

Fred didn't respond; he just looked puzzled.

Grant continued thinking out loud. "So what is the net result of shutting off the pumps?"

Fred shrugged. "I guess it's going to make the flood downstream a little worse. You know, since all the water that was in the aqueduct is now going to stay in Havasu."

Grant considered the idea, then looked back at Fred. "I wonder if that's it. After the bomb at Davis Dam, he must of figured we'd step up security on the other dams. Could this guy's motivation be to flood the hell out of the lower Colorado? I wonder who he hates down there?" Grant pulled the cell phone off his belt. "We need to call Phil. These are all questions for the FBI."

Phil picked up on the first ring. He sounded as if he were losing the war. He had already heard about the bombed aqueduct and had already dispatched a couple of agents to the site. However, they didn't have high expectations on collecting evidence. Police reports from the site reported that water had washed much of the hillside away, not to mention the small lake created in the surrounding area.

"What's next?" asked Grant.

"We need to get together again, talk some more," said Phil.

"I can't leave here," Grant responded. "The water from Glen Canyon is starting to arrive and Lake Mead water levels are rising by the minute. Things are going to get a little dicey."

"That's fine. The trail's cold here anyway. I'm coming to Hoover. You guys have been hearing stuff before us."

Grant hesitated for a second. "Look, I don't want to tell you guys how to do your job, but –"

Phil interrupted him. "No. Go ahead."

"Well, one thing we shouldn't wait to discuss is that our bad guy must have guessed we'd beef up the security around the dams. So that might be the reason he switched to the aqueduct. I think it's only reasonable —"

"I'm way ahead of you. There's another one farther down, isn't there? I agree; I can have the police tighten security there, too."

"There's more than one, Phil. There's a couple that go to Arizona, including the Central Arizona Project, CAP, and one that goes to the Indians. There's another huge one called the All American Canal that goes to Imperial Valley. That one even splits and sends a fork over to Palm Springs. And then there's the Gila, another big one, but it's in Mexico."

Phil didn't say anything.

Grant continued. "The bottom line is, these things stretch for hundreds of miles through the desert. The police aren't going to be able to guard 'em. The bombers probably waltzed right up to the last one. It's in the middle of nowhere."

"I see your point."

Grant continued. "Look, I still don't know this guy's motive, but he seems to be concentrating on the lower Colorado River. It's almost like he wants to damage something or somebody downstream. I think we need to get aggressive. Shut down all the roads in and out. String the National Guard along the aqueducts. You name it. Our targets cover a lot of space out there."

"That's going to be tough, Grant. They are still trying to evacuate many of those cities downstream. There are thousands of people on the roads. We can't impede the evacuations."

Grant rubbed his forehead. "I know, I know. But we have to try. Maybe you can randomly stop some of them. Who knows, we might get lucky at a roadblock somewhere. Isn't that how they caught the guy that blew up the Oklahoma Federal building?"

"We'll see what we can do, Grant."

"What about the dams and aqueducts in Mexico?" Grant asked.

Phil hesitated. "You know the FBI can't go into Mexico."

Actually, Grant didn't know. "But this is an emergency."

"Grant, the FBI cannot go into Mexico. We have no jurisdiction. Their government will have to handle it."

Grant hated politics, but saw no way around this one. "Well, have we talked to them yet? We need to at least give them a heads up."

"Not yet. I'll need to make some calls to the big wigs. It won't be my decision. In the meantime, I need some help with maps of all the aqueducts, something I can pass to local law enforcement."

Grant knew Phil wouldn't like the answer. "Phil, the Bureau doesn't handle the aqueducts. In fact, I'll bet every one is handled by a separate agency or municipality." He hesitated. "But I can give you a contact at the Bureau, somebody who should at least be able to help accumulate the info, or if nothing else, send you in the right direction."

"I appreciate it, Grant."

Grant gave Phil the number of a woman in the Denver office. Since it wasn't even 7:00 a.m. in Denver, he told Phil where she lived, so he could call information if necessary. He added her supervisor's info just in case.

When Grant hung up the phone, Fred stood nearby waiting. "Did he take your advice?"

"Yeah, kind of. I recommended some big stuff like the National Guard. But that's over his head. He'll need to bring in his superiors."

Fred smiled. "You want to go for a walk again?"

Grant stood, stretched, and tried to stop a yawn that wouldn't quit. "Sure, what's up?"

"The spillways are now full." Fred looked like a kid with his first bicycle. "You wanna go look at 'em again?"

Disaster or no disaster, Grant wanted to see them as much as Fred did.

"Let's go."

* * *

6:15 a.m. - Hoover Dam, Nevada

With the sun having just risen above the horizon, a large group followed Grant and Fred out to the Nevada Spillway, including Governor Jenkins and Commissioner Blackwell and their entourages. A man and a woman with cameras and a separate guy with a video camera had materialized from nowhere and joined the caravan. Grant noticed that there were two helicopters hovering over the dam shooting pictures of the sandbag dike. Both of them, a white one and a blue one, had logos of news organizations stenciled on the sides.

When they reached the dike, Grant saw that a makeshift stairway had been built with sandbags, up one side and down the other, to facilitate the crossing. He wondered whose idea it had been. The large group meandered over the wall and through the parking lot toward the Nevada spillway. Grant noticed that the water had risen to within a few feet of the top of Hoover Dam, burying the fifty foot white band of rock normally seen around the perimeter of Lake Mead. A few more feet and it would flood the parking lot where they stood.

As they walked closer, the rumbling noise increased until it vibrated the ground. When they reached the chain link fence surrounding the spillway, Grant saw the water now higher than the fifty-foot-diameter spillway tunnel. The water level was slightly lower near the tunnel itself, dropping a few feet, as the spillway was taking the water faster than it flowed down the channel toward it.

The volume of water movement was intimidating. Commissioner Blackwell was holding the fence so tight that his knuckles were white, one foot next to the fence and one noticeably behind, in case a quick exit became warranted. He looked shaken, as if he had just seen a ghost.

Governor Jenkins smiled and talked to someone near him, but his high eyebrows showed that he too wasn't completely comfortable.

"You're finally looking at 200,000 cubic feet per second," yelled Fred from a cupped hand. "More than Niagara Falls."

Grant only nodded, gripping the fence tightly himself.

"These spillways have waited almost seventy years to show their stuff." Fred's voice faltered with emotion, and his eyes looked misty.

An incredibly loud screeching noise made the whole group jump and then cover their ears. A large whirlpool had formed above the spillway tunnel and the noise continued for several seconds before it and the whirlpool both disappeared.

After the group regained its composure, the photographers moved everyone away from the governor, then took some pictures of the governor with the spillway behind. The guy with the video camera unfolded a tripod and another person held up a poster-sized card. The governor buttoned his coat and checked his tie. A small microphone was clipped on the governor's lapel. Grant figured that the governor was going to make a statement.

Sighting the large group, and sensing something was up, the two news helicopters moved from the crest of the dam over near the spillway. Both had tethered cameramen hanging out open doors. They jockeyed for position in the small space.

With wind blowing his hair and the loud rumbling, the governor began. "It's just after 6:00 a.m. at Hoover Dam. As we speak, Lake Mead rises at a staggering rate as it combines with the water from the Glen Canyon Dam and Lake Powell. Since the tragedy upstream yesterday, the water has traveled over three hundred miles, having passed through the Grand Canyon." The governor motioned to his side. "Behind me is the Nevada spillway."

The governor hesitated as some wind buffeted him. The noise had also increased, not from the water, but from the helicopters. Grant felt a brief wet spray and looked up. Both helicopters had come in much closer, too close. He couldn't believe they dared fly so close together. Their rotors seemed only a few feet apart.

"Get them out of here," the governor yelled, waving his arms.

Most of the group reacted and waved frantically at the choppers. Both aircraft hesitated, as if waiting for the other to move first, but then gradually moved a short distance away.

The governor brushed at his hair, then quickly regained his composure. "Behind me is the Nevada Spillway. It is mirrored by its counterpart over on the Arizona side. As a tribute to the many thousands of dedicated men who risked their lives in the construction of this dam, these spillways are now running at full capacity for the first time ever. Only in the spring floods of 1983 have these spillways ever been needed, and then at only a small fraction of what you see now. I'm told the current flow is approximately 200,000 cubic feet per second, each." He emphasized the last word with a smile. "Together, they are passing almost forty times the normal flow of the Colorado River."

"Over the next few hours, these two spillways will likely save Hoover Dam, the first great dam in the world. They will allow us to move the floodwater downstream in a controlled manner."

Grant wondered how the governor could consider forty times normal flow a controlled manner.

The governor continued. "I regret that you cannot all come here yourselves and see this amazing spectacle. Unfortunately, the situation precludes that possibility."

"As your governor, I would like to personally thank all of you who heeded last night's call for volunteers to fill sandbags. Without you, our efforts to save Hoover Dam would surely have been in vain."

The governor's face became very serious. "The next few hours at Hoover Dam will be critical. The water will shortly rise above the original structure and will test the integrity of our sandbag extension. As your governor, I commit to make every attempt to keep you informed. May God be with us." He remained still for a moment, then drew his finger across his throat.

Many in the crowd clapped, Grant among them. Another whirlpool formed and repeated the loud screeching noise, but this time the group knew what to expect, and as quickly as it formed, it disappeared.

Roland worked his way over to Grant. "Pretty amazing, isn't it?"

Grant nodded. "Incredible."

"What'd you think of the governor's speech?"

"Pretty good, in spite of the helicopters."

The commissioner looked back out over the spillway. "About this morning." He looked back at Grant. "I was caught off guard."

Grant knew Roland was struggling, but still didn't want to let him off the hook. He let it drag out for a while, and then smiled at him. "You should be sorry."

Roland smiled back. "Don't get cocky, Stevens. Only time will tell if your little sandbag dam will hold."

But Grant knew that if the dam extension held, as he expected it would, he would have saved all of their butts. And he figured Roland knew that too.

* * *

6:20 a.m. - Grand Canyon, Arizona

David felt Judy stretch. Although he was not asleep and in fact had not slept all night, he kept his eyelids closed and chose not to stir.

Judy sat up and then jerked savagely. "Oh my . . ."

"What's the matter?" Afram asked.

David and Afram sat upright to see what Judy had reacted to. David gasped and pulled himself away from the edge. The sun was just beginning to rise up in the top of the canyon, providing barely enough light to see below. During the night, the floodwater had receded dramatically, dropping hundreds of feet. They were now stranded on a ledge with no way to go either up or down.

David looked below and saw all the places where they had climbed the night before as the water pushed them higher and higher on the canyon wall. He couldn't help but scan downstream to see if his friends had somehow landed before reaching the narrows. He saw no raft or sign of them.

"Now what?" Afram asked.

Judy craned her head upward. "We might be able to –"

"We're not going anywhere," David said. "We're staying right here."

Judy pointed above. "If we could just make it up to that ridge, we might be able to traverse –"

"Judy, if we fall, we'll be dead. We're almost three hundred feet in the air."

She looked ready to argue. "Then how are we going to get out of here?"

Afram pointed down at the river. "There will be search teams looking for survivors. They'll find us. We'll just have to wait."

David nodded in agreement.

"What if they don't?" she asked.

"They have to," David answered. "Because we can't get down."

CHAPTER 30

7:00 a.m. - Hoover Dam, Nevada

At 7:00 on the dot, Phillip Sutherland and a dozen other FBI agents arrived in the Hoover Dam visitor center. The agents quickly claimed a small room as their own, setting up a folding table and chairs. It seemed like every time Grant saw Phil, different agents accompanied him. He wondered briefly where they had sent Special Agent Williams, who had inspected the bomb the night before at Davis. She was probably out looking for evidence on the California Aqueduct bombing.

Phil looked the way Grant felt. His eyes had rings under them and lacked the sparkle of when they'd first met. His hair looked oily and uncombed. His tie hung loosely around an unfastened top button. He slouched over the table and held onto the coffee mug as if it alone were holding him up.

Grant felt tired too. His lack of sleep was wearing on him. At least the Advil had dulled the aches and pains from Davis Dam.

Phil motioned at a seat with his coffee mug.

Grant sat, and his body thanked him. Two of the other agents, previously standing, sat at Phil's sides.

Phil spoke mostly to his agents. "Okay, as Mr. Stevens put it, we just got the third piece of our puzzle. So how does blowing the aqueduct fit in with the bombs at Glen Canyon and Davis Dams? What are these guys trying to accomplish and why?"

Although spoken to the agents, Grant knew the question was meant for him, even though he didn't have the answer they wanted. "Well, before, when it was just dams, you thought it might be aimed at boaters or vacationers. The aqueduct definitely doesn't fit in that scenario. The only thing we came up with is that one of the main results of all three bombings is more water is channeled downstream. It's like they want to flood somebody or someplace downstream." He looked up at them. "I know it's kinda flimsy."

"Can't that still be interpreted as going after boaters? What about the boaters downstream?"

Grant shook his head. "The vast percentage of recreation takes place in the big lakes: Powell, Mead, Mojave, and Havasu. There's not nearly as much recreation south of there."

"What's down there, then?" Phil's voice showed frustration.

"Not much; there's only a couple of hick towns and an Indian reservation before you get to Yuma, Arizona."

"Farmers?" Phil asked.

Grant nodded. "Yeah. The Indians farm a little. One of the small dams diverts irrigation water to them. But overall, the land's pretty barren."

"What about Yuma?"

"Yuma's small, less than a hundred thousand people. There's some farming around Yuma though. Why? Do you think they might be after the farmers?" Grant hadn't considered that.

"No, I'm just thinking out loud. Why else would they want to flood Yuma? What about Mexico?"

Grant laughed briefly. "The Mexicans would love to be flooded."

Phil didn't laugh. He didn't even smile. "Why? What do you mean?"

The thought sunk in and Grant wondered why he hadn't thought of it before. "The Mexicans don't get hardly any of the Colorado River, and what little they do get, they pipe over toward Tijuana in a big canal. The whole area south of Mexicali is barren."

"What do you mean, what little they get?" Phil asked. "The river's huge."

"Not by the time it gets to Mexico. We take most of it. The Great American Canal diverts most of it before the Colorado gets there."

Phil wiped at both of his eyes. "Most of the river? How can they do that? Isn't it regulated?"

"Every drop," explained Grant. "We have a treaty with Mexico that stipulates they get at least 1.5 million acre feet per year. But, that's not all – by the time the Colorado River gets to Mexico, the salinity is so high that the water's not drinkable and will kill most crops."

Phil looked surprised by this. "And they put up with this?"

Grant shrugged. "Oh, they've been complaining for years. Finally, the U.S. had to guarantee the purity of the water at certain levels, and one of Imperial Dam's main purposes at the border is to desalinate it before it gets to Mexico."

"Isn't that expensive?" asked Phil.

"It's the biggest reverse osmosis desalination plant in the world. I think I heard that the U.S. spent over a hundred and fifty million dollars to build it, not counting yearly operating expenses."

"So Mexico is still not happy with their allotments from the Colorado River?"

"I don't think happy would be the right word. They know they're at the end of the line. I'm sure they'd like to have a lot more. But they're probably happy that what they do get is guaranteed, both in quantity and quality. At least that's something."

"So could this be some pissed-off Mexicans? Could they be our bombers?" Phil didn't sound very convinced.

"I don't think so. Remember that both of our bombers were white, and had credentials," Grant pointed out.

"What about an American group that's sympathetic to the Mexicans?"

Grant shook his head. "I can't imagine a group of Americans being sympathetic enough to blow the Glen Canyon Dam for Mexico."

Phil stood abruptly. "Then what have we got?" He walked around his chair, and leaned on it from behind. "Motive?" He let the word hang in the air. "What's the motive here? Do we have any idea? How about objective? We don't even know that." He paced over to the wall and stared at it for a second, finally returning. "Glen Canyon, then Davis, then the aqueduct. What's next? Can we at least figure that out?"

Grant shrugged. "Well, we don't know for sure. But like I said this morning, all the other aqueducts and dams downstream have to be considered targets."

Phil motioned his hand at Grant. "I forwarded your National Guard idea, but I haven't heard back yet. However, my superiors liked it. The FBI is trying to set up a conference call with Mexico this morning to fill them in on what's going on. Hopefully it's not the Mexican government behind this, or we'll be feeding information to the perpetrators."

Grant didn't believe Mexico was behind this, and he didn't think Phil did either.

"What about boat accident data?" Grant asked. "You were going to try to find out how many people had been hurt in boating accidents on the lakes."

Phil scratched his head. "There were thousands of accidents on the two lakes, plus a ton more where car accidents involved trailered boats. It's going to take a long time for my people to filter the lists. Anyway, now that he's blown the aqueduct, I'm not sure this guy is after boaters."

They were interrupted by a knock on the door. Fred poked his head in. "Sorry to interrupt, but you asked for updates." He waited for objections before proceeding. "The employee parking lot is underwater and the level will be higher than the original concrete dam in a few minutes."

Grant smiled at Fred and nodded. "Thanks, Fred. I'll be out in a while."

Fred withdrew and shut the door. There was no doubt that Fred was restless, but Grant thought it was more than that. In addition to the fear and anticipation, Grant sensed that Fred was just plain excited, glad to be there, to be a part of it. His face had shown it at the spillways, just like his voice now. The funny thing was, to a lesser extent, Grant felt the same way.

Phil took a long swig on his coffee mug. "If you need to go, don't let me stop you. But if you have a minute, I need more info from you dam guys." He smiled. "No pun intended, of course."

Grant nodded.

"I need to know what's going to happen today. Where's all this water going to end up? When will it hit? Damage estimates, etc." He pointed casually at Grant. "Are you going to hang around here all day, at Hoover? If not, where are you going to be?"

Grant considered the question. "I have an assistant here with me from Denver. She has put together a timeline of what's going to happen downstream. It shows our estimates for when the water will reach each dam, all the way to Mexico and the Gulf of California. I'll get you a copy. As far as damage is concerned, if Hoover holds, we don't expect to lose any of the three major dams. But with Hoover's spillways at capacity, we're going to have just under 500,000 cubic feet per second going downstream."

Phil looked confused so Grant clarified. "That's almost fifty times normal for the lower Colorado River, basically twice the flow of Niagara Falls. Anything next to the river is going to be flooded, badly. Laughlin will be a total loss."

Phil frowned. "You said you don't expect to lose any major dams. What does that mean? Does that mean some small ones are going to fail?"

Grant nodded. "By far, the two biggest are Davis and Parker, which hold back Lake Mojave and Havasu. Both of those have spillways that, theoretically, should be able to keep up with Hoover. Downstream are two small dams, Head Gate Rock and Palo Verde, which have comparatively little storage. Their primary purpose is to divert water for irrigation. As a worst case, we expect both of these dams to fail. However, neither should substantially affect floods downstream. The one we're worried about is the Imperial Dam, just north of Yuma, Arizona. It'll definitely be breached and we'd like to figure out a way to minimize the damage. As I explained before, Yuma is where the United States desalinates the water going to Mexico. So we want to protect the desalination plant."

"Approximately how many hours will the flood last? How soon will you be able to get people in to access the damage and make repairs?"

Grant stared at Phil. "It's not hours, Phil, it's months. It'll be almost two months before Hoover drops below the spillways. If we're lucky, the people can move back in and start sifting through their stuff by September 1st."

Phil's jaw dropped and he walked over and sat down. "Two months of Niagara Falls?"

"Two months of Niagara Falls times two," Grant corrected.

"I had no idea." Phil looked around, then back at Grant. "What about Mexico? What's going to happen there?"

"Well, before it gets to Mexico, there's the Laguna Dam. It's less than ten feet high. It won't even slow the water down. The dam in Mexicali, Mexico is called the Morales Dam. Its primary purpose is to divert the water into the Gila canal. It's not very big, and if the water destroys it, maybe the United States can help them rebuild it."

"What about downstream from Morales? Any more dams?"

Grant shrugged. "No, that's it."

"And your girl's list shows timelines for all these dams?"

"Yeah, she did a good job. She wrote a crude model for the whole thing. It lists estimated times for each reservoir to fill, and water travel times between dams."

Phil stood. "All right, we have a lot of phone calls to make. Hopefully we'll get some National Guard personnel to help us."

Grant got the distinct impression that the interview was over. He walked toward the door of the small conference room. "I'll send Shauna up with your info." He heard Phil respond that he appreciated it as he walked out the door.

* * *

7:20 a.m. - Riverside, California

The skinny man took the exit. The truck needed gas. After blowing up the aqueduct, he had continued west and skirted the south side of Joshua Tree National Park, then joined I-10, which passed by Palm Springs and all the windmills. The exit put him in Riverside, California.

Back when he planned this day, he wanted to follow the Colorado River south, but he knew the cops would be looking for him. There would be road checks and detours, and staying near the river would be too risky. It would be bad enough to get caught, but especially out on the open highway traveling between targets. Ultimately, he had decided he had plenty of time. The long detour through Southern California would almost guarantee he would go unnoticed.

After starting the gas pump, he fished through his glove box and found the address of his next destination. A map had been printed from his computer. Days before, after calling numerous persons advertising on *recycler.com*, an online classified advertising company in Southern California, the skinny man had found the vehicle he was looking for. A deal had been made. Now all he needed to do was show up on the guy's doorstep before noon. The seller was expecting him.

When the tank was full, he looked at his watch. He saw a few fast food restaurants just down the street and decided he had time for breakfast.

* * *

7:30 a.m. - Hoover Dam, Nevada

Grant and Fred had climbed to the top of phase one of Hoover-Two. They walked carefully along the sandbags. Where they walked, it was only ten feet wide. Looking north over the lake, the employee parking lot was gone, covered with water. A slight breeze blew down Black Canyon, rippling the surface, but the breeze was not refreshing, as the air temperature crept toward 100 degrees, even early in the morning.

For the last hour or so, the construction of the dike had transitioned from phase one to phase two. The ten-foot-high dike was finished and stretched from the cliffs on the Arizona side to the cliffs on the Nevada side. Phase two called for widening the dike from half the width of the dam to the full width, and building it up to a full height of twenty feet. The transition meant that trucks would no longer be able to drive across the dam and turn around, but would need to back up to unload sand bags. Phase two was gradually being built from the Arizona side toward the Nevada side.

Over the noise of the trucks and men, one could still hear the rumbling sound of the two spillways. By referencing off the concrete handrails on the top of the dam, Grant could approximate that the water level had risen about two feet above the concrete, meaning that two feet of water would be flowing over the top of

Hoover if the sand bag dike wasn't there. So far, the dike was doing what it was supposed to do, a very satisfying feeling.

Fred seemed to read his mind. "This place would look a little different with a small waterfall stretching all the way across the dam, wouldn't it?"

Grant laughed. "I wouldn't mind a small one; it's a fifteen or twenty footer that I don't want to see."

Grant turned to Shauna who had just joined them on the dike. "How are we doing on water levels?"

She adjusted her glasses. "The rate at which the water is rising has started to slow slightly, even though the floods entering the lake are still peaking. That's mostly due to increased flood area of the landscape upstream as the water rises."

Fred laughed out loud. "In English?"

Shauna looked uncomfortable. "What that means, Mr. Grainger, is that the higher Lake Mead rises, the more it spreads out. It therefore takes much more water to make it rise. Basically, the surface area of the lake is growing faster than the flood, therefore the rate the water is rising in the lake is decreasing."

Fred, still laughing, struggled to talk. "I thought I understood, Miss Kingsly. I just wanted to see if you could say it in simpler terms."

Grant and Fred both laughed again.

Shauna smiled in spite of being the object of their joke. Grant didn't want to upset her, even if she did have a vocabulary problem. She had been invaluable on this trip, and her estimates had been near perfect.

"Are the levels still within our projections?" Grant asked.

She nodded. "Yes. In fact, I've reduced my projection for maximum depth from Hoover plus thirteen to Hoover plus twelve and a half."

"That's great. I'll take all the 'halves' you can give me," said Grant. "By the way, did you get that table of downstream stuff to the FBI guys?"

She nodded. "Yeah."

"Thanks." Grant considered the information. "What about time? Have you changed when you expect Hoover to peak?"

"No. I monitored the reports of peak flood stages as they moved through the Grand Canyon last night, and I actually expect peak flows to be entering the other end of Lake Mead within the hour, then decreasing gradually. However, flow into the lake will remain greater than 500,000 cubic feet per second until late this evening, approximately 9:00 p.m. After that, the lake should start to drop very slowly."

Grant remembered something that had crossed his mind while talking to the FBI. "Were you able to get a hold of anybody at the three small dams downstream yet?" He worried about them, because they were not under direct control of the Bureau of Reclamation. Headgate Rock Dam, whose major purpose was to divert water to the Colorado River Indian Reservation, was actually controlled by the Bureau of Indian Affairs. The Palo Verde Diversion Dam was managed by a bunch of farmers in the Palo Verde Irrigation District. And Imperial Dam, way down by Mexico, was managed by the Imperial Irrigation District, the same group that managed the All American Canal, the largest of all the Colorado River aqueducts.

She nodded. "I'm glad you brought that up. I got ahold of them all, but the person I talked to at Headgate Rock said he couldn't do anything until the big wigs show up for work."

"You're kidding, right?"

"No, he was serious. He said the offices for the Bureau of Indian Affairs are in Phoenix, and they didn't have any home numbers for them at the dam."

"So what are we going to do?"

Shauna looked at her watch and then back toward the visitor center. "Well, we should be able to try them pretty soon. They answer their phones early, since much of their communication is with offices on the east coast."

"What about Imperial and Palo Verde? What did they say?"

"Imperial had already put two and two together. They knew they'd get flooded; they just didn't know when. I told them we were concerned with the desalination plant, and they said they had been sandbagging around it all night."

"What'd they say when you gave them the time frames?"

"It was later than they expected. They were actually relieved."

"And Palo Verde?"

"The guy I talked to was very concerned. He wanted to know how much higher the water would be, which I didn't know. He asked me to estimate, so I told him about ten feet. He told me ten feet would put the water level over his dam, which I told him I already knew. He asked what the plan was to save his dam and I had to tell him there wasn't a plan, that we knew it was going to fail. He didn't like that."

"Did you recommend that he break it himself?"

Fred laughed and Shauna looked up, surprised. "No. Should I have?"

Grant explained, "We need to call them back. It would cause a lot less damage if he breaks his dike before the water gets there. Why don't you call them back and explain it to them. Since both Palo Verde and Headgate Rock are landfills, an intentional controlled break before the water levels get out of control would be better. It would not only mitigate upstream flooding and reduce the amount of water released, but more importantly, they would be able to choose where they wanted the dike to break. That'll help them later, when they have to rebuild it."

Fred laughed. "I want to listen to their reaction when you tell them to break their own dams."

Shauna looked nervous. "I wonder how they'll react."

Grant nodded his head. "Oh, they'll be shocked when you suggest it. But once you explain why, they'll understand."

Shauna looked nervous and put her head down. Grant touched her shoulder. "Have you called your family? Is it okay for you stay out here for a few days?"

She looked back up and nodded. "I don't need to call. I can stay as long as you want me to. " She smiled. "It's been interesting."

"Had you ever been here before?"

She shook her head. "Not at Hoover. But when I was in high school, my parents took us to Lake Powell. We didn't have boats or anything, but we took a tour boat over to see Rainbow Bridge. We toured the Glen Canyon Dam while we were there. They let us go down and see the turbines and everything. Glen Canyon seems very similar to Hoover."

"Not anymore," said Fred.

Shauna's head turned toward Fred before her eyes bulged. She looked back at Grant. "Oh! I keep forgetting. Was it terrible to watch?"

Grant nodded. "It was amazing and terrible at the same time."

Fred's eyes looked dreamy. "I wish I could have seen it."

Grant tried to visualize. It seemed like weeks ago. "When I left, there were two concrete outcroppings, one from each side of the canyon. That's all that was left of the dam. Lake Powell was running down the canyon like a gigantic river, 600 feet deep. The Glen Canyon Bridge was gone, buried in the bottom of the river."

Shauna's hand went to her mouth.

Grant broke out of his trance and motioned along the crest of Hoover Dam. "Now we have to save this one." He peered over the 600 foot drop to the river below. "If you believe in prayer, say a prayer for Hoover Dam."

* * *

7:45 a.m. - Wahweap Marina, Lake Powell, Utah

Julie stood in the Mastercraft and looked east toward Castle Rock at the early morning sun. Hundreds of people must have started hiking at first light. They had formed into multiple lines that snaked over the hill from Warm Creek Bay. It would be hours before they had hiked around Wahweap Bay to the marina. She did not envy them.

She looked down at the water and marveled at how far it had dropped during the night. Was it possible that it had dropped another hundred feet? There were literally hundreds of boats stacked two wide below them on both sides of the launch ramp. Although boats had continued to enter Wahweap Bay the night before, the darkness had halted further attempts. That or the parks service had finally figured a way to prevent boaters from attempting the risky journey.

She wished she could see over to the main channel. What would it look like, with the water so low? Maybe it was too low to permit entry into Wahweap Bay. What if there was some sort of obstruction? What if there were still boats heading south, but they were all being swept over the remains of the dam? She hoped that was not true. She wondered how many people actually had been pulled over during the night. It was unreasonable to believe that nobody had. What if fifty people had died last night? What if a hundred?

"You're awake?"

Julie turned to see Erika walking down the ramp from above, with Paul following behind.

"You ready for breakfast?" Erika asked.

Julie was starving. "Is the restaurant open?" She couldn't imagine it was.

"They're not cooking, with the power out. But they put out some bagels and fruit on a table for the people that are arriving." Erika reached over and ran her fingers through Julie's hair. "Were you able to sleep much last night, with everything going on?"

Julie shook her head. "I might have gotten 15 minutes." She remembered the night being a series of boaters debating whether to ground their boats like the Crawfords had, then after finally doing it, walking up and down the ramp talking to anyone who would talk.

Greg pointed up the ramp. "Has anyone said anything about clearing this off?" He motioned at the slimy surface.

Paul shook his head. "Everybody is asking about it, but I didn't hear any answers."

"Have you seen any equipment show up? Any cranes?"

Paul shook his head.

Greg pointed at the Mastercraft. "Can you watch the boat? I want to go talk to some people."

Erika held out her hands. "That's why we came down here. We'll watch the boat while you guys go up and get something to eat, and get cleaned up. Take your time."

Julie liked the idea. She pulled Greg along and started up the hill.

* * *

8:00 a.m. - Hoover Dam, Nevada

The governor had arranged for breakfast to be brought in from the Hacienda Casino. A group of men wearing white shirts and hats carried in the long rectangular silver platters with lids. They set up a buffet along the west wall of the visitor center with a stack of plates on one end. The aroma of sausage, bacon, and maple syrup drifted through the visitor center.

Grant's entire body begged for sleep, and he'd actually considered allowing himself to take a quick nap, but that was before the food arrived. Another urge, more powerful than sleep, changed his mind. His last meal had been cut brutally short by the second bombing. And his stomach now told him that a breakfast buffet took priority over naps and dam discussions.

He, Shauna, and Fred lined up behind Governor Jenkins and Commissioner Blackwell's parties. Phil's team from the FBI lined up behind them. Grant scooped liberally from the first platter, which was filled with bacon and sausage.

"Easy on the cholesterol," Fred said, smiling.

Grant picked up one of the links with his fingers and took a bite. "Hmm . . . That was worth at least a year of my life."

Shauna smiled. "Don't laugh. It may have cost you a year."

Grant looked over at her. "Since it was my last year, I probably saved myself a year of cancer and chemotherapy."

"Pass the sausage," Fred said, laughing.

With no large table, everyone found wherever they could to sit. Grant's group found three chairs over by the wall. The whole lobby was surprisingly silent as they ate. Grant had to force himself to eat slowly enough to chew. He noticed that even Shauna ate like she didn't know where her next meal would come from.

About half way through breakfast, the governor stood. "Ladies and gentlemen, attention please. I've just received word that phase one of Hoover-Two is officially completed."

The crowd erupted with clapping and some yells. Grant couldn't believe the governor used the "Hoover-Two" nickname.

When the noise settled, the governor continued. "As you know, without Hoover-Two, there would be a waterfall all the way across Hoover Dam right now." More cheers and a couple of playful boos could be heard.

"If all goes well today, the Bureau," Grant noticed that the governor motioned to where he sat, not to where Roland's team sat, "the Bureau expects Hoover Dam and Hoover-Two to be holding back Lake Mead at an elevation of twelve hundred forty four and a half feet, which would be twelve feet over the top of the original Hoover Dam." More applause.

"And some time in the next sixty days, we expect the lake to have dropped back below the concrete, after which Hoover-Two will be torn down again." Grant could tell by looking around that not all had expected it to take that long.

The governor continued. "So, since this is a historic moment, I need everybody to walk out right now," he motioned, "and we're going to take a picture in front of Hoover-Two. Come on. Your breakfasts will wait."

With many still chewing, the group headed out the doors of the visitor center.

Almost an hour later, after the photos were taken and the breakfast was cleaned up, Grant inquired of Shauna as to what was happening downstream. He felt satisfied with what they had accomplished at Hoover and was starting to worry more about downriver.

She pushed her glasses up on her nose and paged through a bound notebook, stopping on her latest entry. "A little before 7:30 a.m., the levels stabilized at Davis Dam. We think the spillways have caught up to Hoover."

Grant considered the information. "Caught up?"

"Yeah. Davis handled the flood, and passed it on, just as we hoped it would."

"Any damage?"

Shauna hesitated. "Well, the level of Lake Mojave didn't rise that far, so —"

Grant interrupted, "I meant downstream."

Shauna read from her notebook. "They're reporting major flooding in the casinos in Laughlin along the river, including the Edgewater, Colorado Bell, Golden Nugget, and the Riverdale Resort." She looked up briefly. "Basically, anything on the edge of the river is getting inundated. They said that the Colorado Bell has four feet of water running through the lobby."

Grant shook his head. "Ouch. Two months of that and some of those hotels will be floating down the river."

Shauna continued reading from her notebook. "The cities of Laughlin and Bullhead City spent quite a bit of time sandbagging in preparation, and except for the buildings near the river, they've held. So there are a few wet places in the cities, but the major flooding has been contained to the river."

"Well, I guess that's good news."

Shauna continued. "However, just south of Riverfront Drive . . ." She motioned around with her hand. ". . . where the river curves east, it overflowed and flooded out the Needles Highway."

"Any damage farther down?" Grant asked.

"Maximum flow hasn't got to Needles yet, but we expect it during the next hour. I-40 and the Burlington Northern & Santa Fe Railroad's main lines go right next to the river there. The railroad's been trying to build dikes around the tracks for the last 18 hours, but they're afraid it's hopeless. It's their main east-west corridor out of the shipyards in Los Angeles. They average over 25 trains a day through there. A flood would shut 'em down."

Grant rubbed his eyes. "What's next downstream?"

"South of Needles, the river flows into Lake Havasu. Havasu's already rising fast, but it's going to double when maximum flow hits at around . . ." She turned the page and searched with her finger. ". . . 11:00 a.m. The lake will then quickly fill and top out sometime between 11:30 and 11:45 a.m."

Grant looked confused. "That doesn't sound right. The lake fills up less than an hour after peak flows get there?"

Shauna looked up. "It's right. Havasu is pretty small comparatively. Only 18,000 acres, compared to Hoover, which is more than ten times bigger. Plus, ever since Davis Dam opened its spillways early this morning, Havasu has been getting a full 500,000 cubic feet per second."

Grant thought about the damage being done in Laughlin to the casinos and the flooding by Needles. He wondered what kind of damage the railroad would sustain. He wanted to be at Parker Dam and make sure everything was done correctly. He looked at his watch. Here at Hoover, water levels would not peak until later in the evening. Today was going to be a disaster downstream. He had already written off two dams that he thought would fail downstream in the afternoon, not to mention the desalination plant at the Imperial Dam that they needed to protect. They might need him downstream. It was someplace where he could help out. Besides, the terrorists seemed to be moving that direction anyway. Grant made a quick decision. He was leaving.

"We'll be there when Havasu fills," he said. He noticed her head come up abruptly from her notebook. "You can come too. We need to be at Parker Dam when the spillways reach capacity." He hesitated, then added, "In case something comes up."

"What about Hoover-Two?" she said, almost pleading. "Who'll monitor the rising water levels?"

Grant motioned to Fred. "Fred'll take care of it. His guys can forward you the numbers. I want you to stay with me. I may need some quick calculations." He waved at Hoover Dam. "It's too late to do anything here. Hoover-Two is going to either hold or fail this afternoon, and it's too late for us to make a difference either way."

She hitched her glasses up on her nose and casually paged through her notebook, but Grant knew she wasn't really looking for anything.

"Don't worry," he said. "We can't be everywhere. Downstream is where we need to be. If there's anything to be done it will be down there."

Grant pointed at Fred. "I need another helicopter. See if you can reserve it for the whole day. And I'd better call the FBI and tell them I'm leaving."

Fred smiled. "Aren't you forgetting something?"

Grant shrugged. "What?"

"Don't you need to tell the commissioner?"

CHAPTER 31

"You're what?" The commissioner looked shocked.

"I'm going downstream to the other dams, to make sure everything gets done," Grant replied.

Roland motioned out the windows toward Hoover-Two and the monumental effort in process to complete the second phase of sandbags in time. "What about that?"

Grant shrugged. "My part is done. They can handle it from here."

"You are not done!" the commissioner yelled. "This project is far from finished, and we are far from being out of the woods, and you are responsible."

Grant held out his palms. "I'm not doing anything. They don't need me anymore."

The commissioner yelled, "Then start doing something. Go make sure they are doing everything right. Make sure we're not going to run out of sandbags. Make sure we are building it fast enough. Make sure we have enough volunteers. Who is doing all that?"

"It's all being handled. The governor's people are handling the sandbags, and the National Guard is managing the dike. They are all doing a great job. It's under control."

"Yeah, but what if something goes wrong? What if the water rises too fast or the dike breaks? These people consider you their leader, even the governor. Who would they go to?"

"Fred," Grant said. "He is taking over while I'm gone."

The commissioner turned on him. "Fred Grainger? What the hell does he know? They're not going to consider him in charge. He's not a dam builder."

Grant had had it. "How about you, Roland? You're here, aren't you? What about the other executives? Are they all worthless? How much more horsepower do you need?"

The commissioner looked surprised.

Grant continued, "Right now we have major flooding occurring downstream in Laughlin and Needles. Bridges and railroads are going to be lost. People will die.

We will likely lose three dams this afternoon, maybe four if we don't manage them correctly. Are you going to go down there and take care of those problems?"

Roland had no response.

"I didn't think so." Grant pointed at him. "You belong here, in the limelight, with the governor and the cameras. I'm leaving. I'm going to try to save some dams downstream. If you get in trouble, call me." He held up the cell phone. "And I'll tell you what to do."

Commissioner Blackwell said nothing as Grant walked away.

* * *

8:40 a.m. - Grand Canyon, Arizona

David felt Judy stiffen on the ledge.

"What's that?" she asked.

David heard it too. It was the unmistakable sound of a helicopter. "Thank God!"

All three of them were physically and emotionally exhausted from the events of the night before and the lack of sleep. David was still cold and over the last hour had become incredibly thirsty. He craved a hot cup of coffee. Finally, they would be rescued.

When the helicopter rounded the bend downstream and became visible, it was much lower than they expected, flying just above the river.

All three of them waved their arms frantically. They jostled on the small space to prevent knocking each other over.

"OVER HERE!" David yelled.

Afram waved his arms back and forth to try to get the helicopter's attention, but the helicopter was too far below them. It could not see them. It was obviously flying low to search along the river. The eyes of the searchers were surely aimed downward. When it passed by them, they could only see the rotors. The three rafters continued to wave and scream as it passed. A moment later, it had flown upstream and around the bend.

"I don't believe it," Afram said.

Judy wiped at her forehead. "They didn't see us."

David spoke the obvious. "We're in big trouble."

* * *

9:30 a.m. - Hoover Dam, Nevada

The helicopter had "Las Vegas Tours" painted across the side just like the last one. It would stay with them throughout the day. The owner had been all over the idea of an all-day charter. With the rotor still spinning, Grant climbed into the front seat and restrained his urge to reach out and shake the pilot's hand, since the pilot didn't seem to have a free one.

"You Grant Stevens?" said the pilot without looking at him.

The pilot wore wire rim sunglasses and sported a full beard and mustache. The earphones he wore held his shoulder-length hair out of his face. Although not long, the beard was scraggly and the growth on his neck had not been trimmed. The tour company shirt was clean and pressed, and looked out of place with the man's worn jeans and tennis shoes. Grant guessed his age in the mid fifties.

"That's me," Grant yelled to be heard above the rotors.

He saw Shauna jump in one of the rear seats, place the computer case down by her feet and pull the door shut.

Grant pointed back toward the visitor center. "We're waiting for one more person."

The pilot pointed at the headphones hanging on the console. "Put those on."

Grant complied and positioned the microphone in front of his mouth.

"Makes it easier to talk." Grant heard the voice in the headphones and he noticed the guy was smiling at him. "I'm Lloyd."

Grant motioned for Shauna to put on her headphones.

"So I understand the first destination is Parker Dam?" said Lloyd. "What about after that?"

Grant looked over at him and could see he was genuinely interested. "We'll follow the river. There are a few small dams downstream from Parker. We'll probably stop at a few of those. Eventually there's Imperial Dam down by Yuma. We'll probably go at least that far."

Lloyd nodded with an excited look on his face. "I hear things are getting a little outta control downstream."

Grant sensed Lloyd was anxious to be going with them. "You know it. How'd you get assigned to us for the day, anyway?"

"Volunteered," Lloyd said, smiling. "I would have killed to get this gig."

Grant looked at Lloyd's eyes and decided he might be telling the truth. "Why?" Grant asked, although he thought he could guess the answer.

Lloyd looked at Grant as if he was his counselor. "I started flying choppers for the rush, the excitement. Flying low with bullets zinging past my head in Nam upped the ante. But since Nam . . ." He stared straight ahead. "It's not what it used to be. The most excitement I ever get anymore is when I'm flying around at night while somebody joins the mile-high club in the back seat."

Grant turned back toward Shauna, hoping she hadn't put her headphones on yet, but saw that she had, and that her eyes had grown at Lloyd's comment. The Vietnam story fit perfectly with Lloyd's looks. Grant wondered for a moment if they were safe, but remembered hearing that helicopter pilots who survived Vietnam were the best in the world, able to fly over a hundred miles an hour only inches off the ground.

"Yesterday, they had me flying down in the Grand Canyon. You know, to warn the rafters about the flood. That was good. We never get to fly that low in the canyon. I almost got my feet wet." Lloyd's teeth showed a devilish smile, one that Grant was glad Shauna couldn't see. Lloyd pointed over Grant's shoulder. "Is that your other passenger?"

Grant turned and saw a small female FBI agent in blue coveralls running crouched toward the helicopter. When she looked up, he recognized her as Agent Susan Williams, the one who'd met him at Davis Dam the night before. "That's her," he said into the microphone.

The pilot watched the woman approach the chopper and suddenly his jaw dropped and his expression showed fear for the first time. "Are you guys all FBI?" He must have seen the insignia on Agent William's coveralls. His nervousness made Grant wonder if Lloyd was hiding something under the seat.

Grant suppressed the laugh and smiled instead. "No, Shauna and I are with the Bureau of Reclamation out of Denver. The dam builders," he added for clarification.

"Hi," said Shauna, speaking for the first time.

"Hello, Miss."

Grant continued, "Agent Williams is an explosives expert from the FBI. She's coming along in case we encounter the bad guys or another bomb."

Lloyd's eyes lit up. "You think we might run into some explosives today?"

Grant heard the door shut behind him. He turned and smiled at Agent Williams. She returned the smile briefly, then reached for the seatbelt. Shauna reached over and handed her a pair of headphones. Grant felt the turbine accelerate and heard the sound of the rotors increase.

Grant gave her a minute, then said, "Agent Williams, nice to see you again."

His stomach dropped as the helicopter lifted. Agent Williams must have had the same sensation, because the response didn't come back for a few moments.

"How's your body?" she asked, meriting a quick glance from Lloyd.

"The toe's still a little sore, but the Advil is helping." Grant's soreness was mostly gone, or masked by the painkillers. It was replaced by an overwhelming desire to sleep. "I'm bushed, though. How about you?" Grant felt rude for not turning to face her during the conversation, but with her seated directly behind, combined with the G-forces from the helicopter, it was easier to look straight ahead.

"In the FBI, we're used to all-nighters."

Lloyd looked over and winked, showing Grant he'd interpreted her comment differently.

Lloyd flew south, roughly following Black Canyon. None of the three passengers spoke, all of them craning their necks to stare down at the river below. On last night's ride in the darkness, Grant hadn't been able to see much. But now he could look down into the canyons. He could see whitewater occasionally on the Colorado River, and knew he was seeing big waves that either hadn't been there two days ago, or had been much smaller. After a few minutes the canyon widened and Grant could see the water of Lake Mojave.

"How low can we fly?" Grant asked and immediately regretted it.

Lloyd smiled. "I can drag the landing gear if you want."

"No, that's not necessary." Grant pointed ahead to where he could see what looked like cabins on the side of the lake. "I just want to be low enough to see the effects of the higher water line."

"No problem," he said, and Grant felt the helicopter drop. Lloyd was smooth and maneuvered the chopper down to about a hundred feet of elevation with no erratic maneuvers. Even a hundred feet seemed way too low and accentuated the feeling of speed. Grant caught himself gripping the sides of his seat. Like Lake Mead, the water lines along the banks were noticeably missing, covered by the all-time-high water level.

For a while they didn't see any boats, but fifteen minutes into the journey, they saw a water-ski boat. Over the next few miles they saw many more, including a few houseboats. Evidently, not everyone heeded the warnings to clear the lake.

"Shauna, how much higher is the water?" Grant asked.

"Less than ten feet," she responded off the top of her head. "They don't vary the levels here near as much as they do at Mead and Powell."

"So basically, if there weren't a million warnings, they wouldn't be able to tell the difference? Except for the water marks?" he asked.

"No. The only difference would be the drift in the channel, and that would only be noticeable upstream where the lake is skinny."

They watched in silence again for a while. Grant knew the calm feeling on the lake was deceiving. There was chaos ahead. He could feel it.

Shauna broke the silence. "What are all those houses on the left?"

Grant stared at a hillside of homes, many of them at the lake's edge. He had remembered seeing their lights the night before.

"It's called Kathrine's Landing," Lloyd said.

"There's the dam." It was Agent Williams's voice.

Grant saw it, but Davis Dam was not nearly as obvious at low elevation and lacked the lights to make it stand out in the dark.

"Lloyd, can you slow us down so I can get a good look at the dam and the spillways?"

"No problem, Mr. Stevens."

Right up until the helicopter reached Davis Dam, everything seemed normal. The water levels seemed close to the top of the earth dike, but not enough to panic an untrained eye. However, as the helicopter passed over the dike in view of the concrete spillways, the normalness quickly disappeared. Unlike Hoover's spillway tunnels, Davis Dam's spillways did not disappear into the mountain. The concrete superstructure was built like a small dam itself and the spillways were positioned slightly lower than the maximum water level, channeling the excess water over the top of the concrete.

Close to 500,000 cubic feet per second was rolling over the top of the two spillways. Like Glen Canyon, the crashing water generated so much mist that it was difficult to see where the water was landing. One thing that was all too evident was that the river had leaped out of its channels. The concrete pool below the spillways was gone, covered in water. The whole area below the dam was underwater.

Grant turned and saw both of Shauna's hands in front of her mouth.

He heard Lloyd's voice in the headphones. "I assume this lake ain't supposed to be here?"

Grant nodded and thought Lloyd's classification of the flood below the spill-ways as a lake was an accurate description. The water covered the entire landscape below the dam, filling the riverbed and covering the entire parking lot and roads. He looked around for Blaine or Billy, the two security men he met the night before, but he couldn't see them. He could only see policemen.

"No, this lake wasn't here last night," he finally responded to Lloyd. He motioned with his hand. "This whole area below the dam was an old stream bed, dry gravel."

"You wanna look around some more, or move on?" Lloyd said.

Grant realized the helicopter had stopped in mid air, hovering, and that the pilot had been waiting for him. "No. Keep going, but stay low over the river."

The helicopter immediately banked and headed downstream. Just south of the dam, they passed by the large casinos lining the Nevada side of the river. Most of them featured riverfront amenities such as spacious pools and sun decks. None were visible, being covered with dirty water.

"Unbelievable," said Agent Williams from behind. "This is going to cost billions to clean up."

Grant noticed a couple of guys in a rowboat between two casinos trying to retrieve something wrapped around a tree. The Showboat, a casino shaped like a riverboat, was built right on the river, and suffered the most damage, with water flowing in one side of the building and out the other.

Grant only saw a few people around the casinos. He figured most of them had been evacuated. The ones he did see wore hip boots and carried shovels. Obviously, there had been a lot of effort to sandbag, as sandbags were piled next to most of the casinos to channel water around them. He wondered if he would have evacuated if he lived in Laughlin. He didn't think so. He tended to relate more with those who tied themselves to a tree before the hurricane hit, or climbed on the roof when the river bottoms flooded. Of course those were the ones that always died, too.

He tried to remember the name of the guy who decided to stay when Mount St. Helens blew in Washington. They tried to evacuate everyone, but he wouldn't budge. He said he'd lived there his whole life and he'd take his chances. It was the last time anybody ever saw him. Was Grant that stubborn? Maybe not.

But this was different. If he lived on the banks of the Colorado River and they told him it was going to flood, he couldn't imagine driving away. He might pack some stuff, and be ready to go at a moment's notice, but he wouldn't go miles away. Just up on the hill a little, so he could rush back down after the flood subsided. Maybe the people didn't have any choice. Maybe the police forced them to leave. That was something to consider. Besides, this flood would last almost sixty days. How would someone get supplies with all the stores closed?

Living in Denver, he didn't ever remember hearing about evacuations, other than localized ones for gas leaks or something. But it seemed like every spring, the news would show pictures of places in the Midwest getting flooded by the Mississippi or the Missouri or some other river, and those disasters were always followed by some governor declaring a national disaster area, and promising millions or billions in relief funding.

Grant was no fan of disaster relief. Isn't that what insurance was for? He remembered one year, one of the news programs talked to an old-timer who had lived by the river all his life. That guy was no fan of the government bailouts either. He said that the river had flooded the bottoms every five years as long as he could remember. Nobody got hurt until they started building housing developments in the river bottoms. He figured if anybody was dumb enough to build down there, they deserved to lose their homes. And sure enough, when the flooding started, it was them that were flooded out. The old-timer on TV did not want his taxes to bail out a bunch of idiots, and Grant agreed with him.

But this might be different. The lower Colorado River hadn't flooded for over seventy years.

Leaving Laughlin and the casinos behind, only desert remained. In fact, aside from green vegetation on the sides of the river, the valley seemed almost lifeless. There were places where the river had broken out and flooded some of the dry lowlands. Grant wondered if it would make a difference. Would long-dormant flower seeds germinate and sprout, and transform the extended banks into something beautiful? Not likely. True, in the early 1900's, before Hoover Dam, the river flooded the valley every spring. But Grant didn't recall hearing about any fields of flowers, only the pictures of flooding and devastation.

"How many miles to the next city?" Agent Williams asked.

Shauna responded with no hesitation. "It's just under thirty miles to Needles. You can see it ahead, over there." Grant couldn't see her pointing, but he could see the small town.

"Lake Havasu is just beyond, through that small mountain range," Shauna said.

"Tighten your belts and we'll be there in a quickie." Lloyd smiled and Grant felt the helicopter tilt forward and accelerate.

Looking down, it was easy to see the river was higher than normal. In many sections it had spilled over the sides and made small lakes on either side of the channel. Grant saw many places where riverside homes were surrounded by water. He saw water flowing over the top of a bridge in Needles and water on many of the streets close to the river. There were people all over the place, which meant the evacuation order had been largely ignored. After Needles, the damage was less obvious. Grant noticed that the BNSF railroad had given up, and water had breached their sandbags and buried the tracks just south of the city. He shuddered at the thought of unburying and repairing the rails when the flood was over.

When the river ducked into Topock Gorge, Lloyd followed it, causing Grant to clutch the seat again. After a few minutes the water spread out into a beautiful canyon of jagged red rock. Lake Havasu, like Lake Mojave before, showed no signs of flooding or disaster. The water looked turquoise and calm. No boats were visible on the north end of the lake, but Grant looked ahead and saw a few farther south defying the warnings.

After a few minutes, Lloyd laughed loudly. "Check out those guys in the red boat at three o'clock."

Grant scanned for a second to see what Lloyd was talking about, while Lloyd and Agent Williams laughed in his earphones. A long red and white boat pulled two water-skiers while being chased by a police boat with blinking lights. From a distance it looked like the tanned bodies, both skiing and in the boat, were naked from the waist up, but as they got closer, he saw that the girls wore swimsuits, just incredibly tiny ones.

"Whatever it takes to get smooth water," said Lloyd.

Ahead, Grant could see a growing city spreading up from the east shore. "Is that Parker?"

Lloyd answered. "No, that's Havasu City, Arizona. The city of Parker is a couple of miles downstream from the dam."

Grant nodded. He had never been to Lake Havasu before and was amazed at how isolated the turquoise lake was, surrounded on all sides by the red rock cliffs.

He heard Shauna's voice in the headphones. "If you look over on the right you can see pipes going up over that hill, and the pumping station on the edge of the lake. That's the California Aqueduct. That's the one that was blown up this morning."

The pipes were larger than Grant imagined. And the hill they went up was tall and steep. He guessed the amount of electricity to pump the water up the hill wasn't trivial. And with that much water, no wonder the bombed aqueduct made a huge mess.

Lloyd looked over at Grant. "When did that happen? I hadn't heard about that."

"It was a few hours ago, just before the sun came up."

"It looks okay to me," Lloyd said.

Shauna explained, "It was out in the desert about twenty or thirty miles from here. The flood made a big lake before they finally shut off the pumps."

"You want to go check it out?" Lloyd asked, hopefully.

Grant thought about it. The aqueduct had supposedly torn up the hillside and flooded acres of desert. He would like to see it too, no doubt about it. But they were far too late to do anything. There were more pressing issues at the dams downstream.

"No, it's out of our way. Besides, we need to get to Parker. We may still be able to accomplish something there."

Lloyd's mouth twitched slightly, which Grant thought might've been an indication of his disappointment. But it happened too fast to be certain. Up ahead, Grant could now see the concrete structure of Parker Dam. He had a feeling that there would be plenty of action there.

CHAPTER 32

11:00 a.m. - Parker Dam, California –Arizona Border

As the helicopter approached Parker Dam, Grant could see the place was crawling with police. Agent Williams had called ahead so the helicopter was expected. However, the entire roadway on top of the dam was covered with police cars and they had to hover for a few minutes while some of the cars were moved to make room for the helicopter to land.

Parker Dam, compared to Hoover and Glen Canyon, seemed unimpressive. The concrete dam rose only 85 feet from the river below, and the superstructure another 60 feet above the roadway. But Grant knew looks were deceiving. When building a concrete arch dam, it was necessary to dig through all the substrate until bedrock was reached, to anchor it. In the 1930's when Parker was built, the Bureau of Reclamation dug 320 feet down before hitting bedrock, making Parker the deepest below-ground dam in the world, with almost seventy five percent of it underground.

As soon as they landed, Lloyd killed the engine, and the rotors started winding down. Grant turned and looked at Shauna. "What time was the water level supposed to peak here?"

"11:45," she said with no hesitation.

"All right, that gives us 45 minutes. See if you can find out who's tracking the water levels, and let's get an update on how soon it'll reach the top of the spillways."

"Where are you going to be?" she asked.

"I'll be over by the spillways themselves to see if there's anything we need to worry about. I'm certain that these spillways haven't been used in years, and never at full capacity."

Agent Williams spoke from behind. "I'm going to go talk to the police for a few minutes, then I need to check in with Phil. I'll find you later."

Lloyd was looking at Grant. He was hurrying to shut down all the electronics. "You mind if I hang with you for a while?"

Grant laughed. It was obvious the pilot was excited to be in the middle of everything. "No. Come on." Grant jumped out of the helicopter.

No sooner had Grant walked out from under the still spinning rotors than a short, fat man appeared to greet him. The man wore a white polo shirt with the words *Parker Dam* embroidered above the pocket. The pocket itself sported three pens in a plastic pocket protector. He rested his pudgy arms on his extended stomach and his black slacks barely reached down to the tops of a pair of black tennis shoes. The guy wore thick glasses and attempted to hide his nearly bald head by combing his hair across it. In spite of the sunny location, this man had no tan whatsoever. Grant guessed he was in his early fifties.

The man reached out with one of the pudgy arms. "Mr. Stevens? Hi. I'm Charlie Jorgensen. I've been expecting you. Fred Grainger called from Hoover and said you were coming."

"Nice to meet you, Charlie." Grant noticed as soon as he released the handshake that Charlie returned the arm to its resting place on his stomach. An awkward moment of silence ensued as Charlie just stood looking at Grant with a weird smile on his face.

"Well, how about you show me the spillways?" Grant started to walk around him before the man suddenly snapped out of his trance and hustled alongside.

"Sure, Mr. Stevens. Right over this way." He motioned to where Grant was already headed.

Unlike Hoover, Parker's spillways did not rely only on the water levels to operate. There were huge gates that opened upwards to allow the water through. Like Davis Dam, the spillways were built at the top of the concrete structure, channeling the water through the top instead of around the dam. At the moment, four of the five gates were partially open, allowing an impressive amount of water to pass.

"Why isn't the west spillway open?" Grant asked.

Charlie adjusted the thick glasses. "That's number five. It jammed. We're working on it."

"How long since it's been used?"

"The only time we ever used the spillways was 1983, the year of the big spring runoffs. Other'n that, we've been able to keep up with Davis using only the penstocks."

Grant wasn't surprised. It was the same at Hoover and Davis. "I understand they haven't been used for a while, but don't you ever test them?" Grant thought he knew the answer.

Charlie adjusted the glasses again. "Yeah, we test the gates a few times a year, but we don't move 'em very far, usually less than a foot. Number five jammed at about a foot and a half. It hasn't been moved that far since '83."

They reached the spillways, and Grant stopped and looked over the edge of the upstream side toward Lake Havasu. Parker Dam's five spillways, each separated by a wall of concrete, were built right in the center of the arch. Each measured twenty-five feet high and twenty feet wide. Looking at the five huge holes made Grant relax a little. They were bigger than he'd expected. His instincts told him that if they were all open, they would be large enough. But then again, what if they weren't? And they definitely weren't all open.

Grant walked along the dam until they were above the unopened spillway. He could hear someone banging on the metal gate below. "What about the others? Why aren't they open all the way?"

Charlie looked down at the ground. "I didn't feel it was necessary yet. We're still within acceptable levels on Havasu."

That didn't surprise Grant either. None of the people at the dams upstream were gutsy enough to do anything until they were ordered – why should Parker be any different? "Well open 'em now — all the way! The penstocks aren't going to be able to handle 500,000 cubic feet per second."

Charlie's face contorted. "What about number five?"

Grant motioned at the other four. "Opening the others will take some pressure off number five. Tell the guys working on it that they have another half hour before we get some demolition guys in here to blow it open."

This time Charlie took off the glasses and wiped the sweat off his brow. "Blow it open? But then it would never close, not without major repairs. And we'd have to lower the whole lake to get access to it."

"That's tomorrow's problem, Mr. Jorgensen. Today's problem is getting 500,000 cubic feet per second to go downstream without overtopping this dam."

Grant raised his head and looked around. The area on both sides of the dam seemed flat and at nearly the same elevation as the dam itself. If the water rose too high, it was not evident where the low point was. As he took in the surroundings, he noticed that Charlie was moving around, trying to see what Grant was looking at.

Grant explained. "If the spillways don't keep up, where's the water going to go?"

Charlie looked around, panicky. "What d'ya mean, where's it going to go? The spillways were designed to keep up."

"Yeah, but they have never been tested, have they? And besides, right now you can't open all of them anyway. We have to have a contingency. That's why I'm here." Grant looked at his watch. "And we have at most forty minutes to figure it out."

Charlie lowered his head again and prepared to leave. But Grant stopped him. "Oh, Mr. Jorgensen, be sure to call a demolition team. I want them here and ready if your guys can't open the gate on number five." Grant glanced at the top of the metal gates. "Oh, and tell them to bring some of that stuff that burns through metal, the stuff they use underwater to sink ships." Grant considered that it was doubtful they had any of that in Parker, Arizona.

The small man adjusted his glasses one more time and scurried off to relay the instructions. Grant noticed Lloyd standing next to him for the first time since they left the helicopter. He looked at Grant and a large smile appeared across his face.

"You're gonna give the poor man a heart attack," Lloyd said. "He's not used to that kind of pressure."

"Maybe he needs a heart attack. If he'd seen how much water was going through the spillways at Davis, maybe he'd pull his head out."

Grant looked again at the dam and surrounding hillsides and decided the dam itself was probably the lowest point. He walked past a group of police officers, over to the downstream side of the dam. Looking down at where the spillways exited the top of the dam, he decided there was probably less than ten feet of concrete between where he was standing and the top of the spillways.

He had a thought. "Hey Lloyd, if we had the demolition guys blow the top off the spillways, you think that would make a huge difference in how much water we could get through here?"

Lloyd looked down at the spillways, and then back across the dam. "Mr. Stevens," he said, "I don't think Charlie Jorgensen is going to like having you around."

* * *

11:10 a.m. - Carlsbad, California

The skinny man climbed into the back of the truck and checked the tie downs. He verified that the four-wheel ATV he had just purchased was secure and would not move around. The other items, including buckets, shovels, and gas cans, were stacked around it.

"Good luck with it," the other man said. "It's never given me any problems."

The skinny man nodded. "I think it'll work out just fine."

After arriving at the man's house he had taken the ATV for a short test drive in the cul-de-sac where the man lived. The engine was stronger than he expected and the tires were practically new. The muffler was quiet as claimed, which was one of his most important criteria. The four-wheeler had been stored in the garage and seldom used according to its owner. It looked almost new. Besides, he only needed it to run for the next 24 hours.

Satisfied that it was tied securely in the back of the truck, he hopped down and shut the tailgate. The seller stopped counting the wad of twenties for the third time and reached out to shake hands. The skinny man quickly glanced at his watch and then shook. He climbed into the pickup and started the engine. When he glanced one last time at the seller, he was busy counting the bills again.

As he drove the truck back toward the freeway, he wondered how far south the floodwater had traveled. According to reports on the radio, flooding was bad around Needles, which wasn't far from Parker Dam. That put it an hour or two later than he had estimated, but well within the worst-case calculations he had made. He smiled. He had plenty of time. Forty-five minutes south to San Diego, then an hour east and he would be right back in the action.

* * *

11:15 a.m. - Grand Canyon, Arizona

The three rafters were prepared. They couldn't afford to miss any more helicopters. Two had already flown past without seeing them. The problem was how to be noticed.

They were getting desperate. All three of them were thirsty, and the sun was almost directly above them, beating down on them. Additionally, there was no telling how much longer the helicopter searches would continue before they were called off. David wondered how long they could survive on the small outcropping with no food or water. And the space was becoming even more confining as the day went by. David's calves hurt from standing on the jagged slope, and sitting or laying down provided little relief.

The only upside was that over the last four hours of looking over the 300-foot ledge, David was finally becoming more comfortable with heights. It still scared him to look down, but nothing like the first time this morning. Gone were the shakes, sweating, and dizzy spells. Now it was just subdued fear.

The last four hours had oscillated between conversation and silence. They had speculated over and over, all the possible ways for their friends to have survived. But logic told him otherwise. It would be a miracle for any of them to be alive.

The second most popular topic had been how to attract the attention of the helicopters. They had discussed ways to get their attention: noise, fires, mirrors, all to no avail. They did not have the resources to communicate in any of those ways. They agreed that something visual had to be done, and waving arms hadn't worked the previous times. A smoky fire would be best, but all they had at their disposal was rock. Afram had suggested that if only he could throw a rock and actually hit the helicopter, they would be noticed. But both David and Judy knew that the probability of making contact was extremely small.

They needed something to draw the pilot's eyes upward. All three agreed that seeing something catapulting down the cliffs would do the trick. And that ultimately had given them their final idea.

"I think I hear one." Judy cupped her hand to her ear.

David stood and listened. "I can't hear any—"

"I hear it too!" Afram said. "Get ready!"

David crouched and so did Afram. Judy would be first. They had agreed on the sequence in advance. David held on to Judy's legs to stabilize her. The helicopter flew around the bend and became visible. Judy threw her life jacket and it started to fall down the cliff. The life jacket fell 75 feet, then hung on a rock outcropping. Judy crouched and David stood and threw his life jacket as hard as he could, the motion almost carrying him off the ledge. David's jacket dropped slightly farther before hanging on some sagebrush a hundred feet below. The helicopter showed no sign of recognition, maintaining its speed and trajectory. David crouched.

Afram, who had assured them his idea was best, rolled a large rock off the ledge that he had worked out of the hill. His lifejacket was wrapped tightly around the rock. The rock fell twenty feet before impacting rock below it. The collision sprayed dust in all directions and catapulted the rock farther down the canyon. In the next impact, it broke into two smaller pieces and the life jacket came off in another spray of dust. The two rocks continued rolling, unsettling other rocks in their path.

"Wave!" Afram yelled.

All three stood and waved their arms. One of the rocks bounced all the way to the river and splashed. The helicopter slowed.

"They saw it!" Judy said, jumping up and down on the small ledge.

"Wave!" Afram yelled again.

The helicopter veered as if it was searching for something. It climbed higher.

"Keep waving!" Judy encouraged. "They're looking for us."

The helicopter climbed and headed directly toward them.

"I think they see us," David said.

Judy shook her head. "Don't stop until we're sure."

The helicopter climbed higher and moved directly in front of them. David could see someone inside pointing at the three rafters.

"Hello." The sound was metallic and came from the helicopter's PA. A man inside the helicopter waved.

David had never been so happy in his life. The three rafters stopped waving, although Judy was still jumping up and down. The men in the helicopter pointed up at the rock cliffs. It looked like they were talking strategy. David realized the helicopter could not get close enough to help them without causing the rotors to hit the cliff. The men inside continued talking and pointing. The rafters waited.

The metallic voice returned. "Unfortunately, we are not going to be able to retrieve you from that location. We'll need to send another helicopter, one that can get you from above." He pointed up.

David felt disappointment that they would be on the ledge longer.

"Don't worry," the voice continued. "We'll be back." The man smiled widely. "Don't go anywhere while we're gone."

And with that, the helicopter flew up the river and was gone.

* * *

11:20 a.m. - Parker Dam, California/Arizona Border

Spillways one through four were now completely open and the volume of water was scary. Grant guessed that they were each running at eighty percent capacity, needing Lake Havasu to rise only a few more feet to max them out. According to Shauna, just before Charlie opened the gates, Lake Havasu was rising just under an inch every two minutes, which meant the full volume of water from Davis and Hoover was entering the lake. Opening the four spillways had slowed the rate considerably, but it was still rising. They needed the other spillway open.

Charlie's guys had rigged some scaffolding off the downstream side of the dam allowing them to climb down into the spillway itself. Grant now stood on the scaffolding inside number five, looking up at the stuck gate. The metal head gate was designed to slide down two slots in the concrete. Electric motors pulled huge chains to move the gate up and down. With the right side stuck, the left side had dropped enough to wedge the entire gate. One of Charlie's men had climbed up the ladder and was banging on the top of the head gate, where it was jammed. Now Charlie was worried about burning up the motors, since the one on the right started smoking during the last attempt. Obviously, the more pressure on the gate, the harder it would be to break loose, and the rising water on the other side wasn't helping. The worker on the ladder continued pounding mercilessly with the sledgehammer to break it loose. He stopped hammering for a second, mopped the sweat off his brow with his glove, and gave Charlie a thumbs up.

Charlie stood next to Grant, looking up at the worker. "You want to try it again?" The worker nodded.

Charlie held a radio to his mouth and prepared to have someone inside the dam try the motors, when Grant interrupted him. "Can you separate the motors?"

Charlie shrugged and adjusted his glasses. "What do you mean?"

"Can you try raising it with just the left motor?" Grant pointed up at the top. "That might un-jam it."

Charlie relayed the request into the radio. The response came back that there was only one switch.

"Aren't there separate circuit breakers for each motor?" asked Grant.

The person on the radio answered that there were. Charlie thumbed the radio. "Turn off the right motor, then try to raise it."

They waited for a while then they heard the gate screech and Grant saw the left side move up slightly.

"Stop!" Charlie yelled in the radio.

A couple of the men started cheering, including the man up on the ladder.

"Okay, now turn the right motor back on," Charlie said into the radio. He gave the operator a few moments to flip the switch. "All right, now try both motors down." He motioned for Grant to cross his fingers.

The gate started moving down. The workers cheered again.

"Stop!" yelled Charlie into the radio.

The gate stopped and Grant heard the response from the radio. "What's wrong now? Did it jam again?"

Charlie explained in the radio. "No. But we need to get out of here before you open it — or you'll drown us all," he added.

That made perfect sense to Grant. He headed for the scaffolding, at the same time noticing the man with the sledge hurrying behind him. When Grant reached the top, climbing onto the safe concrete structure again, he saw Shauna and Lloyd waiting.

"So you fixed it?" said Lloyd.

"It's not open yet," Grant answered.

He turned to see Charlie climbing over the rail. He looked terrible. His un-tucked shirt was smeared with dirt and soaked with sweat under both arms and in the middle of his chest. The three other workers followed, handing the ladder up as they came. With everyone on the deck, Charlie first nodded at Grant, then keyed the radio. "Okay, we're all out. Let 'er rip."

Grant watched over the side of the dam at number five as the switch was activated. He could hear the metal gate moving. After only a few seconds the small stream exiting the spillway increased. The stream quickly grew until it was almost half the size of the other four.

Charlie's head showed up next to Grant's. He yelled to be heard over the water. "The right motor is smoking like hell."

Grant looked over at him. "What'd you tell him?"

Charlie grinned. "I told him to let it smoke. We'll replace the motor later."

The sound of the gate raising was barely audible with the noise of the water. But Grant knew it was still moving because the water exiting number five continued to grow, now almost equaling the other four.

Charlie's radio squawked something indiscernible and he walked to the middle of the dam where it was quieter. He said something into the radio, but Grant couldn't hear. Charlie looked back at Grant, then walked toward him. "We burned up the right motor. It's on fire."

Grant looked back at the streams of water blasting from the spillways. If number five's flow was less than the other four, it wasn't by much. He turned back to Charlie. "Is it all the way up?"

Charlie adjusted his glasses and shook his head. "It's still got a couple feet to go."

Surely, a couple of feet wouldn't make much difference. But Grant knew it was a wish more than a fact. Grant grabbed Shauna's arm and led her to the middle of the dam where the sound wasn't as loud. "I need you to watch the water levels, by the minute. Number five is jammed again and this time we're not going to be able to fix it."

"We're already monitoring the levels every minute. But Havasu needs to rise higher until the water reaches the tops of the spillways. Only then will the spillways be at full capacity. That's when we expect the water levels to stabilize."

Grant nodded. "How soon?"

She looked at her watch. "Next half hour?"

Grant nodded again. "Okay, keep me informed." He watched her turn and walk quickly through the police officers until she was out of sight.

Grant turned and looked at Charlie again. "Order a new motor and get it installed ASAP. These spillways are gonna be open for two months. The longer we wait to open the spillway that last two feet, the more likely the water is going to damage the head-gate. Besides, if it turns out that it isn't open enough, and water starts going over the top of the dam, you'll need that motor to fix the problem."

Charlie nodded and walked away. Grant returned to the edge of the dam and stood next to Lloyd, observing the water leaving the spillways. Both stared for a few minutes without saying anything. Finally Lloyd broke the trance. "All right, Mr. Stevens, what's next?"

Grant straightened and they both walked slowly across the dam. "As soon as Shauna's water levels start to stabilize, we're off." He pointed downstream. "With all that water, Headgate Rock Dam, fourteen miles downstream, is probably getting topped already."

"You can't do anything about it?"

"We already tried. We told them to dynamite it, you know, open it up to let all this water through. But they refused."

Grant saw Lloyd's eyes grow and his mouth contort before he continued. "It's not going to matter anyway. The water'll tear the dam apart in a couple of hours. It'll just flood a little upstream before it lets go."

"What's upstream?"

"The reservoir is called Lake Moovalya. It's tiny compared to Lake Havasu, or Mojave, let alone Mead. More like a wide spot in the river. There's not much on the banks. They might get a little flooding. It shouldn't last long, though. I think Shauna's numbers predicted that at full flow, it'd take less than fifteen minutes to fill up the whole lake and spill over the top of the dam."

Lloyd pointed toward Parker Dam's spillways. "Doesn't Headgate Rock Dam have spillways?"

"Sure. But nowhere near big enough to handle 500,000 cubic feet per second."

"Why not? The other dams upstream got 'em."

Grant shrugged. "The dams downstream from Lake Havasu were only built to divert water for irrigation and aqueducts. Relatively speaking, there was no intent to do water storage or flood management. That would be handled upstream, primarily at Hoover and Glen Canyon."

"But what about a disaster like this?"

"You mean a complete failure of the Glen Canyon Dam? Believe me, that was never planned for at any of the dams, including Hoover. Keep in mind that all these dams – Hoover, Davis, Parker and even Headgate Rock – were all built before Glen Canyon. So they were mostly worried about controlling spring runoff and generating electricity. Handling flood waters from a failed mega-dam wouldn't have even been considered."

"Well, right now, you're probably wishing they had been designed for it, aren't you?"

Grant considered Lloyd's comment. What if all the dams downstream were equipped with red buttons: press here to engage management system for failed dam upstream. It definitely would have made life easier over the last thirty-six hours. But realistically some disasters are too big to warrant contingency plans. What if all 747's were to crash in one day, or what if California's big earthquake finally hit and everything west of the San Andreas fault sank into the ocean, or what if all the nukes self-detonated? These are all "what ifs" that are too expensive and unlikely to prepare for. The strategy, instead, is to do everything possible to prevent the events from occurring, versus contingency planning for the events themselves. Grant would place the failure of the Glen Canyon Dam in this category. How could you possibly prepare for it?

Grant smiled at Lloyd. "Right now I'd be happy if we just end up saving Hoover, Davis, and Parker. I might get fired for it, but I expect the flood to wipe out all the other dams downstream. That, I would consider a huge success, considering the cards I've been dealt. We could rebuild all of the small dams in a year if we had to."

"Then why would you get fired for it? Aren't your bosses going to see it the same way?"

Grant smiled at Lloyd. "Is your boss logical?" He didn't wait for an answer. "No, this thing is going to be a media circus. When they finally get a death count from Lake Powell and the Grand Canyon, show video of all the floods including flooded farmland, floating houses, dead cows, damaged casinos, stranded houseboats, nobody's going to be saying 'just think how bad it would have been if Grant Stevens hadn't saved Hoover Dam'. They won't be looking for heroes, and if they do, it'll be some park ranger who dragged a fat lady out of the Grand Canyon before she drowned. More likely, the media is going to come down hard on the Bureau of Reclamation on this one. They'll want a scapegoat. And I can't see my boss volunteering."

"You really think they'll come after you?"

"Hey, look at what happened in Oklahoma. Remember when that whacko blew up the Oklahoma Federal Building and killed all those people including the kids in the daycare center?"

"Yeah, but he intentionally blew them up."

"The bomber is not who I'm talking about. If you remember, the president vowed to track down everyone responsible. The bomber had a friend who supposedly taught him how to build fertilizer bombs on his farm."

"I remember him. Isn't he the one they want to re-try in Oklahoma?"

"Yeah. He's only serving a life sentence, but they want the death penalty." Grant overemphasized the word "only" to make the statement sound more sarcastic.

Lloyd looked confused. "I don't understand what that has to do with —"

Grant interrupted. "He's a fall guy. When the feds prosecuted him in Colorado, the jury acquitted him on all the murder counts. They couldn't prove that he knew anything about the bomber's plans to blow up Oklahoma."

Lloyd's brows furrowed. "That doesn't sound right. If that were true, why'd he get life in prison?"

"The jury found him guilty of two crimes – involuntary manslaughter and conspiracy to make a weapon of mass destruction. Then they leaned on the judge to throw the book at him."

"Well, if he's guilty of those two things, why shouldn't they throw the book at him?"

"Do you know what involuntary manslaughter means?" Grant continued. "Involuntary manslaughter means there was no intent to kill and that you were only indirectly responsible for someone's death. Involuntary manslaughter is the law we use to punish people for accidents. You know, it's the law district attorneys use when a child drowns in a swimming pool, or a parent accidentally backs over their kid in the driveway."

Lloyd raised his voice. "Yeah, but what about the other one? What'd you call it, mass destruction?"

"That's one of the government's 'big brother laws.' It's a selective prosecution law."

"What do ya mean?"

"They make a law where everybody's guilty, and then big brother can decide when to come in and prosecute. This law, Conspiracy to Make a Weapon of Mass Destruction, is broadly written. Hypothetically, let's say I'm a smart guy, and we sit down at your kitchen table one day over a couple beers, and you ask me how nuclear bombs work. Let's say I build a small model using apples and toothpicks. We could both be guilty of the conspiracy law."

Lloyd shook his head. "I don't think so; just talking about it can't be illegal. There are books in the library that tell you how bombs work, and internet sites. How can we make it illegal to teach somebody how to make a bomb?"

"That's just it. They don't prosecute everybody, just who they want. That's why the other guy is in prison for life, and in jeopardy of being re-tried so they can get the death penalty, even though re-trying someone for the same crime in this country is supposed to be against the law."

"But that bomb was actually used to kill people."

"But the second guy didn't know that. At least they couldn't prove it or he would have been guilty of murder. They couldn't prove he knew anything about the plan to blow up Oklahoma. They only knew that he taught the bomber how to make fertilizer bombs. That's it."

"Well, building bombs in your corn field is illegal."

"Yeah. But it doesn't warrant life in prison, or the death penalty, does it? No, he was a scapegoat, a fall guy, someone that the president could throw to the masses."

Lloyd was quiet for a long time. Both of them had stopped walking without realizing it. Lloyd finally looked up at Grant. "And I thought *I* was into conspiracy theories."

Grant smiled.

Lloyd's smile vanished. "You're not saying they're going to prosecute you for these floods, are you, all the deaths and everything?"

"No, but they will look for scapegoats, both the government and the media, especially if they don't catch whoever's blowing up the dams. And firing somebody like me from the Bureau of Reclamation is a small price to pay, to be able to say that you've . . ." Grant made a sign in the air for quotation marks with his fingers, ". . . implemented corrective action."

Grant saw Shauna walking through the crowds, scanning her head back and forth, obviously looking for Grant. He yelled at her. "Shauna!"

She turned at the sound and her face lit up when she saw them. She quickly walked toward where they were standing.

"What's happening with the water levels?" Grant asked.

"The water is still rising, but just barely. After you opened number five, the rate changed from an inch every two minutes to almost five minutes per inch. Since then, the lake has risen another six inches and now the rate has slowed to almost ten minutes for the last inch. And we're still six inches below the tops of the spillways."

"So you think it'll handle it?"

"No problem," she said immediately.

"All right then. Let's go."

Shauna stepped back. "You mean leave? Before the water level stabilizes?"

"Yeah. You said it'd handle it." He knew he was pushing her. She didn't like leaving loose ends. But then, neither did he. Unfortunately, there just wasn't enough time to eliminate every reasonable doubt. If there were, he'd still be at Hoover; actually, he might even be at Glen Canyon. He pointed downstream. "Right now, the water's probably topping Headgate Rock. We need to go."

"Yeah, but what if —"

"They'll call us, believe me." Grant motioned for the helicopter.

At that moment, Charlie walked up, followed by a guy in a hard hat. "Well the demolition guys are here." The guy in the hard hat nodded toward Grant. Charlie adjusted his glasses then returned his hand to its resting place on his stomach, which was now stained from the sweat and grime from the last hour. "Guess we don't need them anymore, since we got the gate open. Right? You want me to send 'em home?"

Grant glanced over at Shauna before answering. "No, we were just talking about that." Grant stepped closer and reached out toward the guy in the hard hat. The man responded and they shook hands. "Grant Stevens."

"Duane." Duane's hands felt dry and rough.

Grant pointed toward Lake Havasu. "The water levels haven't stabilized yet. We expect them to, probably sometime in the next hour." He checked Shauna's expression to verify accuracy, and since he saw no changes, assumed he was okay. "But we'd like to have you hang around for a few hours until the water level does stabilize. Just in case."

Charlie looked surprised and quickly adjusted the glasses again. "The spillways are pretty much open now. And we couldn't get Duane down there to blow it anyway."

Grant knew where this was going. "Charlie's right. The spillways are as open as they're going to be. If that's not enough to stop the water from rising, then we have to do something else." Grant saw Charlie's mouth drop open. "Lloyd and I were thinking that the concrete at the top of the dam that goes over the top of the spillways is probably, what, about six to eight feet thick?" Grant looked at Charlie for affirmation.

Charlie nervously adjusted his glasses. "Yeah, sure. That sounds about right, but —"

"So if the spillways can't handle it, you could blow the top off a few of them. That would definitely open them up enough." Grant looked directly at Duane. "You think you could open up that much concrete?"

The man in the hard hat shifted uncomfortably and glanced over at Charlie. "Well, sure, I guess. But I'll need to check to see –"

Grant held out both of his hands. "Look, we're pretty confident we're okay. You're probably not going to have to blow up anything. But we'd like you to hang around and be ready. You can work with Charlie."

Charlie looked over, concerned. "Why? You're not leaving, are you?"

Grant nodded quickly at Lloyd, who immediately left toward the helicopter. "Yeah, Charlie, we are."

"How soon?" he asked, adjusting his glasses again.

"Right now."

"But the water —"

"Don't worry, you can call us if anything goes wrong." Grant felt confident that Charlie wouldn't blow up anything without calling first.

"But —"

"Shauna will tell your people what we expect the water levels to do. If it varies much, call me and we'll figure it out. If it gets bad enough, we'll come back. Don't worry."

Grant heard the whine of the turbine on the helicopter and started walking toward it. Grant saw Shauna dart away, most likely to brief the person watching the water levels. Charlie hustled up to walk next to Grant. He looked like he wanted to say something, but wasn't sure what. As they reached the outer perimeter of the now spinning rotors, FBI Agent Susan Williams joined them. She looked surprised.

"Are we leaving? I heard the helicopter."

Grant nodded. "Yeah. You ready?"

"Yeah. I guess."

Grant turned back to Charlie and shook his hand. "Nice working with you, Charlie. Hopefully we'll run into each other again sometime."

Charlie's lips moved, but he didn't say anything. He looked nervous, but realistically the hard part was behind him. Parker Dam's spillways would be at full capacity for the next sixty days. He'd settle in after a while. He'd have to. Looking at Charlie Jorgensen, Grant realized he kind of liked the guy, in spite of his weirdness.

Grant broke the handshake, patted Charlie on the shoulder to reassure him, then walked under the rotors toward the passenger seat of the helicopter. Right before he opened the door, he turned and pointed to Charlie. Grant motioned a phone at his ear and mouthed the words "call me."

Charlie nodded weakly.

Grant climbed in. Lloyd held out the headphones, which Grant pulled on. He saw that Agent Williams was doing the same.

"Are we waiting for your girl?" It was Lloyd's voice in the headphones.

"Yeah. She'll only be a minute."

They waited without talking. When the door opened and Shauna jumped in, the rotors had already begun to accelerate. She was still attaching her seat belt when the chopper lifted off.

As they rose quickly into the air, Grant noticed the water exiting the five spillways. The aerial view didn't do it justice. You had to be standing right next to it to get the real feeling for how much water was heading down the Colorado River.

* * *

12:00 p.m. - Lake Powell, Utah

Julie was ecstatic. Finally, a crew had arrived to clean the launch ramp. They brought five power washers, and had started scouring back and forth at the top of the ramp. The moss was washing right off, although many of the boaters were now considering that the power washers might have been the wrong approach. It seemed that after being exposed to the dry desert air through the night, then baked in the sun all morning, the moss could almost be swept off the ramp. But with a crew busy cleaning, nobody wanted to throw a wrench into the works for fear the effort would stop.

They had yet to see any equipment arrive that was capable of lifting the boats onto the trailers. The equipment was available in Page, as it was frequently used to move boats around in the repair lots. But the bridge across Glen Canyon was gone. The Crawfords had been surprised to find out that it had collapsed in the flood.

Paul pointed at the team of men power-washing above them on the ramp. "How much longer before you think we can load up?"

Greg shrugged. "It'll be a while." He motioned at the boats farther up the ramp. "We'll have to wait for all these guys to go first."

"Do we have a couple of hours?" Paul asked.

Greg nodded. "Sure. This will take a while. Why?"

Paul pointed in the direction of where the Glen Canyon Dam had been. "I thought maybe we could drive over and check it out. It's only a few miles."

Greg looked up at the men working. "I'd better stay here by the boat, but Julie'll probably want to go." He looked at her.

Julie nodded enthusiastically. She was dying to do something besides wait.

Paul waved at Julie and Erika. "Let's go, then."

A few minutes later they had made the hike up the ramp and climbed into Paul and Erika's SUV. It was a short drive to the highway, but the road was blocked as they neared the dam. Paul parked off the side of the road like many other vehicles, and the three of them jumped out and started walking. As they approached, the canyon opened and they could see more with each step. Another barrier had been set up to prohibit pedestrians. About 40 or 50 people were crowded along the barrier for a look.

Julie's eyes locked onto both ends of where the Glen Canyon Bridge had been the day before. The highway abruptly ended on both sides. It looked like an optical illusion for a road to just end like that.

Paul led them to the far right of the barrier so they could see better around the visitor center, which was partially obscuring their view of the dam. Like Julie had seen the night before, jagged concrete protruded from the sandstone walls where the dam had been. The water had dropped substantially since she and Greg had almost been sucked over the dam. Julie could see that the water flow had also decreased from the night before.

She looked upstream and saw the wet vertical rock canyons. She tried to imagine what Lake Powell must look like upstream. The large bodies of water like Padre Bay must be empty. She couldn't believe it. Lake Powell was gone, replaced by a narrow winding river.

CHAPTER 33

12:10 p.m. - South of Parker Dam, California/Arizona

The helicopter followed the Colorado River downstream from the dam as it wound gracefully through jagged rock canyons. The river was lined with mobile homes, cabins, and houses, leaving almost no gaps. The few small spaces were filled with trees and other green vegetation. The river bottoms contrasted dramatically with the dry barren mountains just a hundred feet away.

The increased flow from all five spillways had upset the serenity. Many of the homes that bordered the river were partially underwater. Only a mile downstream from the dam, the river had torn out a row of mobile homes and piled them in a small park. Grant could still see the tops of a playground. From the air it was obvious the water flowed out of its banks, swirling around homes, through back yards, and even down a small street, the road only identifiable by the protruding mailboxes.

Normally the river ran turquoise and clean below the dam, but today was different. Garbage, papers, trashcans, clothes, and whatever else the river had encountered littered the surface of the water. In one place Grant saw something incredibly large rolling in the water downstream briefly before it sunk. Only afterwards did he realize it had been a car, a Volkswagen Beetle. It took a moment for his mind to assimilate it. Farther downstream, he saw two mobile homes in the middle of the river.

Grant saw many residents, standing, huddled together in groups at higher elevations on the shores. They all acted the same, standing stationary like zombies, staring at the destruction of their lives and property. At least they'd had the presence to hike a few feet up the hill and save themselves.

Grant heard a scream in his headphones.

"It's a body!" Shauna said, pointing ahead to the left of the chopper.

The corpse floated face down still fully clothed. The long-sleeved flannel shirt and the worn denims were still identifiable. The hair, which was either white, or more likely gray, gave Grant the impression that the unlucky victim was an old man.

Grant knew there were two types of drowning cases. One group resisted taking the water into their lungs until the very end, the carbon dioxide building up and increasing their panic level until they finally lost consciousness. When divers found this type of body, they were tense with eyes wide open and teeth clenched. The other type sucked in the water and tried to breath it. In these cases the panic was replaced with a calmness or state of well-being right before they died. These bodies were found relaxed with eyes closed, and sometimes with smiles on their faces.

Grant had read a study on the two types of drowning, where the hypothesis was verified by interviewing survivors, people who had drowned and were later revived. The ones that respired the water described the calmness that followed. More than one had used the words "this isn't that bad" in their descriptions.

Hopefully the old man floating face down on the Colorado River had ultimately breathed in the water. The fact that he was still floating was not a good sign. It could mean there was still air in his lungs.

He heard sniffling in the headphones as they passed over the body and flew downstream. He didn't have to look back to see that Shauna was crying. He wanted to say something to reassure her like "don't worry, everything will be all right." But that wasn't true, was it? Especially for the old man. He couldn't think of anything to say, so he said nothing. Although Grant knew many had died on the Colorado River over the last two days, it was the first he or Shauna had witnessed.

Up ahead the river widened. A dam was barely visible downstream - Headgate Rock Dam. Headgate Rock was only fourteen miles below Parker Dam. The resulting reservoir, Lake Moovalya, was even smaller than he expected. In fact, it hardly seemed like a lake at all.

Only one hotel, the Bluewater Casino, had been built on the banks of the lake. Since the casino sat on the Arizona side of the river, Grant knew it had to be owned by the Indians. In fact, that explained why it was the only structure on the lower part of the lake. The land was probably part of the Colorado River Indian reservation.

The hotel was huge with walls of glass facing the lake. A medium-sized marina extended from the hotel. On the river's edge sat a small shack with a bar right on the river. However, all was not right with the Bluewater Casino. The jetty supporting the bar was underwater, only visible from the helicopter. Two men sloshed through waste-deep water with armfuls of bottles from the bar. The docks in the marina floated and were safe, but the base of the hotel and the dockside sidewalks were underwater.

On his right Grant could see where the highway bordering the west side of the lake now ran right down into the water. Stranded cars had stopped and their drivers stood next to them. No boats could be seen on the small lake.

"Now I know why they call it Headgate Rock Dam," said Lloyd.

Grant nodded in agreement. In the middle of the river channel, just past the Bluewater Casino, was a large black rock formation, obviously Headgate Rock. On the west side of the rock, stretching to the California shore, was an earth dike, topped with dark red and black rocks. On the east side, slightly downstream from

Headgate Rock, was the concrete waterworks including seven square spillways. A smaller earth fill dike connected the concrete structure to the big rock. Like Parker, this dam had a large square concrete structure above each square spillway to pull the head gates up into. Unlike Parker, the head gates were already up all the way.

Lloyd's voice was in the headphones. "Where do you want me to put us?"

"When we get closer, slow down a little, get a little lower, then fly across the downstream side of it. It looks like the water hasn't breached yet. We're going to be just in time to see this fiasco." Grant wondered why it hadn't breached yet. He'd expected the water to be high enough already.

Without looking back, Grant spoke into the headphones. "Shauna, didn't we expect the dam to be getting topped by now?"

"Yeah, but only a few minutes ago." As she spoke, the helicopter flew over the crest of the dam.

Grant had meant to look down, check out the spillways, and assess the dam itself, but something else had caught his eye. Immediately below Headgate Rock Dam, right in the river bottoms on the Arizona side, was a whole community of mobile homes. They were packed together like sardines, stretching all the way down toward a railroad bridge about a mile downstream. They would be obliterated when the dam let go. It was unavoidable and he knew it. He didn't see any people walking around. Hopefully they had cleared out. If not, there would be many more floating bodies.

When he finally looked down, the spillways were blasting. "Wow, look at 'em. No wonder it hasn't breached yet. They're dumping a ton of water. They must have lowered the lake to get ready." He turned and looked over his shoulder at Shauna. "What's the exact capacity of those spillways?"

"Originally they were designed for 200,000 cubic feet per second, but when they modified the dam to generate electricity, they actually built the water works into a couple of the spillways. That reduced their total capacity to around a 140,000."

Grant considered the numbers. Headgate Rock could handle a 140,000, and almost 500,000 was headed for it. It did not take a genius to understand that Headgate Rock Dam was not going to survive.

"Hey, should those guys be standing down there?" Grant recognized the FBI agent's voice in the headphones. He turned and saw her point off to what was now their right side, as the helicopter had turned and now faced upstream.

Lloyd pivoted the helicopter slightly and Grant saw that a pickup had driven down the steep road and parked in the small parking lot near the generation plant. Three men stood by the truck looking up at the dam. One of them wore a yellow hard hat. The truck was close enough for Grant to make out *BIA* on the truck door, for Bureau of Indian Affairs.

Shauna answered. "No, they shouldn't be there. If the dam breaks on that side, they won't stand a chance."

Grant heard the pilot's voice. "How much time do we have?"

"It can't be long. Let's fly back over the crest and see if we can see any low points."

The helicopter tilted forward and dropped toward the dam.

"Look on the left side of the spillways," yelled Shauna, a little too loud for the headphones.

Grant saw a small stream of water was now running over the top of the cement.

"It's on both sides now," said Agent Williams.

"Does that mean the concrete part of the dam is what's going to fail?" asked Lloyd, somewhat unsure of himself.

Grant shook his head. "No, the dikes are way softer. The water's going to carve into that gravel right next to the concrete. They would have been much better off if they had listened to us, and broken the dike themselves. Now it looks like it's going to break right next to the concrete."

"Is that bad?"

"It might be. Remember this flood will last for two months. With all that water flowing right next to the structure, it'll definitely damage it."

"Look," Shauna said. "It's starting to carve into the banks. Look how dirty the water's getting."

Grant saw that the volume of water had increased substantially over the top of the concrete. He remembered the truck and the three men. "We better get back and tell those guys to get outta there." He looked over at the pilot. "You got a PA in this thing?"

"Sure thing."

The helicopter banked hard and flew back toward the truck. Grant saw that the men hadn't stayed put, but had walked closer to the dam. As Lloyd maneuvered the helicopter lower, the rotors blew toward the men, making them put their arms in front of their faces.

Lloyd flipped a switch and gave Grant a quick thumbs up, before grabbing back onto the controls. At first Grant didn't know what to do, expecting a hand-held mic. He looked over at Lloyd, confused.

"Just speak," said the pilot, and Grant heard Lloyd's voice from the outside as well as through the headphones.

Grant tried to remember what he needed to say. "People, the dam is about to break."

None of them seemed to be looking as they shielded their eyes from the turbulence.

"Please, hurry back to your truck and get clear of the area!"

Incredibly, one of the three men, the one in the hard hat, waved the helicopter aside. They weren't moving. Grant looked over at Lloyd and the pilot shrugged. The man continued motioning for the helicopter to move.

Lloyd flipped the PA switch off. "What do you want me to do?"

Grant was angry. "We warned them. What else can we do?"

Lloyd immediately lifted the helicopter out of their way. Grant wondered if the man was the moron Shauna had talked to on the phone at the Bureau of Indian Affairs. That guy was an idiot. She had tried everything to reason with him. But the guy wouldn't budge. He kept telling Shauna there wasn't any way he was going to intentionally break his own dam. Deep down, Shauna didn't think the guy actually believed Headgate Rock Dam would fail. He had chosen to not believe it, as if that would prevent the whole tragedy from happening.

As soon as Lloyd had moved the chopper out of their way the men continued walking toward the concrete structure.

"Look, there are two more guys over by the spillways," Agent Williams said.

Sure enough, two men stood next to the spillways. Grant wondered if they had been inside the structure a few minutes before.

Lloyd moved the helicopter higher and back toward the concrete structure. Looking up where the breach first occurred, Grant saw that over five feet of water was pouring over the top of the structure, both edges being noticeably dirty water. He wondered if the five idiots below had noticed the breach.

Grant reached over in front of the pilot and flipped the PA switch himself. "Attention below. Look up at the top of the structure. The dam is breaking apart. Get out of there! Now!" He flipped the switch back down.

One of the two guys by the spillways pointed up toward the breach, and the other shielded his eyes and looked up too. The water was now tearing into the dike on the right side of the dam. Both men started running toward the pickup.

"About time," Shauna said, obviously relieved.

However, when the two men reached the three who had arrived in the truck, they argued. Grant could tell by their body language, plus they were all waving their arms and pointing. Grant saw the guy with the hard hat shake his head back and forth.

"That idiot doesn't think it's going to fail," said Grant

"Look at the dam," cried Shauna.

Grant looked up in time to see a large piece of the gravel dam break off and fall into the river that was now tearing into the dike on the right of the spillways. Looking down, he saw water standing where the two men had stood only moments before. Glancing to his left, he saw that the two men had abandoned the argument and were running toward the steep road out of the parking lot. But the three that arrived in the truck stood still, gazing up at the spectacle.

"We're gonna have to watch these idiots die, aren't we?" It was Agent Williams' voice in the headphones.

Grant looked up again in time to see another large chunk of earth slough off. Grant estimated the water to now be ten feet deep into the dike. It looked like the stream was equal to one of the spillways. The entire stream was now dark brown from the debris it was cutting.

"Looks like two of them got religion," Lloyd said.

Grant glanced over and saw two of them running, but the guy with the yellow hard hat stood still, staring up at the dam.

When Grant looked back at the dam, he couldn't believe how fast the flow had increased. He'd only taken his eyes off of it for a few seconds. It seemed twice as big as a moment ago. Yet now it dwarfed the volume of the spillways. Another large section broke off and was swept out immediately. Grant could now see Lake Moovalya through the cut.

"Oh my . . ." It was Shauna's voice.

"It's history," said Lloyd.

For the next few moments, Grant could only stare. The volume of surging water grew at an alarming rate. Large chunks of the dike fell every couple of seconds. A part of him wanted to look down to see if the guy in the hard hat ran, and make sure the others had made it, but his eyes wouldn't let him. They stayed glued to the scene unfolding in front of him. Time stood still. In one final motion, a fifty-foot-wide piece of the dike let go, and the Colorado River broke loose and barreled down the riverbed in a large wave of frothy brown water. The first two guys had climbed up the road far enough to be safe. The next two had reached the truck and were climbing in the back, even as a wave of water smashed into the side of it. The truck started moving and swapped ends. Within moments Grant guessed the water would pull the truck off the elevated parking lot and into the channel. There was no sign of the guy in the hard hat.

"Those guys in the back of the truck need help!" Agent Williams yelled.

Grant saw the truck swap ends again and teeter dangerously as the water moved it toward the edge. Both men waved their arms back and forth. Lloyd reacted and the helicopter headed toward them.

"What are you gonna do?" Grant asked.

Lloyd concentrated ahead on the men. "Their only chance is to grab onto our landing gear."

As they accelerated toward the truck, the truck jerked sideways and one of the men fell into the water. The other one reached over the side and quickly pulled him back in.

"Hurry," cried Shauna from behind.

When the helicopter arrived, before the two men could reach out, the chopper dropped quickly and the landing gear hit the top of the pickup's cab, putting a large dent in it. The impact scared the two men, making them hesitate. Grant could see the terror in their eyes, since they were only a few feet away.

"Why'd you do that?" asked Grant.

Lloyd brought the landing gear over the men's heads and they both grabbed on. Grant couldn't see them anymore, since they were on the pilot's side.

"I had to ground us first," said Lloyd, not taking his eyes off them. "The rotors build up static electricity. We could have electrocuted 'em."

Grant saw that Lloyd was lifting them toward the cliffs above the dam, although the motion was so smooth that Grant felt no acceleration. He wondered how many times Lloyd had done this trick in Vietnam, and how many years it had been since his last attempt.

Grant turned and looked back at Shauna, who sat crouched over looking out at the men hanging on the landing gear. He saw her nodding her head and mouthing words of encouragement to them.

"How're they doing?" Grant asked.

"Hurry," she coaxed, ignoring the question.

When Grant looked forward again, he saw the helicopter had reached the height of the cliffs. Lloyd moved the helicopter sideways until they were over dry land, then lowered slightly.

"They let go," said Shauna. "They're okay."

Lloyd set the chopper down and the men approached, still crouching. Grant saw that the first two had hiked to the top of the road and now came running toward them. Lloyd opened his door.

"Thanks, Mister," one of the men yelled. He was a Native American. All of them were.

"What happened to your friend in the hard hat?" asked Lloyd, also yelling.

"He didn't think it would fail," he answered. "The water got him."

"Well, you guys almost waited too long yourselves."

They both smiled, not in happiness, but in relief. Grant could see their faces. They knew they were lucky to be alive.

Lloyd shut the door and the chopper took off.

"Let's make one more pass over the dam," said Grant.

Grant watched as they headed back toward Headgate Rock Dam. The whole area beneath the dam was now flooded and white caps were visible. The cut in the dam now stretched over a hundred feet from the left side of the spillways. The water level in Lake Moovalya had dropped almost fifteen feet and was no longer breaching the concrete.

Grant shook his head. "Idiots. We warned 'em."

Lloyd spoke without turning his head. "Some guys can't be told. They have to figure it out for themselves."

"Unfortunately," said Grant, "the guy in the hard hat is dead because of that."

When the helicopter passed back over the broken dam, Lloyd looked over. "You want to see anything else?"

Grant shook his head. "No, let's go. Head downstream."

When the helicopter pivoted and pointed downstream, Grant could see the community of mobile homes for the first time since the dam had broken. The entire row of homes bordering the river was gone, torn out. A couple of them drifted in the middle of the channel, but the bulk of them were piled up against the railroad bridge downstream. Most of the second row of mobile homes had held, but water pushed against them. Then, as Grant watched, the second row let go like dominoes, and the river pulled them out into the channel.

A large group of people stood up on the Arizona bank, out of the danger. Even at a distance, Grant saw a couple of them cover their eyes with their hands. Another had his hands on top of his head. The group was large and Grant guessed they were the inhabitants of the trailer park. He imagined there would be lawsuits against the Bureau of Indian Affairs for not breaking the dam earlier.

Lloyd had been hovering, allowing them to witness the destruction below. Finally he looked over at Grant. Grant understood the unspoken question.

"Go ahead. I've seen enough. Head downstream toward the next one. Hopefully they listened to us and busted their dam already. I don't think any of us want a repeat performance."

Lloyd's reaction, as usual, was immediate. The helicopter banked and headed downstream.

* * *

12:40 p.m. - Farmland, south of Parker, Arizona

Daniel Tahbo shifted the Massey Ferguson into high gear and his long black hair blew in the wind as the tractor accelerated. His father didn't like Daniel to use the high gear of the old tractor on gravel roads. The bumps would rattle the tractor to pieces. But Daniel's father worried too much. Everybody knew that. Besides, Daniel was already 15 years old. He would have his license in another year, and he had been driving tractors since he was eight. He could tell when the road was too rough. He knew where all the bumps were on the road, and could easily dodge them.

Daniel's father would not approve of this trip anyway. Daniel needed to hurry, hook onto the ditcher, and take it back to the house. If Daniel's father caught him, he would be furious, but after he made it home safe with the ditcher, and his father discovered it later, he'd be happy. Sure he'd still grumble and swear and tell Daniel he'd acted like an idiot, but he'd be pleased to have the ditcher just the same. Daniel would retrieve the ditcher and be home before the river flooded.

The three hundred acre Tahbo farm was part of the Colorado Indian Reservation, a small farm compared to most of the neighbors. They worked hard on their farm, too hard to lose the ditcher in the flood. Daniel had argued this fact with his father that morning, but his father was a stubborn man. His father believed in the old ways, simple and conservative, no unnecessary risks.

Although the Tahbo farm was small, it was good land, right next to the Colorado River, and only two miles south of the bluffs. The family had great water rights too, being so close to Headgate Rock Dam, where the canal was diverted from the river.

Daniel's father was nervous, with the terrorists and all. Ever since the bombing the day before, the farmers had talked of nothing else. Who blew it up? Why? When would the water reach the reservation? How bad would it flood the farms? How fast would the soil recover? Would the government help? If so, how much? His father had attended a meeting the night before at the high school with representatives from the Bureau of Indian Affairs. The officials had practically guaranteed that Headgate Rock Dam was safe, but his father did not believe them.

Daniel's father worried too much, especially when there was actually something real to worry about. His mother said that his father didn't sleep a wink last night, and Daniel believed it.

Daniel thought all farmers worried too much. They worried when it wasn't raining, then they worried when it was. They worried when the wind blew, or when it was too calm. They worried when crop prices moved. If the prices were stable, they worried that they would change in the future. Daniel didn't want to be a farmer. He didn't want to worry about anything. He liked driving better. Tractors were okay, but driving something big like bulldozers or excavators would be even better, maybe even an eighteen-wheeler. At least then, Daniel would be able to get off the reservation.

As Daniel approached the end of the gravel road, he slowed the tractor, choosing a slower gear. He could see the Colorado River just past the fields at the end of the road. He had never seen it this high or rough before. Usually the river floated lazily past the Tahbo farm, but today it filled the river bottoms, spreading out from its main channel and flooding the willows and grass that grew around the river. There was strength in the river today, a power that Daniel had never seen before.

The ditcher lay in the corner of the field at the end of the road. As he got closer, he noticed water on the road and around the ditcher. A small stream had washed through the bank of the river and now flowed right in front of the ditcher and out into the cornfield. Daniel pulled past the ditcher, stopped, then flipped the steering wheel and backed around toward it, stopping while the rear wheels were still on the gravel. He stared at the small stream and wondered how long it had been flowing past the ditcher. If the water had time to soak into the soft soil in the cornfield, the Massey Ferguson would get stuck in the mud. If the stream had only been flowing a couple of minutes, it would not have had time to soak in, and the small tractor would be fine. Daniel cursed his father for not buying a four-wheel drive John Deere tractor like the neighbors. If he had, getting stuck would not be an issue.

Daniel put the transmission in neutral and climbed down off the tractor, leaving the diesel engine idling. Walking around behind, he stopped and stared at the ditcher, so close and yet so far away. He felt reluctant to back the tractor into the mud. He had gotten tractors stuck before and his father always kicked his butt. Besides, this was no time to bury the tractor, especially if the flood materialized as his father expected it would. Better to sacrifice the ditcher than his father's tractor.

Wait. If he could drag the ditcher up onto the road, then hook it up, he wouldn't need to get the tractor in the mud. Daniel ran around the tractor to retrieve a small log chain stored in the tractor's toolbox. He returned a moment later, dragging the chain behind. He looked over at the ditcher, judging the distance.

For a moment Daniel didn't notice it. His eyes, after all, were focused only a few feet away at the ditcher. But his subconscious mind noticed something and sent a warning to his brain. Something on the horizon didn't look right. Daniel looked up. He blinked. His eyes must have been deceiving him. But blinking did not correct the problem.

Daniel saw a line of water that covered the whole valley between him and the canyons upstream. The wave was less than a mile from where Daniel stood, but it was hard to tell how high. It did not appear to be moving, but Daniel knew better. What could it mean? It could only mean that his father had been right to worry about Headgate Rock Dam. The dam had failed.

Daniel dropped the chain. He forgot about the ditcher. He ran around the tractor and climbed on it. He fumbled with the gears and selected high. Feathering the clutch, he attempted to go, but the gear was too high. He quickly selected a lower gear, popped the clutch, spun the steering wheel, and the Massey Ferguson leaped forward and headed back down the gravel road. A moment later, when the tractor had reached speed for the lower gear, Daniel crammed it into high gear. The Massey reacted, pouring black smoke from the stack.

Initially, he thought he could outrun it, but the gravel road headed east and crossed in front of the flood. For safety reasons, most tractors did not go much faster than twenty miles per hour due to poor handling characteristics. Daniel suddenly wished the Massey was an exception. He would gladly take the risk. Unfortunately, the Massey topped out at about nineteen. Daniel watched the approaching water on his left and forgot to watch for the bumps he had memorized. The tractor bounced through a large pothole, almost tearing the steering wheel out of his hand.

Daniel had only traveled a half mile before he saw the water breach the gravel road a hundred yards in front of him. The water hit the raised embankment of the road hard, curling upwards briefly before being pushed across by all the water behind. A few seconds later, the water was in front of the Massey Ferguson. Daniel steered into the water with the tractor still at full speed. Water sprayed everywhere and Daniel swerved to regain control. He had no choice but to clutch and shift to a lower gear.

As the tractor plowed through the rising water, Daniel was forced to continually choose lower gears. Creeping along with almost four feet of water flowing across the road, Daniel knew the water would soon be over his feet. The front tires were completely underwater, and he could not see them anymore. When would the engine stall? He looked ahead. The water had buried the road for almost a mile in front of him. The dry road seemed so far away.

Suddenly the rear of the tractor slid a few feet. Daniel spun the steering wheel to stabilize it. He felt the water move the tractor again, just as the water started flowing over the deck where his feet were. He hadn't been able to see the road for a while, looking instead at the disappearing road ahead. The water moved the tractor again, and this time it didn't stop. He felt the tractor slide sideways over the downstream embankment and in one motion the right tire dropped and the water pushed the Massey Ferguson over.

Daniel was pulled underwater in one quick motion. He reached out to push off the steering wheel and realized it wasn't there, the current had already pulled him away from the tractor. He lunged for what he thought was the surface of the dirty water, only to plow his fingers into the ground underneath. He was confused by his disorientation and lunged again. Nothing. He panicked. He could swim, but he wasn't a strong swimmer. He would never dare swim in a flowing river. His lungs were bursting and his eyes felt like they were going to pop out. He flailed his arms in an inefficient effort to propel himself.

Suddenly his head came out of the water. He gulped for air a second too late and got a breath of water. His body tried to reject the water with coughing and gagging contractions. Daniel knew he only had one more chance. He kicked hard to get back up and made it. He coughed out some of the water and involuntarily inhaled again, sucking more water in.

This time when his head went back underwater, his body had lost the strength to fight. The panic had also subsided. He gulped in another mouth full of water. But his body stopped trying to reject it. He felt calm. With no apprehension, he wondered what his father would say about the Massey Ferguson. Surely his father would not be happy. But at the moment, the thought didn't seem to bother him. Instead his entire body felt calm. He felt himself going to sleep. He closed his eyes and relaxed. Then 15 year old Daniel Tahbo drowned.

* * *

12:45 p.m. - South of Parker, Arizona

Viewed from the helicopter, the landscape changed dramatically downstream from Headgate Rock Dam. The rock canyons ended, opening up into a wide valley that stretched as far as Grant could see. Huge square grids of green, yellow, and occasionally brown painted the unmistakable picture of farming. The river wound lazily back and forth along the valley's west side. An extremely large canal accompanied the river out of the canyon, having been diverted by Headgate Rock Dam. Countless other irrigation canals stretched east from the river.

Native Americans of the Colorado River Indian Reservation owned the farms just downstream from Headgate Rock, but looking south over the endless farms, it was impossible to tell where the reservation ended and non-Indian farming began.

When the floodwater hit the valley, it spread out, burying the north end of the valley under a shallow brown lake. The helicopter sped past the flood and followed the river south toward the Palo Verde Diversion Dam. In the helicopter, at well over a hundred miles per hour, they expected to arrive at the dam by 1:00 p.m. The floodwater wasn't expected until 2:15 p.m.

With no disasters to stare at through the windows, Grant decided to catch up with the FBI. He was beginning to think they had no idea what was going on. It had occurred to Grant that he had as much chance of solving the crime as the FBI. "So, Agent Williams, what'd you learn from the cops at Parker Dam?"

Grant couldn't see her face behind him, but disappointment resonated in her voice. "They didn't know anything. They didn't even know we were looking for a guy in a white pickup. He could walk right up to them and they wouldn't recognize him."

"Would we?" asked Grant.

She hesitated. "I talked to Phil on the phone. They're working on some leads."

Grant doubted the leads were serious. "Really. Like what?"

"I'm not sure if I should say."

Grant cast his eyes over at Lloyd and they traded smiles. Grant pushed her. "Why not? You afraid me and Lloyd here are gonna leak it to the press, and spoil the investigation?"

She hesitated. "It's not that. It's just that Phil probably needs to —"

He interrupted. "Needs to what? Run down all the leads before he asks me for more?" He swiveled in his seat to look her in the eyes. She seemed surprised at his line of questioning. He swiveled back forward. "You know, even when I watch TV, when cops communicate, it's only in one direction. I tell the FBI everything I know. And they tell me nothing." He swiveled again. "I've come to the conclusion that passing information one way is not the best way to communicate."

"What are you saying?" she asked.

"I'm saying that if we want to solve this thing, I need to know what's going on. I need some facts."

Agent Williams stammered. "Well, I'm not authorized to say anything. I would need Phil's —"

Grant interrupted. "Look, I understand. If the FBI wants to try to solve this in a vacuum, without interaction with the Bureau of Reclamation, who am I to complain?" Grant pointed ahead toward an open hay field. "Lloyd, you can set it down in that field over there. Agent Williams wants to get out."

Lloyd smiled again. "That one just up ahead?" The helicopter started dropping.

Agent Williams sounded nervous. "Phil said we're going to meet with you again, and trade information. But we need to chase a few things down first. Maybe this evening, or maybe tomor –"

"This thing will be over by tomorrow!" Grant yelled, "and Lloyd and I have commitments this evening at Palo Verde and Imperial Dams. Don't we, Lloyd?"

They had almost reached the hayfield and Lloyd looked over at Grant. "You want me to put it down?"

"No," said the agent.

"Yeah. Go ahead," Grant said.

The chopper dropped quickly toward the ground.

"You can't leave me here," she said. "You agreed to take me along today. You'll be impeding the investigation."

Grant laughed. "No, the way I see it is, we can't keep you with us. We'd risk you accidentally telling us something we shouldn't know, spilling some piece of secret information in a non-secure environment. We couldn't allow that. You know, for national security reasons."

The landing gear touched down.

"I'm not getting out," she said.

"Does your cell phone work out here?" Grant asked. "You can call one of your secret agent buddies to pick you up. You could talk more freely with them."

Agent Williams hesitated. "All right, I can probably share some information, but only with you. We can walk a few feet away from the helicopter."

"No deal," Grant said. "The government trusted Lloyd in one of their multi-million-dollar helicopters in Vietnam. You ought to be able to trust him now." Grant turned to Lloyd. "Lloyd, didn't you have a security clearance?"

Lloyd nodded.

Grant laughed. "Besides, Lloyd came with us today to see some explosions, not create them, didn't ya Lloyd?"

Lloyd nodded again, smiling.

"We're not worried about Lloyd," she said, barely loud enough to hear.

This caught Grant off guard. He and Lloyd both turned around and looked first at Shauna, who also looked surprised, then agent Williams, who wouldn't meet their eyes.

"The FBI's worried about Shauna?" Grant asked.

She hesitated. "It's not Shauna per se." Agent Williams glanced nervously between them. "It's the Bureau itself. Both of the attempts at the dams were executed with credentials. Both attempts required detailed information about procedures and the dams themselves. We suspect that our bad guy might be –"

" – an insider," Grant finished.

Grant turned back around facing forward, nodding for Lloyd to take off. The rotors accelerated immediately and a few moments later they were back in the air.

The agent spoke again, almost pleading. "Look. We don't suspect either of you, but we wanted information to be minimized through your organization."

Grant had to admit when he first heard about the credentials, he wondered if it could have been an inside job. He'd dismissed the idea mostly due to motive, but it was certainly possible for someone in the Bureau to become disillusioned with the organization. When it came right down to it, he felt disillusioned with the Bureau, especially his bosses. Of course, he never considered blowing up any dams. His bosses maybe, but not dams.

"All right, Agent Williams, we accept the FBI's notion of an insider as a potential suspect. But don't you think it would've been better to bring us in earlier? We could have discussed how Shauna and I would handle ourselves when communicating back to Denver."

"Absolutely. But things have been happening so fast. We just haven't had enough time to sit down and talk it through."

Grant tried to remember the last time he had a few minutes to relax. He wondered about the next twenty-four hours – would they be any different? He didn't think so. They still had Palo Verde and Imperial Dams to worry about, not to mention Hoover-Two. Then there was the dam in Mexico. Although the Bureau of Reclamation had no responsibility or jurisdiction below the border, Grant had a nagging feeling he might end up getting involved, even if only as a consultant.

Without looking back at the agent, Grant talked into the headphones. "Okay, so let's say we suspect somebody in the Bureau. How do we go about figuring out who it is?"

"We're generating a list of any employees that were absent over the last three days, vacation, sick, or even traveling. Our contact in the Bureau is pretty confident about generating the data quickly. She said the Bureau is pretty anal about attendance and time keeping."

That made sense. Grant had personally been written up for time card violations a few times. And he had only been a day behind on the information. He tried to think whether he personally knew anyone who had been out for the last few days. No one came to mind. Wait, Howard, his boss, was in Yellowstone. Oh, that would be too good to be true. He snickered silently, imagining his boss being escorted between two FBI agents with his head bowed and his wrists cuffed. But Grant knew it could not be Howard. He wasn't smart enough. His expertise centered more around politics and less on planning and execution, and he didn't like to get his hands dirty.

"So once you get the list?" Grant asked.

"We'll run it past some of the other data we're already looking at – cellular phone usage near the dams, credit card usage, hotel records, and even the list we put together about boating accidents."

Grant considered that for a moment. "When they crashed into the World Trade Centers, I seem to remember you guys figuring out all the names of the terrorists within a few hours."

"That was different. We received flight numbers from all four planes within minutes. It was only a matter of calling the airlines and getting passenger lists."

Grant tried to phrase his next question correctly. "So in cases like this, where the bad guys don't leave any obvious clues, how long does it usually take, you know, to sift through all the data and everything?"

Agent Williams seemed to resent the question. "That's kind of hard to answer. Every case is different."

"Best case?" said Grant. "What's the fastest it's ever happened?"

"Well, when the Oklahoma Federal Building was blown up, we got him within a couple of hours."

"That's different. That wasn't the result of sifting through data and suspects; you got lucky when he drove through a stop sign and the cops nabbed him."

"Yeah, but we would have caught him eventually. We found the truck rental agreement and we figured out where he bought the ammonium nitrate."

"Sure, days later. That's my point. Without a lucky break, it'd be unreasonable to expect all these lists to be whittled down until after it's all over. The most likely scenario is to arrest the perpetrators next week, after the damage is already done. Even September 11th was like that, way too late."

Agent William's voice sounded defensive. "Don't underestimate lucky breaks. All criminals make mistakes. We'll get one here, too. You'll see."

"Will it be in time though? That's what worries me. Will it be in time?"

"In time for what?" Agent Williams asked.

Grant turned around to face her again. "In time to prevent whatever other pandemonium they have planned."

Lloyd interrupted them. "Is that your dam up ahead?"

Grant looked ahead. He had never actually seen the Palo Verde Dam before, only pictures. It seemed smaller than he expected. Even from the distance Grant could see two bulldozers at work on the dike. It meant the Headgate Rock fiasco would not be repeated.

"Good job," he said.

* * *

12:50 p.m. - Grand Canyon, Arizona

David watched as a large red helicopter lowered a cable with an orange padded loop. The helicopter was at least a hundred feet above them.

The white helicopter that found them hovered just off the cliff as before, relaying instructions. "Be careful. Don't let the harness pull you off the ledge."

Afram grabbed the harness. The noise was loud with both helicopters so close, and turbulence buffeted the rock ledge. David sat down to ensure he didn't fall.

"YOU FIRST." Afram motioned to Judy with the harness.

Judy put the harness over her head and looped her arms over the padded material. She gave a quick thumbs-up sign to the white helicopter. Immediately she was lifted. Seeing her dangling out over the canyon made David sick and he had to shut his eyes for a few seconds. When he opened them Judy was almost up to the helicopter.

Before long, the empty harness was sent back down to them. Afram pushed the harness toward David, but he wasn't ready.

"NO. YOU GO."

Afram looked unsure, then pulled it on and allowed himself to be lifted. Again David winced when Afram's body lifted out over the edge of the cliff. He was not looking forward to this.

When the harness was lowered back down, David held it in his hands and looked at it. Suddenly the fear of heights was back and he was afraid to stand and try to put it on. What if he fell while putting it over his head?

"Go ahead, son," the metallic voice coaxed. "You'll be fine."

Still sitting, David pulled the harness over his head and looped his arms over the pad. He intended to take a minute to catch his breath before motioning he was ready, but they didn't wait for him. As the harness lifted David, his body went rigid and he screamed. He tried to hook his feet on the jagged rocks, but he was pulled up and out. Once in the air, the tension in the cable made him feel more secure and the panic subsided. But he didn't dare look. He kept his eyes firmly shut. The chopper's buffeting air grew stronger as he was hoisted. Before he knew it, he was in the chopper and a man was removing the harness. When he was free, he collapsed in a seat next to Judy and Afram.

* * *

1:00 p.m. - El Centro, California

The skinny man took a long swig from his Big Gulp. Too much driving. From San Onofre beach, he had driven another hour south into San Diego, then east, parallel to Mexico on I-8 for an hour and a half, and according to the last sign, El Centro should be the next exit, the heart of California's Imperial Valley. That would be just in time. He needed to get out and walk around. He needed to find a restroom. And he was hungry.

The All American Canal ran parallel to the Mexican border on his right almost five miles south of the freeway. He'd already passed over the Westside Main Canal, the last and westernmost of the six major diversions off the All American.

Below Imperial Dam, for all practical purposes, the Colorado River became the All American Canal. Most American's didn't know that, but he did. Imperial Dam diverted more than twice as much water west into the canal than it allowed to flow into Mexico. No one cared if the river dried up before it reached Mexico.

Certainly not the farmers of the Imperial Valley, that's for sure. If the United States had not agreed in a treaty to guarantee a fixed amount to Mexico, the Mexicans wouldn't get anything, and they knew it.

Only a few miles back, when he first drove into the valley, he passed a dirt field too dry to grow sagebrush. No bushes, weeds, or anything, just dirt. An empty irrigation ditch ran right next to the freeway, which explained why nothing grew. Without water from the Colorado, Imperial Valley would be a dust bowl, just like it once was.

Up ahead was the main exit for El Centro. Good. There were some fast food joints where he could eat, visit the restroom, and stretch his legs. He needed it, because he had a big day ahead of him. After all, he was going to blow up the All American Canal.

CHAPTER 34

1:10 p.m. – Palo Verde Dam, California

Don Simpson from the Palo Verde Irrigation District was nervous. He'd been venting on Grant since the helicopter landed. Don looked to be about fifty, a little under six feet, and bulky, maybe 220. He wore shiny brown cowboy boots and a western shirt with snaps instead of buttons. He would have looked complete with a felt cowboy hat, but instead, he wore a green baseball cap with a Palo Verde Irrigation District logo on the front.

"You're sure there's nothing we can do to save this dam?" he asked.

"Absolutely," said Grant. "We just watched Headgate Rock fail from the helicopter. We just came from there. One guy from the Bureau of Indian Affairs didn't believe us, and he's dead right now."

Don's face softened. "Well, we're ready; I just wanna be sure. The farmers in my district rely on this dam for irrigation, and it's not natural to bust a dam intentionally."

Grant laid it on the line. "You're gonna have almost 500,000 cubic feet per second of water coming through here for the next sixty days until Lake Mead settles back below its spillways. Your dam can't even handle close to that much. You tell me how your dam is going to survive."

Don didn't answer.

Grant looked around. The Palo Verde Diversion Dam had three gates for the Colorado River and a separate gate for a diversion canal. The concrete structure sat on the California side of the river, right next to an old house, still occupied. A big willow tree shaded the front yard and a friendly white dog walked from person to person, nudging their hands with his nose. A dirt dike over a thousand feet long connected the head gates to the other side of the river. No other homes were visible. The California bank of the river rose into a small dry mountain range. On the Arizona side, endless farms were visible. Like Parker and Headgate Rock Dams, police cars littered both sides, and many officers could be seen walking around on the dam itself.

Even from the helicopter, Grant could tell they had lowered the reservoir. All three Colorado River gates were completely open and a wet line circled the upstream side of the river showing that the water had dropped at least five feet. Upstream, the reservoir veered east a quarter mile from the dam, making it impossible to see the full size of the reservoir.

"How long before the bulldozers will be done?" Grant asked. "After they open it, the water'll need time to clean it out before the flood gets here."

Two extremely large bulldozers had carved a 70 foot section down to the water level by pushing the dirt and substrate off the downstream side of the dam. This resulted in a huge pile of dirt and gravel below the cut.

Don checked his watch. "Both dozers've been going since 10 a.m. They're both D-11 Caterpillars, the biggest suckers available. They're almost at water level now." Don turned back toward Grant and pointed upstream and motioned at the wet banks. "As you can see, we already lowered the reservoir."

Grant nodded. "Yeah, I noticed, but that may work against us."

Don furrowed his brows. "What do you mean? I thought that would be better."

Grant watched a bulldozer push a blade of dirt into the water. "Well, you're gonna need to dig five feet deeper now, before the water starts helping." Grant pointed upstream. "And I'm a little worried whether there's enough water to really open the dike, you know, wide enough for the flood."

Don turned and looked at the river. "I didn't consider that. I just figured the less of a flood I cause downstream, the better."

Grant held out the palms of his hands. "Any flood you cause will pale compared to the flood that's on its way, Don."

Don's head jerked back toward the dam. "Hey, what if I shut all the head gates while they're digging? We could start filling the reservoir again."

Grant looked at his watch as a bulldozer pushed another blade off the dike. He figured they still had almost an hour, but no sense cutting it too close. "Yeah, that sounds like a good idea. The more water the better."

Don barked orders to a young guy with a John Deere hat. He lowered the gates, one by one. Grant stood on top of the concrete structure, looking straight down into the three spillways. In spite of the dam's small size, the amount of water churning and swirling under the three gates was respectable. After a few minutes, all three gates were shut and the water downstream stopped churning.

Agent Williams stood in the shade of the tree by the house, talking on her cell phone. Shauna had walked over next to the reservoir, and was staring down at the wet rocks as if measuring how fast the water had risen since they closed the head gates. Lloyd walked over and joined them, with the white dog from the house nudging at his hand.

"So what's the agenda, boss?" Lloyd asked.

Grant smiled back at the pilot. "I'm making a small flood, just for you." He pointed toward the bulldozers. "They're going to continue lowering the middle of the dike and in a few more minutes they will meet the rising water. Then they'll make a few cuts below the water level, and get the hell out of there before it comes tumbling down. Should be pretty spectacular."

Lloyd smiled wide. "Wow, you guys put on a good show. How much you charge for this kind of entertainment?"

Don glanced over at Lloyd. Grant guessed Don didn't know what to think about the pilot.

* * *

1:25 p.m. – Palo Verde Dam, California

In the ten minutes since they closed the head gates, the bulldozers had lowered the 70 foot-wide notch another couple of feet. At the same time, the reservoir itself rose a few feet, and now some small streams began trickling through the large notch.

"Okay, this is the critical part," Don said to an already tentative audience.

Everyone on both sides of the river, including the cops, stood watching. One of the bulldozers headed up the slope out of the dike away from Grant, a slope that had been intentionally left for their escape. Halfway up he stopped. The operator jumped off the bulldozer, and shortly appeared dragging a chain around the back.

"What's he doing?" asked Lloyd.

Don answered, "He's getting a chain ready; in case the other one gets in trouble, he can hook onto him and pull him out."

While the first operator stretched out the chain, the other D-11 Caterpillar pivoted, placing the right track on the downstream edge of the dike and the blade facing away from them. He stopped. Even from a distance, the group saw the water streams through the notch had increased slightly in the last few minutes, and the tracks of the bulldozer glistened wet. After the two drivers waved to each other, the second D-11 dropped his blade and cut a two-foot deep swath, stopping after only ten feet, as dirt piled up in front of the blade. The D-11 reversed back through the two-feet-deep water. Grant guessed it would take four more passes to open the dike.

"Why is he starting downstream?" asked Grant.

Don glanced over at him and shrugged. "I don't know; maybe he's afraid if he starts on the upstream side, the downstream side will wash out."

That made sense. Either way, after the last cut he figured the bulldozer wouldn't stop but hustle his rig up the slope as fast as he could.

After the bulldozer completed its second pass and again reversed through the water, Grant looked at Don. "How deep of water can they drive through?"

Don smiled. "I asked the same question. They said they could go to the top of the tracks, if the ground under them was firm. That'd be over four feet."

The bulldozer reversed from his third pass and prepared for what they knew would be the final assault on the notch in the Palo Verde Diversion Dam. Grant felt some sweat run down the center of his back.

"Here comes the hard part," said Don.

The D-11 hesitated for an instant, sitting with its right track on the edge of the dike, then black smoke poured out of the exhaust stack and it lurched forward.

Almost immediately Grant saw water flowing off the dike from behind the blade and through the crawlers tracks. As the dirt piled up in front of the dozer, he lifted the blade and continued over the top of the dirt he had just pushed and the driver raced for the slope. The other D-11, seeing that he wouldn't be needed, accelerated forward out of his way. Both of them climbed up the slope onto the other side, not stopping until they both sat on top of the dike.

Behind them, the two-foot deep by ten-foot wide channel cut by the second dozer flowed off the downstream side of the dike.

Lloyd turned to face Grant and shrugged. "Doesn't seem like enough to do anything."

"Don't take your eyes off it," Grant said.

Grant suddenly wished he had a video camera. He looked around and saw that somebody else did, likely one of Don's guys from the irrigation district.

For what seemed like a minute or two, the water appeared to only be increasing slightly. Then suddenly Grant realized it had doubled. The rising reservoir itself was making it harder to focus on the ditch, since water now flowed across the entire notch, making a 70 foot wide waterfall, and obscuring the deeper ditch in the center. But the water in the center ditch grew swifter by the second. Unlike the waterfall that simply dropped off the dike, the ditch water shot through, causing the water below to churn into a brown froth. Grant guessed the ditch was much wider than ten feet now.

For the next few seconds, the water volume and trajectory increased almost as fast as a hose while opening the valve. Then Grant saw something spectacular and unexpected which drew an "ooh" from the other bystanders. The volume in the ditch suddenly increased enough to drop the reservoir right next to the dike, which killed the waterfall over the top like curtains being drawn, as the waterfall disappeared from inside to out.

With the waterfall gone, they could see the ditch better, and it looked to be at least 30 feet wide and 25 feet deep. A loud cracking sound startled the group. They all looked downstream in time to see a large tree in the river bottoms get toppled by the raging river.

While everyone watched, a large section of dirt on the Arizona side broke off and sloughed into the water only to disappear immediately. Not a second later, a similar slab followed from the California side. The combination of the two seemed to double the flow. Grant looked upstream and saw the water in the reservoir had dropped over five feet right next to the dike. And the previously still water could be seen moving quickly toward the cut. More of the dike sloughed off every few seconds until the ditch had widened to almost the entire 70 feet cut down by the two D-11s. This perspective was reinforced when part of the slope the dozers had used to climb out collapsed into the stream. As a result, both D-11s poured black smoke out their exhausts and surged away, heading along the dike toward the Arizona riverbank. The policemen and others standing on the dike ran to distance themselves from the cut.

When Grant thought the flow had decreased, he looked upstream. He saw the wet band around the reservoir all along the river had dropped another five feet.

Downstream, the river was a mess. The color ran an ugly brown and had spread wide, filling the old river bed for what Grant guessed was the first time since spring floods before Hoover dam was built, during the 1930s. The river bucked, jigged, and swirled around trees and other obstacles that hadn't been threatened for the last 70 years.

The water blasting out of the cut in the dike was less visible now, as the water level downstream had risen almost as high as the reservoir upstream.

"Wow," said Lloyd.

Grant nodded. "Yeah. That's a good way to describe it."

Don turned and faced Grant, visibly shaken. "What now?"

Grant looked at his watch. "Now we wait. The water should be arriving here some time in the next twenty minutes." Grant patted Don on the shoulder. "Hey, the hard part's over. You did it. That was a lot better than waiting for the reservoir to rise another twenty feet to the top of the dikes and let it break itself. Now, in a couple of months when Hoover's spillways stop and things get back to normal, you can fix your dike and you'll be back in business."

Don forced a smile. "You act like it's no big deal."

Grant looked serious. "It isn't, compared to what happened to the Indians upstream. There's dead people up there, homes washed away, farmland flooded," Grant pointed at the concrete structure, "and their dam is gonna suffer over the next couple months, millions of dollars worth of damage."

Don seemed to think about that. "Speaking of the structure, you think I should open my head gates again?"

Grant looked upstream. "Yeah, why not? The more water that flows through the gates, the less to wash away your dike." Don nodded and walked off to get the gates open.

"So we gonna hang around? Wait for the flood water?" said Lloyd.

"Absolutely." Grant pointed downstream at the raging brown Colorado River. "According to Shauna's numbers, it'll take almost three and a half hours for the water to work its way down to Yuma and the Imperial Dam."

* * *

2:00 p.m. - East of El Centro, California

The skinny man slammed his fist against the steering wheel and cursed loudly.

National guardsmen swarmed along the banks of the All American Canal, not just the bridges and the overpasses either. They were everywhere, and the canal was over eighty miles long.

His plan had been perfect. The whole area between El Centro and Yuma was an off-roader's dream with sand dunes as far as the eye could see. All he needed to do was stop at one of the many OHV spots, find an isolated parking spot next to the canal, set a ten-minute timer, and be five miles down the road when the canal blew and started watering the desert.

Now what? He had already driven past all the places he had scouted, and the soldiers were crawling all over the thing. They weren't even letting motorcycles approach the canal, let alone his pickup.

He pulled into one of the lots and stopped next to a motor home, letting the engine run. The All American Canal was still 50 yards away, 50 yards of deep sand. The soldiers carried assault rifles. He wondered if they would shoot him if he drove over there. He knew they'd be reluctant to shoot a civilian. But then again, they were probably hot and bored and he wouldn't put it past them. The idea of planting his bomb was unthinkable.

He wished he had one of those anti-tank weapons, the ones that shoot a little rocket out of a tube. He could stand next to the motor home, take aim, pull the trigger, and bingo. He salivated at the thought. He imagined it blowing sand all over the place, in a bright fiery ball, with soldiers flying head over heels in all directions.

A year before, when he planned the bombings, he knew everything would be easier with the good stuff: missile launchers, plastic explosives, and wireless detonators. Although everything could be had for a price, his finances wouldn't allow for that. Besides, it would have required that he work with others, and broaden his circle. And he didn't trust anybody. If he could do it alone, without anyone else, that would be the best way.

He hadn't done too poorly, either. The Glen Canyon Dam was history, and the California Aqueduct. Too bad about Davis Dam; the three of them would have made a nice little package, a portfolio of success. But two out of three wasn't bad. Besides, if that sandbag fiasco the government was building didn't work, Hoover and Davis would get busted.

He was proud of the aqueduct, but Glen Canyon was a miracle. He couldn't think of a better word. Sure, he had prepared for a year, but he couldn't help but feel that God had intervened for him, a strange thought for a guy who normally considered himself an atheist. But there had definitely been a god at Glen Canyon, a god who had mourned for the river as he did.

He forced his mind back to the issue at hand. At this point he had no ideas how to blow the All American Canal. It had been an important part of his agenda, being the largest by far of the diversions off the Colorado River, over twice as big as the aqueduct. Blowing the canal would have forced Imperial Dam to send the water downstream into Mexico where it belonged. As soon as the explosion occurred, they would have radioed the dam and closed the gates immediately. If only he knew the phone number and could make the call himself.

The thought made him pause. Could it work? What if he didn't blow up anything, but just called in a report of an explosion, or a bomb scare? Would they shut the gates? He didn't think so. They had too many eyes on the canal; they would know immediately that there had not been an explosion, and they were unlikely to shut the gates until they confirmed a large leak. Even if he had the phone number, he couldn't think of what to say to make them shut the gates.

He scratched his chin. Maybe the All American Canal would have to survive. It was a thought that took the energy out of him, and put a knot in his stomach.

He reached forward and pulled the shift lever into reverse. Turning his head from the canal, he looked over his shoulder and backed away from the motor home. If only there was something he could do to make them shut the gates. But what would possibly make them shut down canals that furnished water for irrigation and drinking to so many people?

He slammed on the brakes. The truck skidded to a stop in the sand. Of course! Why hadn't he thought about it before? What would make farmers want to shut it off? How would you get households to demand that their drinking water was turned off? He laughed out loud.

He shifted the truck into drive and headed back to the freeway. He needed a phonebook. The phone number for Imperial Dam would be best, but even the cops would do. It was starting to look like God loved the river as much as he did.

* * *

2:05 p.m. - Hoover Dam, Nevada

Fred Grainger watched the national guardsman place the last sandbag on Hoover-Two. The soldier slid it effortlessly in the gap between the two other bags. And it was done. The dike was complete.

For the first time since the construction began, the mass of national guardsmen stopped moving. They hesitated, glancing back and forth between each other. Then they started yelling. Arms pumped into the air, whistles were heard, clapping. Fred couldn't stop the smile from stretching across his face. They had done it, and none too soon. The water in Lake Mead was still rising, and had eclipsed the original height of Hoover Dam hours ago.

An hour earlier it had been touch and go, as the water had reached the top of some of the sandbags near the visitor center, and started to flow over the first phase of the dike. Since the twenty-foot-high second phase started from the Arizona side, the section on the Nevada side, by the visitor center, was the last to be finished. For a half hour the team scrambled to keep up, and Fred had worried that the water would open a large gap and get ahead of them, but it didn't happen. The men stayed one step ahead of the water until the larger dike grew west and closed the weak point. Since then, the soldiers had been building the dike up to its full twenty-foot height.

Fred looked east to the Arizona shore, and admired the sandbag extension. From a distance, the sandbags blended together perfectly, and the dike looked like it was made of concrete, but with an interwoven texture where the bags fit together. Fred was proud of what they had done, and he wished Grant and Shauna were here to see it. So far it was working, just as Grant had planned. Lake Mead was higher than ever in history: crest plus almost eleven feet. Although the next few hours would be nerve-racking as the water continued to rise, Fred was confident that the dike would save Hoover Dam. With that thought in mind, he headed back into the visitor center to call Grant.

* * *

2:10 p.m. - Palo Verde Dam, California

According to their watches, the floodwater from Headgate Rock was due any moment. Grant did not expect anything spectacular. If everything went as planned, the water behind what was left of the Palo Verde Diversion Dam would rise between ten and fifteen feet for an hour or more, then gradually subside a few feet. The water being dumped through the head gates plus through the new notch in the dike would stabilize at just under 500,000 cubic feet per second, and remain like that for about two months. Five hundred thousand flowing through Palo Verde would be the most water in 70 years.

Lloyd stood next to Grant, watching upstream. Shauna had walked over by the reservoir and peered at a measuring stick again, while Agent Williams remained separated from the group, talking on her cell phone.

Don Simpson walked toward Grant and Lloyd from the house. The white dog followed him, wagging its tail. "I was just thinking," he said.

"I hate it when that happens," whispered Lloyd.

Grant laughed, but put his hand on Lloyd's to signal him to be quiet. "Thinking what, Don?"

The irrigation manager stopped in front of them. His cowboy boots weren't shiny anymore. "I was just thinking that when Headgate Rock broke, it let all its water out at once, just like we did. Doesn't that mean that we're going to get a tidal wave down here?"

Grant shook his head. "When we flew over it in the helicopter, it had already jumped out of its channel and spread out. Looked like it was going to flood all the Reservation farms upstream. Anyway, that will disperse it. We might get more water during the first hour, but I don't expect any tidal waves."

Grant felt a wet nudge under his hand and looked down at the dog's pleading eyes. He scratched behind its ears. Living clear out here, the dog probably only encountered visitors occasionally. But with all the people on the dam, the dog was getting lots of action. The dog had no sense of the flood to come. In a way, Grant envied the dog.

"It's started," yelled Shauna from the reservoir. "The level just rose an inch."

Grant saw a group of policemen sitting in the shade under the willow tree stand and move toward the water. Grant walked over to where Shauna stood.

She pointed at a measuring stick in the water. "Look at it for a second, you can almost see it rising."

Grant stared at the stick, while the water lapped against it. He couldn't see anything move, but sometime during the thirty seconds he stared, it went up another inch.

"See?" Shauna said.

He stood and looked upstream. One of his clearest memories from Headgate Rock Dam was the trailer houses being piled up against the railroad bridge. Although illogical, Grant couldn't help wondering if he would see a mobile home drift around the corner.

"Another inch," called out Shauna to a growing crowd.

Don arrived and stood next to Grant. "When will the peak —"

"Another one," said Shauna.

"Now," answered Grant. "We only expect the peak to lag the leading edge by five or ten minutes."

"Two more," called Shauna. She pointed at the stick. "Now you can actually see it rising."

Grant looked back at the stick. Sure enough, he could see the water rising on the index marks. If he hadn't known better, he would have sworn it was the stick sinking into the mud, not the water rising.

He left the small crowd gathered around the stick and walked back to where he could look downstream. If the current had increased below the dam, it wasn't visible, at least not to him.

"What do you think?" Lloyd asked.

Grant shook his head. "I can't see any difference over here."

"Did you expect to?"

"No, not yet." Grant cocked his head around and looked downstream.

When they first arrived at Palo Verde, two clean green streams exited the dam, the river itself and a large canal. Both flowed in man-made channels, which only covered a small percentage of the original riverbed. Trees and other bushes grew in the other sections. Now, brown water covered the entire expanse, having toppled most of the trees. Brush poked up through the water in places and wet marks were visible on the banks.

"Looks kind of like a lull in the storm, doesn't it?" Lloyd said.

Grant looked back at Lloyd and nodded. "Yeah, hopefully whatever wildlife lived in the riverbed will take the hint and get out while the getting's good. Heaven knows there's not going to be anymore lulls for several months."

Lloyd pointed toward the slice where they broke the dike. "I have a question. What's going to happen to the dike, after two months of floodwater? Won't that tear it up even worse?"

Grant shrugged. "Sure. It'll probably be two or three times wider by August, when Hoover's spillways shut down. That's the whole reason we wanted a controlled break. Even if it grows by a factor of three, it'll still be a ways from the concrete structure and the head gates, and that's what we wanted to save."

Lloyd held out his hands. "It all comes from us taxpayer's pockets anyway, don't it?"

Grant laughed. "Yeah, but that doesn't mean I like the government throwing money down holes when people are stupid."

"Then why are you working for the Bureau? I bet you guys waste as much as anybody in the government."

Grant nodded. "You have no idea. I ask myself why I work there every day. Unfortunately, it's too late to go anywhere else."

Lloyd raised his eyebrows. "You don't really believe that, do you?"

"Sure. Where would I go? You think your company would hire a washed-up dam engineer as a helicopter pilot?"

"No, but there's got to be some place."

"Oh, it happens, occasionally. Other countries are still building dams. But then I'd have to move my family to Brazil or China. I could always try to slide sideways and become a bridge or freeway designer, but then I'd be starting over and competing with college grads."

Lloyd shook his head. "You're an engineer. You talk like you're all washed up."

Grant smiled. "I am. For the most part, American engineers as a breed are headed for extinction."

"What are you talking about? Engineers are the brains behind everything. They design our cities."

"Not if we can outsource it," Grant said. "Haven't you noticed how many electrical engineers have been laid off over the last twenty years? U.S. companies are figuring out that they can outsource more than labor to third-world countries. Have you called tech support for your computer lately?"

Lloyd smiled. "You got a point there. Some guy from India answered the phone. He was smart, but I had a hard time understanding him."

"Case in point. If it can be outsourced, they will outsource it."

Don and Shauna led a group of people over to where they were talking. Grant glanced over at the water funneling through the dike and noticed that it had increased considerably during his conversation with Lloyd.

Don pointed. "It's up over five feet."

"Is it still rising?" asked Grant, more to Shauna than Don.

She responded. "Oh yeah. We just wanted to see how it looked down here."

Grant looked again. The wet marks on the far bank told him that the water had been at least ten feet higher when they broke the dam.

"So far, so good."

Shauna turned to go. "I'm going back to watch the levels. I'll tell you when it peaks and starts to fall."

They didn't have to wait long. Less than ten minutes later, she called out that the water had started to drop slowly. By then, the water levels below the dam were almost as high as when they broke it. The brown water heading downstream flowed fast and dirty. Grant heard a couple more trees collapse in the current downstream.

"There it goes again!" Don pointed as another large slab of the dike sloughed into the cut. "It's gonna wash the whole thing away."

Lloyd winked at Grant.

"It will keep doing that for a while," Grant said, "but it'll stabilize, hopefully before it gets to the concrete." Grant knew it wasn't easy watching the water wash the dam away, especially for Don and the other irrigation guys.

While they stood staring at the spectacle, Grant felt a tug on his sleeve. He turned to see Agent Williams. He hadn't seen her for at least a half hour.

"We need to talk," she said.

"Not now." He pointed at the cut. "We're at peak flow right now."

"I know, but –"

He cut her off. "Can't this wait a few minutes?"

"No!" she said. "It's the bomber. He's struck again, at the All American Canal."

CHAPTER 35

2:30 p.m. – Palo Verde Dam, California

Grant, Lloyd, and Agent Williams stood in the shade under the willow tree. Shauna, who wouldn't leave her post, remained at the measuring stick, writing down water levels and times.

Grant scratched his head. "So nothing was actually blown up?"

Agent Williams shook her head. "No. The caller only stated that he inserted 200 gallons of a biological agent in the canal."

Grant wondered what type of biological agent it could be. He knew that the Bureau of Reclamation spent time thinking about terrorists poisoning the water supply, and what could be done in reaction. But it was something he knew nothing about, information he generally let wash over his head. Unfortunately, right now he'd feel better if he knew more about it. He wondered who at the Bureau to call. "I thought the National Guard was guarding it."

"They are," the special agent responded.

Grant shook his head. "Then how did he get close enough to dump four 55 gallon barrels in it?"

"We don't know."

Grant had a thought. Wouldn't the bomber have guessed that the canal would be guarded, especially after he blew the aqueduct? Maybe he planned in advance for it. There would be ways to get the poison into the canal, even if it was guarded, if you planned in advance. "What if he didn't do it today?"

Agent Williams and Lloyd looked confused.

Grant continued. "Maybe he set it up weeks ago, underground, then flipped a switch and pumped it in. The soldiers wouldn't see anything."

Agent Williams nodded. "That would explain why nobody saw it."

An idea occurred to Grant. What if this wasn't what they thought? "Hang on. You say that nobody actually saw him dump it in?"

She shook her head. "No. No one has reported —"

Grant interrupted, "And nobody knows where he dumped it?"

"No."

It all fit. It all came down to why. The net result of poison in the All American Canal was what? Grant turned to Agent Williams. "Have they shut the head gates yet, the ones feeding water into the canal?"

"Yes," she said. "They shut them as soon as the report came in."

Grant smiled. "He's bluffing."

Agent Williams looked uncomfortable. "What makes you say that?"

"Isn't it obvious?"

Agent Williams looked over at Lloyd, who shrugged his shoulders.

Grant rubbed his forehead. "Look, what's the net result of poisoning the water?"

Lloyd answered. "Kill a ton of people?"

Grant shook his head. "I could buy that if this were somebody else. But assuming this is the same guy that blew the Glen Canyon Dam, Davis Dam, and the California Aqueduct, it wouldn't add up. What was the first thing that we did after the call came in?" Grant answered his own question. "We shut the head gates, the same as when he blew the California Aqueduct. He knew that's what we would do."

Agent Williams seemed to be catching on. "Okay, I can see why dumping poison in the canal would make us shut it down – that makes sense – but what makes you think it's a hoax?"

Grant smiled. "There's one thing inconsistent with the other bombings."

"Yeah, this wasn't a bombing, it was a poisoning," Lloyd said.

Grant shook his head. "Okay, but even more inconsistent is the fact that he phoned. That's the first time he's done that."

Agent Williams looked confused. "I don't know what difference it makes. Even if we believe he's bluffing, we still need to check it out, just to be safe. It's not like we can open the gates and take the risk the poison really exists."

Grant knew neither the agent nor Lloyd was following his line of reasoning. In fact he wasn't sure he knew himself. All he knew was that he'd just been given clue number four, and it fit. All four attacks were intended to send more of the Colorado River downstream. He felt it more than knew it.

"No, you're right, Agent Williams. I'm not saying we shouldn't close the gates. The point I'm trying to make is about the bomber himself. He doesn't care what happens to the canal, and by warning us, he's telling us his intent is not to kill, he just wants us to divert more water downstream."

"But what's downstream? Just Mexico."

Shauna walked over from the river and joined the conversation. "The Mexican Dam is called Morales. It's similar to Imperial Dam in that its primary purpose is to divert water for irrigation."

Lloyd looked confused. "So even if our bomber's intent is to steal all this water for the Mexicans, would their canal even hold it?"

"No way," said Grant. "Their canal isn't even as big as the All American."

"Then what's below that?" asked Agent Williams.

"Nothing," said Shauna, "just a dry riverbed. Morales diverts almost the entire river west."

Agent Williams sounded surprised. "Then where does the water go that continues downstream?"

Shauna shook her head. "Basically nowhere. There isn't much left. By then the riverbed is almost dry."

The special agent looked confused. "All the water? Dry riverbed? You mean the Colorado River is gone after Morales?"

Grant winced. It was like he had just been gut punched. His mind began racing and the voices of the others started to fade. The puzzle fit. He had all the pieces. And now that he did, he felt like an idiot for not seeing it before. It was the damn Mexican border; he hadn't been thinking beyond it. He had been hypnotized by the old "that's not my job" theory, the same theory he hated when others adopted it. In order to understand the intentions and motives of the Colorado River bomber, he needed to look at the Colorado River as a whole.

Shauna continued, "Yeah. Like I said before, we ended up signing a treaty with Mexico to guarantee what they get today. Without the treaty, the river wouldn't even make it there. The Americans would use it all."

Agent Williams thought about that for a minute. "What about where the river hits the ocean?"

Shauna laughed. "The delta? There isn't one. The water doesn't make it there any more. The whole thing is dried up."

Grant jumped back in, but his voice was dreamy. "People who visited the delta in the early 1900's described endless marshes, filled with millions of waterfowl. Huge fish hunted in the brackish water. The delta stretched across almost fifty miles. Explorers considered the Colorado River Delta one of the most incredible places on earth. Jaguars were even seen hunting there."

Agent Williams looked between Shauna and Grant. "And it's all gone now?"

Grant nodded. "All of it. The river bed dries up almost sixty miles from the ocean; it just kind of disappears into the sand."

Lloyd, who had been silent, argued, "But every map I've ever seen, shows the Colorado River emptying into the Gulf of California."

Grant looked him in the eyes and shook his head. "Not any more. Not for decades."

Lloyd rubbed his eyes, then responded with vigor. "Hey, I'm no tree hugger, but that stinks. So we need water. Fine. Divert a little here and there, okay. But, all of it? Every drop? We dry up a delta that big so we can have water fountains and palm trees in Los Angeles and Las Vegas? That seems a little over the top."

Agent Williams spoke again, almost pleading. "I don't understand how this could happen."

Grant hung his head. "Well, it did. It was a different time." He knew how it happened. Everyone had been looking out for number one. When the U.S. government allocated the water in the Colorado River between the western states and Mexico in 1930, the squeaky wheel got the oil. California squeaked the loudest, and the delta didn't squeak at all. Early in life Grant learned that water flowed downhill. But, after joining the Bureau, Grant learned that water flowed uphill, toward money, and in the West, nobody had more money than California.

Grant continued. "Well, I think we finally have a plausible motive for our bomber."

"Do we ever," Lloyd said.

Grant felt funny. They had just cracked the case wide open. The Colorado River bomber was an environmentalist. He was sure of it. Now the FBI would know where to look. They could track him down. But Grant didn't feel as good as he should, and he sensed that the others didn't either. It had been easier when they thought the bomber wanted to destroy, maim, or kill. Now the motive turned out to be restoring a wildlife habitat. Now what? Grant knew what they had to do, but his feelings had changed.

"So what's next?" asked Agent Williams.

Grant considered. "First, we need to tell Phil."

Agent Williams nodded.

Grant pointed south. "Then somebody needs to contact Mexico again, and let them know what's happening."

Grant knew what else they needed to do. Subconsciously, he'd known it all along. "And finally, we need to start making arrangements to go into Mexico. With all the water that's headed downstream, the Colorado River Delta is going to be wet again, after over fifty years. And I have a feeling our environmentalist is going to be there to celebrate it."

* * *

3:00 p.m. - Palo Verde Dam, California

The helicopter blew dust in all directions as it lifted off from the Palo Verde Diversion Dam. Grant caught a final glimpse of Don Simpson from above. The head of the Palo Verde Irrigation District still looked nervous. He had been extremely anxious when he found out they were leaving. But, all things considered, things were fine at Palo Verde. The water levels had been slowly dropping since peak, and the rate at which the dike was washing away had slowed. The farmers were lucky, especially compared to what might have been if they had not intentionally broken their dam. Grant had tried to reassure Don of that fact before leaving. Not that Grant could blame him. Many of the farmers would hold Don personally responsible for the dike's failure. Blame waited on both sides of tough decisions.

As the helicopter followed the river downstream, Grant marveled at the way the river had changed, transformed from a calm green to a rushing brown. Sometimes, when it left its banks and spread out, it almost reminded him of the upper Mississippi, or maybe the Missouri. That probably made sense as the upper Mississippi averaged a little over 600,000 cubic feet per second, and for the next two months, the Colorado would be very close to that.

Soon after the helicopter left Palo Verde, Grant saw a small town shimmering beyond the countless grids of farm land, about five miles ahead.

"What town is that up there?" Grant asked.

"That would be the thriving metropolis of Blythe, California," Lloyd responded.

There were many words Grant could use to describe Blythe, but neither thriving nor metropolis came to mind. He looked at his watch and noted it was after 3:00 p.m. "Shauna," he said into the headphones, "how long before the water gets to Imperial Dam?"

"5:45," she responded immediately.

"All right, that's almost three hours; we have some time." Grant pointed ahead to Blythe. "Lloyd, head over there. Let's see if we can find a burger or sandwich place with a vacant lot next to it."

Lloyd looked over at Grant, surprised. "You want me to land the helicopter next to a fast food joint?"

"Sure, unless you can fly through the drive-thru. I haven't had anything since breakfast, and I'm starving."

Lloyd grimaced "It'll blow dust all—"

"I'll buy," Grant added.

"Why didn't you say that to start with?" The pilot smiled broadly.

"I'm in," Shauna said, from behind.

"Me, too," said the FBI agent.

Lloyd covered the five miles in a couple of minutes. "How about that one on the other side of the freeway? There's a whole field to land in behind it."

Grant saw it at the same time. "That'll work."

"I was kinda hoping for something cold, like a deli," Agent Williams said.

Lloyd glanced back at her. "They've got ice."

When the helicopter landed, Grant opened the door and hopped out. Turning back toward Lloyd he cupped his hands. "What do you want?"

Lloyd hung his headphones on the hook and opened his own door. "I'm coming too."

Grant saw that both women were already out. He instinctively crouched to avoid the rotors and jogged out from under the helicopter, meeting Lloyd on the other side.

As they walked across the sand toward the parking lot, Grant noticed a family standing next to their car. By the way they were staring, he guessed that helicopters did not often land next to hamburger places in Blythe.

Grant caught up to the pilot. "You could have kept the engine running, then we could have left when I got your food."

Lloyd held out his hands. "Driving with a cheeseburger and fries in my five-speed jeep is tricky, but if I were to try it in the helicopter, well let's just say you guys would be better off watching from a safe distance."

Grant nodded, realizing suddenly that both the pilots' hands were always occupied in a helicopter.

After they ordered and were seated, they ate in silence, all of them stuffing food in their mouths.

"Good idea," said Lloyd, with a mouth full of french fries.

Grant nodded a response. He glanced out the window and saw two men standing near the helicopter, looking it over. He swallowed a mouthful of food, and motioned to Lloyd. "Should I worry about the Lookie Lou's?"

Lloyd glanced up, then responded while still chewing. "Nah, people are always checking out the choppers. They won't hurt anything." He swallowed and rolled his eyes toward Agent Williams. "Besides, if they try something, the FBI here can put a bullet in 'em."

Agent Williams made a thumbs-up sign with her hand.

Grant swallowed, took a swig of his soda, and looked at the agent. "So what did Phil say?" Grant knew she called her boss just before they left the Palo Verde Diversion Dam, but he hadn't heard the result.

She took her time and finished chewing before responding. "It's hard to tell for sure what Phil's thinking, but it seems like he agrees with your delta theory."

"What about Mexico?"

She shook her head. "That, he was very clear about. We are not to cross the border. He's going to charter a jet from Hoover Dam to either Yuma or El Centro. He said he'd call the Mexicans while he waited for the jet."

"They can't get a jet from Hoover Dam," said Lloyd through a mouthful of french fries, "but a sea plane might work."

Agent Williams glared at Lloyd. "I know that. They're using the Boulder City Airport."

Grant laughed, which caused the agent to glare at him too.

After a few minutes, when they were done with their hamburgers, both women excused themselves and walked to the restroom. Lloyd helped himself to both women's extra french fries. Grant glanced over his shoulder to make sure they were out of earshot.

"What kind of paperwork would we need to fly into Mexico?"

Lloyd stopped chewing. "Didn't the FBI just tell us not to cross the border?"

"I'm just asking a hypothetical question."

Lloyd raised his eyebrows. "Well, in that case, if we just wanted to fly over the border and look around, kind of an aerial tour of the delta, then nothing."

Grant glanced around again. "Nothing? No permits?"

Lloyd shook his head. "As long as we don't try to land."

"Good."

Lloyd held up a finger. "There are other issues, besides the Mexicans and pissing off the Feds. I don't think my chopper's insured in Mexico."

Grant hadn't considered insurance. "How much would it cost to replace?"

"More than I'll make the rest of my life," Lloyd said.

"How about we worry about that problem later?"

Lloyd lowered his voice. "We'll need fuel."

"Can you get fuel in Yuma?"

Lloyd nodded. "Sure."

Grant lowered his voice. "All right, when we get to Imperial Dam, you take off and get some fuel."

"Won't it look suspicious, leaving you guys at the dam?"

Grant saw movement in Lloyd's eyes and looked over his shoulder to see both women exiting the restrooms.

Grant rushed his words. "Doesn't it need gas anyway?"

Lloyd winked.

"Hey, what are you guys whispering about?" said Agent Williams.

Grant stammered, embarrassed about getting caught.

Lloyd filled the silence. "We were just talking about how flattering those FBI coveralls look."

Both women looked at Grant, not Lloyd, and he felt his face flush.

Lloyd smiled. "No. That's not what I meant. What we were saying is that they're very practical in this hot weather, especially if you don't wear anything under them."

Grant saw Shauna gasp while Agent Williams looked over at her, then both women looked at Grant again, although this time Grant sensed that they were not sure whether to believe Lloyd.

Agent Williams shifted her look to Lloyd. "Are you messing with me?"

Lloyd shook his head. "No, ma'am. I have a policy to never mess with anybody who's packing." He pointed at her forty caliber Glock.

Grant wondered if Lloyd was making it worse, but the pilot didn't seem nervous. In fact, he seemed to be enjoying himself. During the standstill, Lloyd reached over and stole a couple more of the uneaten fries from the special agent.

She stared hard at him. It made Grant nervous. Finally her expression broke, and a slight smile appeared. "You touch one more of my fries, and I'll gun you down right here."

The pilot looked nervous for a second, pulling his arm back, then suddenly lurched forward, grabbing her whole carton of fries. She reacted as if she were under fire, broadening her stance and grabbing the handle of her weapon.

Grant saw a man at the next table jump in his seat, his eyes wide, and mouth hanging open.

Agent Williams released her hand from the weapon and pointed at Lloyd, smiling wider. "You're just lucky my gun was snapped in, or my reflexes might have taken over."

The pilot stuffed the fries in his mouth and took a swig of his drink. "That's the story of my life with women, just one snap away from the action."

Grant was laughing so hard he couldn't breathe. After he regained control of himself, he stood and gathered the garbage from the table onto his tray. "Enough comedy. Let's head out. We got another 80 miles to Imperial Dam."

The two women pitched in while Lloyd refilled his soda. A moment later Lloyd held the door and they all headed back into the desert heat.

* * *

3:45 p.m. - *Border between the United States and Mexico*

The thin man passed from Calexico, California into Mexicali, Mexico. The security on the border reminded him of a two-way mirror, where you could see out, but not in. The entrance into Mexico was a straight shot; he hardly had to slow down. Yet cars were lined up for a mile going the other way, and he could see that each driver entering the United States was being stopped and questioned.

Before he crossed, he passed many stores that advertised Mexican car insurance. On all of his past trips he had always paid the money. He knew his normal car insurance wouldn't cover him in Mexico, and he'd heard the horror stories of Americans getting thrown into Mexican jails after an accident due to lack of insurance. It just wasn't worth the risk, not for twenty bucks a day.

But this particular trip was different. He had worried about all those things before when he couldn't afford to be locked up in Mexico. He could not afford to jeopardize his goal over a trivial issue such as car insurance. But this time when he pulled up to the insurance store, he sat in the car and wondered what to do. For the last year he had planned meticulously for this. It had consumed him. But today he realized that he had given no thought to his life after. To be honest, he was surprised to have gotten away with it, expecting to either be caught by the police, or more likely, killed. But he was not dead, nor incarcerated.

Sitting in the parking lot he realized that he didn't know what came next. One plan included heading farther south into Baja for a couple of days. He could camp and kill time until he felt safe crossing back into the U.S. But he had never spent any time thinking about the details, and realized now that he had no food, sleeping bag, or even water jugs for such an excursion. And what of the car insurance?

Realistically, the police would eventually track him down. He felt sure of it. Yet now that he had made it this far, he wondered if there were things he should have done just in case he was successful. Fake I.D. would have been a good start. Maybe even airplane tickets out of Tijuana or Cabo San Lucas. But where would he go? And what would he do when he arrived? He had no money for a life of exile. But he couldn't really go back to work on Monday either. Or could he?

In the end, he bought the car insurance, a seven-day policy. If he wound up wandering around in Baja, at least he wouldn't be thrown in jail for an auto accident. He laughed at the thought of the FBI finding him in a Mexican jail, being held for a fender bender. Actually, if he told the Mexicans that he was the one responsible for releasing the Colorado, they just might let him go. It was an interesting thought. But how would he tell them? He didn't speak Spanish.

A horn honking behind him brought him out of his daze. He was in the wrong lane. He waved his arm out the window and moved left to where he should have been. The street signs were just different enough to give him an uneasy feeling when driving in Mexico. He rubbed his eyes and focused ahead.

Mexico's Highway 5 headed south through Mexicali. After exiting the city, it would eventually run alongside the last of the Colorado River. Forty miles south of Mexicali, the river dried up completely. From there, the highway continued another fifty miles along the edge of the dried-up river delta, and eventually went through San Felipe on the coast of the Gulf of California. His map showed the road continuing south, finally linking with Highway 1 that stretched all the way to Cabo San Lucas, a thousand miles away at the bottom of the Baja Peninsula. But south of San Felipe, the line on his map was small indicating a dirt or gravel road. Maybe he would head south after tonight. Cabo sounded like a good place to get lost. But the road was unknown to him, and it reminded him how little preparation he had made for success.

He glanced at his watch. There was plenty of time. A news report on the radio estimated the floodwater was traveling about twenty miles per hour. Another station said twenty-five. Either way, the water should reach the delta sometime late that evening. It would be better to have firm time estimates, but that was a luxury he didn't have. He would reach it in time; that was the main thing. He would be there to see the delta restored.

CHAPTER 36

─────────

4:10 p.m. - North of Yuma, Arizona

From the helicopter, they could see the concrete structure of the Imperial Dam. Unlike the last two dams, Imperial was entirely concrete and stretched all the way across the small canyon, for a total length of over 3000 feet. In spite of its length, the dam looked unimpressive, only thirty-one feet tall in the middle, with slightly larger concrete head gates on both sides.

As they flew over the structure, Grant could make out three streams flowing from the dam. From west to east, the first and by far the largest was the All American Canal on the California side. Next to it, and only a third as big, was the remainder of the Colorado River. Then, on the far eastern shore, the Gila Main Canal flowed from gates into Arizona.

In the middle of the concrete structure, between the Colorado River and the Gila Canal, was a thousand-foot-long section that was twenty feet lower than the rest of the structure. Water constantly trickled over this entire section, creating a green carpet of moss on the concrete slope down to the river below. This lower middle section at Imperial Dam was designed to handle any overflow and therefore acted as Imperial Dam's spillway system.

Most people know that dams will eventually silt up as the river deposits its dirt and debris into the mouth of the reservoir. After hundreds of years, the silt will eventually fill the entire reservoir, leaving no storage space for water and rendering the dam useless. Although Imperial Dam was only built in the late 1930s, it was already completely silted. Being less than thirty feet deep, the dirty Colorado made quick work of the small reservoir. Grant heard that only three small channels remained in the reservoir, one to each set of head gates, though he couldn't see them through the murky water. What he could see, however, was a huge patch of reeds and other water plants growing right out of the middle of the lake, leaving no doubt as to the reservoir's depth, or lack thereof.

A quick visual inventory of potential damage spots indicated a small mobile home development on the east bank of the reservoir, but most of it looked to be located at high enough elevations so as to not be affected by the next two months of flooding. Below the dam, however, it was obvious that everything would be underwater. A flat gully almost three miles wide, littered with willows and other brush, marked the original Colorado River channel. The gully looked to be just over five miles long before it opened into the farmland just north of Yuma, Arizona. Access roads, both to the trailer park and to the dam itself, connected to a small highway in the bottom of the gully, and Grant knew that both would shortly be inaccessible. Both sides of the dam were littered with police officers and their patrol cars, as Grant had seen at the other dams upstream.

Grant pointed to a gravel patch near the main head gates on the west side. "Put us down over there."

The helicopter banked immediately before descending to the gravel. Before anyone could exit, Lloyd's voice could be heard in the headphones. "You guys hop out. I'll run into Yuma and get some fuel. I should be back in an hour."

Grant looked over at the pilot and they made eye contact. "Okay, we'll see you in a while." Grant looked at his watch, then added, "Things should look different when you get back."

"Will I be able to land here?"

Grant looked around, trying to predict what would be flooded. He pointed just west of the concrete structure. "If not, that little knoll oughta work."

"10-4," said the pilot.

Before Grant removed the headphones, he heard Special Agent Williams' voice. "Look around in the Yuma airport for the FBI team. They should be arriving pretty soon in a private charter."

Lloyd looked over at Grant, his eyes prompting a response.

"Just do what you need to do," Grant instructed Lloyd. "If anyone asks, tell them we expect our flood by quarter to five, and we'll meet them at the Yuma airport sometime between 5:15 and 5:30."

Lloyd nodded, and the three passengers opened the doors and hopped out. Grant crouched and jogged from under the rotors, and by the time he was clear, the helicopter had already taken off. Grant watched the chopper disappear into the distance.

A middle-aged guy in a suit and tie approached with a policeman alongside. "You from the Bureau?"

Grant reached out his hand. "Yeah. Grant Stevens." When they shook, Grant noticed the man's hands were sweaty.

"Name's Frank Kennedy. I'm the site supervisor for Imperial Dam."

"Nice to meet you, Frank," said Grant. He released the sweaty hand and wiped his on his pants. "What's happened so far at your dam?"

Frank pointed back toward the middle of Imperial Dam. "Well, in spite of how big that spillway looks, it ain't big enough for a half a million cubic feet." He looked up at Grant with an almost pleading look on his face. "You sure we're going to get that much water?"

Grant nodded. "Afraid so, Mr. Kennedy."

Frank glanced upstream.

Grant pointed north. "We just came from Palo Verde. We were there when they broke the dam. All that water's headed this way." Grant continued. "So your spillway won't handle it. What's the backup plan?"

Frank hesitated. "Well, our priority is to protect the canal and its desalinators." He pointed back toward the west end of the dam.

Grant's eyes were drawn to the head gates for the All American Canal, where the water was separated into three large ponds where the sediments were extracted. After the extraction, the sediment was flushed back into the Colorado River and sent to the Mexicans. He wondered if the Mexicans approved of the way the canal cleansed itself at the cost of dirtying their water. Kennedy had constructed a new dike almost ten feet high to protect the desalination ponds. Grant thought about the raging brown water racing down the riverbed below the Palo Verde Dam an hour before. Obviously, a ten-foot dike would not be nearly enough. He thought about telling Frank Kennedy, but decided there wasn't any point. It would just distract him from what Grant knew was a more important issue.

"What about opening up the dam a little bigger?" Grant asked.

Frank Kennedy looked back toward the middle of the structure, then back at Grant, a terrified look in his eyes.

"You did bring in some demolition guys like we told you to?"

"Yeah, they're here, but . . ." Frank couldn't finish the sentence. His eyes went down.

Grant shook his head. He felt the skin on his neck tighten. Nobody had guts anymore. He wondered if these guys would have reacted the same if they had seen the water pouring out of Lake Powell, or if they had seen the bodies floating in the water below Parker Dam, or the flooding below Palo Verde. He tried hard not to lose control. "Well, Mr. Kennedy, get 'em out on both sides of the spillway right now and start planting the charges." He looked at his watch. "We only have about forty minutes."

"But Mr. Stevens –"

Grant couldn't hold back. His anger took over as he shouted at Kennedy. "No buts, Mr. Kennedy! Get 'em out there right now! Either you widen the dam, or the river will, and the river most certainly will not do it the way you want it. It'll tear it apart in the place you least want it to."

"Where exactly should I —"

"There's no time for exactness, Frank! You already pissed all your exactness time away. Get them to blow both sides of the spillway now." Grant saw the man look over at the dam with a blank look in his eyes. Grant couldn't stop himself. He reached out and grabbed the man's shoulder, a little too forcefully, and pointed to the concrete above the main river head gates. "There!" he said. He then swiveled toward the Gila Canal head gate on the other side. "And there!"

"But Mr. Stevens," pleaded the supervisor. "That will destroy both gates."

"I thought you wanted to save the All American Canal." Grant said, pointing back toward the settling tanks.

"Yeah, but what about the —"

Grant stretched out his hands. "You can't save it all, Mr. Kennedy." He hesitated for a moment. "You'll be lucky if you save anything."

Frank Kennedy slowly raised a radio to his mouth. He pressed the button to talk, but looked like he didn't know what to say. Finally the words trickled out. "Okay. Let's send in the demolition guys. Split 'em up. Both sides of the spillway. Open it all the way from the Gila to the main river gates." His voice trembled when he finished.

He looked back at Grant. "I hope you know what you're doing Mr. Stevens."

Grant looked over and imagined water pouring over the top of the Imperial Dam. He looked back at Frank Kennedy. "Frank, I'm not worried about doing too much." He shook his head. "I'm worried we're not doing enough."

Forty minutes later Kennedy approached with his radio in his hand, his thumb on the button. "Okay. They'll be ready to detonate in a few minutes."

Frank Kennedy had changed in the last forty minutes. Once the decision was made to open up the dam, and the task switched from strategy to implementation, the man had acted like the supervisor he was. The indecisiveness was gone, replaced instead with pointing, directing, counseling, and tactical planning. Grant could tell the men respected Kennedy and responded to his directions. Obviously, the decision to blow up the dam, the dam he was in charge of, had been a little too much.

Grant was just about to respond, to tell them to go ahead and blast, when Shauna came running up. "Aren't you going to blow under the spillway? How come they're not putting any explosives there?"

Both Grant and Frank Kennedy stared at her for a moment before Grant answered. "What do you mean?" He motioned toward some dirt just downstream from the dam. "There?"

"No." She pointed at the center of the dam. "The spillway itself. If you blow the bottom out of it, the rest of the structure might survive." When both Grant and the supervisor mirrored blank stares, she continued. "You might not have to blow the head gates on both ends if you make the spillway deeper. It would be almost twice as deep," she added.

Grant felt confused. "But the dam is full of silt . . ." He realized his error as soon as he spoke. Yes, Imperial Dam was full of silt, but the floodwater would wash that out in no time. If they blew the bottom of the spillway, the spillway would be twice as tall, and would theoretically be able to flow well over 400,000 cubic feet per second. They could save the rest of the dam.

Grant looked at his watch, 4:50 p.m. Now they had less than an hour before the water arrived. "Shauna, that's brilliant. Where were you a half hour ago?"

Frank Kennedy shook his head. "That won't work. The dam's full of silt," he said, still looking confused.

"No, she's right," said Grant. "If we blow the bottom out of the spillways, the water will take care of the silt in no time. It would more than double the capacity of the spillway."

Frank nodded slowly, comprehension setting in. "She's right."

Frank lifted his radio to his mouth. He hesitated and looked at Grant who nodded confirmation. "Demolition team, hold everything. We have a last-minute change of plans. I need all available people to stop what they're doing, and instead, start planting explosives on the lower part of the spillway. We need the spillway to be deeper."

Grant heard a response from the radio, which he guessed was the guy in charge of the demolition team. "But Mr. Kennedy, isn't the water almost –"

Frank keyed the mike and shouted into the radio. "Yes, the water is almost here! That's why you need to hurry!"

"But if we're not done in time? Then we won't have blown anything."

Frank looked over at Grant.

"Have them leave a small team on the Gila side," said Grant quickly. "We can blow that as a backup."

Frank forwarded the instructions into the radio and almost immediately they saw the results as the men on the dam started hustling toward the center.

Grant looked anxiously at his watch again.

"I wish you still had your helicopter here so we could scout the water upstream," said Frank.

Grant nodded. He agreed. Hopefully Lloyd would be back soon. Grant wondered if the pilot had beaten the FBI to the airport.

The thought of sneaking past the FBI into Mexico was starting to bother Grant. What was driving him to do it? It wasn't his job to find the bomber. He had no expertise at apprehending criminals. But for the last two days, the FBI had shown no signs of solving this crime. They'd been two steps behind from the start. The FBI was better when they had time to do computer simulations, run background checks, and analyze information. This whole thing had gone down much too quickly. Grant realized it had been less than eighteen hours since the first bomb at the Glen Canyon Dam, and he was already over 500 miles from there. It felt like a lifetime ago.

And what about Mexico? It seemed like the FBI had no intentions of going past the border. Could they really trust the Mexican police to do this by themselves? What if Grant actually did sneak into Mexico and they found the bomber down there? The environmentalist would surely be there. Maybe they could follow him in the helicopter until the Mexican police could pick him up. But how could they communicate with the Mexicans on the radio? None of them spoke Spanish. What about Lloyd – did he? He had forgotten to ask the pilot. He wondered for a second what Roland and Howard and the other officers in the Bureau of Reclamation would think of his idea to go into Mexico after the bomber against the direct orders of the FBI. It was a line of thought that he did not want to explore. Frank's voice pulled him out of his thoughts.

"Will this floodwater hit hard at first, or gradually build?"

Grant looked up and saw the entire length of the spillway lined with demolition guys busy at work. He realized that even a small amount of water coming over the spillway would disrupt their efforts. He looked back and forth along the dam before returning his gaze to Frank Kennedy.

"Open all the other gates, the All American, the Gila, and the river gates. It'll give them a few more minutes warning." Grant looked back at the men working on the spillway. "Tell them not to wait to wire the explosives. If the water forces them to ditch, I want them to be able to blow what's already done."

Frank spent the next few moments forwarding the instructions. Almost immediately Grant heard the gates on the All American and the river raising.

Grant pointed at a small hill on the west side of the river, just upstream from the dam. "Can we post some police officers up there to watch for the floodwater?"

Frank nodded and keyed the radio again.

* * *

5:30 p.m. - Grand Canyon, Arizona

David and Judy sat on a couch in the South Rim visitor center. Afram paced back and forth. The visitor center had been closed to tourists and had been converted to a make shift crisis center. After the red helicopter dropped them off four hours earlier, the three had been fed, clothed in warm green sweats, and examined by doctors.

Throughout the day, every time someone walked by in green sweats, and there were many, David checked to see if they were his friends. At every opportunity, he asked the doctors or the volunteers if they had any information about Sam, Becky, or Keller. The answers were always the same. "I'm not sure, let me go check," or "I don't have that kind of information, you'll have to talk to somebody else," or "They might be at another facility," or "We are checking into it, somebody will get back to you," or "I'm sure they are fine, now just relax and don't worry."

At one point Afram had gone searching through the building, pulling back curtains where others were being treated and opening doors. But their friends were not to be found.

Finally, a ranger with an orange vest approached them. He had a somber look in his eyes.

"I understand you have been asking about your companions."

"You have some information?" Judy asked.

They crowded around the man. He motioned for them to sit. David and Judy sat, but Afram remained standing.

"Can you give me a description of them, and what they were wearing?"

"Are they alive?" David pleaded.

The ranger held out his hands. "I don't know. That's what I'm trying to figure out."

"Well, take us to them and we'll tell you," Afram said.

The ranger did not even look at Afram, ignoring the question. David had a bad feeling about how the conversation was going. He suspected there was a reason they were not taking him to see his friends.

"How many of your friends were there?" the ranger asked.

"Three," Judy responded quickly. "Two men and a woman."

The ranger looked confused. He pointed at them. "You ran the Grand Canyon with only six of you, in one boat?"

David looked over at Afram. "No. Actually, there were two rafts. If you count everyone, there were fourteen total. But we got separated."

The man wrote down the number in a notebook. "So there were eleven besides you three."

Judy nodded.

"And you say you were separated in the flood?" He looked at Judy. "Can I assume there were six in your boat and eight in the other when you split up?"

Judy nodded.

"And you were all with Colorado River Foam?"

David didn't remember telling anyone that. "How did you know that?"

The man reached in the pocket of his vest and pulled out a bright green emblem like the one from their life jackets.

David's stomach sank. Judy put her face in her hands.

"They're dead, aren't they?" Afram pointed at the emblem. "You found their bodies, didn't you?"

The man nodded. "We found some bodies wearing these life jackets, yes." He waited while it sunk in.

"Eleven?" Afram asked.

The ranger shook his head. "Ten. We found an eleventh jacket, but no person."

David felt perplexed. "Does that mean somebody made it?"

The man shook his head. "The straps on the jacket were torn out. It would take a very violent situation to do that. We don't believe it's possible that the person wearing it could have survived."

"So they're all dead then?" Afram said.

The ranger nodded.

Deep down David had known it already. He had known it since the night before. He felt no shock now, only disappointment at the lack of a miracle.

"The three of you were picked up just above Granite Narrows. We can tell from watermarks that Granite Narrows basically acted like a funnel last night. So anyone that went through during high water . . . Well, let's just say, they wouldn't have much of a chance. There was just too much water."

"We could hear it," Judy said. "Keller knew what it was."

The ranger looked confused.

"Keller was our guide," David said.

The ranger pointed at them. "You three were lucky."

David felt many emotions. He would return to Los Angeles and go back to work without Sam and Becky. He would always remember Keller and the members of the other raft. He knew it was a miracle to be alive, but he definitely did not feel lucky.

CHAPTER 37

5:47 p.m. - Imperial Dam, California/Arizona Border

Grant sat in a folding chair under a temporary shade canopy. His body felt exhausted, and his toe was aching again. He was reviewing the projected timelines with Shauna when Frank Kennedy interrupted them.

"They think the water is starting to rise," he said, pointing to the small hill where the police were watching the river upstream.

Grant stood. "Are they sure?"

He nodded. "Yeah, they said one of the rocks on the river bank, one they were watching, is now underwater.

"How are your demolition guys doing?" said Grant.

"I just called them. They said they only need a few more minutes."

Grant walked out from under the shade so he could look out at the demolition men. He saw a couple of them hustling away with tools and boxes of excess materials. A few remained in their working positions, but Grant couldn't see what they were doing from where he stood. He guessed they were still planting the explosive themselves, or maybe threading in the detonators.

"Did you tell them to finish up and get outta there?" he asked.

Frank nodded. "Already did."

Grant looked downstream from the main head gates to see if he could detect if the water had risen yet. He stared at the water for a while to see if he could see it rise. He finally looked up and saw that only about five men remained below the spillways.

"The water's rising!" yelled Shauna.

Grant's eyes moved back toward the river and he noticed the river had risen almost to the top of the wet marks in what must have been only a few seconds.

Grant turned to Frank. But the site supervisor was already on the radio urging the demolition guys to clear out. "We have to blow it now!" Frank yelled.

Grant heard the response in the radio. "I can't detonate until my men are clear."

"Then get them out now!" Kennedy retorted.

Grant saw the final guy drop what he was doing and begin to run. A moment later a fine film of water breached the top of the moss-covered face of the concrete spillway and streaked it dark gray.

"The water's there. Blow it now!" urged Frank into the radio.

"Not 'til my last man's clear," the radio responded immediately.

Grant saw the man, still running, turn his head to look at the spillway, and suddenly trip and fall down. He was still, not moving.

Grant cursed under his breath.

The man's head came up slowly. Grant could see two other men running back to help. The whole face of the spillway was now dark gray and covered with water. The flow downstream from the head gates had increased noticeably.

Grant tapped Frank on the shoulder. "Ask him if the water flowing over the spillway will screw up the explosives."

Frank relayed the question and the radio responded, "Yes, if we wait too long."

The men reached their fallen comrade and immediately started dragging him away.

"Now!" yelled Frank.

"Just a little farther," responded the guy on the radio.

Grant saw the water running over the spillway had increased. It now splashed when it reached the bottom and the boxes left by the demolition team were washing away. Grant looked back at the two men dragging the third. They were only a hundred feet past the spillway.

The explosion erupted behind them and knocked all three men down. Grant's hands went upwards to relieve the pain in his ears. With his hands still covering his ears he noticed that the lower spillway had a dozen huge openings of up to twenty feet in diameter. Some of the blocks of concrete could be seen downstream from the spillway. Muddy brown water now gushed around the new openings. As he watched, he saw the water open another huge hole, rolling a concrete block out of the way.

Grant saw Frank Kennedy yelling at him, but couldn't hear anything. Suddenly realizing why, he removed his hands from his ears. "What?" he yelled.

Grant saw a group of men splashing through knee-deep water to recover the three men knocked down by the explosion.

"He wants to know if he should blow the upper dam on the Gila side," said Frank.

Grant turned his head around. "Where's Shauna?"

She appeared suddenly from behind some of the policemen. He waved her over. "What do you think?"

Her face revealed a nervous smile. "Wow, that was scary. I was watching the men when it happened. I didn't expect it until they were farther —"

Grant interrupted. "Me neither. But what about the spillway? Is it enough?"

"Oh sure. I think the water will finish it off. No problem."

Grant felt the same, but it felt better that she agreed. "So, no need to open the dam wider?"

"Couldn't hurt," she responded.

It wasn't the answer Grant expected. Why blow up the rest of the dam if it wasn't needed? "But if you think that it's enough . . ."

"The spillway should have been wider from the start," she said quickly. "We might as well open it up like it should have been."

It made sense. He'd only been thinking of saving the original structure, not leaving it the way he would have designed it. "I think you're right."

He waved Frank Kennedy over and told him to have the demolition team unhook some of their detonators and only blow another 300 feet of the Gila side. That would leave another couple hundred feet of concrete to protect the Gila Canal head gate. The man on the radio said it would only take a few minutes.

The amount of brown water flowing through the shattered spillway had grown considerably. The water exited dark and soupy after carving through the years of silt deposited behind Imperial Dam. Although the concrete structure underneath was no longer visible, the general shape could be discerned by looking at the rapids, the higher points revealing the remaining structure. Grant noticed one large rapid move downstream and dissipate, which told him the water pressure had cleared another block of concrete.

While staring at the scene, he heard the sound of a helicopter. He looked up and saw the LAS VEGAS TOURS logo on its side. Lloyd was back.

"How long before the river level peaks?" asked Frank.

Grant looked at Shauna.

"A half hour, maybe forty minutes," she said.

They all watched as Lloyd set the helicopter down. As soon as the landing gear touched, Grant heard the engine begin to wind down with the rotors.

"You guys gonna leave now?" asked Frank tentatively.

Grant looked at his watch – 5:57 p.m. The water would reach the ocean in a few hours. He felt something powerful tugging at him, telling him to move on. The environmentalist was in Mexico, headed for the delta. He knew it. But the strong force tugging at him was pulling him away from his job. Leaving Imperial Dam before the water peaked, before they knew for sure if the demolition team succeeded, would be deemed irresponsible.

"No, Frank. We'll stick around for another half hour to see if we opened enough of your dam up."

Frank's shoulders relaxed a little and he smiled.

Lloyd walked up. "Did I miss all the action?"

Grant wanted to ask the pilot more questions about flying into Mexico, but couldn't. "No, Lloyd, we saved the second explosion for you. We should be ready in a minute." Grant nodded at Frank to verify the exact timing on the radio.

While he waited, Grant pointed south so Lloyd could see him. "Did you run into the FBI while you were in Yuma?"

"Nah, they didn't arrive at the airport until I was ready to leave. We didn't even talk."

Grant wondered if they had even recognized Lloyd's chopper as the one Grant was using. More likely that they were thinking about their own responsibilities and not what Grant was doing.

Frank walked over. "Cover your ears this time; he's going to detonate it in fifteen seconds." Frank turned and shouted for the policemen standing around to cover their ears.

Grant covered his ears and noticed that Lloyd and Shauna were doing the same. He suddenly realized he hadn't seen Agent Williams since they landed.

The explosion blew chunks of debris into the air. It hurt his ears even with his hands clamped over them. He watched a large portion of the concrete dam break off and move downstream. Grant guessed that at least half of a football field length of the dam was displaced and that the water would have no problems finishing the job.

"Awesome," Lloyd said.

* * *

6:25 p.m. - Imperial Dam, California/Arizona Border

Grant, Lloyd and Shauna stood next to the helicopter watching the water do its thing. The level had risen steadily since the first explosion. Now it seemed to have stabilized at about four or five feet from the top of the original dam. There was no doubt in Grant's mind that the decision to blow the 300 foot section on the Gila side saved the dam from being topped. In all, counting the spillway and the extra section, a 1300 foot section of the dam was now flowing full blast. As Grant had predicted, the ten-foot dike constructed to protect the settling ponds of the All American Canal had been breached almost fifteen minutes before. They'd have to wait sixty days for the water to drop before they tried to dig out the mud and attempt to restore them.

The small highway below the dam was underwater. The rushing water had flattened what previously had been an impenetrable mass of willows in the riverbed below the dam. Grant saw no evidence that they had ever existed. Looking downstream, the river had spread out to almost a half mile wide, then steadily flowed downhill for three or four miles before it emptied into the valley of farmland below.

"Unbelievable," said Lloyd.

Grant looked at Shauna. "You know what the bright side of this is, don't you?"

She looked up at him with a confused look on her face. "No. What?"

"It will only take a few days of this to un-silt the dam. It'll be cleaner than it's been in seventy years."

She looked back at the water and nodded. "I'm not sure anybody's going to be celebrating."

As Shauna spoke, Agent Williams walked up to where they were standing. She was covered in concrete dust and her knees were wet and dark.

Grant shook his head. "Well, look who you see! I was starting to think you blew yourself up."

"Not likely," retorted the agent.

Lloyd pointed at her. "So, what do ya like better? Digging around after explosions looking for clues, or blowing stuff up yourself?"

She glared up at the pilot.

"It's okay. You can tell us," Lloyd prodded.

She pointed at him. "This had to be done. It had to be done right."

The pilot's eyes bored into her. "That don't mean you didn't get off doing it, does it? Look, I know you loved watching it blow up. I can see it in your eyes. I liked seeing it. I can admit it."

Grant tried to hide his smile as he watched Lloyd push her buttons. He felt like interjecting, saying something to stop the harassing, but then her composure changed and she finally smiled.

"Okay, it was impressive to watch," she said. "Since it had to be done."

Grant smiled, happy the attack was over. He liked Lloyd, but the pilot scared him sometimes, especially the way he talked to the FBI.

Both the special agent and Lloyd looked up at Grant. He could see that Shauna was also looking at him too. He knew they were waiting for his decision. He looked over at Imperial Dam. The massive stream of water plowed through the huge opening. Downstream a mile-wide river ran into the Yuma farmland, but the water level was stable, he couldn't deny it. He listened for the voice that had been nagging him into Mexico. For some reason the urge had dissipated. But then again, the urge could have subsided because it knew he had already given in to it.

* * *

6:30 p.m. - Lake Powell, Utah

Finally, it was their turn. The boats that had been beached above the Mastercraft were gone. Greg had already backed the trailer down the long ramp, and it was waiting for the boat to be lowered onto it.

In the early afternoon, two cranes had been brought in from Las Vegas to lift the boats. They were unlike anything Julie had ever seen before. They reminded her of a military Hummer, in that they were low, flat, and looked heavy. Each had tires bigger than truck tires, and each had a large telescoping arm right in the middle, with the logo CARRYDECK inscribed on the side. One was slightly larger than the other, and Greg told her it would lift 20 tons, not that Julie knew how that related to the boats they were lifting.

But Greg and Paul could not stop talking about how the cranes were perfect for the job at hand. The large crane lifted the boats on the left side of the ramp, and the smaller one lifted the ones on the right. As soon as they had placed a boat on its trailer, they moved the cranes down a boat length, parked and began lifting the next boat. Two helpers wearing hard hats attached special harnesses that slipped under the bow and stern, then once they lifted the boat in the air, the operator could put it wherever he wanted.

When the Mastercraft was hoisted up, Julie couldn't help being scared that they would drop it, but she had nothing to fear. The crane operator lowered the boat down onto the trailer in a slow, gentle motion. Greg and Paul hurried to tie down the boat, and when they were finished, the two men in hard hats removed the harness and the crane moved to the next boat. Since there was a line of trailers waiting to replace the Crawfords on the ramp, Greg motioned for everyone to get in the truck and they pulled the boat to the top of the hill out of the way.

In the parking lot, Greg pulled over next to Paul and Erika's SUV and turned off the engine. They climbed out of the truck and Greg and Paul began securing the boat for the journey home.

Erika looked at Julie, smiling.

"What?" Julie asked.

"Nothing. Just that we're done. We can go home."

Julie looked at her watch. She tried to remember which day it was, and saw that it was Wednesday. Originally, they had rented the houseboat until Friday. "I guess we're leaving a few days early, aren't we?"

Erika laughed. "I think we left at just the right time."

They both turned and looked down the hill to where Wahweap Bay had once been. It no longer looked like a bay. Most of the water was gone, replaced by a thin stream of water running down to merge with the Colorado River. It was how it must have looked before the dam was built. The entire dock structure of Wahweap Marina including the floating store, gas station, rest rooms, and of course, hundreds of houseboats, were all grounded on the shore. Julie was saddened by the sight. What a waste. Lake Powell had been one of the most incredible places in the world.

"Let's go home," Greg said.

* * *

6:40 p.m. - Hoover Dam, Nevada

Fred Grainger stood on top of Hoover-Two and stared out over the water of Lake Mead. He was uncomfortable. He tried to visualize the scene over a hundred miles upstream where the Colorado River exited the Grand Canyon and emptied into the huge reservoir. What was happening up there? Until the floodwater entering the lake fell to less than what Hoover was dumping from both spillways and all the head gates, the level of Lake Mead would continue to rise.

Over the last hour, since 5:00 p.m., the lake's steady rise upward had slowed, but it had not stopped. And the water was now at crest plus 13 feet 3.2 inches, which was almost a foot higher than Shauna had projected. Fred wondered how much higher it could go.

He was not worried that the water would actually breach the dike. The Hoover-Two dike was twenty feet high, and he knew the water wouldn't go that high. But the crest was never designed to hold horizontal pressure. With the additional weight of the thirteen feet of water, the entire wet surface of the 600 foot dam, from the top to the bottom, had an additional 850 pounds per square foot pressing against it. Fred was no longer worried that Hoover-Two would hold. Now he was worried that the concrete in Hoover-One would hold.

"Level?" Fred called out.

"It's still holding at 13 feet 3.25," one of Fred's technicians responded.

Fred considered that. It had been the same for the last twenty minutes. Had it stabilized? He hoped so. He wished it would start dropping. But he wondered if that was unrealistic. If only Shauna were here. She would know what to expect. Why couldn't Grant have left the analyst at Hoover? Wasn't Hoover more important than any of the other dams downstream?

"3.24!"

Fred looked over at the technician. Had he heard correctly? "What did you say?"

"It dropped a little. 13 feet 3.24 inches."

"Watch it for a few minutes," Fred ordered. "I want to make sure it's really stable."

Fred looked at his watch, 6:45 p.m. He felt a wave of energy radiating from somewhere deep inside. Hoover-Two. They had done it. They had saved Hoover Dam. Governor Jenkins and Commissioner Blackwell had told Fred to notify them immediately when it peaked. He wondered where the two politicians were. They were probably eating dinner in the visitor center someplace. He needed to find them and tell them. They would likely call another press conference and stage another photo for history. Fred was so happy that he didn't even mind.

"Level?" he asked.

"Still 3.24," the technician said.

Fred headed for a telephone. The governor could wait. He needed to call Grant.

CHAPTER 38

6:45 p.m. - Yuma, Arizona

Grant could see the Yuma airport ahead from the helicopter. It was larger than he expected, with four runways. Many small planes were tied off to the side of the runways. Past that was a row of metal hangars where the best planes were stored.

Grant rested his head back against the seat, feeling tired. The pilot and both women in the back must have felt the same, because no one had spoken since they left Imperial Dam. The all-nighter from the night before was definitely catching up to him. He had that urge again to lay down.

One advantage to being a paper pusher was the lack of abnormal hours. Compared to that, the past two days were from a different lifetime, a lifetime that, in spite of the chaos, had been in some ways satisfying. Whether he could sustain that type of lifestyle seemed doubtful. Besides, what kind of career would provide the same kind of action he had lived through for the last eighteen hours? A policeman? An FBI agent? He didn't think so. Even those jobs were probably 90% paperwork and 10% action. No, the reality was that the last two days were an aberration, and he knew it.

His stomach told him the helicopter was descending and he opened his eyes, which he hadn't realized he had shut. He saw a jet parked away from the other planes. Lloyd brought the chopper in next to the isolated jet. This time, Grant resisted the temptation to jump out of the helicopter. He let his head rest against the seat back until the rotors had completely stopped. He heard one door open and shut, which told him Special Agent Williams had climbed out.

Grant heard Lloyd's voice in the headphones. "What's the plan?"

"Still working on it." Grant felt butterflies in his stomach. He hesitated before finishing. "We'll have to let it play out, see what happens."

Grant saw Shauna lean forward from the rear seat. "What are you guys talking about?"

He felt guilty for keeping Shauna in the dark. "We're deciding what to do next."

"I thought the FBI wanted to talk to you about your theory," she said.

"I mean after that," said Grant. "We're thinking about going into Mexico." He turned and looked into her eyes. He wondered why he was telling her.

Her eyes grew noticeably. "I thought the FBI specifically denied that?"

"They did," Grant stated unemotionally.

The rotors of the helicopter had stopped. The three were enveloped in silence. Grant recognized Phil and a few other special agents from Hoover Dam talking to Special Agent Williams.

Shauna sat back in her seat before talking. "I see." There was a moment of silence before she continued. "Aren't you afraid of getting fired or something?"

Grant rested his head back on the seat again. "I should be." He knew Shauna probably thought he was crazy.

Her response shocked him. "I'm going with you."

He sat up and turned, facing her. "No. There's no reason to."

"I'm going, Grant. They can fire me too if they want. We're in this together, to the finish."

Grant wanted to argue and tell her she couldn't go, but they were interrupted when one of the agents opened Grant's door. "Can you guys come out here for a second? Phil wants to ask a few questions."

Grant nodded and removed his headset. Climbing out of the helicopter took more energy than it should have. He hoped Shauna wouldn't spill the beans. After they exited the helicopter, Grant walked toward the FBI agents.

Phil shook his hand. "I would have been better off if I'd told my agents to follow you around for the last two days. You seem to have a nose for the action."

Grant smiled. "It was logical that the water trouble would keep moving downstream. It's where I needed to be." He caught Shauna looking at him.

Phil looked around before continuing. "So tell me how you came up with this environmentalist theory."

Grant shook his head. "None of the other theories worked – the mad boater, the middle-eastern terrorists, the anti-recreationalists. After Glen Canyon, maybe, but not after the attempt at Davis. They just didn't fit. But I knew there was a common denominator, ever since this morning at Davis Dam."

"I remember that. You were sure of yourself. So, what was the missing piece?" Phil prompted.

"The delta." Grant remembered the feeling when he put it together. "I knew the Colorado River dried up before it reached the ocean. But I never thought about it. I knew it, but I never considered the ramifications." Grant looked around and realized he was rambling.

He continued. "Finally, this afternoon, I realized when they closed the All American Canal what the common denominator from all the bombings was. All the bombs were intended to send more water downstream. That's why it didn't matter whether the poison was real or not. We had to shut down the canal either way. Mission accomplished." He looked over at Shauna. "It was Shauna who reminded me what was downstream in Mexico. That delta is dried up. Dead. The river hasn't made it that far in years. All of a sudden I knew why the bomber wanted all the water to go downstream. It made perfect sense."

"It made perfect sense to blow up the Glen Canyon Dam to restore a dried-up river delta?" asked Phil sarcastically.

Grant locked eyes with the FBI agent. "It makes perfect sense if you're an environmentalist, if you've spent years demonstrating for Greenpeace, or the Sierra Club, or the Glen Canyon Institute. If you've fought to elect liberals like Clinton and Gore, but were forced to watch when even they gave the environment lip service, establishing a few monuments, but avoiding the real issues, the issues that might offend the farmers who receive subsidized river water, or the populations of Los Angeles, Las Vegas, and Phoenix, who plant palm trees in an environment more suited for scorpions or rattlesnakes. If you had dedicated your whole life to restoring the Colorado River and one of the most amazing deltas in the world, but deep down you knew that nothing you'd done, or ever would do, would even matter."

When Grant looked up, he saw that everyone was staring at him, some with wide eyes. He felt his hand trembling.

Phil spoke softly. "Wow, Mr. Stevens. If I didn't know better, I'd think you were the bomber."

Grant glanced around. He saw that Lloyd was smiling broadly. Grant shook his head. "I'm not your bomber, Phil. I don't condone what was done, or the lives and property that were lost in the process. But I understand it. And actually, I'm surprised that nobody ever tried it before."

Phil looked down for an instant. "Relax. I bought it. We forwarded your theory to the Mexican authorities over an hour ago."

"And?" said Grant.

"And there's nothing else we can do. It's their problem now."

"Did they discuss their plans with you?"

Phil shook his head. "They said they would get back to us. We told them we would stay here, at the airport, at their disposal, if they need us."

Grant didn't like it. He knew the Mexicans would be in over their heads. "Can't our president do something? Make some calls—"

Phil shook his head. "We have no jurisdiction down there, Grant. It's their problem now."

Grant pointed toward Mexico. "But they don't know what to do. They have no idea how much water is headed their way."

"We told them," Phil said. "They are getting ready."

Grant wanted to argue further, but stopped himself. The silence felt awkward.

Phil broke the silence. "So we wait. Maybe they'll call. If so, we'll be ready."

"I guess, if that's the only option," Grant mumbled. Grant felt the tugging again. He knew the water was already past the border. He couldn't hang around here much longer. If he was going to go, it needed to be now.

"And what about you, Mr. Stevens?" asked Phil. "Can you stay here with us? I'm convinced that you know how my bomber thinks better than anyone else. If the Mexicans need anyone, it's probably going to be you."

Grant looked at his watch, then over at Shauna and Lloyd. Shauna looked nervous and Lloyd looked perfectly calm, as if he didn't have a care in the world.

He locked eyes with Phil. "Sorry, Phil, we need to head back north. All five dams are running beyond capacity. I need to monitor them over the next twenty-four hours." He hesitated to strengthen his lie. "But we can stay available, via cell phone." He held up the phone that the FBI had given him that morning. "We can be back in a flash if they need us."

Phil stared at him, making Grant wonder if he knew. The uncomfortable silence remained for a few moments before Phil finally nodded.

Grant reached out to shake again. "So, unless you guys have any other questions . . ."

"Good luck, Mr. Stevens," Phil said. "Your knowledge and instinct have been indispensable during this investigation."

Grant nodded. Too bad all his knowledge hadn't done any good. Grant turned and started walking toward the helicopter. His heart was racing, expecting any moment he might be tackled from behind. He resisted an urge to break and run. Finally, he reached the chopper and climbed quickly into his seat and put on his headphones. He stopped only then to exhale the air he'd been holding. Shauna and Lloyd climbed in after him. He heard Lloyd start the turbine and felt the rotors begin to turn.

He felt terrible for lying to Phil, not just because Phil represented the FBI and the investigation, but because he liked him. He was a good man. Phil would be furious when he found out Grant had lied to him. It wasn't the way Grant liked to leave things with people. Grant looked south over the trees toward Mexico. The environmentalist was down there. He could feel him. There was no choice. The FBI couldn't go, but he could. There was no other way.

When he looked back, he saw Phil talking to Special Agent Williams. Although Grant couldn't hear, he could tell that Phil was yelling to be heard over the helicopter. Then Grant saw something that made him feel sick. Phil yelled something at the special agent and pointed at the helicopter. She nodded and sprinted in a crouch toward them. Grant heard the door open quickly then shut. He felt the chopper move slightly when she climbed in. Lloyd looked over at him.

Grant waited until she had her headphones on. "What's up?"

"Phil thought I should hang with you guys, just in case."

"Just in case what?" Grant asked.

"Just in case you were wrong and something else happens upstream." She buckled her seat belt. She continued, "In case he's not in Mexico. In case he blows up more stuff where you're going."

Grant felt sick. He wanted to argue but did not know what to say. Lloyd looked over at Grant again and Grant nodded to take off. The helicopter lifted and the agents on the ground waved to them. Grant returned the wave. Lloyd headed north, back toward Imperial Dam.

Agent Williams continued talking. "Phil says the action seems to follow you, that we need to cover that base too, just in case."

Grant let the silence linger for a moment. Ahead he could see the mountain range that housed Imperial Dam. He looked down and realized that half the valley below was flooded. Brown water flowed everywhere. Where a country road had been swallowed by the flood, he saw six or seven cars parked, their passengers standing at the edge of the water. Grant knew what they were feeling. Maybe it was their posture, or their mannerisms, but ultimately it added up to lack of hope.

As they approached the mountain range, Grant spoke into the headphones. "Put her down over there." He pointed to a spot around the edge of the hill where they wouldn't be visible to anyone watching from the Yuma airport.

"Why are we landing?" Agent Williams asked, sounding surprised.

Grant hesitated, then, "We need to drop you off, Agent Williams."

"What?"

"You can't go where we're going."

"Why? Where are you going?"

"Don't worry about it," Grant said. This was turning out to be tougher than he expected.

"Wait a minute. You guys aren't thinking about flying into Mexico, to the delta?"

"Wherever we are going," Grant said, "you can't come with us."

He felt her hands on the back of his seat, pulling herself toward him. "You can't go either, Grant. Phil explicitly said that —"

"I'm well aware of what he said, Agent Williams, but we are going. That's why we have to drop you off. Phil left me no choice when he sent you with us."

"I can't let you," she stammered.

Grant turned and saw her punching numbers on her phone. For an instant, he wondered what to do, but then he saw Shauna do something completely out of character. She reached over and snatched the phone from the agent's hands.

The agent yelled into the headphones. "Hey you can't . . . Give me that back!"

Shauna tossed it in Grant's direction and it fell to the floor in the front seat. Grant wondered if both he and Shauna had crossed the line.

Lloyd set the helicopter down on a flat meadow above the riverbed. As soon as the landing gear touched, Grant jumped out, shut his door, then opened the agent's door directly behind his. "Get out," he said, yanking on her arm.

She glared at him. "No! I won't get out, and you can't make me."

He tossed her phone on the ground twenty feet away where she could see where it landed. He hoped she would go after it. She didn't move.

Still holding onto her arm, he felt the muscles. He was a desk jockey and she was a trained spy and assassin. He suddenly realized he couldn't make her do anything. He relaxed his grip on her. "Get out."

"No."

He had no idea what to do next. Maybe if all three of them tried, they could drag her out of her seat. But it didn't feel right. Besides, she had a gun. She could use it if she wanted to. Another idea finally occurred to him. "So, you're going with us?" he asked.

"Nobody's going into Mexico," she said.

He pointed a finger at her face and he felt his emotions burn. "We are definitely going into Mexico." He motioned at the river. "The guy who did all this is down there, waiting."

"It's not our problem," she said, without much conviction.

"It is our problem!" he yelled. "We're the only ones who know where he's going. Think of all the people this guy has killed and how much damage he's caused."

She pursed her lips. "Don't be so arrogant. You're not the only one that can catch him."

Grant took a step back from her. He motioned at the chopper. "We are going to Mexico, right now. If you don't get out, you are choosing to go with us. So Special Agent Williams, are you going or staying?"

She stared at him with anger in her eyes, then floored him. "I'm going."

His jaw dropped. "Are you serious?"

Her eyes went down for a second before returning to his. "Phil told me to stay with you."

He looked down at her gun. He suddenly pictured her holding the gun to Lloyd's head to prevent them from leaving the country. "You're not going to use that on any of us, to make us turn around?"

She looked down at the weapon. "No."

"I don't trust you," he said.

She unsnapped it, spun it around, and handed it to him, butt first. "I trust you, Grant."

He felt uncomfortable holding her gun. He held it so the barrel pointed at the ground by his feet. "What about Phil? Your job?" he asked.

"What about yours?" she responded.

He didn't know what to say. "You're doing this willingly?"

She smiled. "No, you beat the crap outta me and made me come with you," she shrugged. "I'm supposed to stay with you guys, remember? That is my excuse. Besides, you need me." She pointed at the pilot. "He's the only one of you that's ever tried to sneak up on a bad guy, and that was a million beers ago."

Lloyd smiled, nodding his agreement.

Grant couldn't see another alternative. He couldn't make the agent get out. She'd kick his butt if he tried. "All right then, but no funny stuff. We have a job to do and we need to get going." He took a step backward, and motioned toward Mexico with his thumb. "Lloyd, let's go find our environmentalist."

He glanced at Agent Williams and she nodded. He closed her door. Not that he didn't trust her, but, he didn't trust her. He kept the gun and left the cell phone in the dirt. He climbed back in his seat and Lloyd took off. The helicopter headed east to minimize the chance they would be detected. After a while they turned south. They passed silently over the border from the United States into Mexico about twenty miles east of Yuma.

* * *

7:20 p.m. - Mexico

As Grant looked down over the small shacks and lean-tos that housed most of Mexico's rural population, he felt privileged to live in the United States. He noticed that, just like in the southwest, down below in Mexico, any un-irrigated land had reverted to barren desert.

Like the Americans, the Mexicans diverted as much water from the Colorado as possible. Ditches and canals criss-crossed the entire landscape below. Grant was surprised to see so much irrigated farmland east of the river. It had been his understanding that the bulk of the Colorado River was shipped west from the Morales Dam toward Tijuana. He wondered what had become of the Morales Dam. He felt guilty for not trying to save it, as he had done for the American Dams. He hoped the Mexicans had gotten the message and had taken some sort of action. But if the American managers were any example, then he doubted the Mexicans would have the heart to destroy their own dam, even if that was the only way to save it. In the long run, it probably wasn't that important, since the Americans would end up bankrolling the reconstruction with foreign aid as penitence for allowing an American criminal to cause the damage.

Since they had entered Mexico so far east of Yuma, they had not yet encountered the Colorado River. But as Lloyd headed west, they saw the destruction ahead. The whole area below was covered with brown water. Debris, that Grant could only assume were the remains of living shelters, covered the surface of the water. A woman and six or seven children had sought refuge in a tree. A few old cars were half submerged. In one place, a dozen people were standing on a rooftop of one house.

He knew things would get worse and his fears were realized when Lloyd motioned toward a couple of bodies floating face down near some trees. He felt a knot in his stomach and heard some sniffling in his headphones, but nothing was said. The destruction was everywhere. Grant tried to focus ahead instead of below. Fifteen minutes later, they passed ahead of the flooding.

An unmistakable snaking line of green trees in front of them marked the original channel of the Colorado River.

Grant pointed toward it. "Follow it south."

He knew river levels ahead of the flood would be low, but was still shocked at the actual sight of such a meager stream of water in the Colorado River. It became so small that the trees completely closed the gap as if they lined a creek.

They followed the river southwest until it converged with a small mountain range running north and south. At that point, the river ran almost straight south, paralleling the mountain range. Highway 5 paralleled the river, running along the base of the mountain. During those miles where the river skirted the highway, it ceased to flow, but instead widened into standing water surrounded by reeds and willows. The area seemed more like a marsh than a river. Grant saw a few rundown huts between the river and the highway. One of the huts had a sign that said "Resort." But the grounds looked nothing like any resort he had ever seen.

They followed this marsh for almost five miles until it slowly turned southeast away from the highway and the mountain range. During the five-mile stint, Grant saw run-down dories tied up to trees along the sides. At one point he saw a man in a small boat with an outboard motor winding through the maze. A few miles from where the river cut away from the road, a gravel access road aimed toward the river. Two rundown police cars were parked just off the highway.

"That must be the Mexican FBI," said Lloyd.

Grant pointed at them. "With them parked out in the open like that, he'll drive right by. They'll never catch him."

As the marsh turned away from the highway, the landscape between the mountains and the river was flat and gray with no vegetation for as far as the eye could see.

They traveled a few miles over this flat barren land, keeping the river on their left, before Grant pointed at a spot. "Put her down over there for a second, would ya?"

Sand sprayed in all directions when Lloyd brought the helicopter close to the ground, making it hard to see. Grant waited until the rotors slowed and the dust settled before he opened the door. He stepped out onto the surface. It felt like walking on the beach in California. White flat objects about the size of a quarter littered the sand. He picked one up and rolled it through his fingers. It was a shape that even a small child would recognize. He picked up a half dozen more as they were everywhere. He looked south and the landscape didn't change for as far as he could see. According to the map, this flat surface continued for another forty miles.

Grant climbed back into the helicopter.

"What were you looking at?" asked Shauna.

Grant turned in his seat and handed one of the white objects to Shauna, then to Agent Williams. When he swiveled back, he handed one to Lloyd.

"Seashells?" said Agent Williams.

The pilot swiveled in his seat, holding the shell up. "This whole area used to be underwater, didn't it?"

Shauna's hand came to her mouth. "The delta?"

Grant swept his hand over the landscape. "This is it, the Colorado River Delta. A century ago it used to be a thousand square miles of marshes. Now look at it."

Grant nodded at Lloyd and they lifted off. When they were back in the air, they followed the dwindling stream southeast into the center of the dry delta. Only a mile or two later they came upon a series of square lots bordering the water. They were dirty and separated by wire fencing or rickety wood. Most of these lots looked abandoned, but a few housed small trailer houses or wood shacks. Two Mexican police cars were parked in the last lot.

"And you thought they weren't taking this seriously?" Lloyd said.

"If they saw the destruction and flooding we just saw, they wouldn't be parked there," said Grant. "Not without a boat."

"Hopefully somebody'll warn them on the radio," Special Agent Williams said from behind.

"What is this place?" asked Shauna.

"I saw a sign back there that said Campo," said Agent Williams. "I don't know if it means anything or not."

"Whatever this place is or was, it looks like everybody's either gone or going," said the pilot.

"The water's too salty," said Grant. "Probably very few fish and bad water."

After they passed over the small lots called Campo, the pilot struggled to follow the river. It wound back and forth through the reeds and willows, disappearing for a while, only to reappear later. At this stretch, the once mighty Colorado River had dwindled down to a stream the size of a small ditch, a ditch you could step over.

"Where'd it go?" asked Agent Williams.

"I lost it," Lloyd said.

Lloyd flew the helicopter back and forth across the dense willows for almost ten minutes while the four scanned for the Colorado River. At one point they backtracked to where they lost it, but again they could not locate the river past that point.

"It's gone," Shauna said.

Lloyd hovered the chopper and looked over at Grant, waiting for instructions.

Grant wasn't sure. It had seemed clear to him back when they were in Yuma, that all he needed to do was fly south to find the environmentalist, but now the thought seemed absurd. He looked south over endless miles of barren desert. They could fly around all night and never see anyone. The sun was sinking in the western sky. It would soon fall behind the mountain range bordering the delta's western shore. Grant looked southeast and saw that the dense willows continued for another mile or so. After that, the dry delta stretched in all directions. Vaguely he remembered from a map a small channel where the Gulf of California encroached into the dry delta during high tide. He wondered if it was really there, or if it too was a lie, like the millions of western maps showing the Colorado River draining into the Gulf of California.

Grant pointed in a southern direction where he thought the ocean might be. "Head that way."

* * *

7:50 p.m. - The Colorado River Delta, Mexico

The skinny man slowed and stood on the pegs of the quad. He had ridden east for almost an hour from Highway 5 where he left the pickup. He knew the Gulf of California extended up into the delta for twenty miles. He had taken a tour a few years before where they boated up the small channel. So riding to it on an ATV seemed simple enough. It would be the perfect place to watch the river flow into the ocean again.

He had traveled east much farther than he expected, and he still couldn't see it. Staring at the heat radiating out of the desert for so long while riding made it seem like a constant mirage. Many times he wondered if he was going the wrong direction, but the setting sun behind him was as good a guide as any. He wished he had brought a compass, and wondered if he had aimed slightly too far north and missed the inlet completely.

He rode on. He was moments from giving up and changing direction when he finally saw it, a smudge of green in the distance. It had to be water. Otherwise, nothing could grow. He accelerated. Five minutes later he arrived at his destination.

It was water, but it was not the Colorado River. He didn't need to touch it to know the brown water was salty, and came north from the ocean during high tides. It wasn't the Colorado River, but it soon would be.

Shutting off the engine, he climbed off. He felt sore from the long ride and his mouth was dry. He stripped off the helmet, then fished around in the rear compartment and brought out his water bottle. The water was warm. He took a long swig and looked at the bottle. He felt like an idiot for not bringing more. He had spent way too much time hiking in the desert to be this short sighted. It was just another reminder that he had not expected to get this far. The first few explosions were meticulously planned to the finest details, but this afternoon had been rushed, and he knew it. He felt damn lucky to be in the right place at the right time.

He left the bottle on the quad and clomped over to the water in the awkward riding boots. If it were cleaner, he would jump in. He definitely needed to rinse off the dust and sweat from the long ride. However, when he reached down and touched the water it almost burned his hand. The water had to be well into the nineties. The thought of jumping in made him cringe. He could imagine the salt on his back after he dried off in the heat.

No matter. He looked north into the dry desert. The Colorado River was coming. He expected it within an hour or two. It would change everything. When the river arrived he wouldn't be able to drink it, but he could definitely bathe in it. He stared at the horizon and tried to imagine what the water would look like as it traveled toward him.

He looked across to the opposite shore of the salty stream and realized there would be far too much water to fit in the channel. He looked back at the quad and wondered if he should move it farther away. If only there were a small hill nearby, where he could watch the water approach. Unfortunately, this place was as flat as a pancake for miles in every direction. He thought about the All American Canal, and how much water was in it. It had seemed large, sure, but not much larger than this channel. He admitted to himself that the canal had to have been much deeper. When it came down to it, he had no idea how much water would be coming from the north. But he felt sure that the water would arrive gradually, then build up slowly, giving him time to escape on the quad. Of course, that was all a guess, since he had not been able to witness the floods at any of the dams.

CHAPTER 39

They had been flying across the delta for almost fifteen minutes before they saw anything. Grant saw it first, far on his right, which meant they had aimed too far east.

"Over there." Grant pointed.

"Yeah, I see it," said Special Agent Williams.

The helicopter banked right toward what looked from a distance like a muddy lagoon with weeds growing around the perimeter.

"We almost missed it," mumbled Lloyd. "We could have been flying around all night looking for it."

As they approached, Grant saw a group of people standing around two dune buggies. His first thought was, "why so many?" He expected the bomber to be alone. Could the events of the last thirty-six hours have been a group of environmentalists? Why hadn't he seen the signs? When he decided to fly into Mexico, it had been to find a single person. Although he had no details in his head, he had thought they could potentially apprehend the guy, or at least draw attention to him so the local authorities could get him. But if the perpetrator ended up being a group, not an individual, what, if anything could they do by themselves? Grant had always felt he would recognize the man if he saw him. Now he realized that expectation had been absurd.

"Hey, what are they doing?" Shauna yelled from behind.

Grant looked and saw some of the group pointing at the approaching helicopter and a group of men scrambling toward one of the dune buggies. For an instant he thought they would jump into the vehicle and attempt to escape, but he saw them reach into the truck and retrieve something approximately five feet long and round. As they swung the item around out of the truck toward the helicopter, Grant felt sure it must be some kind of missile launcher. They intended to blow the chopper out of the sky.

Now the folly of this trip, against the direct orders of the FBI, became blatantly obvious. His mind raced. They would all four be killed, because of him. He thought quickly of his wife and children. He loved his wife more than he had ever realized before and ached for her. She would be forced to raise his kids as a single mother. It was tough enough to be a kid without having to deal with a parent's death. He didn't have enough life insurance, he realized. They would suffer.

"Look," Shauna said, pointing.

The group had taken the round device from the dune buggy, and laid it on the ground. They proceeded to unroll it. It was white.

"It's some kind of banner," Shauna added.

When the group finished unrolling, they spread themselves along the banner and lifted it up, revealing the message *THE SIERRA CLUB supports the Restoration of the Colorado River Delta*. The group held the banner high and shuffled their feet to pivot it slightly to align it with the helicopter.

"Want me to land?" asked Lloyd.

Grant didn't know. As they approached the group, he could see some of their faces. A man with a bushy black beard held the banner at one end. A blond girl with a headband and ponytails stood next to him. Both wore worn clothes. Something told him that neither was the bomber. They both looked like demonstrators, or at least like the ones he'd seen on TV. The girl looked like the type to live in a tree. He could easily imagine the man laying down on the tracks in front of a train transporting nuclear waste, or handcuffing himself to the blade of a bulldozer at the site of a new highway.

The helicopter had reached the group now and Lloyd circled around them. They rotated themselves to keep the sign visible. Grant scanned their faces, but the banner obscured some. He could clearly see two blond guys and four women. Grant felt nothing as he scanned for some sign, some indication. What if they got closer? There were too many of them. It would be impossible to get a good look at all of them from the helicopter. He looked back at the man with the black beard and decided he couldn't rule him out as the bomber.

"You want me to land?" asked Lloyd again.

Grant looked up. The pilot was waiting for an answer. "Yeah, okay."

The helicopter sprayed the sand in all directions as it landed. The four passengers waited until the rotors were almost stopped and the sand settled to open the doors. When Grant opened his door he saw that the group holding the sign had approached the helicopter and he could hear them chanting something like: ". . .orado". When he heard it the second time, he understood.

"Restore the Colorado. Restore the Colorado," they chanted.

As Grant and the others climbed out of the helicopter, the rhythm and energy of the chant seemed to increase. "Restore the Colorado. Restore the Colorado." The group seemed energized by the chopper's arrival and Grant realized that the four of them were likely the first audience for this protest.

A few more steps and both groups stopped, facing each other. The pace and volume of the chant increased. Grant recoiled as they began to thrust the banner at him in rhythm with their voices. He waved his arms in the air for them to stop, but it only increased their energy. He scanned the group and focused on a few faces. A blond man directly in front of him, also sporting a full unkempt beard, reminded him of a picture he'd seem on one of the tabloids of Brad Pitt when he grew a beard for one of his movies. The man's eyes looked mean and uncivilized. Could he be the bomber?

A girl to Grant's left caught his eye. She was a beautiful brunette with big eyes and long straight hair over a white t-shirt. She was young. She was chanting like the others, but without the hostility. He would be shocked if she was older than fifteen. He felt sure she had not masterminded the explosion at the Glen Canyon Dam.

Farther left, Grant spotted a man wearing a white polo shirt. Unlike the others, he was clean-shaven and professional looking. He looked more like the sort who just got off work than a protestor. Lacking was the urgency in his eyes like the rabid blond guy directly in front.

Grant wondered how, or if, the stalemate would end. How long could they go on? But he sensed the energy of the group was dying. When he scanned back to his right, the black bearded guy he'd first seen from the helicopter had stopped chanting and was motioning with his free arm for them to stop. It took a while for Black Beard to quiet them, but after a few half-hearted attempts, they stopped.

"Why is the FBI traveling in a tour helicopter?" yelled the blond guy in front.

The question caught Grant off guard, and he instinctively turned to look at Agent Williams. He saw her blue coveralls with the insignia on the breast pocket and realized how they'd made the connection.

He looked back at Black Beard and waved his hands back and forth. "No. No. We're not FBI, we're—"

The blond cut him off, pointing. "That's a lie, we can see her. . ." He didn't finish, but emphasized his point at Agent Williams by shaking his finger.

"What I meant to say," said Grant, "was that we are not all FBI. We're . . ." He stopped and looked back at his group. Lloyd, with his beard and clothing, could easily blend in with the protestors. Shauna, who looked terrified, looked the part of the analyst she was. Special Agent Williams, with the coveralls, well, there was no doubt about what she did. Grant wondered what the protestors thought he looked like. He realized he needed to be careful about what he told them about the group. He didn't want to force the bomber undercover.

"We're here to mitigate some of the damage of the impending flood." He saw that many of the group's eyes remained on Special Agent Williams. Grant pointed to her. "The FBI sent a demolition expert in case we found any other bombs."

"Who do you work for?" asked Black Beard.

Grant hesitated, worried about the effect of his answer. "The Bureau of Reclamation."

The blond in front went nuts and thrust his arm forward, pointing at Grant. "You're the bastards that built the dams. You guys are the ones that killed the river. This delta's dead because of you."

The words stung. He looked straight at the blond guy. "Those dams were built before you or I were even born," he said defensively.

A woman pointed at him. "Well, the river's free again now. The delta's gonna be alive again." She looked behind her to make sure she had their support. "And we're not gonna let the government put it back again. You're not going to re-build Glen Canyon. That dam is history." Grant heard some rumblings of support from the group.

"What are you guys looking for down here, on the delta?" asked one of the protestors.

Grant knew he was on dangerous ground. "We've been following the flood waters. We just came from Imperial and flew over the flooding in northern Mexico." He saw some looks of concern from the crowd.

"How bad's the flooding in Mexico?" asked Black Beard, sounding genuine.

Grant looked around at the now-attentive group. "It's bad, actually terrible. When we flew over, it looked like the river was flooding for miles in every direction." By the positioning of their vehicles, he guessed the protestors had driven down the east side of the river through the farmland. They would have seen the makeshift shacks and huts. "It looked like many of the small homes were decimated."

"We saw some bodies floating in the water," Shauna added, from behind.

Grant saw some heads drop and some shoulders sag.

"What about upstream?" asked the blond guy, who had calmed and now almost looked civilized.

Grant looked around. "Well, Headgate Rock Dam in Parker, Arizona failed, the Palo Verde and Imperial Dams were intentionally broken to prevent breach, but we don't know about the Morales Dam in Mexico."

The blond man's eyes flared. "We don't care about your dams."

Grant considered the rebuff. "How about the destruction we saw south of Parker Dam, and the bodies we saw floating there? How about the areas below Laughlin where a whole community of houses and buildings were washed away? Or what about the trailer park below Headgate Rock Dam that was totally destroyed when the flood carried them downstream and piled them up against a railroad bridge? How about yesterday in the Grand Canyon, when hikers and float trips were caught in the flood? We don't have the death toll from that yet."

"That's not our fault," the blonde said tentatively.

"Oh? I thought that's what you were here celebrating," said Agent Williams.

Grant stared into their eyes, the ones that were still looking up. Most showed compassion. The young brunette looked like she might cry.

"We're here to celebrate the freedom of the river," Black Beard said. "That doesn't mean we're happy about the people who died."

Grant thought they were getting close to the issue. "But you support what was done?" asked Grant. "Blowing up the dams? Isn't that why the Sierra Club sent you?"

Black Beard hesitated.

"Yes!" yelled the blond. "It had to be done."

Grant saw heads nod, but none as enthusiastic as the blonde. Black Beard's face showed concern. Others turned and looked at the blonde as if he were crazy. Grant scanned back and forth quickly to assess how many true supporters of bombing the dams there really were. He guessed that most of this group, like in similar groups, were followers. Although passionate about the environment, they would never consciously kill people to achieve their goals. Even Black Beard seemed reluctant to kill. Only the blonde and one of the women had enough hate in their eyes.

Black Beard spoke. "We're members of The Sierra Club, but they didn't send us out here or make the sign. We did that on our own. I don't know whether the Sierra Club supports the bombing, but a spokesman on the news this morning said the attack was inevitable. It was only a matter of time. We would have preferred the river be restored peacefully, but we all know that's impossible."

"Look!" someone shouted. "Another helicopter."

The conversation was forgotten as both groups turned and looked into the sky.

"Get the sign turned around," said Black Beard, motioning with his arm. "It might be the news."

Grant looked ahead and saw the approaching helicopter. As it approached, he noticed it was in fact a media chopper. A tethered cameraman hung from an open door. The words *Channel 4 News, San Diego*, were printed on the side.

The chant, "Restore the Colorado. Restore the Colorado," started again.

Grant, Shauna, Agent Williams, and Lloyd were suddenly standing alone, having been abandoned by the protestors.

"What now?" asked Lloyd.

Grant scratched his head. "I don't know." He looked over at the group holding the banner. "I don't think anybody in that group is our man."

"What about that tall blonde guy?" Shauna asked. "He scared me."

Grant shook his head. "I don't know. He's got the passion for it, but —"

"He's not smart enough," said Lloyd. "These guys are just a bunch of hippies that decided to drive out here and get on TV." He pointed toward the group who were shuffling their feet to keep the banner aligned. "Look at 'em."

"Restore the Colorado. Restore the Colorado," they chanted enthusiastically.

"I hate to say it, but Lloyd's right," said Agent Williams. "I don't think he's in that group. He'd look different. He'd be different."

"There was one guy who did look different," said Shauna. "He was dressed better, cleaner."

"The guy in the polo shirt," Grant said.

"Yeah." Shauna nodded.

Lloyd shook his head. "Did ya see what Polo shirt he was wearin'?"

They all looked at the pilot. Grant shook his head.

"Dirty Devils," said Lloyd. "It's an off-road accessory store. He's the guy they recruited to bring the dune buggies." He pointed at the vehicles, then back at the group. "You think those bozos could get out here by themselves?"

While they were talking, the news helicopter had made a full circle around the banner. Grant saw that the cameraman then pointed his camera at the Vegas Tours chopper, not the protestors.

The pilot nudged Grant. "I think your secret mission into Mexico is now being viewed nationwide by 20 million cable subscribers."

Before Grant could respond, the helicopter broadcasted a message from its PA system. "Attention below! Floodwater is approaching. We recommend everyone leave this area immediately. Repeat. Floodwater is approaching quickly from the north. Please vacate this area while it is still possible."

Grant shielded his eyes from the setting sun and scanned in a northwest direction. How far out was it? He wondered if the news helicopter could actually see the water, or whether it was still a few miles out. Unfortunately, they wouldn't be able to tell until they got back up in the air.

The warning message had confused the protestors. A few released the banner and were running back toward the dune buggies. At least six or seven still held the banner as if nothing had changed. Eventually, they released it, but stood next to it arguing about what to do. The chant stopped. One of the runners was the guy in the polo shirt whom they guessed owned the buggies. He now waved frantically for the others to follow. Grant guessed that he had no intentions of donating his vehicles as martyrs to the Colorado River.

Grant looked at Lloyd. "Why don't you get on the radio in the helicopter and ask them how far —"

The other helicopter interrupted them. "Flood water is estimated to be less than four miles away". The guy broadcasting the message broke out of his formal tone and raised his voice. "This whole area will be underwater shortly. Please hurry to your vehicles and vacate immediately."

"Never mind," Grant said.

Without speaking, he turned and headed for the helicopter and the others followed. While still walking, Grant glanced back at the protestors. Only two remained at the banner: Black Beard, and the blonde. They were stretching it out on the ground. The rest sprinted across the sand toward the waiting dune buggies. A moment later Black Beard and the blonde abandoned the banner and ran off.

Lloyd reached the helicopter first and the turbine was already starting before Grant climbed into his seat. Lloyd flipped switches on the dashboard. When Grant pulled on his headphones he heard Lloyd talking. "Vegas Tours calling Channel 4 News. Do you read?"

"We read you, Vegas Tours," they responded.

"Do you currently have visual on the water?" Lloyd asked.

By now the rotors were turning fast enough to blur. Visibility was obscured by sand being blown in every direction.

"Negative, Vegas Tours; four miles was only an estimate from when we—" Grant heard another voice from the news helicopter, a woman's voice. "I can see it. Over there."

The first voice came back, "Affirmative, Vegas Tours. We now have visual on the floodwater. Looks to be about 2.5 miles northwest of here."

The helicopter lifted off. After they climbed out of the swirling sand, Grant saw that most of the protestors were loaded into the dune buggies. One of the vehicles had already turned around and faced east. Grant searched the northwest horizon as they gained altitude. The glare from the sun setting over the mountains on the west made it difficult to see. Finally, Grant noticed what looked like a gray line across the top of the sand. "It doesn't look like it's two miles away to me," said Shauna from behind. "More like a mile and a half, or less."

Grant pointed at the flood line. "Let's fly over it. I wanna see it." The helicopter accelerated in response.

"Vegas Tours, this is Channel 4 News." It was the woman's voice. "We couldn't help but notice the FBI coveralls. Can we assume that your party is affiliated with the U.S. government?"

Grant covered his mouthpiece with his hand. "Can they hear everything we say?"

Lloyd shook his head. "Not unless we hit the transmit button."

Grant didn't want to tell the reporter they were official government, especially since it wasn't true. Then again, he didn't want to say they weren't either. A "no" answer, coupled with their sighting of Agent Williams, would communicate some sort of secret mission. The last thing he wanted them to think was that the mission was confidential. It was a sure way to guarantee being broadcast nationwide immediately.

"Vegas Tours, this is Channel 4 News, do you copy?"

Grant swiveled and looked behind at the special agent. "What can I say to get her off our back? She knows we're government."

She stared back at him and shrugged. "I don't know. Denying it could be even worse."

Lloyd spoke. "How about you play it down a little? Tell 'em you're just inspecting damage or something."

Grant looked at Agent Williams and she shrugged again and held out her hands. Why hadn't he thought to make her change or something? That was the second time the FBI coveralls had sent the wrong message. It was a little hard to sneak into Mexico anonymously with an agent in uniform. He turned back into his seat and removed his hand from the microphone. Lloyd pointed to a transmit button on the dash.

Grant pressed the button. "Channel 4 News, we read you."

The woman came back immediately. "You are a US government party, correct?"

Grant could imagine her with her notebook and pencil ready. He wished he had a written statement in front of him. Ad-libbing didn't seem like the way to go on this one. He pressed the button. "We are on an inspection mission only. We're here in an unofficial capacity."

Silence, then, "Can I ask you a few questions?"

Lloyd shook his head. Grant agreed. "Negative, Channel 4. We are not at liberty to talk with the media." Grant grinned; that felt good.

"Mind if we tag along for a while?" she asked.

Grant looked and saw the news helicopter was already following them. "How do I get rid of her?"

"You want me to try and lose 'em?" asked Lloyd, grinning.

Grant stared at him. "Is that possible?"

"Sure. This thing's got way more horses than theirs. I should be able to out run 'em in a straight line, without even swerving around. Besides, they can't go too fast with that cameraman hanging out the door."

"Okay. Let's do it, then."

Lloyd banked and headed east. Grant noticed that they had dropped and were now only about ten or fifteen feet off the ground, traveling at an alarming rate.

"Vegas Tours, this is Channel 4, where are you headed?"

"We need to look around over on the east side," responded Grant.

Grant lifted his hand off the transmit button and looked over at Lloyd, who was in deep concentration. "Why are we so low?"

Lloyd responded without moving his eyes from below. "Just in case they've got radar."

"Vegas Tours, we are unable to keep pace with you." It was the pilot's voice.

Grant smiled at Lloyd, but remained focused ahead.

"How long will it take?" asked Grant. The speed felt comfortable when he wasn't looking down. But looking down made him sick. He imagined Lloyd sneezing and the landing gear digging into the sand, consequently flipping the helicopter into endless summersaults of wreckage.

"Just a few more minutes," said the pilot, without looking up.

Grant realized his hands hurt from clenching the sides of his seat. He forced them to relax. The helicopter swerved right and he clenched the seat again. Lloyd headed south at the same speed and altitude for a while. After a few minutes he swerved again, turning back west into the sunset. "Vegas Tours, we've lost you. Please give us your location," begged the newswoman, but they could hear the lack of hope in her voice.

Grant wasn't even tempted to respond, nor did he think they expected it. He saw that the sun had now dipped completely below the mountains. It would be dark in less than a half hour. The group sat in silence as the helicopter flew into the sunset.

* * *

8:40 p.m. - The Colorado River Delta, Mexico

The skinny man looked at the mountains to the west. The sun had already set and the sparse clouds contrasted ever so slightly with the dim orange sky behind them. He sat on the sand, propped back against a tire of his four-wheeler. Where was the water? He had over-estimated its speed. It should have reached him already. And he should be on the way back to his truck. The thought of it arriving after dark scared him. He might get caught in it.

He couldn't wait much longer. His four-wheeler had no lights. Not that it would've done any good in this desert, since there wasn't anything for them to illuminate. He scanned the sky for the moon, but saw nothing. He hadn't even brought a flashlight.

Something had been worrying him for the past half hour. When he drove out on the delta, he almost missed the lagoon. When he headed back in the dark, how could he possibly find his truck? Just a few degrees off and he would miss it by miles. And he would have no way of knowing whether he'd aimed too far north or south.

He craved another drink, but there was precious little water remaining. It had to be saved. He had spent enough time in the desert to know that things could get worse before they got better.

He pulled himself up and clomped in the boots over to the edge of the lagoon. The water was gone; only dry mud remained. This observation startled him until he remembered the lagoon was connected to the ocean. The explanation was simple enough; the tide had gone out in the last forty-five minutes. But it had gone so quietly he hadn't even heard it. He looked north and wondered if he would hear the floodwater approaching. Maybe not, he realized. All the more important to keep his eyes focused. With the sun already down, it would get dark fast, making it harder to see.

He walked back to the four-wheeler, vowing to wait only a few more minutes. The thought of having to leave before seeing the water arrive made him angry. After all he had done in the last two days, and after so many months of preparation, he deserved to see it. He deserved to take his time and frolic in the water, to feel it running between his fingers, and taste it. He licked his dry fingers as the fantasy passed through him. In hindsight, he should have detonated the bomb at Glen Canyon a couple hours earlier; it would have given him the time he needed.

Walking back to the four-wheeler, he stopped. What was that sound? He cocked his head. There, very soft, almost imperceptible. It wasn't a water sound, though. It sounded more like a broom being dragged through sand, a kind of swishing noise. His head shot up and he scanned the northern horizon. At first he saw nothing, only the endless gray sand. Then he noticed the top of the gray was alive – moving toward him. All at once he knew he had made a terrible mistake. This was much more water than he had anticipated. The entire horizon was pulsating. He sprinted to the four-wheeler and jumped on. He swiveled out the kick-starter and started kicking as hard and fast as he could. The engine turned over, but wouldn't fire. His heart raced. Not now. How could this be? He suddenly remembered the ignition switch between the handlebars. He turned the key and started kicking again. This time it almost took, then nothing. Had he flooded it? He gave it full throttle and kicked it twice to clean it out, then released the throttle and kicked again and it finally fired.

Looking back over his shoulder he saw the water less than 50 yards away. He slammed it in gear and gave it some throttle. As the quad took off, he felt the helmet and goggles, which he had left sitting on the rear rack, roll off the back. He considered stopping for them, but decided it wasn't worth it. It would soon be too dark for goggles anyway. He headed west toward his truck, knowing that the water would soon intercept him. But he couldn't resist. He had to see it. So he veered north toward the oncoming flood. He reached it almost immediately and veered southwest to stay just ahead of it.

The leading edge was small, only a few inches deep. It was traveling much slower than the twenty miles per hour he had heard on the radio. Of course, that was due to it spreading out on the delta. It meandered around small humps before rejoining itself. He was easily able to stay just out of its reach even in first gear, although jogging would have been a challenge. Tempting fate, once he allowed the water to catch his back tires, but when he accelerated, they spun and he wondered if he would be able to extract himself. He had to rock back and forth while feathering the throttle to get back ahead of it, and he felt lucky to have done it.

After a few minutes he saw water to the west, ahead of him. He felt stupid for screwing around. His only choice was swerve south, and go fast enough to get around it. He shifted to second, then third and applied full throttle. He rode that way for a few minutes. Eventually he could not see the water anymore. It was still coming, though. That he knew for sure.

He headed back west toward his truck, not straight toward it, because then the water would intersect him again, but at a southwest angle that would put him miles south of his truck. He rode this way for only a few minutes before he again saw the contrast of oncoming water. This panicked him and he veered directly south. The water was coming too fast for him to cross in front of it. He accelerated, but the four-wheeler bounced uncontrollably over the small dunes and he almost crashed. He slowed slightly and settled on what he considered top speed for the terrain. He knew it was not fast enough, though, and he had little hope of reaching his truck. After gaining some distance, he veered slightly southwest again, just in case.

CHAPTER 40

8:50 p.m. - The Colorado River Delta, Mexico

Grant looked ahead from the helicopter, but it all looked the same, and it was getting too dark. What if the environmentalist wasn't here? He had led this wild goose chase across the border for nothing. They would fire him for sure, and he would be the laughingstock of the Bureau. What if the Mexican police had already apprehended the man? Grant had never really given them a chance, but now he realized he might have underestimated them. They could have him in custody right now. Either way, Grant would look like an idiot, hijacking a helicopter and crossing the border against direct orders from the FBI. What had he been thinking?

"What's that up ahead?" Lloyd asked through the headphones.

Grant jolted in his seat. "What? Where?" He scanned the horizon for a person or some sort of vehicle. Maybe the environmentalist was driving a dune buggy like the protestors.

Lloyd motioned southwest of the helicopter, then quickly returned his hand to the controls. "Looks like bushes or something, in a line."

Grant saw what Lloyd was talking about. It was a line of bushes stretching north and south. At over a hundred miles per hour, the helicopter approached quickly and Grant saw that it was actually two lines of bushes with an expanse of dark sand in the middle. He recognized it immediately as the lagoon coming up from the ocean just south of the delta. The lagoon was mostly dry with only a few puddles, which told Grant the tide had withdrawn.

Lloyd slowed the helicopter. "Where now?"

Grant looked north. "I wonder how far the water is. It should get here pretty soon." He saw nothing, but it was dark and he knew the water was out there on the horizon, coming very quickly.

The helicopter hovered over the empty lagoon.

Grant pointed to the west shore, at the bushes on the shore. "He would be on that side."

"What makes you say that?" Special Agent Williams asked.

Grant considered the question. He had just assumed that the environmentalist would come from the highway on the west. He had no reasoning for it. In fact, the protestors had come from the east. "I don't know. I just figured —"

Lloyd interrupted. "You want to follow it north or south? We don't have much longer until we won't be able to see a thing."

Grant wanted to follow it north. He wanted to see the floodwater, but Shauna pointed out the front of the helicopter.

"Look!" she yelled. "The water."

Grant saw it too. A long, dark line moved toward them over the gray sand, both in the lagoon and outside of it. They all watched it come, mesmerized.

"How fast is that?" Shauna asked.

Lloyd answered. "It's slow, not much more than ten miles an hour." The water passed under the helicopter and Lloyd swiveled it so they could watch it flow downstream.

"Follow it," Grant commanded. He pointed toward the west shore. "Over there."

The helicopter moved forward and they angled southwest. They followed the water for several minutes. Visibility had dropped to less than a hundred feet.

"How long do you want to keep this up?" Lloyd asked.

Grant didn't know what to do. Part of him wanted to tell Lloyd to accelerate off in some direction, any direction. But what good would that do? They were looking for a needle in a haystack.

Just ahead of the helicopter the lagoon widened in front of them. To stay over dry sand the helicopter veered west for a few minutes. Then, as they rounded the wider section of the lagoon, Lloyd again aimed southwest.

"What was that?" Agent Williams' voice boomed through the headphones.

Grant scanned underneath the helicopter. "What?"

"Over there."

Grant couldn't see where she was pointing and had no idea where to look.

"There it is again! It's somebody." She touched Grant on his right shoulder. "He's on your side. He's in front of the water."

Grant finally saw him. It was a man riding a four-wheel off-road vehicle. The man looked like he had his hands full trying to keep the vehicle under control as it bounced over small clumps of sand and dodged the sparse weeds and brush that grew throughout the dry delta. The man swiveled his head as if he had just noticed the helicopter, then swerved hard right and disappeared into the darkness.

"He's gone," Agent Williams yelled.

The helicopter moved in the direction where they had last seen him. Grant felt a wave of excitement. Could this be him? It made sense, except for the fact that this guy seemed so – he couldn't think of the word – well, weak. Or was he overreacting to how skinny the man was?

"Give me my gun back," Agent Williams said from behind.

Grant flinched. That thought had never occurred to him. Was she going to just shoot him from the air, without even finding out for sure if he was the right guy? Grant reached down on the floor between his feet and carefully brought the gun up and handed it over his shoulder to the special agent. He heard the mechanical sound of her checking the chamber.

Lloyd swept the helicopter back and forth along the front of the slow-moving line of water, but they saw nothing. They searched for what Grant thought to be five minutes, but he didn't trust his sense of time with his heart racing. It was almost completely dark. The man could not have gotten away. There was no place to go.

"There he is!" It was Shauna's voice. Grant saw her reach up and point over Lloyd's left shoulder.

The helicopter banked left. Grant saw him again. They were almost on top of him. The skinny man looked up at them for an instant, craning his neck. The quick look nearly cost the man, as the four-wheeler hit something and he was almost bucked off. He must have lost the accelerator in the motion because the helicopter passed over him and they lost him again.

"There he goes!" Agent Williams said. "Due west."

The helicopter swerved and Lloyd positioned himself approximately three car lengths behind the bouncing four-wheeler, enough space to react. The next time when the driver jigged left, Lloyd followed.

* * *

9:10 p.m. - Colorado River Delta, Mexico

He couldn't believe it. How had they found him? He swerved east again and applied full throttle. He bounced over a mound of sand and sagebrush and nearly crashed, which forced him to back off the throttle. The loud whopping sound of the helicopter told him that they were right behind him. He veered south. They were still there.

He applied more throttle and prepared for another swerve to lose them. He scanned ahead, but his visibility was almost nil. Up ahead he saw the lagoon widen in front of him. He was too far east. He would get trapped. He veered southwest and tried to close the gap before the water trapped him. When he finally rounded the corner of the lagoon, the floodwater had only been ten feet away. He stayed in fourth gear full throttle and aimed again in a southwesterly direction. He had to try to get around it. After running in the same direction for a few minutes and no longer able see the water behind him, he swerved west. The helicopter was right behind him.

Since his angle of due west was perpendicular to the direction of the water, he knew he couldn't hold his heading long, or the water would catch him. He was preparing to turn when unexpectedly the four-wheeler spun around in a huge spray of water. He grasped frantically to hold on. He was instantly soaked and he blinked to clear his eyes and gasped for air. He knew in no time at all the water would be too deep for the quad, so he slammed it down one gear and goosed the throttle, aiming in the direction he thought was south. The tires spun. He relaxed the throttle slightly and they bit. He felt the water behind him almost shoving the vehicle ahead. Miraculously, seconds later he was back on dry ground. The helicopter was still right behind him. He aimed due south, forgot the swerving, and accelerated. He needed some distance from the water before he tried anything else.

He maintained a fairly straight course for a few minutes, veering only to miss a clump of brush. Although he hadn't completely given up, he knew that the chances of losing the helicopter were slim. The pilot was too good. And even if he could lose the chopper, the water was going to force him so far south that he would never get back to his truck. He would miss it by twenty miles. A thought occurred to him. How would they be able to apprehend him, with the water encroaching so fast? They couldn't set the helicopter down, or it would get washed away too. Although he saw no exit for himself, the thought that the people in the helicopter had no clear option either gave him a sliver of hope.

With his eyes watering and the lack of light, he didn't see it at first. When he did, it was too late. In a fraction of a second he saw the ground in front of him raise a couple feet into a hard crested bank, then drop off abruptly into a flat wet sandy area. He knew immediately it had to be the north tip of the Gulf of California. At over thirty miles an hour, the quad hit the raised area like a ramp and it shot him into the air over the wet sand. Releasing the throttle at the last minute had only worsened the trajectory of the vehicle, making it land in a severe front-down position. His body was launched forward onto the handlebars by the abrupt landing, causing the quad to veer sharply. The motion was too severe and he was thrown off an instant before the quad rolled. He thought he had landed clear, but felt the quad roll over his leg. The impact only lasted a second, but he felt an unmistakable snapping sensation.

His body slid to a stop, and amazingly he felt no pain. He was lying in a puddle of wet sand. His tongue tasted salt. He struggled up on his side and looked at the quad. It was upside down with a front tire still spinning. He looked at his leg and saw it jutted awkwardly to the side, still with no pain. He needed to get up and get going. But even if a miracle occurred to roll the quad back over, how would he start it with a broken leg?

He looked north toward the crest just in time to see the gray floodwater roll over the top and head toward him. This was it. He laid his head back and relaxed. He had no regrets. A small miscalculation would end his life, but not before a string of successes that would be talked about for generations. The fact that he would be a victim of his own destruction seemed to fit somehow. It was not the way he planned it, but compared to getting caught and living the remainder of his life in prison, it was the preferable alternative. He was ready to die, and wondered how long it would take for the water to reach him. He didn't know much about drowning, or how bad it would hurt, but he welcomed it.

The loud whooping noise of the helicopter was still there in the background. But he didn't care, and tried to ignore it. The noise, however, increased in intensity until it became almost deafening. He was buffeted by the wet spray and sand from its rotors. He turned his head and held his arm up to shield the spray. He tried to roll, to escape from the turbulence, but his leg protested with intense pain. A blindingly intense light illuminated him from the helicopter.

* * *

9:15 p.m. - Gulf of California, Mexico

"Did you see that?" screamed Shauna from the rear seat. "He's probably dead."

The quad had abruptly swerved left when it hit the beach, and then rolled multiple times before stopping upside down. It was hard to focus in the dwindling light.

"The water'll reach him any minute," said Agent Williams.

Lloyd motioned at the silver handle on Grant's right. "Use the spot."

Grant spun the handle and saw that it maneuvered the spotlight just outside the cabin. He aimed it down and flipped the switch to illuminate below. He swept it wildly for several seconds while he got the feel of it. He found the man lying on his back, his right leg bent awkwardly to the side. The man seemed dazed.

Lloyd brought the helicopter in close and the man lifted his hand up to shield his eyes. Grant only saw his eyes for a second, but it was enough. It was him, the bomber. Here was the man who had blown up the Glen Canyon Dam, and the Colorado River Aqueduct, the same guy who tried to blow up Davis Dam and poison the All American Canal. Here was someone who would stop at nothing to restore the Colorado River, even if it meant killing innocent people. He was seconds from drowning in the flood he had created, seconds from being buried in the delta he had tried so hard to restore. What justice did he deserve? If they rescued him and took him back to America, his trial would be a media circus. Lawyers would line up to defend him. The liberals would scream for a presidential pardon. It would divide the country, Grant was sure of it.

But even in that fraction of a second, Grant had seen something else. Although Grant did not agree with what this man had done, he understood.

There was no decision to make. Grant shucked the headphones, opened the door and jumped from the helicopter, which was now only six feet from the ground. He landed off balance, fell, and rolled in the wet sand. Disoriented from the dark and the rotor turbulence, Grant stood, shielding his eyes from the swirling wet sand. His knees and arms were wet from the beach. An instant after regaining his feet, he felt water run over them. The floodwater.

The floodlight swept erratically after Grant released it. With the light moving back and forth, he searched for the environmentalist. The water had risen almost to his knees. Finally he caught a glimpse of him, and slogged in that direction. When Grant reached him, he was on his back in the water flailing his arms. Grant grabbed his shoulders. He yelled to the man. "Who are you?"

The man stared up at him before reaching for Grant's hand. He didn't answer.

Grant pulled him up and put the man's arm around his neck. The man grimaced in pain, then looked into Grant's eyes. Grant asked the question that was burning in his mind, although he already knew the answer. "You're him, aren't you? You're the one who's been blowing up the dams?"

The man nodded in affirmative, then his eyes rolled up into his head as if he might pass out. The water was rising quickly and was almost to their waists. The man's eyes came back to life and Grant tried to move him toward the helicopter.

"Hurry!" warned Lloyd from the helicopter.

As Grant dragged the man forward in the rising water, he saw the helicopter moving to meet him. They were close when Grant tripped and both men went down. Grant went under. The water felt gritty. He hoisted himself back to his feet and grabbed the environmentalist again. He wondered how on earth they would be able to get the man to the helicopter, but then noticed that Lloyd had positioned the landing gear right in front of them. The pilot kept the chopper close and dipped the landing gear in the water. Grant grabbed on, and helped the man loop his arms over also. The water behind pressed them against the chopper for a second before Lloyd lifted and both men were pulled out of the water. Although Grant had both arms over the landing gear at his armpits, his body and wet clothing felt heavy and he wondered how long he could hold on.

He looked over and saw the other man was struggling. He had the look of pain in his eyes. Grant shouted to be heard over the noise of the rotors. "Hold on!"

The man nodded, but he didn't look like he could go much longer. He looked back at Grant, and stared for a moment.

Grant repositioned his arm over the other man's shoulder to help. The helicopter smoothly accelerated and they skirted the gray water. Grant wondered if Lloyd could find a place to set them down. He knew he couldn't last very long. He saw the environmentalist's eyes roll into the top of his head again, then his eyelids close for a while. The helicopter jerked and the man's eyes opened and focused on Grant's. Although the noise of the rotors made communication impossible, Grant's eyes and the environmentalist's locked. "Who are you?" Grant mouthed.

The man shook his head. Grant thought his lips mouthed, "It doesn't matter."

Grant agreed. It didn't matter. Although he already knew the answer that all of America wanted to know, Grant asked the question anyway. "Why?"

Grant saw recognition in the other man's face. The man looked down at the black water below the helicopter, then he stared upstream at the blackness that obscured the Colorado River Delta. The man stared back into Grant's eyes and smiled. Not a funny smile, nor an evil or mischievous smile. It was subtle and reserved, and communicated satisfaction and happiness. Grant felt the muscles in the man's arms relax. Grant tensed and stared into his eyes.

"No!" he shouted. "Don't!"

But the man just looked back at Grant. He let himself slip down until he was holding the landing gear with only his hands. Grant lunged and put his arm over the environmentalist's hand. The man stared at Grant for a brief moment, then closed his eyes, and released his grip. Grant tried to hold him so he wouldn't fall. He didn't want to let him go. He didn't want to let him get away. He didn't want him to die. But he felt the man's hand slipping out from under his arm. He grabbed at his wrist, but the dead weight was too much. The man fell, still looking up at Grant, still with that subtle smile, still with those haunted eyes, dropping into the black water below. And then he was gone.

They searched for him. The helicopter swerved back and forth where the man dropped. Lloyd circled, and Special Agent Williams swept the spotlight back and forth. Grant hung on to the landing gear, and focused downward, afraid to blink.

But he saw nothing. He knew they wouldn't find him. He was gone. And so finally they gave up. Agent Williams opened the door and encouraged Grant while they flew him to a dry spot where they could land safely. Grant's arms ached from holding on, but he knew he would make it.

Looking down, there was only darkness, an endless expanse of black water, water that might have been in Lake Powell only the day before, and now flowed into the Gulf of California. The fresh water mixing with salt for the first time in seventy-five years.

EPILOGUE

September 10

9:30 a.m. - Highway 89, East of Kanab, Utah

Grant had not been back to Lake Powell since the disaster over two months before. For part of that time he had not been allowed. The two-month stretch since the bombings would always be remembered by him as a period of high highs and low lows, a period when sometimes he hated the world, and other times he could not believe his good fortune.

The previous day, Fred had retrieved Grant from the Las Vegas airport for a day at Hoover, then a drive to Glen Canyon. Hoover had changed dramatically since June when Grant had last seen it. Gone forever was Hoover-Two and the thousands of sandbags that had created her. Gone were the high water levels. Gone were the throngs of National Guardsman. Gone were the FBI special agents in their blue coveralls. All of these had been replaced by a new white high water mark on the rocks around Lake Mead, a testament to the height of the flood that would last for generations.

To Fred's question of whether anything looked different, Grant had responded that it almost looked like nothing had happened at Hoover. Fred had laughed and took Grant to see the spillways. On the way to the Nevada spillway, Grant noticed that two buildings, the snack bar and the gift shop, both which had been on the water side of Hoover-Two, were missing. Fred had explained that the water damage had been severe enough that they would both need to be rebuilt.

The Nevada spillway itself had changed dramatically. The round spillway tunnel dropping into the hillside had been severely eroded. It was no longer round. The concrete had been stripped off the bottom showing exposed jagged rocks. The shape was almost square now, except for the bottom left, which looked like it had a deep tear in it. Deeper in the mountain, Grant could see more places where the concrete was completely gone and where large openings expanded beyond his vision. Inside the concrete retaining walls where Grant had authorized demolition, the ragged concrete edges had been worn smooth by the water. Only a small stream, maybe three or four feet deep, still flowed down the spillway, as the water in Lake Mead had almost dropped below the spillway openings.

Grant asked Fred if the Arizona spillway was worse or better. Instead of explaining, Fred drove him over. Although the erosion seemed less severe inside the spillway itself, the concrete arch bridge spanning the Arizona spillway had been weakened enough to warrant future demolition and replacement.

Fred explained that in a week or two, after the water in the dam had lowered enough to completely dry out the spillways, inspection crews would descend on ropes deep inside. They expected to find huge caverns hollowed out by the forces of the water.

After the tour at Hoover, the two men had headed northeast on I-15 toward St. George, Utah. The two-hour journey and dinner afterwards had given them ample time to rehash the events of the two dramatic days in June. Although Grant had known Fred for years, June had changed their relationship. They were bonded by the experience, and both knew they would be close friends for life.

During the conversation over dinner, Fred asked if Grant had heard from Roland Blackwell. Fred had smiled when he asked the question, knowing the answer. Of course he hadn't heard from Roland, nor would he ever. Roland and Grant had become bitter enemies in the aftermath of those two days. Fred had joked that they should make up and spend Thanksgiving together. Grant laughed and agreed that the only time the commissioner would be allowed in his home would be when Grant had a carving knife in his hand.

Back in June, when Grant and the others had flown back from Mexico into the United States, without the environmentalist, and had told their story to the authorities, federal charges were filed against Grant for illegal pursuit across international borders, illegal border crossing, and even abetting a felon. Although all charges were eventually dropped, Roland and the Bureau of Reclamation had placed Grant on disciplinary suspension while they conducted their own internal investigation. To add insult to injury, the Bureau had filed a restraining order against Grant preventing him from approaching within ten miles of any dam or edifice controlled by the Bureau of Reclamation.

As part of the suspension, Grant had been warned not to talk to any media representatives, or he would be immediately terminated and his pension would be forfeited. Although Grant had thought the treatment was unfair, he had tolerated it, thinking that eventually the truth would be known. However, when the Bureau publicly blamed Grant for the failures of Head Gate Rock, Palo Verde, and Imperial Dams, Grant had heard enough. In mid July, he agreed to a series of interviews on television to clear his name. He told the truth, including the Bureau's lack of support for Hoover-Two, which experts agreed had saved Hoover, Davis, and Parker Dams. Governor Rally Jenkins of Nevada appeared on Larry King Live and backed up Grant's story. The Bureau of Reclamation fired Grant in retaliation. Grant reported his treatment on national news. The public believed Grant. A media circus followed, and editorials around the country screamed for the government to throttle management at the Bureau of Reclamation. The Bureau became a public example of big bad government. A week later, Roland Blackwell resigned, saying that he wanted to spend more time with his family. The next day, Grant was reinstated at the Bureau, and the President of the United

States flew to Colorado and held a press conference, publicly thanking him for his heroic efforts at Hoover and the other dams downstream. The helicopter flight into Mexico was never mentioned.

No, Grant and Commissioner Blackwell would never be friends.

After dinner in St. George, Grant and Fred retired to separate rooms of a small motel on St. George Blvd. They awoke early, ate a quick breakfast, then drove toward Lake Powell. They talked continuously and marveled at how the country had reacted to the bombings.

After the dust settled in late June, the environmentalists went crazy. There were parades in Las Vegas and Los Angeles. T-shirts were sold by the thousands. Many showed a picture of the Glen Canyon Dam being blown up by a mushroom cloud of fire. The Los Angeles Times and other prominent newspapers across the country showed a front-page color shot of some pelicans swimming in the restored Colorado River Delta in Mexico. Environmentalists dominated TV talk shows and speculated how fast the delta would recover. They hypothesized how many birds would return, and guessed at how many fish would nest in the delta next year and the year after. There were environmental theories in abundance and the media seemed willing to oblige them all.

By the fourth of July, a rumor took hold that the bomber had survived. Many claimed to have seen him. Some said he was short, some tall, but all described him as a skinny guy with a limp from his broken leg, both of which had been reported in the news. Some said that he was living in Mexico, but the majority opinion had him moving to Oregon where he was preparing to single-handedly do something to stop deforestation.

For the first few days after the incident, helicopters had flown grid patterns over the Gulf of California searching for his body. They found the four-wheeler, but not the environmentalist. The missing body fueled the rumors that he was still alive, but Grant didn't believe it.

By early July, the FBI had raided the RV storage facility in Page and confiscated the first white pickup. They had already retrieved the second truck, parked just off the highway in Mexico. From the two vehicles, they figured out the bomber's identity, which led them to cell phone records of the phones used to detonate Glen Canyon, credit card receipts for food and gas on the bomber's route, and a rundown house in East Las Vegas with traces of ammonium nitrate fertilizer in the back yard. They also found some unused homemade detonators in one of the kitchen cabinets. The license plate on a motorcycle parked in the garage matched one that passed through a roadblock in Utah the morning of the first bombing. They released the name of the bomber (more commonly referred to in the media as the environmentalist) as Jeffrey Calhoun, an electronics technician employed by a large lighting contractor in Las Vegas. Co-workers described him as a social recluse with no close friends, but very smart, especially with electronic devices. Neighbors described him as private. Most of his acquaintances were aware of his environmental concerns, and in fact many considered him fanatical. An elderly woman next door said that Calhoun refused to water his lawn, eventually converting the landscaping to cactus, and encouraged her to do the same. She refused, however, maintaining a healthy green lawn, which had seemed to irritate Calhoun.

At the public release of the perpetrator's identity, the environmental community vacillated back and forth on whether to embrace or vilify him. The Sierra Club, Greenpeace, and the Glen Canyon Institute all confirmed he had once been a paid member of their organizations, but that his memberships had lapsed. Greenpeace, in a widely attended and televised ceremony, announced an honorary lifetime achievement award to Jeffrey Calhoun and installed him into their hall of fame for positive environmental actions. The Sierra Club, on the other hand, tried to distance itself from him, claiming that they believed Calhoun was not the perpetrator, but had been framed by a right-wing conspiracy cooked up by the federal government. They had no explanation for why Calhoun had not been seen since those two days in June.

As Grant and Fred started getting closer to Lake Powell, Grant started to feel giddy. He knew that seeing the remnants of the dam would bring back strong emotions. The image he saw when the Gulfstream had flown over the dam back in June, where a huge column of water sprayed out of the face of the dam, would haunt him for the rest of his life.

Fred interrupted Grant's thoughts. "Look at that," he said, pointing up ahead. "I thought they weren't going to tell anybody about this."

Grant saw a bunch of cars parked off both sides of the road. "They weren't," he agreed. "There must've been a leak."

When Fred reached the other cars, he had to weave through them like a gauntlet. The crowd converged on the car and yelled. What they were saying was impossible to decipher. One girl held a sign that said "DON'T DROWN GLEN CANYON AGAIN. LET IT LIVE." Grant noticed that a couple of the vehicles were Volkswagen buses. He wondered what was up with environmentalists and the Volkswagen bus. How could someone claim to care about the environment then drive a car that belched out blue smoke?

After passing through the protestors, Fred stopped at a police roadblock. While a policeman checked Fred and Grant's credentials and marked their names off a list on his clipboard, Grant looked back at the group. Among the waving signs, he saw a small girl, who couldn't have been older than ten, waving a sign that said, "DAMN THE DAMS."

The policeman waved them through.

"Wow," Fred said. "They must think something's up."

In the days following the bombings, environmentalism had reigned. The media was flooded with calls for legislation to assure that none of the dams on the Colorado be rebuilt, and that the delta be guaranteed an allocation of water for fishery and waterfowl habitat restoration. Public opinion, at least temporarily, seemed to support the environmentalists. The Democrats in the House of Representatives wrote a bill that would permanently outlaw any repair or rebuilding of Glen Canyon, Head Gate Rock, Palo Verde, or Imperial Dams. Additionally, they suggested that the United States immediately negotiate a treaty with Mexico, prohibiting Mexico from rebuilding the Morales Dam. The legislation would essentially leave Hoover as the only major dam on the Colorado. Initially unnoticed, deep inside the bill, was buried text that would have prevented repair of the California Aqueduct.

Although the press initially lauded the legislation as "exactly what this country needs," the farmers in Mexico, the farmers of Imperial Valley, native Americans of the Colorado Indian Reservation, and farmers in the Palo Verde Irrigation District all immediately announced opposition to the legislation, saying it would ruin the lives of hundreds of thousands of farmers on the lower Colorado. A little slower to react were the communities in California, Arizona, and Mexico, who would be starved of their allocations of culinary water from the California Aqueducts, Central Arizona Project, and the Mexican diversions.

The last and most surprising opposition to the bill came from recreationalists. Although millions of middle class Americans loaded up their boats every weekend and headed for the nearest body of water to fish, water-ski, jet-ski, sun bathe, gamble, camp, ride motorcycles, stay in house boats, hike, skinny dip, consume alcohol, and ogle the bronzed flesh of the opposite sex, they had historically been an easy target, legislatively speaking.

Over the years they had endured closures of lakes for endangered fish, restrictions on speed, closures to off-road vehicles for tortoises, closures of hunting areas, no wake zones, restrictions on motor size, restrictions on oil type, elimination of personal watercraft in certain areas, closures of sand dunes to protect milkweeds, restrictions of two-stroke outboard engines, etc. However, the draining of Lake Powell, a mecca for over three million recreationalists a year, had struck a nerve.

In late July, the Sierra Club organized a celebration at the site of where the Glen Canyon Dam had been. Thousands of environmentalists attended. However a much larger group of recreationalists, estimated at over thirty thousand, showed up to communicate their displeasure. Police staffing had been grossly underestimated. The two groups came together and communicated passionately. With virtually no law enforcement present, and a fifteen to one advantage, the recreationalists won handily. Hospitals in St. George, Utah reported treating over a hundred fractured noses. The Glen Canyon Massacre, as it would be known, shifted the momentum. The media took an anti-recreationalist bias, calling the boaters "thugs", and in retaliation, a million newspaper subscriptions were cancelled across the country. A movement began and congressmen and senators were called, emailed, written, and faxed. Republicans wrote a trillion-dollar appropriations bill to rebuild the Glen Canyon Dam and restore Lake Powell, more than a thousand times its original construction cost. The debate was on.

Environmentalists argued that the Colorado River had been overly regulated and diverted, the evidence being a sand dune-swept river delta that no one in the United States had known about two months before. Recreationalists, city dwellers, farmers, Mexicans, and Native Americans, argued that God and the U.S. government had given the river to them for their use, and they had a right to use it. The country was split.

On September 1st, two months after the bombings, the Republican President of the United States, who some called a liberal, and others called a right wing fanatic, flew Air Force One to Yuma, Arizona, where he, along with a smattering of senators, both Republican and Democrat, boarded six helicopters. They first flew to Mexicali, Mexico, to pick up the newly elected President of Mexico, then south over the delta – a place none of them, including the Mexican President, had ever seen.

Although no media representatives were present, a leak in the President's staff described the tour as eye opening. The delta was much bigger than anticipated, covering a thousand square miles. What appeared to be hundreds of thousands of birds, but easily could have been millions, had already returned to the delta in huge flocks. Judging by the activity in the water, millions of fish had migrated upstream into the shallow water. At one point a helicopter flying lower than the others had spooked a flock of birds, forcing the chopper to take evasive action to avoid, at the very least, an embarrassing incident, if not an actual crash.

As a surprise to the entire group, and speculated to have been decided on the spur of the moment, the main helicopter with the two Presidents hovered at water level, and both presidents hopped out with bare feet and their pants rolled up to their knees. The water could not have been more than a foot deep. The helicopters backed off and let the two men wade around and talk about whatever they were talking about. The leak estimated they were in the water for about twenty minutes. Pictorial evidence of the wading party was not released by the White House. The trip had been ten days before. The White House said nothing of the event. No press conferences. No statements to the press. Nothing. However, in the week since the trip to Mexico, the President had been meeting with key members of Congress and the Senate, both Republicans and Democrats. Details of the meetings were not shared with the press, and remarkably, all congressmen and senators declined questions. The media and the entire country knew the subject of the talks, however. Unnamed sources revealed they were talking about appropriations bills to rebuild the dams on the Colorado River.

Environmentalists were not happy. TV, radio, and newspaper editorials called for the President to back off. A million-environmentalist-march was scheduled in the capital. Recreationalists, who now called themselves "working citizens with boats", farmers, Native Americans, and a mixture of smaller groups that stood for all kinds of things from hydroelectricity to culinary water rights, demonstrated all across the country. The number of supporters for the pro-dam movement was respectable, and surprising to many.

As Fred rounded the last turn, and the view opened to what should have been the Glen Canyon Dam, Grant first noticed the roadblocks on both sides of the canyon stopping motorists from driving off the cliffs where the silver arched Glen Canyon Bridge had once been. Although partially obscured by the visitor center, a glance to Grant's left showed the empty expanse where the dam should have been, lined by shards of severed concrete still hanging from the rock wall. Across the canyon and up on the hill was the small city of Page, which was now isolated from the west by the missing bridge.

As Fred pulled the car to the entrance of the visitor center parking lot, they were stopped again. Their ID's and names were carefully checked. Grant was surprised to see that when the man flipped pages on the clipboard, the sheets contained photos of each invitee. They were checking pictures of every person. Grant had never heard of that. Finally they were waved through and told where to park. The front lot was almost full, the rear cordoned off and completely empty. Grant noticed five TV vans behind yellow tape in the corner of the front lot, one from each of the three national networks, one from Fox, and another from CNN. The little guys had obviously not been invited.

Grant and Fred straightened their ties and retrieved their jackets from the back seat before walking into the visitor center. Luckily, the air conditioning was running full blast, as the Arizona heat was much too hot for suits, even in mid September. After his eyes adjusted, Grant recognized Governor Rally Jenkins of Nevada over by the windows in conversation with a group of other men. When the governor saw Grant, he politely excused himself from the crowd and walked over to meet them.

The governor shook Grant's hand firmly. "Mr. Stevens. Nice to see you again."

Grant nodded. "Governor."

The governor winked at him. "You seem to have survived the challenges to your reputation."

Grant nodded. "I appreciated your comments." The governor's statements had gone a long way in swaying public opinion.

The governor looked around to verify that no one else was listening, then leaned close. "Well, off the record, if Roland Blackwell and those other morons had been making the decisions, we would have lost Hoover Dam. And, as you know, things would have been a lot worse downstream."

Grant knew the governor was right.

The governor stood up straight. "So what do you think about what happened in Washington last week?"

Grant shrugged. "I've never seen politicians be so secretive. Usually somebody spills the beans."

The governor laughed. "I agree. The President must have some serious leverage we don't know about." He glanced around nervously. "You guys work for the Bureau. What's going to happen here today?"

Grant smiled. He was going to ask the governor the same question. "We only know what you do. An important press conference. Mandatory. Be there."

The governor nudged Grant. "Come on. A week of political jockeying, followed by a press conference at the site of the Glen Canyon Dam. What else could it be? He's got the votes."

Grant nodded, but held out his hands. "Sounds logical, but then again, this President goes both ways. Who would have expected the trip to Mexico? He might announce that he agrees with the environmentalists, and he's going to let the river run."

The governor smirked. "Are you kidding? This guy has never voted for anything environmental in his life. None of those whackos voted for him, and none of them ever will, no matter what he does. And he knows it."

Grant agreed with the logic, except that none of the Democrats in Washington were talking about the secret negotiations, which meant they had something to gain. Of course, the Republicans weren't talking either, which made it even more confusing. Grant was trying to think of an answer when the governor saw someone else and quickly excused himself. They watched him go.

"At least we're not the only ones in the dark," Fred said.

Grant saw a contingency of managers from the Bureau of Reclamation over by a buffet of hors d'oeuvres. Bruce Godfrey of River Hydraulics was among the group. Grant and Fred walked over and joined them. Bruce was uncharacteristically quiet and nervous. Grant wondered if Bruce had heard something. For the next half hour, the crowd in the visitor center continued to grow. Although Grant didn't know most of them, he recognized many as Washington politicians he had seen on TV. Finally, a few minutes before 11:00 a.m., a helicopter could be heard. It landed in a vacant spot in the rear parking lot. The crowd was ushered outside and to the rear lot, where Grant noticed a small platform had been erected on the edge of the canyon. A podium with a half dozen microphones had been placed in the center of the platform. On each side of the podium were two large easels covered with canvas.

The President of the United States exited the helicopter surrounded by a throng of Secret Service personnel all wearing dark sunglasses. As he worked his way to the podium, he greeted the Senate Minority leader, a Democrat, and they shook hands and smiled at each other, although the entire country knew the two men despised each other. The pack of people from the visitor center jockeyed for good spots close to the podium. Grant and Fred remained farther away under the shade of one of the few sparse trees in the lot. The national news networks had set up their cameras about five car lengths from the podium, so they could get the steep canyon walls and the Colorado River in the backdrop.

When the President approached the platform he was followed by the Senate majority leader, a Republican, and the Senate minority leader. Right behind them were the top-ranking Republicans and Democrats from the House of Representatives. An aid with a clipboard gave them all last-minute instructions. He pointed at the microphones and then at one of the covered easels, raising the canvas slightly, but not enough to uncover the display under it. The president nodded repeatedly. The two Senate leaders were positioned next to the easel on the left side of the platform, and the two representatives next to the one on the right. A woman touched up the President's hair, and brushed something off his cheek. Another aid stepped to the microphones, tapped one a couple times then said "test" until somebody gave him a thumbs up. Grant noticed that almost all the networks were already filming, their news anchors most likely speculating on what the President might say. Grant wished he and Fred were closer so they could listen. By 11:05 a.m., the anxious crowd had waited long enough. The President finally stepped to the microphones.

"Ladies and gentlemen, I speak to you today from the great state of Arizona, the exact site where two and a half months ago a terrible act of terrorism dramatically changed the canyon behind me and caused massive destruction for hundreds of miles downstream. I am joined today by leaders of both parties. . ." He turned and motioned to the four politicians behind him. ". . . on this important day."

"As you all know, this unique period of time since those two disastrous days in June has been eye-opening. Passion has been unleashed by many organizations, factions, communities, and races. Some would have us leave the Colorado River un-dammed and uncontrolled. Their voices have been loud, and amplified by many in the media. Others would have us rebuild these dams immediately, to restore their livelihoods, recreational areas, and in some cases, their drinking water." The President leaned forward and glared into the camera. "Unfortunately, many citizens of our country and the world are celebrating this act of terrorism, in spite of the staggering loss of life and property. I myself will not tolerate anyone celebrating the destruction of property and loss of human life for their own interests."

Grant wondered what the solution would be, since the President had just painted both sides of the argument as extremes, rebuilding the dams and not rebuilding them. Would he propose rebuilding only some of them?

The President continued. "First I'd like to say a few words about these dams and life on the Colorado River before them. According to historians, each spring as snow melted in the Rocky Mountains, the Colorado worked itself into a frenzy for three to five months. North of Black Canyon, for the most part, the river was trapped inside the rock walls of the Grand Canyon and Glen Canyon. However, south of Black Canyon, the river spread out and flooded everything from what is now Laughlin, Nevada all the way to the ocean in the Gulf of California. Nothing was safe. Farming was nearly impossible with too much water in the spring, then almost nothing in the late summer. A typical year on the Colorado was three to four months of floods, followed by a dry river for the remainder of the year."

"In the pre-dam years, Imperial Valley farmers in California discovered fertile soil and built a canal to their farms. With water, their farms flourished. But in 1904 a spring flood caused the canal to break, and the Colorado River changed course, diverting itself entirely into the Imperial Valley where it flowed for three years before the Southern Pacific Railway finally diverted it back into its channel and back to the ocean. That flood filled the valley with water, and refilled the Salton Sea."

"The dams dramatically changed life on the Colorado River. They completely eliminated the spring floods. They averaged the flow and allowed farmers to water year round. They allowed water to be stored and used to sustain life in desert cities like Las Vegas, Phoenix and Los Angeles, none of which could survive without water diversions. The electricity generated by these dams powered the west. The dams have also created recreational areas enjoyed by millions of people each year. Only fanatics would argue that the dams are bad. Only fanatics would argue that we should go back to the way it was before. It would eliminate some of the most fertile farmland in the country, and necessitate the relocation of millions of people."

"The Colorado River is the only large river in the southwest. We have a choice. We can let it run wild, flooding and eroding the landscape, then dumping into the ocean, without harnessing any benefit for man, or, we can completely control it, use it for drinking water, electricity, farming, and recreation for the citizens of the southwestern United States and Mexico."

The crowd cheered, interrupting the President's speech. Grant saw that even the two Democrats on the stand clapped, although not as enthusiastically as the

Republicans next to them. He wondered how the President had swayed them to his side. What about the environmentalists? Why weren't the Democrats siding with them? The President held out his hands and waited for the applause to subside.

"So, my friends in the House and the Senate will send me a bill to rebuild the Glen Canyon Dam." He turned and motioned into the dark red rock canyon where the dam had been only a few months before. "And we will restore Lake Powell."

The crowd clapped and cheered enthusiastically again, forcing the President to wait. Grant knew why the press conference was a private event and the environmentalists were not allowed past security. There would have been booing. There would have been people rushing the stage. Under the right circumstances, Grant knew that the environmentalists would kill the president if they could, for what he had just said.

The President pointed downstream. "The bill will also contain funding to repair the California Aqueduct, Head Gate Rock Dam, the Palo Verde Irrigation Dam, and Imperial Dam. Although Hoover, Davis, and Parker Dams survived, their spillways were extensively damaged by the sustained high flows. They will also be repaired."

Clapping followed, but this time more subdued.

"As a result of this catastrophe, our neighbors in Mexico also suffered deaths and extensive property damage, including the destruction of Morales Dam. This bill will send relief money to Mexico to help them rebuild as well. Senators—" He pointed at the easel and the two senators pulled the cloth off, exposing a map of the Colorado River with the dams marked that would be rebuilt. "This map shows our plan to restore all the dams."

Grant clapped unenthusiastically. He couldn't believe it. This was a rout. The Republicans were getting everything, and the environmentalists nothing. Although Grant wanted the dams to be rebuilt, he had expected concessions. This felt wrong. How had the President convinced the Democrats?

The President waited until the audience was completely quiet. "Now, let me admit something. The Colorado River catastrophe has taught Americans something we did not know, a secret that has been hidden for almost a century. Even most of the environmentalists didn't know about the Colorado River Delta. Over the years, more environmentalists protested to save the Salton Sea than the Colorado River Delta. The delta was just beyond our borders. It was on every United States map we've seen since elementary school. But none of us really knew what had happened to the delta. At the turn of the century, the Colorado River Delta covered thousands of square miles and the sky sometimes turned dark due to the clouds of birds. Historians report that jaguars, cougars, and bobcats patrolled the shores, and the water was teaming with schools of fish and swarms of shrimp. However, all that changed. For decades now, the delta has been reduced to wind-swept sand dunes, as dry as a bone. Our ancestors dried it up before most of us were born. When they killed the delta in the early 20th century, there were no environmentalists. There were no protests. No signs. No lying down in front of bulldozers. I personally feel that killing the delta was a travesty."

It was so quiet you could hear a pin drop. Grant saw that many mouths were gaping open. These were not the words they expected to hear from a conservative President.

"I'm aware that my political party gets a bad rap for its stance on the environment. And in truth, many times we find ourselves on the wrong end of environmental arguments. I would argue that it is because those disagreements generally pit 100% environmental agendas against compromises. I maintain that Republicans do not want to kill the environment, they are only searching for a compromise that they feel protects the environment while simultaneously serving the nation and the communities."

The President waved his hand back and forth.

"But we are not here today to debate party politics, or how parties are perceived. We have a crisis that necessitates a solution. Many in our nation think the Colorado River should be returned to the people, where 100% of the water is diverted to farms and cities and the delta dried up again, like it has been for the last century. We are not going to do that. Others want the river to be completely freed, where 100% of the water would flow into the ocean. They would advocate that the farms be shut down, and the citizens of the desert cities like Los Angeles and Las Vegas be relocated back to the east coast where there is more water. We are not going to do that either."

The President leaned forward and gripped the pulpit with both hands. His brows furrowed and his lips pursed.

"I believe that neither of those alternatives is the correct solution. They are both short-sighted and fanatical. What is needed here is a compromise, a way for the citizens to use water from the Colorado without killing the river. That is why I have been meeting with members of both parties in Washington."

He motioned at the other politicians on the stand.

"And that is why I also met with the new President of Mexico. I believe we all want the same thing here."

The President smiled mischievously. "Even the Democrats don't want to shut down Las Vegas and move everyone to Florida." He turned and casually pointed at the politician behind him. "Do you, Senator?"

The senator was obviously not prepared for the question. His face flushed and he stammered for a second before subtly shaking his head back and forth. Snickers could be heard from the audience, which made the senator blush even more.

"Of course not," the President continued. "So we needed a solution, a compromise that would satisfy both goals. Compromises always require sacrifice, and this situation is no exception. Sacrifices will be required from both sides."

The President gripped the podium with both hands again, and paused. His eyes swept the crowd. All were intently waiting for the finale.

"In 1922, the delegates of seven states – California, Nevada, Utah, New Mexico, Colorado, Wyoming, and Arizona signed the Colorado River Compact, an agreement to allocate an estimated 17.5 million acre feet of water from the Colorado River. A provision to ensure that 1.5 million acre feet per year reached Mexico was later backed up by an international treaty. Although history has shown that the original estimate of 17.5 million acre feet was too high, those two legal documents have guided water allocation on the river ever since. Both documents will be amended over the coming months."

"A small environmental group called The Sonoran Institute, one of the few groups focused on restoring the delta, has maintained over the years that if just 10% of the Colorado River were allowed to flow into the ocean year round, the delta would be largely restored. Our compromise will include that number."

Grant nodded. He looked around and saw that many others in the crowd were smiling.

"Our treaty with Mexico will be amended to double the allocation of water from 1.5 million to 3 million acre feet per year. Mexico will agree to allow half of their allocation to flow freely into the delta. Additionally, Mexico has embraced a plan to create a new entity called the Colorado River Delta National Preserve. They have been told it will be popular with American tourists."

The President pointed to the second easel, which the two congressmen uncovered. "Here is our plan for restoring the delta." The display showed the map of the delta including blue shading where water would cover the delta.

The crowd erupted in applause. The President motioned to the other politicians behind him who bowed and tipped their heads, obviously proud of what they had done.

The President held out his hands to quiet the crowd. "As I said before, compromise requires sacrifice. The allocations to all seven western states will be reduced, some more than others. Although many will be tempted to fight this decision in courts for years to come, I admonish all citizens in these states to accept this compromise, to adopt water rationing and recycling programs, and I promise you the water will do what you need it to do. One of the greatest sacrifices will be losing wonderful sites inside Glen Canyon again when we refill Lake Powell. I recommend that everyone interested come and see them now, while they are still accessible. Last time it took five years to build the dam and eighteen years to fill Lake Powell, so you have a while. But don't wait too long."

The President hesitated, taking a moment to glance at the four politicians behind him. "Although my colleagues and I would like to stay, we have a lot of work to do back in Washington. All seven states' legislators will need to ratify the new Compact, so they will also be busy. Besides, we have a new dam to build, so let's get this stuff cleaned up and get started. Oh, and by the way, we have a new commissioner of the Bureau of Reclamation, the organization that will rebuild all these dams. His name is Bruce Godfrey."

The President waved to a cheering crowd, then walked off the stand and started shaking hands. The news correspondents jumped in front of their cameras and gave commentary. The crowd milled around congratulating each other. Grant and Fred stood quietly under the tree.

Grant could not believe what the President had said at the end. Bruce Godfrey would head up the Bureau? That was awesome. No wonder Bruce had seemed nervous before the press conference. Grant glanced over at Fred, who nodded with raised eyebrows.

"Amazing," Grant mumbled.

"Looks like you guys are going to be busy for a while," Fred said.

Grant glanced down in the canyon and wondered how long it would take to rebuild the Glen Canyon Dam. In some ways the hard part was already done, with the foundation still in place from before. While Grant was thinking, he felt a hand on his shoulder. He thought it was Fred, but turned to see Bruce Godfrey.

"Already planning how you're going to rebuild it?" Bruce said, smiling.

Grant's eyes widened. "What do you mean? Are you saying . . ." He didn't dare say it.

"Well, haven't you dreamed about this your whole life?"

Grant glanced at Fred who was smiling broadly.

Bruce continued. "Of course you'll have to convince your wife and kids into moving out to the desert for a while. You could live in Page, but St. George is a little more civilized. But that would be a tough commute." Bruce tapped his index finger on his chin as if he were perplexing about the decision.

Grant wanted to hear the words. "What are you saying, Bruce?"

Bruce smiled. "I'm saying that I want you to be in charge when we rebuild the Glen Canyon Dam. Do you want the job or not?"

Grant was speechless. He wondered how many men it would take. He needed to put a rough schedule together. And what about the budget? He would need some help with the financials.

"Well?" Bruce asked impatiently. "You want me to get somebody else?"

Grant looked back at Bruce. "No. I want it!"

"Good. You're the man." Bruce turned to leave, then stopped, looking down into the canyon. "Oh, Grant. I want a better design this time. I don't want this dam to crumble for any one-man shows."

"Yes, boss," Grant said. He smiled as he watched his friend walk away. And as far as ideas for improving the dam, Grant Stevens thought he already had a few.

Author Notes

Since Wet Desert was my first book, and since I was in my forties when I finished, it means that I have either been writing for my whole life without success, or I had a mid-life crisis and decided to write a novel. In my case it was the latter.

As an electrical engineer by trade, I do not remember attending any creative writing classes. I never planned on writing a book, although I occasionally wished I were smart enough to write one. When I wrote emails, memos, or manuals for work, I considered myself a blunt and clear writer. But I read fiction at every opportunity.

In the early nineties while working as an engineer in California, I perused a friend's copy of the June 1991 edition of National Geographic and saw a story about the Colorado River. It was one of those stories where the author spends months traveling from one end to the other and meets people along the way. One of the pictures showed the remains of the Colorado River seeping into the sand and dying miles from its destination at the Gulf of California. I did not know before that moment that the river never reached the ocean. It shocked me, and I realized that it must really piss off the environmentalists. Not long after, I started telling my friends that someday I would write a book about an environmentalist taking matters into his own hands to restore the river. The only problem was, I had no idea how to write a novel.

I began collecting research and even visited Hoover Dam. But, I did not write. I didn't know how to start. After eight years, I started waking in the middle of the night thinking about the plot. Originally, my protagonist was to be a team of FBI agents, like Tommy Lee Jones' posse in the "Fugitive" and "U.S. Marshals", but the more research I did, the more I felt my character should be an engineer. In the summer of 2001, I was sorting through the mail and came upon a class listing for Saddleback College. Instead of tossing it, I scanned it for a Spanish class. But, I found something I was not expecting: "How to write a fiction novel." I enrolled immediately for my first college class in over ten years.

When I arrived that first night, I noticed the bulk of the class were not college kids, but old farts like me. It looked as if I was not the only person having a mid-life crisis. The teacher's name was Shelba Robison. She had crutches and a bum leg, so she did not stand. It was obvious she knew some of the other students, but it was not until she began talking that I learned many of the students had attended before, and the ones she didn't know, like me, were referred to as "newbies." She told us very clearly that if we were not writing a book, we were in the wrong class, and that we must all have a specific book in mind and be ready to write. On the first night, two students brought chapters for us to take home and review. All newbies were required to write a two-page outline of our book's plot, and meet Shelba in her office during the week to discuss whether the class was right for them.

I left the first night invigorated, and wrote my two-page outline in a couple of hours. After almost a decade of research, it came easily. When I met with Shelba, she eyed me skeptically, then asked to see my outline. I waited while she read it. Without finishing it, she looked up and asked if I knew enough about dams to write the book, and I told her about my years of research. She nodded and asked me if I was committed to the project. I responded that I was. She asked if I had a family. I confirmed that yes I was married and had four young kids. She grimaced and said the best thing would be to convince my wife I was having an affair until the book was done. I guess I convinced Shelba I was serious, because she let me stay in the class.

I started writing on Aug 30, 2001. I handed in my first chapter the next week. On Sep 12th, the day after the bombing of the World Trade Centers, the class sat in a circle and gave me feedback on my writing. Although I had thought my ten-page chapter was a masterpiece, my peers found it riddled with passive verbs, confusing points of view, and plain vanilla characters. But my classmates liked the story, and they argued enthusiastically about the plot. After a few minutes, Shelba interrupted them. She said, "As you can see, Gary has a very interesting story to tell; unfortunately, his writing is getting in the way of him telling it."

Over the next eighteen months, I repeated Shelba's class twice, and had a dozen chapters reviewed by my classmates. I would like to go on record now that Shelba Robison and my fellow authors from Saddleback College taught me what little I know about the craft of writing. I owe this book to them and wish I could name each of them individually.

Although many gave good input to my story and my writing, I would like to name six who made significant contributions: 1) Bruce Spencer, a pilot friend who flew me to Lake Powell, edited the entire manuscript, and gave invaluable insight into airplanes, helicopters, and houseboat life on Lake Powell, 2) Tom Glazier, a district attorney who edited the entire manuscript and helped with fishing scenes, law enforcement, and houseboats, 3) Uncle Earl Jolley, a lifelong heavy equipment operator who provided key information about bulldozers, building earth dams, and sandbags, 4) an anonymous engineer at the Bureau of Reclamation who helped me with water velocities in floods which established the timelines for flooding on the river, 5) my mother, who read the whole first draft and because she's my mom, saw virtually no problems, 6) and finally my wife Becca, who helped in all phases of the project, who read the manuscript out loud to me during editing, who corrected my grammar, who never gave up on me, and who put up with my fanatical focus through this entire ordeal over the past fifteen years.

Although it seems a little weird to thank God for helping in the creation of a novel about a terrorist, I can't deny that I was inspired to pursue this project, and motivated along the way. Maybe someday I will know why.

Since I began my research in the early nineties, things have changed dramatically on the Colorado River. Almost a decade of drought has lowered the reserves in both Lake Powell and Lake Mead to critical levels. As of midyear 2005, Lake Powell was down over a 130 feet and classified at under 45% of capacity. Lake Mead was also very low. If the Glen Canyon Dam were to fail under those conditions, Lake Mead would be able to capture the entire flood and make my story non-plausible.

As far as the explosives are concerned, I have done enough research to know what steps to leave out of the formula so as to prohibit someone using the book as a recipe. If the book seems real in spite of the fiction, then it means that at least in that regard, I accomplished what I wanted.

Lastly, I'd like to thank you for reading my book. I hope you liked it. Since the story is now published, and I have survived my midlife crisis, if you wonder about me, I will be perusing old issues of National Geographic to see if other stories need to be told, and to see if I learned enough writing craft from Shelba Robison to write a second book.

Gary Hansen

www.wetdesert.net

AWARDS & REVIEWS
for Wet Desert

Whitney Award Finalist - Best Novel by New Author

"It reminded me a great deal of reading a Tom Clancy novel, but it is faster paced and the device doesn't slow down the story. But like Clancy, the author welds together diverse story lines and characters into one highly suspenseful tale that has the reader reluctant to miss a word or to set the book down." – **Meridian Magazine**

"Wet Desert was an exiting novel, I relished the entire book. It was a supremely engaging story with a lyrically drawn sense of place. This is a stellar debut." – **Once Upon a Crime, Minneapolis, MN.**

"I could tell you this is a fast paced page turner. I could also suggest that through most of this book you will find yourself on the edge of your seat, but it would not do justice to this spine tingling thriller. I recommend one last trip down a Colorado River you have never before experienced." – **Sam Weller's Zion Bookstore**

"Wet Desert is a fast paced book that takes place over a three day period. Descriptions of the collapsing dams and muddy, fast flowing water keep the reader involved and turning pages. The reader watches the damage happen while the long-term repercussions are discussed and illustrated. This book by a first time author is worth looking into." – **Mysterious Galaxy, San Diego, CA**

"Wet Desert succeeds in creating gripping suspense while making readers realize that even a behemoth like Glen Canyon Dam cannot be taken for granted. The book keeps you in suspense throughout by using a local "sacred cow" to grab our attention and not let go." – **The Lake Powell Chronicle**

"I was overwhelmed with the magnitude of the river and the force of the water. The damage to the dams down river, the towns, farms and the California aquifer are unbelievable, and Hansen makes you feel that you are right there." – **Southern Utah News**